More Than I Expected

A Novel

By

Amara Wynn

This book is dedicated to

To the ones who stood with me through every storm. My sweet talented handsome husband, thank you for allowing me to be me.

To my children: D – For being an amazing daughter. W – For being chaotic perfection. And J – We miss you every day, this book helped me to learn more about how to process the daily grief of losing you and realizing it is okay to not be okay.

To my best friends, who helped me see that chosen family is just as important. And who are the real "Sloans" (Robin & Adam)

And to Sol, who held my hand through the crucial editing phase that I ignored the first time around. You were right. I fixed it.

And to LJ – My writing buddy. For telling me I was good, even when I realized I use the words "quietly" too much.

Author's Note

This edition of *More Than I Expected* has been lightly revised and re-edited for clarity, flow, and readability. The heart of the story remains the same.

Because this book deals with mental health, grief, healing, and the way people sometimes get stuck inside their own thoughts, some emotional patterns and repeated ideas are intentional. Healing is not always linear. Anxiety does not always sound new every time it shows up. Grief repeats itself. Fear repeats itself. Sometimes growth means having the same conversation with yourself until, one day, the answer finally changes.

This story is very personal to me, so thank you for reading this story. For giving these characters space, and for allowing them to be human in all the messy, tender, complicated ways people are human.

With love,
Amara Wynn

CHAPTER ONE

December 31st — 5:42 PM

Sydni Benton stares into her bathroom mirror like it personally insulted her. Her curls have chosen violence. Not mild chaos. Full rebellion.

"This," she mutters, tugging at a rogue spring spiraling over her eyebrow, "is why people straighten their hair for special occasions."

Behind her, Sloan Hart leans casually against the doorframe, arms crossed, wearing a light gray henley that somehow makes him look like he has his life together. He watches her with that dry, unimpressed expression he's perfected.

"Special occasion?" he says. "You mean the New Year's Eve panic-fest you've been complaining about for three days?"

Sydni throws a hair tie at him.

He catches it midair, of course.

"It's not a panic-fest," she says, rummaging through the five open makeup bags cluttering the counter. "It's just… not my scene."

"There's no scene that's your scene unless it involves pajamas and DoorDash," Sloan says. "Which is why we need to go."

Sydni smears eyeliner so wildly the wing shoots upward like it's trying to escape her face. She groans. "We can still bail. No one will notice."

"Victoria will notice," Sloan says. "She's been planning this party since July. If we don't show up, she'll hunt us down with glitter body spray and a clipboard."

He has a point. Victoria is five-foot-two and legitimately terrifying.

Sydni sighs. "Why am I even going? I don't like New Year's. I don't like crowds. I don't like being reminded that another year passed and I'm still—"

"—smart, attractive, tattooed, and the only person I know who can write a thirty-page grant in eight hours flat," Sloan interrupts.

She pauses. "That was dangerously close to a compliment."

"Don't get weird about it." He moves closer and nudges aside a makeup palette before she knocks it onto the floor. "You need one night of fun. Or at least one night where you're not doom-scrolling WebMD."

"That was one time," she mutters.

"Three," he says. "And two of those times you diagnosed yourself with diseases that don't exist in this hemisphere."

She points her eyeliner at him. "Stop keeping stats on me."

He shrugs. "Someone has to."

Sydni adjusts her shirt. Loose black, cotton fabric, tattoos peeking out from beneath the sleeves. The raven on her left arm. The floral sleeve on the right. The faintest edge of ink on her ribs where deeper scars hide.

She tugs the hem, unconsciously covering more skin.

Sloan notices, of course. He always notices. But he doesn't say anything. He never pushes.

"Okay," she exhales. "Fine. I'll go. But if I hate it, I'm blaming you."

"You always blame me," Sloan says, grabbing her coat from the hook. "I've accepted my role."

"You're insufferable."

He gives her a small half-smile, the kind that means he's actually proud of her. "And yet, here you are. Let's go ruin your night in a festive environment."

She rolls her eyes, but her heart warms anyway.

Sydni slides on her boots, takes one last glance at her unruly curls, and decides the universe can deal with her as she is.

Sloan opens the door. "If we leave now, we can get there early enough for you to hide before the masses show up."

"Perfect," she grumbles. "I love hiding."

"I know," he says.

As they step into the hallway, Sloan pauses and gives her a quick once-over. "You look good, Syd."

She blinks. "Really?"

"Really," he says. Then, after a beat: "Your hair looks like it's plotting something, but honestly? That's very you."

She smacks his arm on the way out.

He laughs.

And Sydni follows him down the stairs. Bracing herself for crowds, glitter, loud music, and forced cheer. She has absolutely no idea her night is about to shift in a way she never saw coming.

For now?

She's just trying not to trip on the damn stairs.

CHAPTER TWO

December 31st — 6:18 PM

The ride to the party was filled with Sloan's commentary about how if Sydni ditched him tonight, he would *absolutely* join a new family and leave her behind.

"You say that like it's a threat," she muttered.

"It is," he insisted. "A very painful one. For me. And maybe slightly for you."

Crowds weren't her thing. New Year's wasn't her thing. Being seen definitely wasn't her thing.

Sloan nudged her gently.

"We'll go in together," he said. "You can stay glued to me, or you can wander. No pressure. The second you want to leave, you say the word."

She looked up at him, grateful.

"Okay," she whispered.

By the time Sydni and Sloan pull up to Victoria's townhouse, Sydni is questioning every life choice she has ever made, including saying yes to rides, friendship, adulthood, and being born in the first place.

Victoria has done what Victoria always does:
too much.

Lights drip from the roof like sparkles. Music thumps faintly through the windows. A glitter-covered banner hangs across the porch reading:

HELLO, NEW YEAR! DON'T BE A JERK!

Sydni exhales. "This was a mistake."

Sloan parks the car with the resigned patience of someone who has heard this exact sentence eighty-seven times this week. "You say that before every social gathering. And afterward, you say, 'See, Sloan? I told you it was a mistake.' And then you eat cookies and forget you had fun."

"Fun is subjective," she mutters.

"So is drama," he says, opening her door. "And yet here you are, queen of both."

She glares at him, but she takes his hand anyway as she steps out, because her boots are cute but dangerously unbalanced, and Sloan has witnessed enough of her wipeouts to know she needs the assist. They walk up the walkway together. Sydni's curls bounce with every step, catching pieces of the twinkling lights and making her look like she's carrying her own chaotic little halo.

Sloan notices. He doesn't say anything, but his half-smile gives him away.

Inside, the party was already buzzing. Warm golden lights. Crowded living room. Music loud enough to vibrate Sydni's bones but not loud enough to cover the sound of clinking glasses, bursts of laughter, and the occasional "OH MY GOD, HI!"

Sydni flinches at the volume. "Nope. No thank you."

Sloan rests a steady hand on her back. "Deep breath, Benton."

She inhales for four, holds for four, exhales for four.

"Better?"

"No."

He smirks. "Good enough."

Victoria spots them instantly, beelining across the room in heels that defy physics. "Sydni! Sloan! My two favorite introverts pretending you're not dying inside! Look at you!" Victoria is glittery everywhere, possibly even in her bloodstream.

Sydni forces a smile. "You look… sparkly."

"I know!" Victoria beams. "Come in! Drinks are in the kitchen, food is on the table, music is everywhere, and singles are mingling! Sloan, don't disappear into a corner. Sydni, do not leave without speaking to at least three new people."

"That is aggressive," Sydni says.

"That's the spirit," Victoria says, already dragging someone else into a hug.

Sloan leans down. "We should pace ourselves. Think of this like a survival scenario."

"Like a zombie apocalypse?" Sydni asks.

"Worse," he says. "People who want to talk about their resolutions."

Sydni grimaces. "Okay, you're right. Zombies would be better."

They navigate through the crowd toward the kitchen, the universal sanctuary of all parties. Sydni clutches Sloan's sleeve, weaving through bodies like she's slipping through enemy territory. Her heart rate is doing gymnastics.

Sloan grabs two sparkling waters and hands her one. "Step one: hydration. Step two: blend."

"Blend into what?" she asks.

"Noise," he says. "Conversation. General festivities."

Sydni takes a sip, wrinkle-nosing at the bubbles. "I don't blend. I hide."

He taps the rim of her glass with his. "Tonight, we're doing both."

Sydni surveys the room. People sparkle. People laugh. People look so freaking comfortable in their skin, like New Year's Eve is a holiday they were built for.

Meanwhile she feels like a walking anxiety cloud with excellent eyebrows.

Her gaze drifts toward the front hallway, where someone walks in at that exact moment. He was tall, with darkish hair, and warm eyes. He was wearing a sweater that looks altogether too cozy for a man who carries himself like he's uncomfortable with attention. And handsome, did she mention that he was handsome? In that rugged kind of way?

He pauses at the door, scanning the room with an expression Sydni recognizes instantly. It is obvious that he doesn't want to be here either. And they make eye contact for a moment, a flicker. Something like mutual annoyance at existing in public.

Then someone shouts his name from across the room, and he gives a polite almost smile before stepping inside.

Sydni looks away, wondering if that was…a moment.

Sloan nudges her. "You good?"

"What? Yeah. Totally. Just—" She gestures vaguely at the crowd like it explains everything.

He doesn't buy it, but he lets it go. They settle into a semi-safe corner of the kitchen, with enough noise to blend, enough privacy to breathe.

Sydni adjusts her curls again. "How long do we have to stay?"

"At least an hour," Sloan says.

She groans. "That's forever."

"Not if you talk to someone other than me."

"I don't like that rule."

"Not surprised."

She kicks him lightly and he smirks. And somewhere in the living room, the tall guy with the cozy sweater and beautiful eyes blends into the crowd. He is completely unaware that the universe is about to shove him directly into Sydni Benton's orbit.

But for now? Sydni just takes another sip of her drink and tries not to melt into the floor.

Sydni is halfway through her sparkling water and halfway through convincing herself she can survive the night when Sloan abandons her, which was frankly rude.

Victoria calls his name from across the room, and Sloan, traitor that he is, sighs and says, "If I'm not back in five minutes, assume I'm trapped in small talk and send help."

"Text me the password," Sydni says.

"It's 'why am I here,' all lowercase." Then he's gone.

Sydni considers disappearing into the pantry until midnight. She's scanning the kitchen for escape routes when a voice behind her says:

"Sorry, is this seat taken?"

She turns. The tall guy from the doorway in the sweater, warm eyes, definitely-not-thrilled-to-be-here energy, stands a few feet away, holding a cup like it might bite him. Up close, he's even more handsome. Actually, annoyingly so.

His hair is slightly messy, like he ran a hand through it on the drive over. His sleeves are pushed up, revealing strong forearms she absolutely does not need to notice. His expression is equal parts polite and uncertain. A man hovered on the edge of the party, trying to look like he belongs.

Sydni blinks. "Seat?"

He nods toward the kitchen stool next to her.

"Oh." She shifts. "No, it's… um, it's free."

He hesitates like he's not entirely sure he should sit, then lowers himself onto the stool with a sigh that sounds like defeat and mild regret.

She bites back a smile.

He takes a sip of his drink, grimaces, and mutters mostly to himself, "Why do people like these?"

Sydni snorts before she can stop herself, but it's too late. He looks over as she covers her mouth.

His eyebrows lift slightly. "Sorry. Didn't mean to say that out loud."

"No, no, it's fine," she says quickly. "I agree. Sparkling water tastes like TV static."

He laughs under his breath. It was kind and genuine. "Oh thank God," he says. "I thought it was just me."

"Nope," Sydni replies. "Millions of people are pretending they enjoy carbonation."

A small smile tugs at his mouth, the kind of smile that doesn't show up unless someone feels safe. "I'm Elias, Elias Monroe by the way," he says, offering a small wave instead of a handshake, which she instantly respects because she despises unnecessary touching at parties.

"Sydni Benton."

"Sydni," he repeats, like he's testing how it feels on his tongue. Her stomach does something weird.

She blames the carbonation.

He glances around the room, then back at her. "You don't look like you want to be here."

"I don't," she says honestly. "You?"

"I was tricked," he says. "My sister told me we were getting dinner, and then she pulled into this driveway like it was the most natural thing in the world."

"Oh wow," Sydni says. "That's evil."

"It is," he agrees. "She said I needed 'social enrichment.' I told her I'm not a houseplant."

Sydni chokes on a laugh.

He smooths a hand through his hair, embarrassed but amused. "Sorry. That was… weird."

"No, I like weird," Sydni blurts then winces. "Not like… weird weird. Just normal weird."

He chuckles. "I knew what you meant."

Sydni actually begins to relax a little.

A song changes in the next room, louder, bass vibrating the walls. Elias flinches, subtly but noticeably.

"You hate loud parties too?" she asks.

He nods. "Noise gives me headaches."

"People give me headaches," Sydni says.

Elias's lips curl. "Same."

Something settles between them. A little bubble of mutual introvert solidarity.

And then…chaos.

Someone stumbles past them, bumping the table. Sydni's drink wobbles, sloshing upward like it's about to baptize Elias's sweater.

Elias reacts fast, steadying her cup with one hand and catching her elbow with the other. His fingers warm, his grip firm, and he didn't even think to hesitate.

"You okay?" he asks, eyes searching hers.

"Yep," she squeaks.

He lets go slowly, making sure she's steady first.

A flush warms her cheeks. She tells herself it's from the near-spill. "Thanks," she manages.

"Anytime."

She hates how much she likes that answer. Before she can think of something else to say, before she can decide if she should ask him a question or hide in the pantry, a voice behind them booms:

"Hey! Elias! Dude, get over here!"

Elias winces. "That's my cousin. He's visiting. He means well. Mostly."

"I get it," Sydni says. "Sloan's the same."

Elias stands but gives her an apologetic smile. "Save my seat?"

She nods before her brain can argue.

"Good," he smiles. Then he disappears into the crowd, swallowed by glitter and noise.

And that is when Sydni exhales. Her heart is beating too fast. Her curls are bouncing too much. Her drink still tastes like static. And she has absolutely no idea why her chest feels warm like someone just plugged her into an outlet.

Sloan reappears at her side. "You look weird," he says.

"Thank you?" she deadpans.

Sloan squints. "Who was that guy?"

"No one," she says too quickly.

Sloan's eyebrows rise. "Uh-huh."

Sydni takes a big, dramatic sip of her drink. "Shut up."

Sloan smirks. "Noted."

The crowd roars as midnight approaches.

Sydni tries to ignore the fact that she keeps glancing toward the doorway, waiting for that damn sweater and warm eyes to reappear. She tells herself it's nothing. She tells herself she's overthinking. She tells herself she'll never see him again after tonight.

Elias returns exactly five minutes later. Sydni knows it's five minutes because she counted every single one of them while pretending she absolutely was not looking for him in the crowd.

He steps back into the kitchen, brushing past glittery strangers with that same slightly overwhelmed expression, and heads straight for her like she's the only familiar thing in the whole house.

Her stomach flips. Not butterflies. More like… drunk moths.

"You saved my seat?" he asks, nodding at the stool.

"I said I would," she says, trying to sound casual. Instead she sounds like she swallowed her entire personality.

He smiles at her, and it was warm and even a little shy.

And the stupid drunk moths start line-dancing.

He sits again, this time closer than before. Their knees almost brush. Almost. Close enough that Sydni feels the ghost of contact and nearly short-circuits.

"You survived your cousin?" she asks.

"Barely," he says. "He was trying to introduce me to people. Multiple people. Consecutively. And I fell over a plant, so there's that."

Sydni pretends to gasp. "Oh no. Socializing. In a social setting. How terrible. And a plant casualty, what will you ever do?"

"Exactly."

She laughs, and he watches her in a way that makes her feel seen, like he's collecting details. Her curls and the tattoos. The chaos she carries. She tries to look away, but nope. Her eyes have abandoned all responsibility and are glued to him.

Elias clears his throat. "So… you doing okay? You looked a little overwhelmed earlier."

"Oh, I'm always overwhelmed," she says. "It's basically my baseline."

He smiles again, that soft, private one.

"I get that," he says. "Mine's 'mildly inconvenienced.'"

They share a look, equal parts amused and conspiratorial. And suddenly Sydni feels it. That weird… suspended thing. The thing movies exaggerate but is apparently real. The slow-motion moment where everything else blurs out.

Her heartbeat picks up. And she hears herself whisper, "Oh no."

Elias tilts his head. "Oh no?"

She blinks rapidly. "We're… we're having a moment."

"A moment?" he echoes, trying not to smile.

"Yes," she says, blushing. "Like a…like a Hallmarky, romantic-comedy moment. Someone should be cueing soft background music right now."

He laughs, surprised and warm. "Is that… bad?"

"No! I mean…maybe? I don't know! I don't do moments." She gestures between them, flustered. "This is very… cinematic."

Elias leans in just a fraction, voice low. "Well… I don't mind cinematic."

Their faces are close. Too close. Close enough that she can see the tiny flecks of gold in his hazel eyes. He smells like cedar and something warm. His knee grazes hers, barely, and she swears her soul exits her body.

He brushes a curl behind her ear. Slow. Gentle. Intimate. And her pulse trips.

"Sydni…" he murmurs.

Oh god. He said her name. Men saying her name should be illegal.

She leans in before she realizes she's leaning. He mirrors her, drawn like a magnet. The noise of the party fades. The world narrows to the space between their mouths. Just inches.

Sydni's heart whispers: *kiss him.*

But right before their lips meet—

"ONE MINUTE UNTIL MIDNIGHT!" someone screams from the living room.

The crowd erupts as the music blasts. People are shouting, clinking their glasses, and cheering.

Elias pulls back, startled. Sydni jerks away like she's been caught doing something illegal.

"Oh god," she mutters. "Nope. Nope nope nope."

Elias laughs softly. "That was… almost something."

"Almost," she echoes, cheeks on fire.

He shifts a little closer again, not quite closing the space, but not stepping away, either.

"Do you want to… I mean, do you have someone you're supposed to kiss at midnight?" he asks gently.

Sydni shakes her head too fast. "Nope. No. Absolutely not. Zero contenders. Zero, anything. No one. I don't really think I'm the holiday special movie moment, kiss a stranger at midnight…but…"

His smile lifts at the edges. "Okay," he says. "Good to know."

Somewhere in the house, the countdown begins:

TEN!
Sydni's stomach flips.

NINE!
Elias looks at her like she's the only person in the room.

EIGHT!
She swallows hard.

SEVEN!
He moves a fraction closer.

SIX!
Her pulse races.

FIVE!
His eyes drop to her lips.

FOUR!
She can't breathe.

THREE!
He whispers, "Sydni…"

TWO!
Her heart screams yes.

ONE!—

SLOAN APPEARS BETWEEN THEM LIKE A WALL OF HUMAN CHAOS.

"HAPPY NEW YEAR!" Sloan shouts, grabbing Sydni around the shoulders and nearly launching her into space. Confetti explodes behind him like a personal betrayal.

Elias startles and Sydni sputters and Sloan? He smiles victoriously. And midnight arrives without the kiss that should've happened.

Sydni stands there blinking, breathless, stunned, cheeks flaming, and painfully aware of one thing:

She absolutely, definitely, 100% wanted him to kiss her.

And now she's completely ruined.

CHAPTER THREE

January 1st — 12:01 AM

"HAPPY NEW YEAR!" Sloan shouts directly into Sydni's ear.

She lurches backward as Elias stumbles forward. Their almost-moment shatters like dropped glass. Sydni tries not to look devastated and she is unsuccessful.

Elias clears his throat, adjusting his sweater, cheeks slightly pink. "Well. That was… surprising."

"You're telling me," Sydni mutters, shooting Sloan a murderous side-eye.

Sloan blinks at her innocently, confetti stuck in his hair. "What? Did I interrupt something?"

"No," Sydni and Elias say at the exact same time. They freeze and look at each other. Elias gives a tiny embarrassed laugh. And Sydni wishes the floor would open under her.

Before she can choke on the awkward silence, a bright, feminine voice calls from the doorway, "Eli! There you are!" A woman bursts through the crowd. She is short, smiling, wearing sparkly gold, and unmistakably related to him.

Elias sighs. "My sister."

Nora arrives at his elbow, linking arms like she's anchoring a helium balloon. "I've been looking everywhere! Come on, you have to meet this group! They're obsessed with your job."

Elias winces. "Oh no—"

"Don't be dramatic," she says, tugging him. "They think physical therapists are superheroes."

Elias glances at Sydni. He seems apologetic, but also hopeful in a way that maybe he shouldn't be. "I'll be right back," he says softly.

Sydni nods, trying not to melt. "Yeah. Sure."

He lets himself be dragged away, still looking back at her once before the crowd swallows him whole.

Her chest squeezes. She tells herself she imagined it. She always imagines it.

Sloan watches her like she's a lab experiment. "Okay. What was that and who was THAT woman?"

"Nothing," Sydni snaps, too fast.

"Mmm," Sloan says, unimpressed. "Very convincing."

She smacks his arm with the back of her hand. "Shut up."

12:51 AM

Elias never found his way back to her at the party, so they decided to leave. They step outside into the sharp winter air, Sydni hugging her coat tight around her. The cold doesn't help the weird ache in her chest.

Sloan unlocks the car. "So. Are we going to talk about the tall guy you were about to kiss?"

"I was NOT about to kiss him."

"You leaned in."

"He leaned in."

"You tilted your head."

"I WAS BREATHING, HART."

Sloan gets in the driver's seat wearing the smuggest smirk in Illinois. "If I'm reading this correctly—"

"You're not," Sydni hisses.

He chuckles.

She stares out the window, watching gold light spill from Victoria's house, replaying that almost-moment again and again like a malfunctioning projector.

Why did she lean? Why did he look at her like that? Why is she even thinking about him? It was one night. One spark. One almost-kiss.

She tells herself it's nothing. Men like Elias Monroe don't remember girls like Sydni Benton. She almost laughs at the trope in so many movies and books. But facts are facts.

12:58 AM

They reach their doors across from each other. Sydni fumbles with her keys, because of course she does, and Sloan grabs her wrist before she drops them.

"Hey," he says. "For the record… you're not nothing."

She swallows hard. "I didn't say I was."

"You didn't have to."

She looks away and Sloan lets go, but he has a strange look in his eyes. Sydni knows that look. It's a small bit of fear. "Get some sleep. You're emotionally dehydrated."

"That's not a thing."

"It absolutely is."

She shakes her head, unlocked her door, steps inside, and closes it behind her. She leans her forehead against the wood and lets herself breathe.

1:06 AM

Her makeup is smudged. Her curls are frizzing. Her tattoos peek out under her shirt sleeve like forgotten constellations. Her eyes look tired and way too honest.

She wipes off her eyeliner, then foundation, then everything else she used to make herself feel "good enough" for a party she didn't even want to attend.

Barefaced, she looks… like herself. Normal and ordinary. Just…fine. And painfully aware that she is the kind of girl men meet once at a party and forget tomorrow.

She sighs and grips the sink. "Maybe it's for the best," she whispers to her reflection.

Her phone buzzes.

Sloan:
Don't forget. Resolve app starts tomorrow. Make your goals or I'm making them for you. Happy New Year, Benton.

She drops her head backward and groans into the heavens.

"Right. The stupid app."

January 1st — 9:42 AM

Sydni wakes up with the emotional fortitude of a potato.

Her face is puffy, her hair is a disaster, and her soul feels forty pounds heavier from embarrassment.

She grabs her phone.

Resolve App:
✦ Welcome to Day One! ✦
Meet your accountability partner!

"Oh god," she mutters. "Please let it be some sweet middle-aged woman who likes knitting."

She taps the notification. The screen loads. And loads. And loads.

Sydni squints. "Come on, Satan's Wi-Fi, work—"

The name finally appears.

Your Partner:
Elias Monroe
Age 33
Physical Therapist

Sydni jerks upright.

"YOU HAVE GOT TO BE KIDDING ME."

Across town, Elias Monroe is staring at the exact same screen, whispering, "…No freaking way."

And somewhere in the hallway, Sloan sneezes and goes, "I sense chaos."

CHAPTER FOUR

January 1st — 9:52 AM

Sydni stares at her phone like it's actively plotting against her. Staring for 10 whole minutes.

Your Partner:
Elias Monroe
Age 33
Physical Therapist

Nope. No. Absolutely not.

"This is illegal," she whispers to her empty bedroom. "This is a glitch. A cosmic glitch."

She taps the screen like she's trying to shake the truth off it. Nope. Still there. Still Elias Monroe. The guy she almost kissed. The guy her curls betrayed her in front of. The guy whose hands were warm on her arms. The guy with soft eyes and cozy sweaters.

Her insides do NOT do a flip. She lies down flat on her back, phone balanced on her chest, staring at the ceiling. "This is karma," she groans. "But like… the enthusiastic kind."

A knock sounds on her door.

Oh no.

She knows that knock.

"Sydni," Sloan calls, tone way too smug. "Did you do your goal assignments? Or am I choosing them and making your resolution of 'stop sneaking Funyuns into bed'?"

"I don't sneak them," she calls back.

He opens her door anyway, because privacy is optional for Sloan Hart and leans against the frame. His eyes narrow. "You look…weird."

"I always look weird. It's my aesthetic."

"No," he says, stepping inside. "This is the same weird you had at the party when I showed up and—"

"STOP," Sydni says loudly, sitting up too fast. "Don't finish that sentence."

Sloan folds his arms, head tilted. "So… who's your partner?"

Sydni freezes like someone hit her with a tranquillizer dart.

Sloan grins slowly. "Oh. Oh THIS is going to be good."

"I cannot tell you," she says, clutching the phone to her chest.

"You literally have to, because I'm the reason you're doing the app," Sloan says. "This is part of the agreement, besides, you and I are going to be friends on the app, so I'll see anyway."

"It was not part of any agreement."

"It was implied," he says. "Now tell me. Who'd you get?"

Sydni squeezes her eyes shut.

Sloan sits on the edge of her bed. "Syd. You're scaring me. Did you get someone awful? Is it Victoria? Did Victoria hack the app? Is she going to make you do yoga with her in her sparkly leggings?"

Sydni whispers, "Worse."

Sloan sits up straighter. "Worse?! Did you get my ex? Oh my god, please tell me you didn't get my ex."

She holds her phone up just far enough that he can see the name.

Sloan reads it. Sloan goes silent. Sloan blinks once. Twice.

Then bursts into laughter so loud she throws a pillow at his head.

"STOP!" she shouts. "STOP STOP STOP."

He wheezes. "E—ELIAS?! ISN'T THAT THE GUY YOU ALMOST KISSED?!"

"I DID NOT ALMOST KISS HIM."

"You absolutely did," he says. "I was THERE."

"You CAUSED IT," she counters.

He points at the phone. "This is fate."

"This is a curse."

"This is destiny."

"This is a DERANGED ALGORITHM."

Sloan collapses onto her duvet dramatically, clutching his stomach from laughing. "Sydni. Sydni. Listen to me. Listen." He grabs her hands like he's about to announce a prophecy. "You got matched… with Tall Soft Sweater Guy."

"Please stop calling him that."

"No."

"This is a nightmare."

"This is the BEST THING THAT HAS EVER HAPPENED TO ME," Sloan says, wiping his eyes.

"You're not supposed to enjoy this."

"Oh, I'm absolutely supposed to enjoy this," he says. "My neighbor slash best friend just got paired with the man she almost swapped New Year's oxygen with."

Sydni flops backward onto her pillows and lets out a noise that is neither human nor dignified.

"This cannot be happening," she groans. "I'll look insane if I message him."

"No," Sloan says, grabbing her phone. "You'll look like someone participating in the program she signed up for."

"YOU signed me up!"

He shrugs. "Technicalities."

"Sloan!"

"What?!" he laughs. "It's a perfect setup. Look, you're not desperate, you're not clingy, it's literally your assignment. It's the most normal way to talk to a man ever."

Sydni covers her face with both hands. "I'm going to die."

"You're going to text him," Sloan says. "Right now."

"I can't!"

"You will."

He taps her unlock code. She snatches the phone back.

He smirks. "Ready?"

"No."

"Too bad." Sloan pats her knee. "I'll be right across the hall waiting to hear you scream."

He leaves with the energy of someone already planning popcorn. The door clicks shut. And Sydni stares at the screen again.

Elias Monroe.
Her partner.

Her almost-kiss. Her fate. She groans into her pillow for a full thirty seconds…then sits up. "Well," she mutters. "May as well get the humiliation over with."

She opens the chat. Her thumbs hover.

Types.
Deletes.

Types.
Deletes.

Finally, she sends:

Sydni:
Hi. Um. So I guess we're… partners. This is weird. Please ignore anything embarrassing I said last night.

She hits send and immediately regrets every life choice she's made since 1993.

~*~

Elias sits at his kitchen counter, staring at the exact same app notification he's convinced is a prank.

Your Partner:
Sydni Benton
Age 33
Freelance Grant Writer

He exhales slowly, a stunned sound. Of all people. Of all matches. Of all luck.

Nora pokes her head in from the living room. "Did you see? Who'd you get?"

Elias turns his phone over before she can see the screen.

"No one," he says softly. Then, after a pause, "…Everyone."

His phone buzzes again. It is a message from her. He opens it, reads it twice, then rubs a hand over his jaw to hide the smile he can't stop.

"Yeah," he murmurs. "This is definitely weird."

But good. Way too good.

~*~

Sydni hits send and immediately regrets it. She goes to her bedroom and she drops the phone beside her like it's radioactive and rolls onto her stomach, face buried.

"Nope," she mumbles. "Delete me. I can't live here anymore."

Her phone buzzes.

She flails for it like she's rescuing a drowning hamster.

Elias:
Hey Sydni. I... definitely remember you. And don't worry, you weren't embarrassing. I'm the one who almost tripped over a plant stand.

Sydni stares. "Oh god," she whispers. "He remembers me. Why."

She types:

Sydni:
That plant stand came out of nowhere. Honestly, I blame the décor.

His reply comes quickly, too quickly for her heart to handle.

Elias:
Same. I don't think Victoria believes in safe furniture spacing.

She snorts.

Sydni:
She believes in "aesthetic over survivability."

Elias:
Accurate. Are you... okay with this match? I know it's a little weird.

Sydni freezes.

Okay. Okay, that's TOO perceptive.

She types:

Sydni:
*Weird is my specialty. So yeah. I'm fine. Totally fine. Perfectly
normal over here.*

She hesitates.

Then types again:

Sydni:
Mostly normal.

Elias:
*lol
Just so you know, I was forced into the program. My sister signed
me up. I didn't have a choice. So if you're only "mostly normal,"
I'm even less than that.*

Sydni smiles, a real one this time.

Sydni:
*Oh thank god. I also had no choice. Sloan (my best
friend/neighborhood goblin) forced me too.*

Elias:
Goblin?

Sydni:
*Gremlin?
Imp?
Small chaos wizard?*

Elias:
I feel like I need to meet him.

Sydni chokes on air.

Sydni:
*You did, sort of last night. But that was the last time.
He'll interrogate you. He interrogates everyone. He once made a
delivery guy cry.*

Elias:
Oh. Good. I love high-pressure social situations.

She laughs so hard she drops her phone on her chest.

Sydni:
Are you always like this?

Elias:
Like what?

Sydni:
Quietly sarcastic. Deadpan but polite. Soft-grumpy.

Elias:
Soft-grumpy? That feels… too accurate.

Sydni:
Sorry lol
Just… first impression.

Elias:
What was your first impression? Besides "this man hates parties."

She bites her lip. NOPE. Not saying the truth. The truth is illegal.

She types:

Sydni:
You seemed nice. And overwhelmed. And like you didn't want to be there. Which made you relatable.

Elias:
That's fair. My first impression of you was:

Elias:
You have really great curls.

Sydni forgets English.

Elias:
And you seemed…comfortable to talk to. Easy. In a good way.

Not easy-easy. I'm—I didn't mean—Sorry. This is coming out wrong.

She laughs into her pillow, smiling harder than she wants to.

Sydni:
It's okay. I understood you.

Elias:
Good. Because I'm apparently bad at words before 10 a.m.

Okay. She can do this. She can pretend she's normal and not a chaos gremlin.

Sydni:
So. What exactly are we supposed to do first? The app says to "Introduce yourselves through three facts."

Elias:
Right. Okay. Three facts.

I'm a physical therapist.

I hate loud parties.

I make excellent pancakes.

Sydni:
Okay pancakes, that's impressive.
My turn:

I'm a grant writer.

I panic at parties.

I have accidentally set my oven on fire. Twice.

Elias:
… … ….
Twice?

Sydni:
I panic-cook.

Elias:
I feel like that's a red flag.

Sydni:
It's fine. I have a fire extinguisher.
Somewhere.

Elias:
Sydni. Please tell me you know where your fire extinguisher is.

Sydni:
… … …
In spirit.

Elias:
Oh no.

Sydni:
Oh yes.

Elias sends a laughing emoji, the simplest one, and for some reason it feels like an entire hug.

Then:

Elias:
Okay. This is actually… fun. Talking to you, I mean.

Her heart trips.

Sydni:
Yeah. It is.

Elias:
Do you want to keep talking later? I have family lunch in a bit, but I'll be free after.

Her pulse jumps into orbit.

Sydni:
Sure. I'll be around.

Elias:
Good.
Talk soon, Sydni.

She sets her phone down. Blushes. Covers her face. And kicks her feet like she's fifteen again.

CHAPTER FIVE

January 1st — 11:38 AM

Sydni cracks her bedroom door open and finds exactly what she knew she'd find.

Sloan Hart was in her living room again, on her couch, wrapped in her favorite blanket like a smug burrito. He was eating one of her granola bars like a man who did not pay for it.

He grins the moment he sees her. "There she is," he announces. "My little accountability romance gremlin."

She groans. "Oh god."

He pats the spot beside him. "Come. Sit. Tell Papa Sloan everything."

"Absolutely not."

"You literally have to," he says. "You matched with Elias Monroe — aka the man you were going to kiss before I saved you from terrible decisions — and now you're texting him."

"You did NOT save me—"

"You're deflecting," he sings.

She flops onto the couch face-down, muffled voice whining into the cushions. "I regret everything."

Sloan leans over her dramatically. "Tell me."

"No."

"Tell me."

"No."

"Tell me or I'm reading your texts."

She lifts her head just enough to glare. "YOU WOULD NOT."

Sloan raises an eyebrow. "…Try me."

She sits up, groans, grabs a pillow for emotional support, and says in a tiny voice:

"We talked a little."

Sloan's entire face lights up with unhinged glee. "OH MY GOD YOU DID. YOU TEXTED HIM. YOU INITIATED CONTACT WITH A HUMAN MALE."

"It wasn't, I mean… It was the app!"

"THE APP IS JUST A VESSEL," Sloan shouts. "THIS IS FATE. THIS IS DESTINY. THIS IS—"

"Sloan," she interrupts. "Stop being dramatic."

"I cannot," he states. "I physically cannot. You're glowing."

"I AM NOT GLOWING."

"You look like someone who got a good morning text from a man with kind eyes and well-defined shoulders."

"I — Sloan, I swear to god —"

"Oh, I know NOTHING," he says, hands raised. "Except that YOU are acting extremely suspicious."

Sydni pulls the blanket up over her face. "It was small talk!"

Sloan gasps. "SMALL TALK is the gateway drug to EMOTIONAL VULNERABILITY."

"Shut up!"

He smirks. "Okay, then tell me, what did he say?"

She kicks her feet under the blanket. "NO!"

"Oh REALLY?" he says. "So you're blushing over the alphabet?"

"STOP IT."

"Did he use punctuation? That's how nice men flirt."

"He did, actually," she mumbles.

Sloan gasps so loudly she jumps. "HE USED PUNCTUATION."

"Sloan—"

"He's in love with you."

She screams into the pillow. After a moment, she sits up. "Okay. Fine. You want to help? Then let's do something useful."

He narrows his eyes. "Go on."

"We should... cyberstalk him."

Sloan's face transforms into the grin of a man who has waited his whole life for this moment. "That is," he says reverently, "a terrible idea."

"I know."

He pulls out his laptop like he's starting a mission. "So OBVIOUSLY we should do it."

She scoots closer. "Thank God. I can't stalk him alone."

"Sydni," he says solemnly. "This is what best friends are for."

He opens Google with deadly precision.

"Elias Monroe physical therapist Illinois"

Sydni leans in. "This is illegal."

"Yes," Sloan says. "But it's the fun kind."

Search results load. Sloan reads aloud.

"Okay... first result... his clinic. Legit. No mugshots. No FBI watchlists. Slightly disappointing."

"Check Yelp," Sydni whispers.

He clicks. "Twenty-three five-star reviews."

She gasps. "Is that good?"

"It's PREPOSTEROUS," Sloan says. "People do not leave good reviews unless someone saves their life or gives them free food."

"Maybe he saved their knees?"

"Or their hearts," Sloan says dramatically.

She covers her face. "STOP."

He keeps scrolling. "And look, people say he's patient. Gentle. Very kind."

She kicks her feet like an anxious horse. "WHY DOES THAT MAKE ME NERVOUS."

Sloan sets the laptop down and looks at her seriously. "Sydni," he says. "You deserve someone kind."

Her eyes sting. She hates it. So, she does what Sydni Benton does best. She deflects. "Check his Instagram," she says.

Sloan beams. "NOW we're talking."

This time he grabs his phone.

Sydni pulls the blanket up under her chin. "Oh god," she whispers. "I'm not ready."

"You never are," Sloan says. "And I'll be here the whole time."

Sloan types "Elias Monroe Illinois physical therapist Instagram" with the intensity of someone hacking into the Pentagon.

Sydni is hugging her blanket so tight she looks like she's trying to fuse with it. "This is wrong," she whispers. "This feels like spying. I am a professional. A grant writer. A responsible adult. I cannot just—"

"He has a public account," Sloan says calmly. "Therefore, he WANTS us to stalk him."

"That is not how that works," Sydni hisses.

"Hush," Sloan says, tapping the screen. "We're approaching the truth."

The search results load.

Sydni peeks between her fingers. Then she covers her face again. "OH NO."

Sloan grins like the devil at brunch. "Found him."

He clicks. "Username… **@_monroe_mobility**." He pauses. "Adorable. A little cringe. Perfect."

"Do NOT scroll," Sydni orders. "Promise me you won't scroll. Don't do it."

Sloan scrolls immediately.

Sydni screams into her pillow. "I AM GOING TO THROW UP."

"Okay…" Sloan narrates. "Profile picture is him at a park. Fall leaves. Golden light. He has a dog??"

Sydni's soul leaves her body. "NO. NO DOG. THAT MAKES HIM MORE ATTRACTIVE."

"Dog is a golden retriever," Sloan says. "Named… oh my god… Clementine."

"OF COURSE IT'S A GOLDEN RETRIEVER NAMED CLEMENTINE," Sydni cries. "That's the MOST EMOTIONALLY STABLE DOG NAME ON EARTH."

Sloan scrolls more. "Oh look. Gym photo."

"STOP SCROLLING."

"Oh look," he continues, "Him holding someone's new baby at the clinic."

"STOP SCROLLING."

"Oh look," he says louder, "A Halloween picture where he and Clementine dressed as a matching slice of pizza."

Sydni's brain short-circuits. "Absolutely not. I refuse. Take it away. BURN THE PHONE."

"Are you kidding?" Sloan says. "This man is a walking green flag."

Sydni closes her eyes. "I cannot be normal about this."

"Then don't be normal," Sloan shrugs. "Normal is overrated. Be honest."

She lifts her head just enough to glare. "I am not texting him saying I saw his pizza-dog costume."

"No," Sloan agrees. "You will NOT text him that. You will text him something chill."

"What's chill?" she asks.

He thinks. "Something like, 'Just checking the app. Hope your morning's going okay.'"

"That is not chill," she says. "That is MILDLY DESPERATE."

"Fine," Sloan says, typing on his own phone. "Then you need a vibe. Something casual. Something effortlessly cool."

"I am NOT effortlessly cool."

"No," he agrees. "You are accidentally charming."

"That's worse!"

He pats her knee. "It's okay. I'll help you fake cool."

She groans loudly. "This is humiliating."

"Yes," he says. "And also deeply entertaining."

"No texting. Not yet. I need to act like a functioning adult with priorities."

"Name one priority besides panicking about Elias," Sloan challenges.

She opens her mouth and immediately closes it and frowns. "…Breakfast?"

"That is survival," Sloan clarifies. "Not a personality."

She throws a pillow at his head. He dodges it, but just barely.

"Okay, okay," he says. "Just breathe. Be normal."

"I am normal."

"You are currently wrapped in a blanket like a haunted couch burrito and hyperventilating because a man has a dog."

She points accusingly. "A dog named Clementine!"

"Which is adorable."

"WHICH IS A RED FLAG OF BEING TOO PERFECT."

He nods calmly. "Yes. That's fair."

She drops the blanket and stands up, pacing. "I cannot get invested. I don't even know him. He might be too nice. He might have a weird laugh. He might be a bad texter. He might be a close talker. He might—"

Her phone buzzes and she freezes mid-rant.

Sloan freezes too.

Slowly, like a horror movie scene, they both look at her phone on the coffee table.

A new notification from the Resolve app.

Elias Monroe:
Hey, hope your morning's going okay. No pressure to respond.
Just checking in. :)

Sydni whispers, "Oh no."

Sloan whispers, "Oh YES."

She grabs the phone like a hot coal.

"I can't answer."

"You HAVE to answer."

"I don't know what to say!"

"Then say what NORMAL Sydni would say."

"I am not normal!"

"Exactly," Sloan says. "So say something awkward."

"What?! Why?!"

"Because that's you!" he says, waving his hands. "And it WORKED last night!"

She paces harder. "I'm going to faint."

"NO fainting," Sloan orders. He grabs her shoulders and spins her toward the phone. "Text. Him. Back."

"I can't."

"You CAN."

"I—"

Her phone buzzes again.

Elias:
(Really no pressure.)
I know mornings can be rough. Just wanted to say hi. That's all.

Sydni's heart falls directly out of her body.

She whispers, "Oh god he's NICE."

Sloan fans her with a throw pillow. "RESPOND, WOMAN."

45

CHAPTER SIX

January 1st — 12:04 PM

Sydni stands frozen in the middle of her living room while her phone buzzes gently in her hand. Her heart is beating too fast. Her palms are sweaty. Her brain is sprinting in circles like a hamster fueled by anxiety and iced coffee.

Sloan watches her like she's defusing a bomb. "Okay," he says. "You've run out of time to panic. Now you have to respond."

"I can't respond," she whispers. "What if I sound weird?"

"You ARE weird."

"That doesn't help at ALL!!"

"It should!" Sloan cries.

Another Resolve Notification:

Elias:
Here is my phone number if you ever want to text me outside of the app.

She flops onto the couch, blanket dragging behind her like a cape of defeat. His actual phone number.

"What if he's expecting something cool and I send something like 'hi, my hair is really frizzy today'?"

"Then it's honest," Sloan says, sitting beside her. "And trust me — men do not expect cool. They just want coherent."

She groans. "This is so much pressure."

"Then remove the pressure," he says simply.

She looks up. "How?"

"Don't try to be anyone else," he says. "Just be you."

She makes a tortured noise. "But I like him!"

"I know," Sloan says gently. "Which is exactly why you should be yourself."

She stares at the message again:

Elias:
Hey, hope your morning's going okay. No pressure to respond. Just checking in. :)

She tugs a curl. "This is too nice. Like… unreasonable levels of nice. Why is he nice?"

Sloan sighs. "Sydni. Reply."

She inhales deeply, then types.

Deletes it.

Types again.

Deletes it harder.

Types a third time.

Throws the phone across the couch.

Sloan retrieves it, reads the half-draft on the screen, and sighs. "You cannot send 'hi sorry I was panicking.'"

"I was panicking!"

"Yes," he says patiently. "But you don't lead with that."

After a long pause, Sydni bites her lip. And that is when something shifts. She sits up straighter. "Okay," she says. "I think I know what to say."

Sloan watches her like she's a toddler learning to walk for the first time.

She takes back her phone, and finally types an actual text message, not the app:

Sydni:
Hey! Sorry for the slow reply. I'm good, just trying to figure this whole Resolve thing out. Do you know what your goals are going to be yet?

She stares at it. It's simple. Not overly emotional. Not overly eager. Not overly… Sydni. It's normal. It's safe.

She presses send and immediately launches her phone onto the other end of the couch like it's a cursed object.

Sloan claps. "THAT WAS PERFECT."

"No it wasn't!"

"Yes it was. That was relatable. Adult. Not psychotic at all."

She curls into herself. "I feel exposed."

"That's because you're doing something new," he says. "Which is good."

She peeks at him. "I hate growth."

"I know," he says, patting her knee. "But you're doing great."

A rare moment passes. He looks at his best friend before he clears his throat. "Now," he says, businesslike. "Time to set your goals."

She stares into the existential abyss. "Do I have to?"

"Yes," Sloan says. "And also, yes."

She scrolls through the app's goal categories:

- Health
- Social connection
- Creativity
- Daily habits

- Physical activity
- Stress reduction
- Organization
- Hobbies

Sydni groans. "All of these require effort."

"That is the POINT."

"This feels like self-improvement."

"Yes," he repeats. "That is the POINT."

She drapes the blanket over her head. "I can't choose."

"You CAN and you WILL," Sloan says. Then he pulls the blanket back. Gently but firmly. Like dealing with a cat in distress.

"Pick three," he says.

She chews her lip.

Thinks.

Finally types:

Goal 1:
Walk 10 minutes a day (outside, even if it's cold).

Goal 2:
Cook one actual meal a week that does NOT involve fire hazards.

Goal 3:
Write something that isn't work-related (journal, list, anything).

Sloan peeks. "These are great!"

"They're terrible."

"They're perfect," he insists. "Achievable. Personal. Safe."

Sydni sighs dramatically but secretly feels… something. A flicker of hope? Maybe.

Sydni's phone buzzes again. She doesn't move.

Sloan stares at her. "Answer it."

"No," she whispers. "If he says something nice again, I'll combust."

"We already talked about this," Sloan says calmly. "You combust no matter what. Just open the message."

She glares at him, and he raises an eyebrow. And of course, she caves first. She reaches for the phone like she's picking up a live grenade.

Elias:
I'm still figuring mine out too.
But for now:

1. *Walk every morning before work*
2. *Cook three times a week*
3. *Read one book a month*
4. *Stretch or do mobility work daily*
   (None of this is as intense as it sounds, I promise.)

Sydni stares at her screen like she's reading the résumé of a man who lives inside a wellness magazine.

"Oh," she says faintly. "He's… functional."

Sloan leans over her shoulder. "Functional? He's an Olympian compared to you."

"EXCUSE ME?"

"Cooking three times a week? Walking every morning?" Sloan scoffs. "That's—what is that? Discipline? Routine? Who does that?"

Sydni collapses backward dramatically. "I can't compete with that!"

Sloan sits beside her, stretching out like he owns the couch. "Good news: you're not supposed to."

"Yes I am!" she argues. "This is literally a partner-based app. I have to be… impressive."

Sloan lifts an eyebrow. "You? Impressive? Sydni, babe — you're the woman who set an oven on fire twice."

She groans into a pillow. "YOU SAID YOU'D NEVER BRING THAT UP AGAIN."

"I lied," he says cheerfully. Then more gently: "But seriously… this isn't a competition."

She peeks at him.

He shrugs. "You go at your pace. He goes at his. The point isn't to keep up, it's to not do it alone. And you have to stop hiding behind that pillow, it's getting annoying. And you may be dramatic, but my friend, you are not annoying.

Her chest tightens for a different reason. This time she felt warm, accepting his words, which has been hard for her for a long time.

"And Syd," Sloan adds, nudging her knee with his. "Some men do too much because they don't know how to sit still. You're not in a race. You're in a partnership."

She swallows hard. "Why are you being wise? I don't like it."

"It's inconvenient for me too," Sloan mutters. Then taps her phone. "Text him back."

Her thumbs hover.

Sydni:
Wow, your goals are really good.
Like… adult good. Mine are more "barely hanging on but trying." I hope that's okay.

She hesitates a moment and adds:

Sydni:
And if you ever want to share pancake recipes, let me know.
(That was a joke. Mostly.)

She sends it and as per usual, she immediately regrets everything she's ever typed.

Sloan claps her on the shoulder. "Look at you! Look at that vulnerability. I'm a proud papa."

She shoves him lightly. "You're only proud because you're nosy."

He grins. "Correct."

Sydni's phone buzzes and she inhales sharply. She knows she is being dramatic. She knows this about herself, but she is just not good at peopling.

Sloan whispers, "This is it. This is the moment."

She kicks him lightly and then opens the message.

Elias:
They're not "adult good."
They're just things I've been trying to do for a while. Yours are real. Honest. Not everyone needs to be running marathons at 6 a.m.
(Definitely not me.)

Sydni's relaxes a little. That was a good response that she might melt into the couch.

Another message follows instantly.

Elias:
Also… in case you couldn't tell, I saw your goals in the app. They're really good. Walking outside in the cold is braver than anything on my list. And writing something non-work? That's actually harder than daily stretching. So you win this round.

Sydni squeaks internally.

She wins? She WINS?

Before she can process that, another message appears:

Elias:
And as for pancakes…That wasn't a joke for me. I take breakfast very seriously.
It is a sacred art.

Sydni's jaw drops. "He's flirting," she whispers.

Sloan nods solemnly. "He's flirting."

Another buzz.

Elias:
But if you really want recipes…I can share. Assuming you're not planning to set anything on fire.
Again.

Sydni feels her soul exit her body.

"How does he KNOW?!" she shrieks.

"You TOLD him," Sloan says, wiping tears of laughter from his eyes. "You literally confessed your oven crimes."

"Oh god I did."

"He's teasing you," Sloan sings. "This is foreplay."

"STOP SAYING THAT."

"Never."

Before she can combust, another message arrives:

Elias:
Seriously though, we don't have to match goals. Go at your own pace. We're just supposed to encourage each other. No pressure. Promise.

Sydni presses her phone to her chest.

"Okay. That's… actually really nice."

Sloan nudges her with his elbow. "See? Not a competition."

"I know…"

"And you don't have to be him," Sloan adds. "He doesn't want that."

"He doesn't?"

"No," Sloan says. "He wants to talk to you. And he wants you to talk back. That's it."

She feels her shoulders relax.

Then types:

Sydni:
Okay… you win too. Your goals are great. Mine are chaotic but honest. And I guess we'll both try our best (and hopefully avoid house fires).

She thinks for a minute and then types:

Sydni:
Also, I take breakfast seriously too. I'm just more of a cereal girl. But I'm willing to expand my horizons.

She considers deleting that last line, but she doesn't. Instead, she hits send.

Sloan claps like he's watching a sporting event. "THAT'S MY GIRL!"

Another buzz.

Elias:
Cereal counts. Though I feel morally obligated to fix that. Eventually.

Her heart does something violent.

Sloan groans dramatically. "Oh, he WANTS you. This is not subtle."

. He smiles at Sydni, widely, but a tiny hint of something hides behind his eyes. She notices.

CHAPTER SEVEN

January 2nd — 9:14 AM

Sydni Benton has regrets.

Many regrets. But none so immediate as the one currently freezing her face off while she trudges down the sidewalk like a resentful penguin.

"This was a mistake," she mutters into her scarf.

The Illinois winter air bites at her cheeks. The wind is rude. The sidewalk is rude. The entire concept of "walking outside" is rude. But she stomps onward anyway.

"Ten minutes," she whispers, counting it down like a prison sentence. "Ten stupid minutes."

Cars hum past and a lady walking her dog waves at her. Even joggers sail by like smug, overachieving gazelles.

Sydni glares at them all. How dare they enjoy movement. Her breath puffs into little clouds. Her boots crunch over patches of old snow. And even though she hates every second of this, something in her chest unwinds a little.

She notices things she hasn't paid attention to in months. The pink dawn light stretching over the rooftops. The hush of a neighborhood waking up. A kid scraping ice patterns on a frosty window. The way the trees look like black lace against the morning sky.

She stops walking. When was the last time she saw this? Really saw it? She'd been living like a hermit. Trapped in her apartment, inside her head, inside her computer. Eating meals over the sink. Sleeping at odd hours. Breathing only recycled indoor air and worry.

She tugs her coat tighter. And it hits her again. That tiny ache that comes from realizing how much life she's been missing.

A poodle in a puffy jacket trots past her. THE DOG HAS A JACKET.

She gasps. "Ma'am, your dog is better dressed than me."

The dog's owner laughs. "He's a bit dramatic."

Sydni nods solemnly. "Me too."

They share a smile before parting ways.

Her phone buzzes in her pocket, but she ignores it. She's trying to stay present. Trying to be… what did Elias call it? Honest?

Another minute passes. Her cheeks sting and her legs protest. Her nose is definitely considering falling off. But there's also something warm simmering beneath all of that. A tiny spark of pride.

She actually did this. Outside. In winter. Before noon.

When the Resolve app dings, she finally pulls her phone out.

Resolve:
Congratulations! Your partner completed their morning walk.
Encourage them?

"Oh," she whispers. "He already did his."

Of course he did. He's a functional adult with functioning limbs.

She taps the notification.

A message pops up from Elias.

Elias:
Morning! Took my walk earlier, yours done yet?
(Sending moral support either way.)

Sydni stares at the screen, and, unexpectedly, she smiles. She stands under a leafless tree, breath fogging the air, freezing toes and all, and types back:

Sydni:
I'm outside right now and this is awful but I'm doing it.

A second later:

Elias:
Proud of you.
Seriously.

She pauses for a moment, looking at her phone. No one says that to her. Not about things this small. Not about things that feel like nothing but require everything.

She types:

Sydni:
It's cold. And I'm 99% sure my face is frozen. And a dog walked by wearing a better outfit than me.

Elias:
😄 *Illinois winters are savage.*
And yes, the dogs here have more money than I do.

A laugh escapes her. A real one.

Sydni:
I'm heading back now. Please tell me I get a sticker for surviving this.

Elias:
You get TWO stickers. One for the walk and one for the dog jacket incident.

Sydni:
Thank God.

She pockets her phone and walks home. Her steps were lighter. Her heart felt oddly warm.

When she reaches her apartment building and stomps snow off her boots, she whispers to herself, "I guess… this isn't the worst thing."

Behind her, the morning light catches on frosted branches. Inside her chest, something small blooms. Hope, maybe. Or maybe just frostbite. But… maybe hope.

Sydni trudges up the stairs to her apartment, cheeks still pink from the cold, legs heavy … but lighter than it was when she left.

She opens her door and Sloan is already inside. The man has a sixth sense for personal breakthroughs. He's at her kitchen counter pouring cereal into a bowl like he lives here. Without looking up, he calls out, "You survived."

Sydni blinks. "I… yes? How did you—"

Sloan taps his phone. "Resolve app told me. It gave me a sticker for 'supporting my friend.' Which honestly feels like they're pitying me."

She snorts. "They should."

He turns to look at her taking in her flushed cheeks, messy hair, the tiny puff of accomplishment in her posture. "Well," he says, leaning back against the counter, "look at you."

"What?" she asks, suddenly self-conscious.

"You did it," he says simply. A genuine smile spreads across his face. "I'm proud of you."

Sydni freezes. The words hit her like a warm wave and an electric shock at the same time. Two "proud of yous" in one morning?

"You… what?"

"I'm proud of you," Sloan repeats slowly. "That's not sarcasm. That's not a joke. That is sincere, heartfelt, best-friend pride."

Sydni's gut twists, but not in a bad way. In a way she wasn't remotely prepared for. She avoids his eyes, pulling off her coat. "That's weird, Sloan."

"It's not weird," he says. "It's called support."

She scoffs lightly, uncomfortable. "I don't know what to do with that."

"You don't have to do anything with it," he says, stepping closer. "You just did something hard. You left your apartment. You followed through. You put effort into yourself. That deserves recognition."

She stares at him, blinking too fast. "It's just a walk," she mumbles.

"Yeah," Sloan says gently. "But you've been avoiding the world for a long time, Syd." He continues, voice low and steady. "And today, you stepped back into it. Even if it was cold. Even if it sucked. Even if you hated every second. You showed up. That matters."

Her chest tightens, in a way that feels like something thawing. "It's… weird," she says again, voice small. "Nobody says they're proud of me."

"Then they're stupid," Sloan replies instantly.

Her eyes sting, the way they do when someone hits an old bruise you forgot about.

Sloan nudges her arm with his elbow…light, careful.

"You don't realize how much you carry," he says. "How much you do for everyone else. But today was about you. And yeah… I'm proud." And then something shifts in his expression. So small she might've missed it if she weren't looking directly at him.

A flicker. A shadow. A fear he tries to swallow down before it fully surfaces. His voice changes a little, not for her, but from something inside him slipping through the cracks. "Just… don't disappear on me, okay?" he says lightly, too lightly. "I don't handle people leaving very well."

She looks up sharply. He's still smiling. But it doesn't reach his eyes.

A ghost of Robin's name drifts between them unspoken, heavy. Sydni feels it. The pain he felt when she left him. She feels the ache sitting just beneath his joke. The moment is small, but it lands.

Before she responds, her phone buzzes.

Elias.

She flinches. Hope flickering up where she doesn't want it, crashing into the worst timing imaginable.

Sloan notices. His expression shifts, barely, just a tightening around the eyes. He wasn't jealous, he looked scared. That old, fear he never says out loud.

He masks it with a smirk. "Oh? Breakfast Boy strikes again?"

"Sloan," she mutters, heat rising in her cheeks, "don't call him that."

But she already saw the flicker. And he already knows she saw it.

"Make me," he tosses back automatically.

But she's already looking at her screen. Not trying to make him uncomfortable, just… overwhelmed. Because between Sloan's words…and Elias's encouragement earlier…Sydni feels everything hit her at once. There is warmth, pressure, nerves, and the cold still clinging to her skin

Sloan watches her and says, "You're not used to people rooting for you, huh?"

She shakes her head once. "Only you."

"Well," he says, getting up and tossing an arm around her shoulders and pulling her into a lopsided side-hug, "get used to it."

And she lets herself lean into him a little.

Two people in one day. Two people saying they're proud of her. Two people seeing her. Somehow, it's both too much and exactly what she needed. Underneath Sloan's warmth, she feels the tremor of something else, the fear he tries so hard to hide.

It's a lot. It's almost too much. It was definitely unexpected. But maybe she needs this. Maybe she deserves this.

And maybe Sloan needs her, too. More than he ever says out loud.

CHAPTER EIGHT

January 3rd — 10:22 AM

Sydni is halfway through peeling off her boots when her phone dings.

Sloan, sprawled on her couch again (because he has no shame and apparently no home), looks up. "You okay?"

"No," she says flatly. "The app just notified me that Elias finished his stretching routine."

Sloan grins. "Ohhhh. Someone's jealous."

"I'm NOT jealous," she snaps, kicking her boot across the room. "I am ANNOYED. There's a difference."

"Right," Sloan nods sagely. "You're annoyed that he's doing better than you."

"I NEVER SAID THAT."

"You didn't have to."

She scowls at her phone like it personally betrayed her.

Resolve:
Your partner completed their mobility goal for the day! Encourage them?

She glares harder. "No. I will NOT encourage him. He is too accomplished already."

Sloan laughs so hard he nearly drops his cereal bowl (he brought his own this time, because he knows she's suspicious).

"You're ridiculous," he says. "This is adorable."

"STOP calling me adorable."

"When you stop BEING adorable."

But then something shifts in her expression. "I want to check something off too," she mutters.

Sloan perks up. "Oh? Is this motivation I'm hearing?"

"Don't make a big deal out of it."

"It's already a big deal."

She marches to the kitchen like a soldier heading into battle. Today was not a day for cereal, no toaster waffles, and absolutely no emergency granola bars. Today, she was going to cook.

She throws open a cabinet. It is chaos with mismatched spices, a box of pasta, a jar of peanut butter, and one lone bag of oatmeal that looks older than democracy. She shuts that cabinet.

After searching around, she comes to the conclusion that the ingredients to use are simple.

Eggs.
Bread.
Butter.
Possible hope.

"Okay," she says, trying to sound confident. "Toast and scrambled eggs. That counts as a real meal."

Sloan gasps. "Sydni Benton. Chef extraordinaire."

"Shut up."

"I'm so proud," he whispers dramatically.

She points a spatula at him. "Not again. I can't emotionally handle another person being proud of me in 24 hours."

"Okay, okay," he says, holding up his hands. "No pride. Just… a thumbs-up." He gives an exaggerated awkward thumbs-up.

She rolls her eyes but grins until her phone buzzes again. She freezes.

"Is that him, is it Breakfast Boy?" Sloan asks gleefully.

"No. It's the app telling me I've been inactive for 20 minutes."

He snorts. "The app is petty. I respect it."

She moves to crack the eggs.

Sloan watches her like she's operating heavy machinery. "Need help?"

"No. I'm a grown woman."

The first egg cracks beautifully. The second egg… goes everywhere.

Sloan applauds lightly. "Art."

"Oh my god," she groans, wiping egg off the counter. "I hate cooking."

"Yet here you are. Conquering breakfast."

"It's literally eggs."

"Symbolic eggs," Sloan says. "This is you choosing yourself."

And in reality, he's not wrong. She can't remember the last time she cooked for herself. As the eggs start to sizzle and the toast pops up unevenly browned, something warm curls in her chest. She's… doing it. Trying. Showing up. Even if she still kind of wants to die from embarrassment at the thought of texting Elias again.

Sloan, like he can read her mind, says, "You're thinking about texting him."

"No, I'm not."

"You SO are."

"No. Because then I look needy."

"He literally sent you seven encouraging messages yesterday."

"That's different."

"How?"

"Because I'm ME," she dramatic whispers.

Sloan tilts his head. "You think he's waiting for your texts?"

She ponders that for a moment. "Yes. No. Maybe. WHY IS THIS SO HARD?"

She serves the eggs onto a plate with toast with as much finesse as she can muster. "Well," she says, grabbing her fork, "I'm not texting him right now. I don't want him thinking I'm clingy."

Sloan shrugs. "Fine. Don't text him."

"Thank you."

He smirks. "But he's totally going to text you first again."

She nearly chokes on her toast. "NO HE WILL NOT."

"Oh he will," Sloan says. "Because he likes you. And he hasn't even realized how much yet."

She doesn't look up. "I hate you."

"No you don't."

She doesn't. Not even a little. As she takes a victorious bite of her very uneven eggs, the app dings again.

But this time… It's not Resolve.

It's Elias.

Sydni wipes her hands on her pajama pants, grabs her phone, and steels herself. Because if Elias Monroe has texted her again, she needs to read it with poise. Grace. Dignity.

She absolutely does NOT need to squeal like a middle schooler.

She unlocks the screen.

Elias:
Just finished my third goal for the day. Not showing off. Just keeping the momentum. Hope your morning's going okay. (No pressure to reply…I know we all have lives.)

Sydni stares at the screen.

Lives? LIVES? She is in pajamas with egg on her sock.

Sloan leans in. "What is it? Is he sexting? Should I get popcorn?"

She elbows him so hard he yelps. "NO. He's just… doing stuff."

"Ooh. The horror."

She glares. "He finished another goal."

Sloan nods. "Yes. Because he is a person who… how do I say this nicely… functions."

"I function!"

"You hibernate," Sloan corrects. "Different animal."

Sydni huffs, grabs her plate, and sits on the couch with exaggerated dignity.

Sloan watches her a moment, then stands. He grabs his jacket from the back of the chair. "Okay, I'm gonna go."

She blinks. "Wait—you're leaving?"

He smirks. "Gotta let you have some space. Also, Elliot's dropping off my drill set."

"You don't drill anything."

"No," he agrees. "But I enjoy owning tools."

She narrows her eyes. "You're being weird."

"—Sydni—" He hesitates, picking his words carefully. "—I'm leaving so you can process your feelings without me narrating them."

She crosses her arms. "I don't HAVE feelings."

"Sure," he says, zipping his coat. "And I don't let my mom guilt me into Sunday dinner." He shrugs. "We all lie."

Then he opens the door and stops in the doorway. The sarcasm dissipates for a moment. "You don't have to answer him immediately," he says gently. "But you should keep living your life. Not just waiting for messages."

"I'm not waiting for messages," she insists.

He raises a brow. "Good. Then act like it."

As he leaves, his shoulders sag a touch as the door clicks shut. But Sydni notices. For a moment, Sydni sits frozen on the couch, fork hovering mid-air. Then she narrows her eyes at the notification on her screen.

"Oh," she says. "Oh, it's like THAT?"

Because Elias Monroe accidentally initiated something dangerous. A productivity death match. He doesn't know he's in it. But she does. She jumps up and starts getting things done. Quickly, with determination.

**10:58 AM — Resolve App
Add Achievement?**

Sydni taps it with the speed of a woman fueled entirely by spite and pride.

**Completed:
– 10-minute walk
– Didn't Die Yet
– Made breakfast
– Cleaned kitchen counters
– Washed dishes
– Opened curtains
– Took trash out**

She adds them all and hits save, and looks at the screen like a gladiator waiting for applause. But the app only gives her a tiny sparkle animation. "Rude," she mutters.

But something feels different. She looks around. The kitchen is cleaner. The sunlight is actually hitting her floor. There is fresh air coming through the cracked window. Her breakfast was real. Her legs are tired in a good way.

She sits slowly and exhales. She feels a little proud of herself. And not because Elias did anything, or not because Sloan pushed her.
Not even because the app shamed her. But because she did it. Even if it was fueled by silent competition.

Her phone buzzes again.

She snaps her head up, but it's not Elias.

Resolve:
   Great job! Elias just saw your new achievements. Would you like to send encouragement?

She snorts. "Absolutely not."

But she can't help the tiny smile that tugs at her lips. Silent competition or not… Today is a win.

CHAPTER NINE

January 6th

The next few days slip past in a blur of cold mornings, small victories, and the hum of winter in Illinois.

Sydni keeps walking. She doesn't like it. She still resents the wind. And she still mutters curses under her breath at joggers who look aggressively joyful at 8 a.m. But she goes. Ten minutes every day. Even on the day her hands feel like ice pops, and she spends the whole walk glaring at a snowplow like it personally offended her.

She cooks… once. It ends with a very burnt pan and two smoke alarms screaming at her like furious smoke detector parents.

She logs it anyway. She checks off her goals. Every day. And by the end of the week, her apartment looks noticeably different. It's not perfect or even fully transformed. But it feels lighter, maybe not Instagram worthy but definitely lighter.

She made her bed three times. She cleaned the bathroom sink, which had not seen a sponge since the last presidential administration. She did laundry, actual laundry, and folded it instead of leaving it in the dryer for a week. She opened the curtains every morning. She even organized the top of her dresser, which had been a chaotic shrine to miscellaneous objects: hair ties, receipts, a single spoon, at least four pens, and a notebook she thought she lost in 2022.

Each small task made the air feel a little easier to breathe.

And today…It's writing day. Not grant writing or emails. Today was the day to do her own writing. This was going to be harder that it looked. Not to-do lists. She made herself comfortable and sat staring at the blinking cursor on a blank Google Doc.

She's avoided this for days. But now that her apartment isn't suffocating, her mind feels clearer, so better time than any to get started.

She cracks her knuckles and pulls her knees up to her chest. She finally, types:

Non-Work Writing — Day 1:

I don't really know what I'm doing with this. But I'm trying. I guess that counts for something.

My apartment is cleaner than it's been in a long time. It's weird how much space opens up when you move something, even something tiny from "I'll get to it someday" to "done."

I don't know if this is progress. But it feels like breathing again. Even if it is awkward and slow and sometimes painful.

And I think… I think the Resolve app is helping. Not just because it reminds me to walk or to stretch or to eat something besides cereal. But because someone else is doing it, too.

She stops, fingers hovering, and thinks about what her next words, before she types:

Elias has been sending encouragement. Not texts, just app messages. But they feel real anyway. And I send encouragement back. Which also feels real. But the fact that neither of us has texted outside the app in four days makes everything weird.

It feels like we're in a silent standoff. Both waiting for the other to speak first. Both pretending we don't care. And both absolutely caring. Or do we?

She rubs her temples lightly before a moment and then keeps typing:

I don't know what he's thinking. And I don't want to look desperate. But I also don't want him to think I'm ignoring him. Or losing interest.
Or uninterested. Or—

God, this is ridiculous.

She closes the laptop halfway. Presses her forehead to the lid. It shouldn't be so hard to write. But this whole, showing up for yourself was new.

Then her phone buzzes. A Resolve notification.

She doesn't even check it right away, she knows it's him. It always is around this time. She lets the phone sit beside her. Just sits with the feeling.

The strange warmth that comes from changing your life one tiny habit at a time. And from knowing someone else is out there, doing their own tiny habits, sending her encouragement without pressuring her.

It's a new and comforting feeling, and unexpectedly comforting.

She finally reaches for the phone.

Resolve:
✦ **Your partner completed their walk.**
Encourage them? ✦

She rolls her eyes affectionately. "Show-off," she mutters. But she smiles as she taps Encourage.

Even if they're not texting…even if this is awkward…even if she's overthinking everything…She doesn't feel alone.

Sydni taps her laptop back open after a long minute of staring at the wall. She doesn't even know why she shut it so quickly. Instinct, maybe, or old habits. The reflex of someone who's used to hiding parts of herself she can't quite name.

But she types again. This time, her fingers move slower. More intentionally. Paragraphs forming instead of scattered lines.

Non-Work Writing — Day 1 (continued):

Maybe I should admit something here, in this space that no one will read but me.

These past few days have been… surprising. Not groundbreaking. Not transformative. But surprising in the quietest way. Like realizing you've been holding your breath for a long time without noticing, and suddenly you're inhaling real air again.

I don't think I understood how much my apartment had started to reflect the inside of my head. Every pile of laundry, every untouched corner, every undone task felt heavy. Like proof that I wasn't keeping up with life. Proof that I was slipping. And maybe I was.

But doing one thing, just one small thing, shifted something. Like knocking over the first domino. It makes me wonder what else I've been putting off because it felt too big. Or because I felt too small.

I still feel small. But I don't feel… stuck. Not today.

She pauses, rereads, surprised by the honesty.

Then types more.

And then there's Elias.

I don't know what to make of him. We barely text. Yes, I'm back on that. We only send those little Resolve nudges, those tiny "You got this" bubbles that feel like patting someone on the shoulder from across a room. It's nothing. But it isn't nothing.

He didn't have to encourage anything. He didn't have to say he was proud. He didn't have to be gentle. Or consistent. But he is. And for reasons I don't fully understand, it matters.

Maybe that's what scares me the most, the idea that someone else notices whether I show up or not.

She swallows, fingers hesitating before she pushes forward.

We're in this strange holding pattern right now. A quiet standstill. Neither of us texting first. Both of us pretending it isn't weird. Both of us knowing it definitely is. Or am I just assuming how he actually feels? Am I just projecting?

But maybe it's okay. Maybe silence isn't rejection. Maybe we both just needed space to see what this feels like without the pressure of words. Or maybe we're just awkward. Or maybe we are awkward AND he finds me boring as hell.

She snorts at that one.

Just as she finishes the sentence, her phone buzzes loudly beside her, vibrating against the table like it's trying to escape. She jumps.

It's not the Resolve app this time. It's him. Her heart flips in her chest. She pulls the phone closer, hesitation thick in her fingertips. She knows that real people don't act like this. Real people are calm, normal, but not her.

She shakes herself at her nearly childish behavior and reads it.

Elias:
Hey! Hope I'm not interrupting anything. I'm putting together my goals for next week and one of them is socializing more (my sister says I've become a hermit). I was just wondering…Have you thought about your new goals yet? No pressure. Just curious what you're adding.

Sydni stares at the message, pulse thrumming.

Her journal entry still glows on the screen in front of her, heavy and honest and braver than she meant to be today. She looks between the text and journal and feels something unfamiliar and warm threading between them.

Elias broke the silence, in the most "him" way possible. Or what she imagines is "him."

He didn't ask why she hadn't texted. He didn't push. He didn't hint at anything flirtatious. He just… reached out. And asked about her goals. Her. Her progress. Her choices. Her next steps. Like he genuinely wants to know what she's trying to build.

Her fingers hover over the keyboard, but she doesn't feel pressured to respond instantly. She just feels seen.

She whispers to herself, "Okay… okay. I can do this."

And she clicks back into her journal. Typing one last honest paragraph before she answers him.

I think I'm finally starting to want something more from myself again. Even if I'm scared. Even if I don't know what next week's goals will be yet. But maybe choosing something new is the point. Maybe letting myself change, just a little, is the point.

She sits back and then picks up her phone to reply.

CHAPTER TEN

Sydni stares at Elias's message for a long moment, chewing on her thumbnail. Partly because she's nervous. Partly because she genuinely doesn't know what next week's goals should be.

And partly because Sloan hasn't told her yet.

He would tell her, of course. Sloan always tells her. He dictates her weekly schedule, her emotional processing, and sometimes what shoes she should wear because, quote, "Your boots make you walk like a newborn giraffe."

But he's been actually busy: meetings, shifts, his volunteer thing he will never admit is volunteer work. So, he hasn't been hovering over her shoulder like a professional life coach. Which leaves Sydni in the dangerous position of… Making her own decisions.

She sighs and opens a new message to Elias.

Sydni:
Hey! You're not interrupting anything. I was doing some writing. (Not work writing. The other kind.)

She pauses, grimaces, and adds:

Sydni:
As for next week's goals… I'm still thinking. My best friend usually "helps" (Bosses? Dictates? Rules my life?) But he's actually had a busy week, so I'm on my own until he resurfaces and tells me my entire list is wrong.

Her thumb hovers. Too self-deprecating? Too weird? Too honest? She shrugs. It's who she is, so she keeps going.

Sydni:
But I have a feeling he's going to vote for socializing too. He thinks I'm turning into a cryptid. His words, not mine.

She snorts at her own message.

Then hesitates again. Does she ask about his list? Does she keep it light? Does she pretend she's totally fine and not spiraling?

She decides to be a little brave. Just a little.

Sydni:
What about you? Adding anything besides "talk to humans" to your goals?

She rereads it twice. It's playful. It's not desperate. It's not nothing. She hits send. And instantly wants to bury her face in a couch cushion. Instead, she closes her messages and returns to her journal, heart thudding louder than she likes.

She types:

I don't know what I'm doing. I don't know what next week is supposed to look like. But maybe I don't have to know yet. Maybe it's okay to figure it out one day at a time. Or one text at a time.

She rests her hands on the keyboard, staring at the screen. She's not used to this part, the part where she has choices. Where she's allowed to want things. Where she's allowed to hope.

Her phone buzzes again. She startles so hard she almost knocks her water over.

Elias has replied. She steadies herself before she reads it.

Elias:
Your best friend "helps"? That sounds suspiciously like code for "runs my entire existence." I respect it. I also fear it slightly.

She snorts so loudly it startles herself.

Another message pops up before she can recover.

Elias:
But... just my two cents: What you want matters too. Not just what he thinks you should do. Your goals should be yours first.

Sydni stares at the screen, unsure of what to make of that. She felt partly affirmed and partly grateful. People don't usually ask what she wants. Even Sloan, who has been her best friend for a long time, is pretty good about dictating. People usually tell her what she should want. Before she can spiral into that feeling, Elias sends another message.

Elias:
Anyway, you asked about my new goals. I'm keeping my basic ones the same, but adding two things:

> 1. *Socializing once a week*
> 2. *Doing one thing that isn't work (outside my apartment)*

Her eyebrows lift.

She reads it again.

Then the follow-up arrives:

Elias:
Apparently, I've become "monastic," according to my sister. (I don't think eating alone with your dog every night counts as a monastery, but she was pretty determined.)

Sydni laughs again, an embarrassingly warm, chest-deep sound she hasn't made in months.

Then the final message:

Elias:
Anyway... that's what I'm adding. Nothing fancy. Just trying to actually live a little. What feels good for you this week? Anything you've been wanting to do?

Sydni stares at that question for a long moment. What feels good for you? What do you want? No one asks her that. Not really. She feels it land deep. She starts to feel guilt for thinking this way because she does have Sloan.

She doesn't reply right away. Not out of fear this time, but because she actually wants to think about it. To consider what she wants her life to look like next week, not what Sloan insists it should look like.

She closes her eyes, thinking about it, and starts to type. But she doesn't hit send yet. She's… thinking. For her. Maybe for the first time in a long while.

Her chest warms. It isn't panic though, it is this realization that he genuinely cares about her answer, and it is not just Sloan. Someone who actually wanted to real answer, not the polite one, or even the "I should say this" one. But the real one.

Her thumbs hovering over the keys.

Then she types:

Sydni:
Okay, honest answer: I don't actually mind my best friend running my life. He's the best person I know. Heart of gold. Annoying as hell. Constantly pushing me outside my comfort zone. But always for the right reasons.

She pauses, surprised by her own honesty. She keeps typing.

Sydni:
But if I'm talking about my goals…I think I want to do something simple. Like visit a bookstore. Pick out a book that isn't for work. And get a coffee. Like a real, normal person who leaves the apartment sometimes.

Her face warms, but it feels right.

She adds:

Sydni:
And I want to make my bed every day next week, even though I have done it three times this week. (It sounds small but trust me… it's not small for me.) And maybe even change my sheets once a week. Because… lord knows how long it's been.
We're not going to talk about it.

She rereads it.

It's honest. It's human. It's her.

She hesitates for only a second, then presses send. Her phone makes that tiny whoosh sound.

And suddenly, Sydni feels something shift inside her. It was not dread. She didn't even feel embarrassment. This feeling was new, and something quieter. A small, tentative swell of wanting something better for herself. She sits back, wrapping her blanket around her shoulders. And she waits, not anxiously this time, for whatever comes next.

CHAPTER ELEVEN

Elias Monroe sits at his small kitchen table, coffee growing cold beside him, Clementine curled at his feet like a living weighted blanket.

His phone buzzes. He doesn't look at it right away. He's been trying to break the habit of leaping for his phone every time it lights up, especially these past few days.

He'd told himself the silence wasn't weird. That Sydni probably needed space. That he wasn't disappointed. He lies to himself often. Just not very successfully.

When he finally picks up the phone, he expects the little blue Resolve bubble. Another achievement. Another check mark. Another tiny digital nudge. But it's not Resolve.

It's her. He sits up straighter, thumb hovering before he opens the message. He reads slowly. And then immediately reads it again. He has this feeling that he doesn't quite recognize. It feels like surprise and something he doesn't want to name yet.

I don't actually mind my best friend running my life. He's the best person I know. Heart of gold. Annoying as hell. Constantly pushing me outside my comfort zone...

Elias smiles at the screen. He knows that tone. That mix of fondness and exasperation. Someone loving someone loudly and complaining about it anyway. He thinks, I want someone to write about me like that someday. But he pushes that thought away and keeps reading.

...if I'm talking about my goals... I think I want to do something simple. Like visit a bookstore. Pick out a book that isn't for work. And get a coffee.

He feels like the Grinch. It wasn't in a flashy, cinematic way, but the grounding warmth of seeing a person choose a small joy for themselves. Yes, he had that feeling that his heart grew three sizes.

He leans back in his chair, eyes lingering on her words. Bookstore. Coffee. Something normal. Something gentle. It tells him something important: Sydni isn't looking for a big overhaul. She isn't chasing perfection. She's chasing… air. Space. A life that doesn't feel like drowning.

He respects that more than she'll ever know. Then he reads the final part:

And I want to make my bed every day next week. even though I have done it three this week. (It sounds small, but trust me… it's not small for me.) And maybe even change my sheets once a week. Because… lord knows how long it's been.
We're not going to talk about it.

He huffs out a laugh, shaking his head. She has no idea how endearing she is.

Clementine lifts her head at the sound, tail thumping once. "Yeah," Elias murmurs, scratching behind her ear. "She's… something else."

He reads the message a third time. Then he lets his elbows rest on the table, phone held in both hands, the way a person holds something delicate.

He'd been trying to figure out whether he should text her outside the app. He didn't have to, but he wanted to. More than he's wanted to talk to someone in a long time.

He'd waited, though. Wanted to respect the space. Wanted to let her set the pace. But now? Now he feels like she offered him a small doorway into her world. A real one. Not a polite one. She trusted him with honesty. With vulnerability wrapped in humor.

Elias smiles, thumb poised above the keyboard. He starts typing, slowly, carefully. He isn't unsure, but he wants to get this right.

She asked what he's adding to his routine. But he realizes…That isn't what she really asked. She asked if he wanted to share the next steps with her.

And he does. More than he should. And before he knows it, he is sending her a message, asking if she wants to get coffee with him.

CHAPTER TWELVE

Sydni is having an argument with her reflection. "You are a functioning adult," she tells the mirror. The mirror disagrees, showing a woman who looks like she woke up in a tornado. Her curls exploding in multiple directions, a nervous flush across her cheeks, and a mascara wand she's holding like a tiny weapon. She hasn't seen Elias since New Year's Eve. Since the almost-kiss she's replayed far more times than she'll ever admit out loud. Since her "this feels like a Hallmark movie" humiliation. Now she's sweating over coffee.

Sloan lounges on her bed like a judgmental cat, arms folded behind his head. "You're panicking."

"I'm not panicking," she lies, stabbing a curl with a bobby pin. "I'm adjusting my expectations."

"For what? Basic social interaction?"

She points the wand at him. "I will poke you."

He grins. "There she is. I missed this version of you."

"What version is that?"

"The Sydni who cares."

He means it. She hates that he means it. Before he can get any more sincere, she grabs her coat and heads out.

The walk to the coffee shop feels longer than usual. Her heart can't decide whether to sprint or collapse, so it does a ridiculous mixture of both. She stops at the door and forces a deep breath. If he doesn't show up, she'll survive. If he does, she might combust. Either way, her stomach is staging a rebellion.

She pushes open the door. The warmth inside hits her, and she is thankful for the heater. Then she sees him.

Elias.

He's sitting by the window, long legs stretched out, fingers curled around a mug like he's absorbing the heat into his palms. His hair is a little messy from the cold, and the faint stubble along his jaw sends an unexpected shiver through her. When he looks up and sees her, something in his expression opens. A smile forms, slow, warm, pleased, and it feels like a private moment meant only for her.

"Hey," he says. His voice is gentle enough to make her knees feel unreliable.

"Hi."

He stands halfway, awkward, and charming at the same time. "I, uh, got your drink. I hope that was okay."

"You ordered for me?" She tilts her head, pretending she's teasing, but the truth is her pulse jumps.

He blushes, actually blushes, and it does dangerous things to her. "Yes. But I fully accepted the possibility that I got it wrong and have to drink it myself."

"That's very brave of you."

"Only when caffeine is involved," he says, motioning to the chair across from him.

She sits, and their knees almost touch beneath the tiny table. The nearness sparks something warm at the base of her spine, and she pretends she doesn't feel it. The drink is perfect. They only one had tiny exchange about coffee in passing

"You remembered," she murmurs.

He toys with the side of his mug. "I pay attention."

She conveniently ignores that butterfly feeling.

They fall into conversation, but not the surface kind. He tells her about a patient's dog that ate a sock. She tells him about a grant report that nearly made her retire early. They compare bookstore philosophies. He laughs and the sound is deep, genuine, and unfairly attractive.

At one point he studies her for a moment too long. "You seem lighter today."

"Lighter," she repeats, unsure if that's good or bad.

"Yeah." He gestures gently toward her. "Brighter. More present."

"I made my bed. That might be it."

"It looks good on you," he says, eyes steady on hers.

She hides behind her mug because she cannot handle being perceived like that.

They talk for nearly an hour and a half, and it feels easy. Loosened. Like she slipped into a version of herself she hasn't worn in a long time.

When they leave, Elias holds the door for her. The cold air brushes her cheeks, and she sucks in a breath that feels fresh instead of harsh. As they walk, he drifts to the side closest to the street in a casual, protective, and unthinking kind of way. She acts like she doesn't notice, but her chest knows.

When they reach her building, she stops. "Thanks for… this."

"For coffee?" he asks, amusement hinted in his voice.

"For showing up."

His expression shifts, gentle and careful, like he's afraid of mishandling the moment. "I liked today." His eyes darted briefly to her mouth before returning to her face. "A lot."

Her faces feels hot and she desperately hopes isn't obvious.

He smiles. "Same time next week? Maybe we make it a routine."

She nods too fast, and the corners of his mouth curve as if he finds that adorable. "Okay," he says. "See you then."

He walks away with his hands in his pockets, shoulders relaxed. She watches until he turns the corner and realizes her face aches. She's been smiling this whole time.

~*~

Sydni doesn't even have her key fully in the lock before the door swings open from the inside. Sloan stands there with the energy of a man who has been pacing behind the peephole like a deranged raccoon waiting for food. He crosses his arms, squints at her, and says nothing. Just stares.

"Don't you dare," she warns, sliding past him.

He follows her into the apartment like a shadow with opinions. "I haven't said a word yet."

"You're saying a word with your face."

"I have a very expressive face," he replies, closing the door dramatically behind them. "Now sit. You reek of emotional development."

She groans and shrugs out of her coat, tossing it over a chair. "Can I breathe for five seconds?"

"Five seconds? Sure." Sloan pulls out his phone, sets a timer, and then stares at it intensely. After exactly one second, he clicks it off. "Time's up. Spill."

Sydni laughs despite herself. She tries to play it cool, walking into the kitchen like she's not being hunted for information. But Sloan simply follows her, leaning against the counter like he's preparing for a crime interrogation.

"So," he begins, tapping the counter rhythmically, "how was it?"

"It was coffee," she says.

"Aha," he declares. "A confession. She admits she had coffee. And with whom did she caffeinate her feelings?"

"Stop."

87

"Was the coffee hot? Or was it… steamy?"

"Oh my God."

Sloan lifts both hands dramatically. "Fine. Fine. I'll be normal."
He pauses. "Normal-adjacent."

Sydni pulls a mug from the shelf, filling it with water just to have
something to do with her hands. She can feel him watching her
with those dark eyes that see way too much.

"So," he says again, softer now, "it went well?"

Her shoulders loosen. "Yeah," she admits. "It… actually went
really well."

Sloan grins, wide and bright, the kind of grin that makes his
dimples show. He looks genuinely happy for her. The kind of
friend who wants her to have coffee dates that make her smile.
Underneath though, there is still a hint…of something

Then, very smoothly, he pushes away from the counter and
stands straighter. "You're glowing."

She narrows her eyes. "Stop saying glowing."

"But you are," he insists, stepping closer. "I can tell when you're
faking it, Syd. Today? You're actually happy. I like seeing you
like that."

The sincerity almost knocks the wind out of her. It always does.
Sloan's tenderness hits harder than teasing ever could. It's too
much and not enough at the same time.

"I'm not falling in love with him, Sloan," she says defensively.
"It's not like that."

He tilts his head. "Maybe not. Maybe not yet. But I saw you walk
through that door. And I haven't seen you smile like that in a
long time."

She looks away, gripping her mug a little too tightly. "It was just… nice. Being around someone who doesn't expect anything from me."

Sloan's voice loses all humor. "Ok, first of all. Ouch. Secondly, I don't expect anything from you."

She looks back at him then. Really looks at him. "Yes, you do," she says, not accusingly, just honest. "You expect me to live. To show up. To not disappear. But that's because you love me. And I love you. And Elias…" She trails off, not sure how to finish that sentence.

Sloan steps closer and places a warm hand on the back of her head, his thumb brushing one of her curls. It's the kind of touch that says you're not alone.

"You don't owe him anything," he says gently. "Not vulnerability. Not explanations. Not your heart. But if you want to give him pieces of yourself, you get to choose that. Not your past. Not your fear."

She closes her eyes for a moment, pressing her lips together. "He remembered my coffee order."

Sloan hums, thoughtfully. "Men who remember coffee orders are exceptionally dangerous."

She smiles weakly. "And he said I looked lighter."

"Well that's because you do," Sloan says, brushing a curl off her forehead. "You've been taking care of yourself. Making your bed. Doing your walks. And now you're letting someone new be part of your life. That's big, Syd."

Sydni feels heat rise behind her eyes. Not tears, just overwhelm. Kindness always does her in. "I don't know what I'm doing," she whispers.

"That makes two of you," Sloan replies, pulling her into a sideways hug. "But hey, this is the good kind of chaos. And for the record… I'm proud of you. I was proud of you before Elias.

I'll be proud of you long after. This part?" He squeezes her shoulder. "This is just a bonus chapter."

Sydni lets out a breathy laugh into his hoodie. "All this pride just coming out of nowhere. You're insufferable."

"And handsome. And wise. Don't forget wise."

She rolls her eyes and nudges him. "We may be making it a weekly thing, part of our goals, you know?" She hesitates for a moment. "Sloan? Thank you, really."

"Always," Sloan says, squeezing once before stepping back. "Now… tell me every detail. And don't you dare skip the parts where you blushed."

She groans. "You're impossible."

"And yet here I am. Go on. Start from the top."

After nearly an hour of teasing, lecturing, comforting, and what he called "therapeutic cross-examination," Sloan finally stands from the couch, stretches, and grabs his keys from the counter.

"I'm leaving you to your feelings," he announces, slipping on his jacket like a dramatic Victorian widow. "Don't drown in them without adult supervision."

"I'll try not to," she says dryly.

"I'll check on you later," he adds, heading for the door. He pauses in the doorway and throws her one last look, half protective, half proud. "And Syd?"

She looks up.

"You're allowed to enjoy this. Whatever this becomes."

Then he's gone, leaving the apartment warm and quiet, like the air has finally settled.

When the door clicks shut behind Sloan, the apartment settles into a gentler silence. It doesn't feel heavy or lonely, just still.

Sydni pulls her blanket tighter around her shoulders and wanders toward her desk, the glow of her computer waiting like a small, steady lighthouse.

She sits, pulls her knees up into her chair, and opens a new document. She likes the sound the keys make when she types. It's grounding. Predictable. A rhythm she can control.

Her fingers hover for a moment, as they always do.

She begins to type, letting the words come without overthinking.

I didn't expect today to feel like anything. I told myself it was just coffee, a box to check, something I could survive and then hide from for the rest of the week. I didn't plan on enjoying it. I didn't plan on feeling... safe.

I haven't seen Elias since New Year's Eve, and I wasn't ready for what that would do to my stomach. I don't like admitting that, even here. But when I walked into the coffee shop and saw him sitting by the window, smiling at me like he meant it... something shifted. Something small. Something I'm not sure I'm prepared for.

He remembered her coffee order and got it right. I keep thinking about that. People don't usually remember things about me unless it benefits them somehow. Unless I'm helpful or convenient or useful. But he remembered because he pays attention. And that scares me more than I want it to.

He made me laugh today. Real laugh, you know the one. The kind that shakes loose stiffness you didn't know you were carrying. I don't laugh like that anymore. I don't even smile like that unless Sloan is harassing me. But with Elias... it wasn't forced.

And he looked at me the way people look at sunrises; soft, curious, surprised that something quiet could be beautiful. I don't know what to do with that. I'm not used to being seen in a way that isn't dissecting or judging or demanding. I kept expecting the moment to flip into something uncomfortable, but it didn't.

I felt normal with him. Not perfect, not healed, not performing, just… normal. And it has been a very long time since normal felt possible.

I keep telling myself this doesn't mean anything. That it's just Resolve pushing us to be social. That it's just coffee. Just conversation. Just two lonely people doing their goals for the week.

But there was a moment , when he said I seemed lighter, that felt like someone opening a window inside my chest. I didn't know people noticed things like that about me. I didn't know there was anything to notice.

I don't know what this is. I don't want to put pressure on it. I'm not ready for romance or labels or any of the things I used to daydream about before life happened the way it did. But I think… I think I want to see him again.

And that terrifies me. Because wanting anything has always felt dangerous. But avoiding everything has made me feel even worse.

Maybe wanting something small, like another coffee next week, is a good place to start.

She stops typing at the quiet click of the final period.

Seeing the words on the screen, honest and a little raw, makes her chest tighten. Like stretching muscles she hasn't used in a long time.

She rereads the final paragraph twice before saving the document.

Then she closes the laptop, draws her knees to her chest. And now, she doesn't dread what comes next. She's nervous. She's uncertain. But she's here.

CHAPTER THIRTEEN

The following week unfolds in small, manageable pieces. For once, life doesn't feel like a tidal wave threatening to knock her off her feet. It feels more like a series of steps she can take one at a time, even if she stumbles on a few.

Work resumes with its usual chaos. The grant calendar on her wall blinks red with deadlines she'd been avoiding, and her inbox looks like it's been multiplying out of spite. But there's something different this time: she doesn't feel crushed by it.

Just… tired. Human tired. Not soul-crushing tired. And that's progress.

Most mornings, she forces herself out the door for her 10-minute walk. The first day feels like dragging concrete legs through wet sand, but the cold air wakes her up enough to make it bearable. On the second morning, she notices a neighbor's dog greeting her through a window. On the third, she sees a kid wearing a dinosaur backpack and smiles. On the fourth, she buys herself a pastry for no reason at all.

It's not joy, exactly. But it's closer to something like it.

Resolve keeps nudging her, sending those little encouragement badges that used to annoy her but now feel a bit like tiny digital pats on the back.

And then there's Elias. They don't text constantly. Nothing overwhelming. Just gentle, steady check-ins woven throughout the week.

The first comes the day after their coffee:

Elias:
Hope work wasn't too brutal today. Did coffee refill your life force or did you require backup caffeine?

She sends back a picture of her third cup beside the most chaotic section of her desk.

Sydni:
Current status: 78% caffeine, 22% chaos. So… pretty normal.

His reply is instant.

Elias:
Acceptable ratios.

She finds herself smiling at her screen more times than she admits to Sloan.

By midweek, Sydni is deep into writing a difficult grant. The kind that demands logic models, measurable outcomes, and a willingness to pretend she hasn't been staring at the same sentence for forty minutes. She leans back in her chair, rubbing her eyes.

Her phone buzzes.

Elias:
Resolve says you completed "10 minutes of focused productivity." What does that even mean? I folded two shirts and stared at a wall.

She snorts, typing back one-handed.

Sydni:
It means Resolve has very low standards and we should all be grateful.

His response makes her laugh harder than she means to.

Elias:
So… they made it to YOUR level?

She throws a crumpled sticky note at her monitor. The sarcasm is refreshing. Not harsh, not mocking. Just familiar. Comfortable.

Sloan would be horrified to know she's enjoying this much.

By Thursday, Sydni's grant draft is half-finished, the apartment is marginally cleaner, and her bed has been made every morning except one. The morning she overslept because she'd stayed up rereading her journal entry (something she refuses to admit aloud).

She and Elias exchange messages about their upcoming weekly outing.

It's not "a date." She won't call it that. But it feels more intentional than before. A little more chosen.

Elias:
Same time? Or do you want to try a different place this week?

Sydni:
Different place might be good. (As long as no one tries to talk to me.)

Elias:
I can handle any necessary human interaction. I'll act as your social bouncer.

She chokes on her tea.

Sydni:
A what?

Elias:
A social bouncer. Someone gets too close, I bounce them.

She covers her face with both hands, grinning like an actual idiot. She hates how much she likes talking to him.

On Friday night, she finishes the first draft of her grant and clicks Save with a dramatic flourish. Standing from her desk, she stretches until her back pops, then sinks into her couch with a blanket and a quiet sense of pride.

Her phone lights up again.

Elias:
Did you just complete "Major Work Task"? Resolve just congratulated me for knowing someone productive. Which feels like favoritism tbh.

Sydni:
Yes, I finished the grant. Yes, I'm dying. Yes, I deserve a medal.

Elias:
I'll bring you a coffee instead. Cheaper than a medal.

She stares at that message a few seconds longer than she should. He's thoughtful in ways he doesn't even seem to notice.

She types back:

Sydni:
Coffee is acceptable payment. Maybe even preferable.

He answers with a simple:

Elias:
Good.

Just that. And she's good with it.

When Sydni finally crawls into bed that night, her sheets are clean, her journal has a new entry, her grant is drafted, and for the first time in a very long time she doesn't feel like she's barely surviving. She feels… steady. Balanced. A little hopeful.

Maybe it's the routine. Maybe it's the progress. Maybe it's the fact that Elias Monroe somehow manages to be both grounding and disarming at the same time.

Whatever it is, she's looking forward to their next outing in a way that scares her.

But not enough to make her run. Not yet.

CHAPTER FOURTEEN

Their second weekly outing is supposed to be casual. A simple, low-stakes outing. Nothing fancy, just two people fulfilling their Resolve socializing requirement like responsible adults who can totally handle being around another human without spiraling.

That's what Sydni tells herself as she walks through the side streets toward Oak & Ink, a tiny bookstore café tucked between a florist and a thrift shop. The place smells like old paper, lavender, and espresso. The kind of shop where the world feels quieter in all the right ways.

She spots Elias through the window before she even reaches the door.

He's sitting at a corner table, coat draped over the back of his chair, absorbed in a paperback with his thumb marking the page. He's wearing a gray sweater that clings to his shoulders in a way that should be illegal. His hair is slightly messy, like he ran his hands through it one too many times. He looks cozy and comfortable. Like the kind of person who belongs in quiet corners.

And when he looks up and sees her, that small, subtle smile appears. "Hey," he says when she steps inside.

She closes the door behind her. "Hi."

"Got here early," he admits, setting the book down. "Mostly because my sister insisted on ironing my sweater and then lecturing me about 'being presentable in public.'"

Sydni smiles. "My best friend made me practice breathing exercises."

Elias nods solemnly. "We are two fully grown adults who definitely need supervision."

"Absolutely."

This time, sitting across from him doesn't feel nearly as intimidating. The nervous flutter is still there, but there is also a growing familiarity, by the comfort of someone who doesn't fill silence with judgment or expectation.

He pushes a small pastry plate toward her. "I wasn't sure if you'd eaten. I took a gamble again."

She raises an eyebrow. "You're very confident in your pastry gambling skills."

"I contain multitudes."

She giggles as she breaks off a piece of the almond croissant. It's perfect.

They fall into conversation easily. Somehow even more naturally than last time. He tells her about a chaotic week at the clinic, clients rescheduling, Clementine stealing half a loaf of bread off the counter. She tells him about finishing the grant, about nearly throwing her laptop out the window, about Sloan insisting on "reward dinner" by ordering three different kinds of takeout because she "looked like she'd been wrestling demons."

Elias listens in that same careful way, attentive but not intense. So present it's almost startling.

At one point, he leans back in his chair, fingers tapping his mug, and asks, "Do you like your job?"

The question is genuine but feels deep. Most people ask what she does, not what she feels about it.

Sydni hesitates, looking down at the croissant flakes on the table. "I do… most of the time. I like helping. I like writing. I like the purpose. But it also… takes a lot out of me. More than it used to."

He watches her for a moment, not dissecting, just understanding. "That makes sense. You carry a lot. Maybe more than people realize."

She swallows, caught off guard by how true that feels. Even more shocking that she had heard Sloan say that exact thing to her.

"And you?" she asks. "You like the clinic?"

He thinks for a second before answering. "I do. I like helping people get stronger. I like the quiet nature of the work. But there are days that are heavy. Harder than I let on."

In the moment between conversation, it doesn't feel uncomfortable. It feels more like two people realizing the other is human in familiar ways.

"I'm glad you told me that," she murmurs.

"I'm glad you listened."

The warmth between them settles like something fragile and new. It isn't some spark of lust or dramatic tension, but something gentler, something that feels like recognition.

After they finish their pastries, Elias stands and gestures toward the bookstore shelves. "Want to look around? You mentioned wanting a non-workbook."

Sydni hesitates. Not because she doesn't want to, but because she's never done something like this with someone she barely knows but is starting to like. But she nods anyway, letting herself follow him.

They move slowly through the aisles, their fingers brushing the spines of books, sharing little glimpses of who they are. He points out a nature photography book he likes. She admits her obsession with cozy mysteries and self-help titles she buys but never finishes. He laughs, telling her he understands that impulse far too well.

In one moment, he reaches past her to pull down a novel and their shoulders bump, a light, accidental touch that sends a jolt through her.

He doesn't comment. She doesn't either. But her skin remembers it.

Near the front of the store, he hands her the book he's picked for her. "This one made me feel… steadier. I thought you might like it."

She runs her fingers over the cover, surprised by the thoughtfulness. "Thank you," she says, and she means it more than he knows.

As they leave the shop, the winter light bounces off the dry snow on the sidewalk. Their steps fall into sync without effort.

"Same time next week?" he asks when they reach her building, quieter this time, like he's giving her an out if she wants it.

But Sydni doesn't want an out. She surprises herself with how quickly she answers. "Yes."

Elias nods. "Good. I'll find somewhere new."

She watches him as he walks away, gray sweater pulled tight against the cold, hands tucked into his pockets. When he glances back once, just briefly, as if making sure she made it inside safely, her heart twists in a way she doesn't have a name for.

Inside, with the book still in her hand, Sydni realizes something unsettlingly hopeful. She's starting to look forward to these moments. And wanting something, wanting someone, is terrifying. But she isn't running. Not today.

By the time Sydni gets home from the bookstore outing, her cheeks are flushed in a way she can't blame entirely on the cold. She hangs her coat on the back of a chair and toes off her boots and before she even finishes the second, there's a knock on her door.

It's not a polite knock. It's a Sloan-knock. Impatient, rhythmic, like a drumline of judgment.

"Open up," he calls, muffled. "I brought pizza and emotional stability."

Sydni opens the door. Sloan holds up a pizza box with one hand and a bottle of sparkling water with the other, eyes narrowing like he's scanning her for evidence.

"You're glowing again," he accuses.

"Oh my god, STOP saying glowing," she groans, stepping aside so he can come in.

"I stand by my assessment," Sloan says, brushing past her and heading straight to the kitchen counter. He opens the pizza box, inspects it, and nods as if it has passed quality control. "So. Spill. Did he look at you with those dreamy physical therapist eyes and make you feel seen?"

Sydni goes to get her own drink, since she still hates sparkling water. "He did not give me 'therapist eyes.'"

"Oh he absolutely did," Sloan says, grabbing a slice. "That man looks at you like you're a sunrise he didn't know was scheduled."

She chokes on a laugh. "Sloan—"

"Don't deny it." He sits on the couch, tucking one leg under himself. "You like him."

"I don't— I mean, I'm not— It's not like that," she sputters, and Sloan raises both eyebrows in the "try again" expression she hates.

She sighs and sits beside him. "It's just… easy with him. Comfortable. He's really gentle."

"That's because he's a golden retriever in human form," Sloan says through a mouthful of pizza. "He deserves a treat and maybe a nap."

She nudges him with her shoulder. "It was nice. Okay? I had a good time."

Sloan relaxes at that, his teasing shifted into something warmer. "I'm glad. Really."

They eat together for a few minutes in comfortable silence. Sloan keeps glancing at her like he's checking that she hasn't evaporated back into her shell. Eventually, he wipes his hands on a napkin and stands. "Alright, I'm going back to my place before I get emotionally attached to your throw pillows."

"You already are," she says.

"True," he admits. "Call me if you need anything. Or if you start spiraling. Or if you decide you want to psychoanalyze his sweater choices."

Sydni lifts a hand in a mock salute. "Will do."

He gives her one last look. A "you're doing great even if you don't believe it" look, and leaves.

The apartment feels quiet again, but not empty. Her thoughts feel full, humming, warm around the edges. She drifts back to her desk, turns on her lamp, and opens her laptop.

She hesitates for a moment before opening her journal document. Then the words begin to flow.

Today was... unexpectedly good. I didn't think the second outing would feel easier than the first, but it did. There was no spark or dramatic moment. Nothing like romance novels or cheesy movies. It was just real. Steady. Two people choosing to spend time together without pretending to be anything else.

I liked seeing him in the bookstore. He looks like he belongs in quiet spaces. He moves slowly, deliberately, like he doesn't want to disturb the air. He chose a book for me. No one has done that since I was a kid. It made something in my chest feel warm and tight at the same time.

I don't know what worries me more, that I'm starting to enjoy these moments, or that I'm allowing myself to want more of them. Wanting anything feels risky. Wanting someone feels impossible.

But here I am, sitting at my desk, writing about a man who makes me laugh and breathe easier and walk into public spaces without wanting to vanish.

Maybe that's progress. Maybe I should be proud of myself. I don't know. All I know is that it felt good to be around him today. Safe. Not in the "hide behind walls" way but in the "I don't have to hold my breath" way.

And I don't feel that very often.

She pauses, fingers still on the keys. Her chest feels heavy and light at the same time. Such new feelings, that most people are probably used to.

Just as she's about to close her laptop for the night, her phone buzzes with a Resolve notification.

Your partner Elias Monroe has completed:
— Weekly Socializing Goal
— Daily Kindness Reflection

Her heart stutters. For a moment, she just stares at the screen.

It shouldn't bother her. It's literally what they were supposed to do. It's a goal, a checkbox, a task. But some small, insecure voice in the back of her mind whispers:

Was today just a requirement to him? Just a box to check? Just a task with her name on it?

That warmth in her chest? Well, it flickers. It doesn't die exactly but it definitely dims.

She closes her journal slowly, sitting back in her chair. She tells herself she's being dramatic. Overthinking. Reading into something harmless. But she can't help it.

For all the softness she's found in him, in herself , there's still a part of her that wonders what she is to someone like him.

A goal?
A nice gesture?
A person he helps because he's kind?
Or something more?

She doesn't know yet. But that not knowing feeling? It is terrifying, but also, somewhat exhilarating.

CHAPTER FIFTEEN

Saturday morning begins with a knock at Sydni's door so aggressive it could qualify as a wellness check.

She freezes mid-sip of her coffee. "Oh God," she whispers to herself. "He's here."

Before she can get up, Sloan's voice bellows through the door like a Broadway performer who has never once been asked to lower his volume.

"OPEN UP, YOU BEAUTIFUL DEPRESSION WAFFLE!"

Sydni nearly spits her coffee all over her laptop.

She swings open the door to find Sloan standing there with two grocery bags, a grin too big for his face, and the kind of energy that should require a permit.

"What—what is happening?" she asks.

"We," Sloan announces, dramatically brushing past her, "are making waffles."

"I—why?"

"Because your boyfriend bought you a book, and that deserves culinary celebration."

"He's not my boyfriend."

Sloan sets the grocery bags down with a thud. "Keep telling yourself that, sweetie."

Sydni covers her face with both hands, already regretting being alive today. "I'm going back to bed."

"You can't," he says, already unpacking ingredients like a man possessed. "We have batter to make. Emotions to avoid. Carbs to consume."

She groans and flops onto the couch. "Why are you like this?"

Sloan pulls out a waffle iron she doesn't remember him buying. "Two things, Syd: One, I contain multitudes. Two, I googled 'how to romance someone on Sydni's behalf,' and waffles were on the list."

Her eyes snap open. "YOU DID WHAT—"

"Nothing. Shut up. Get over here and whisk something."

The next thirty minutes are an unhinged blend of cooking, bickering, and Sloan insisting he knows what he's doing despite having no evidence to support that.

Flour ends up on the counter. Then on the floor. Then on Sydni's hair.

"You're a menace," she says, brushing flour off her shirt.

"You're welcome."

But the truth is… she's laughing. Like actually laughing. The kind that bubbles up warm and unrestrained, despite the lingering insecurity sitting somewhere in the corner of her chest like a little passenger.

Sloan notices, of course he does, and he nudges her shoulder. "There she is."

"Shut up," she says, smiling.

"Never."

When the first waffle comes out misshapen and slightly burned, Sloan gasps in genuine distress.

"It's abstract!" Sydni offers.

"It's a cry for help," he counters.

The second one is better. The third is perfect. The fourth is a disaster she swears has its own consciousness.

By the fifth, they're standing shoulder-to-shoulder, laughing like children, the kitchen warm and smelling like sugar and butter.

It feels good. Safe. Normal. And yet, somewhere beneath the lightness, a tiny insecurity hums deep inside. He completed his socializing goal. Just checked it off. Maybe she was just… section A of a productivity chart. She tries to shake the thought off, but it lingers.

Sloan casts her a glance while stirring blueberries into a bowl. "You okay? You got quiet."

Sydni shrugs, forcing a smile. "Just thinking."

"Thinking is dangerous," he says. "Avoid it at all costs."

She snorts. "I'm fine."

He raises a brow, unconvinced. "You're thinking about Elias."

"No."

"Yes."

"No."

"Yes."

She lets out a small laugh because there's no winning with him. "It's nothing. Really."

"If it were nothing, you wouldn't be lying," he says gently, but not pushing. Sloan knows when to back off, it's one of his superpowers. "Whenever you want to talk, I'm here. Until then, help me not set this kitchen on fire."

She nods, gratitude settling behind her ribs. He doesn't force her to say more. He doesn't pry. He just stays loud, chaotic, loyal. Exactly what she needs.

They end up sitting at the table, plates piled with waffles, whipped cream, fruit, and the kind of sugar that could kill smaller mammals.

Sydni takes a bite and closes her eyes. "Oh my God. Sloan. This is incredible."

He beams. "I know. If Elias doesn't kiss you soon, he's missing out on waffle-adjacent greatness."

She kicks him under the table.

He yelps. "Abuse!"

"You deserve it."

"Yea, that's probably true."

They fall into easy conversation. Silly things, movies, what they'd name a pet raccoon ("Craig," apparently), why her upstairs neighbor walks like a T-Rex during cardio. And for a little while, her insecurity fades into the background.

When Sloan finally goes home, she's tired but in a good way. The kind that comes from laughing too much. She cleans up the counters, puts the leftover waffles in the fridge, and settles onto her couch with a blanket draped over her knees.

Her phone buzzes once.

Resolve: Your partner Elias Monroe has completed — Daily Mindfulness Moment

There's that flicker again. That feeling of doubt. Like she's a little too aware of being part of his checklist. But she pushes the feeling aside, or tries to, and sinks deeper into the couch.

Tomorrow, she tells herself. She can deal with whatever she's feeling tomorrow. Tonight, she's full of waffles and warmth and just enough courage to hope that maybe she isn't as replaceable as her mind sometimes claims.

After Sloan heads back to his place, leaving her kitchen looking like a flour bomb detonated in the name of friendship, Sydni finally sinks onto her couch with her phone in hand. Her belly is full of waffles, her cheeks hurt from laughing, and her nerves are still buzzing in that post-Sloan chaotic way.

She opens Resolve, mostly out of habit, partly out of the tiny competitive streak she won't admit she has, and taps **"Cook a Meal"** with an overly dramatic flourish.

The app chirps with a confetti animation.

You completed:
— Cook a Meal
You're becoming unstoppable! 🔍 ✦

She snorts. "If only you knew," she mutters.

Just as she sets her phone down, the screen lights up again.

Encouragement from your partner, Elias:
Look at you, Chef Sydni! 🍽️ 💧

She blinks, caught off guard by the feeling that rises in her chest. Proud of her? For making waffles that were 40% edible and 60% chaos? That feels… oddly meaningful.

Before she can overthink it, another notification buzzes, this time a text.

Elias:
Please tell me this "cooked a meal" wasn't just you reheating something questionable in your fridge.

She laughs out loud.

Sydni:
I'll have you know I made WAFFLES. From scratch. With a whisk and everything.

There's a long pause. Long enough for her to wonder if maybe that sounded weird. Or childish. Or—

Her phone buzzes.

Elias:
Hold on. You operated a whisk? Voluntarily?

She rolls her eyes.

Sydni:
It was a supervised activity.

Elias:
Ah. Sloan-implemented culinary enrichment. Checks out.

Sydni:
He says if you don't kiss me after you hear about these waffles, you're missing out on greatness.

She freezes. Then panic-sends a second message.

Sydni:
NOPE. NO. I meant—
NOT LIKE THAT. DELETE THAT TEXT FROM EXISTENCE.

He replies instantly.

Elias:
…
I'm framing it.

Her face goes hot. "I hate everything."

Sydni:
Please don't.

Elias:
Too late. It's already in the Smithsonian.

She buries her face in her blanket.

Sydni:
This is mortifying.

Elias:
It's adorable.

Those damn butterflies do flips. She is *not* prepared for flips. She tries to recover.

Sydni:
Anyway. Waffles. I made them. They were decent. Some were… interpretive.

Elias:
I'm impressed. Truly. Cooking when you didn't want to cook is more impressive than gourmet anything.

She bites her lip, staring at those words longer than necessary.

Her insecurity nudges. *Is he saying that because he means it? Or because he's supposed to? A partner checking off his supportive tasks?*

She pushes the thought away before it ruins the moment.

Sydni:
Thanks. I even saved two. For science.

Elias:
Science = me?

Sydni:
…
Maybe.

Elias:
Then I accept this sacred responsibility.

She snorts, sinking deeper into the couch, with this feeling that she had no idea what to do with.

Elias:
What's next on your list today?

She glances around the tornado of a kitchen.

Sydni:
Cleaning the waffle war zone. And maybe a shower so I don't smell like depression and vanilla.

Elias:
Strong combination. Signature scent of someone who's doing their best.

She smiles. Too big. Too long.

CHAPTER SIXTEEN

By the time Saturday arrives, Sydni has already exchanged three days of texts with Elias. The messages are harmless on the surface, but they carry something under the words that she pretends not to notice. Banter that feels natural. A little flirtier than she will ever admit to Sloan.

She never meant to start a competition, but once Elias discovered she was trying to out-productivity him on Resolve, he turned it into a full-blown challenge. Yesterday he completed two mobility sessions.

Sydni:
Two??

Elias:
Resolve must bow before me. Also everything hurts.

She laughed for five straight minutes.

Now she is standing in front of Cup & Kettle, smoothing her sweater over her hips, and reminding herself to act like someone who does not fall apart the moment a handsome man smiles at her. The cold is a blessing; layers hide everything she is not ready for anyone to see.

When she steps inside, she spots him immediately. Leaning against the counter. Paying for drinks. Shoulders relaxed. That smile forming the moment he turns toward her.

"There you are," he says, offering her a cup. "Today's special is lavender honey. I took a chance."

"You are very bold with your tea selections."

"I know. Truly fearless."

She laughs, and he watches her for a beat too long.

They choose a small table near the window, steam rising from their cups. Elias stretches his legs under the table, posture easy and inviting. He talks about his week, his difficult clients, Clementine's continued efforts to steal bread from the countertop, and his sister signing him up for a pottery class because he apparently needs "structure for his imagination."

He is funny in that unintentional way that sneaks up on her. His humor is softened by sincerity. But Sydni is not fully present. Not yet. She keeps noticing things:

The way he adjusts his pace when they walk, as if matching hers. The way his tone shifts to something gentle when she talks about stress. The way he checks her expression before changing the subject.

Careful, her mind whispers. *He is careful with you.*

She stirs her tea and glimpses her reflection in the window. Her thicker thighs pressed together under the table. Her soft stomach hidden beneath her sweater. Her fuller arms. The ink covering scars that are not small, not delicate, not easy to forget. She feels suddenly exposed, even though everything is covered.

She shouldn't spiral. She tries not to. But the fog creeps in anyway.

"You okay?" Elias asks.

She startles. "What? Yes. Totally. Absolutely. Just analyzing the emotional symbolism of tea leaves."

He tilts his head with a tiny smile. "You drifted.."

"I am a contemplative person."

"Are you?" he asks, amused.

She rolls her eyes, and he leans in just slightly. Not close enough
to invade, but close enough that she feels the shift in the air.
"Come back to me," he says, tapping her mug with his fingertip.
"I like it when you are here."

The words land warm and sudden. In a way that makes the world
tilt a little to the right. "Sorry," she murmurs. "I am here."

"Good," he replies, his smile deepening. "I like your company."

It is simple and sweet. And it brings her back into her body in a
way that feels surprisingly safe.

After their drinks, they wander into the craft shop next door. The
air smells like cedar and beeswax. Sydni reaches for a ceramic
dish, lifting her arm just a little higher than she means to. Her
sweater shifts.

This time the fabric reveals more. A flash of ink. A curve of one
of her larger scars, thick and deep, sort of hidden by the tattoo.
But it's obvious and impossible to miss.

Elias's eyes flick down for a single second. Just one. But she sees
recognition in that glance. Not fear or pity. He isn't
uncomfortable, there is just an understanding. When he looks
back at her face, his expression is exactly the same as before.

She reaches to put the dish back, embarrassed despite herself, but
he gently stops her hand and picks up the dish himself. He places
it into her palms.

"I think this one suits you," he says. His voice is calm and
certain, not forced. "It is stronger than it looks."

"Is that your attempt at being smooth again?"

"Maybe," he replies, eyes brightening. "Is it working?"

She bumps his arm. "A little."

They browse for longer than necessary, talking about candles and pottery and the fact that he is apparently terrible at sculpting anything that has limbs. She teases him about it. He pretends to be offended. Their shoulders brush once, twice, and the third time she does not pull away.

Near the doorway, she laughs at one of his jokes, and he smiles at her with a look so…him…she feels it in her ribs. He tucks one hand into his pocket as if stopping himself from reaching for her.

Outside, the air is crisp and bright. They walk slowly, neither fully ready to part. Their hands sway a little too close.

"Same time next week?" he asks, sounding almost hopeful.

She nods without hesitation. "Yes. Definitely."

He steps backward slowly, as if he is waiting to see whether she will change her mind. When she doesn't, his smile deepens into something tender and unmistakably fond.

"See you then," he says.

He starts walking, but after several steps he glances back over his shoulder to make sure she is heading inside safely. When he sees her watching him, he gives her the faintest smile before turning the corner.

Inside, holding the ceramic dish against her chest, Sydni realizes that he saw her. Parts of her that she had been hiding. And he said nothing. He just stayed interested, which was terrifying. He didn't ask questions, he just existed. It was beautifully hopeful.

~*~

Sydni opens her apartment door and nearly screams. Sloan is on her couch eating her leftover waffles.

He freezes mid-bite. "Before you get mad, remember that you love me."

"I didn't say you could eat those!"

"They were sad and alone in the fridge," he argues. "I rescued them."

She groans, tossing her keys onto the table.

"So?" he asks. "How was your flirty meet-cute continuation?"

"It wasn't—" she starts, then sighs. "It was good. Really good."

"Uh-oh," he says with a grin. "You said that with feelings."

"I didn't." She did.

Sloan studies her face. "Something's off. Spill."

"Nothing's off."

"Lies."

"I'm fine!" she insists, voice cracking slightly.

He gives her a look. The "girl, please" look.

She collapses beside him. "It's just… he's so nice."

"Gross. Disgusting. Hate that for you."

"Sloan!"

"Are you scared?"

She shrugs. "Maybe a little. Or a lot."

"Do you like him?"

117

"Shut up."

"That's a yes."

She covers her face. "I hate being perceived."

He pats her knee. "You'll figure it out. And when you inevitably panic and call me at 2 a.m., I'll bring snacks."

God, she loves him.

~*~

Later that night, wrapped in a blanket burrito, Sydni opens Resolve and logs her social outing. Immediately, her phone lights up:

Elias completed:
— **Socializing Goal**
— **Mindfulness Moment**
— **Daily Reflection**

Of course he did. Of course he's good at everything.

She laughs. Then her phone buzzes with a text.

Elias:
I'm up one point in our unofficial contest. Prepare for battle.

She smiles despite the ache in her chest.

Sydni:
You only THINK you're up. I haven't logged my bathroom cleaning yet.

A few seconds later:

Elias:
...You win.

CHAPTER SEVENTEEN

Elias doesn't go straight home after leaving Sydni.

He tells himself he needs groceries, or fresh air, or a moment to clear his head but none of that is really true. He just… isn't ready for the silence of his apartment. Not after the way today felt.

He ends up walking three blocks past his own building before he finally loops back, hands in his coat pockets, breath fogging into the cold night air.

But even then, even unlocking his door, even tossing his keys onto the table, even greeting Clementine who wiggles furiously like he's been gone for a month instead of an hour, he still feels too full. Full of thoughts and impressions and little moments he didn't expect to matter as much as they do.

He sets a pot of water on the stove without really thinking about it. He's not hungry. He's not even planning to eat anything. He just needs the sound, the simmer, something to occupy him while his brain runs laps around itself.

Because the truth is, he can't stop replaying the afternoon. Not the big things. Not the obvious moments. The *small* ones.

The way she smiled when he handed her the lavender honey tea. That surprised curve of her mouth that felt like watching the sun peek out from behind clouds. The way she looked at him when she laughed. God. That laugh. He hadn't expected that. He hadn't expected *her*.

When they walked through the shop next door, he noticed her drifting in and out. Present one moment, distant the next. He recognized it. He sees that look on patients sometimes. People who live inside their heads because there's something there they're trying to negotiate with.

He didn't want to push, so he didn't ask. But he noticed. He noticed everything.

He saw the way she pulled her sleeves down when she got nervous. He saw the way she hesitated when they started walking side by side, like she wasn't sure how close to stand. He saw the way she ducked her head when he complimented her laugh, like she wasn't sure if she was allowed to accept it.

And then, the moment her sweater lifted. He hadn't meant to see. He hadn't been looking.

It happened in a blink, a flash of skin, the edges of ink, and beneath it, scars he recognized instantly. Not the exact cause. Not the story behind them. But the shape of wounds that weren't accidents.

He wasn't afraid but he felt a fierce, protective ache that scared him with its intensity. He didn't say anything. He knew better than that. He knew exactly what it felt like to have someone stare too long at the pieces of you that weren't meant for the world.

He just handed her the ceramic tray. He didn't want to embarrass her. He didn't want her to think he pitied her. He didn't want her to pull back, not when she had just begun stepping closer.

But he keeps thinking about it now. Keeps thinking about *her*. Keeps thinking about how much he wants to know her without pushing too hard.

Elias exhales, rubbing a hand over his jaw. He didn't expect to like her this much. He didn't expect to look forward to her texts, the chaos, the humor, the charm she doesn't even realize she has. He didn't expect that her waffle confession would make him grin like a teenager.

He sits on his couch, Clementine happily curled against his thigh, and opens Resolve. He logs his reflection because it feels fitting after today.

Before he closes the app, he sees her name pop up:

Sydni Benton completed:
Cleaning Task.

He smiles. She's absolutely going to win this week. He's accepted his fate.

And as he sets his phone down, a truth nudges its way into his chest with certainty. He wants to know her. Not the polished, polite version she shows strangers. Not the guarded version she hides behind humor. *Her.* The real one. The one who spirals mid-sentence. The one whose smile lights her whole face. The one who carries pain she doesn't talk about. The one who tries so hard, even when she's tired.

He wants to know her. More than the app intended. More than he should. And despite everything, despite the way she tenses around vulnerability, despite the walls she pretends aren't there, despite the scars she clearly doesn't want to explain, he's not afraid of any of it.

He just hopes she won't be afraid of him, either.

CHAPTER EIGHTEEN

Sydni doesn't even hear the knocking at first. She's too focused on her phone, curled up on the couch with a blanket over her legs and her hair piled messily on top of her head.

It's the third knock. The impatient "I'm two seconds away from breaking in" knock that finally makes her jump.

She opens the door to find Sloan standing there holding two iced coffees, despite the fact that it's thirty-two degrees outside.

"Emergency caffeine delivery," he announces, brushing past her into the apartment. "Because you did that *smiling at your phone* thing earlier, and I need details immediately."

"I did not smile at my phone."

He gives her a look that could peel paint. "Sweetheart. You made a noise. A happy noise. An *unattended baby goat* noise."

She groans, grabbing her coffee. "You are out of control."

"And you are in denial," he singsongs, kicking off his boots and flopping onto her couch. "Now tell me what he said."

"I'm not telling you—"

Her phone buzzes.

Sloan grabs a throw pillow like popcorn. "OH. MY. GOD. He's texting right now. This is better than reality TV. This is real-life, unscripted, emotionally unstable romance."

"Sloan."

"I'm ready to be normal, continue."

Elias:
Made coffee this morning without destroying my kitchen. Please check Resolve and admire my adulting.

She grins. Sloan sits up straighter, clutching the pillow.

"WHO TAUGHT HIM TO FLIRT LIKE THAT?"

"It's not flirting."

"Sydni. Open your eyes. Open your heart. Open your legs…actually no, keep your legs shut…but you get the idea."

Her face goes red. Before she can argue, another text arrives.

Elias:
Also, Clementine attempted to eat my sock again. Send help. Or send waffles.

Sloan grabs the phone out of her hand.

"Sloan!"

He reads it and gasps dramatically. "HE MENTIONED THE WAFFLES. This man is in LOVE with you."

"He's not—"

"HE IS," Sloan declares. "He is flirting like a man who thinks he's subtle but is actually glowing in the dark with romantic energy."

Sydni's phone buzzes again, and Sloan shoves it at her.

"Reply. RIGHT NOW."

"I don't know what to say!"

"Say something charming, but not too charming, funny but not too funny, flirty but not desperate, casual but not disinterested. Easy!"

"Sloan, I swear—"

But Sydni takes her phone and types:

Sydni:
If she ate your sock, you probably deserved it. Just saying.

Elias:
Impossible. I am flawless. Except for socks. And mornings. And probably taxes.

Sydni laughs so loudly she snorts.

Sloan's eyes widen. "THAT WAS A SNORT."

"It wasn't!"

"Oh it WAS a snort. You snorted like a woman in LOVE."

"I hate you."

"No you don't. You love me. I'm your emotional support raccoon."

She covers her face with one hand. "Oh my god."

Later, after an hour of over analysis and caffeination, Sloan drags her out of the apartment.

"You need fresh air and sunlight," he announces. "And probably therapy, but Target is cheaper."

They walk through town, bundled in warm jackets, the winter chill biting at their noses. Sloan talks animatedly about the latest drama in his office, involving someone stealing yogurt from the break room fridge. Sydni listens, laughing, trying to stay present.

But under the humor, Sloan keeps noticing her drifting, just a little.
A glance away. A twitch of her shoulders. Like she's carrying something she hasn't told him yet. He lets it go for now.

They round the corner toward the little artisan shop. The one with plants, candles, and overpriced mugs and Sydni is mid-laugh at Sloan's dramatic retelling of a yogurt-related office feud when she freezes.

Like, actual *statue mode*.

Sloan walks two steps before realizing he's suddenly alone. He turns around, ready to deliver a dramatic monologue about abandonment, when he sees her face.

"Oh," his eyes following her line of sight. "Ohhhhhhhh."

There, inside the shop, holding a plant like he's contemplating adopting it, stands Elias Monroe. Cozy-fuzzy sweater Elias. Gentle-eyed Elias. Totally-unprepared-for-this Elias.

He looks up. And the second he sees Sydni, his whole face softens into a real, genuine smile. It wasn't just polite friendly smile. He looked delighted which surprised in the best way. And she looks over at Sloan and her stomach drops through her shoes.

"NO," she whispers to Sloan.

"Yes," Sloan whispers back.

"We can NOT go in there."

"We absolutely CAN go in there," Sloan says, already reaching for the door handle because he has the impulse control of a toddler in a candy store.

"Sloan, DON'T—"

Too late. The door swings open with a cheerful jingle that Sydni hopes the universe punishes. Elias turns fully toward them, adjusting the plant in his hands.

"Wow," he says with a little laugh. "Didn't expect to see you here."

Sydni tries to speak. What comes out is… not English. "Hi..I…plant…hello—"

Sloan beams, stepping forward like he's meeting a celebrity he doesn't trust. "Elias Monroe, I presume."

Elias looks at Sydni. Sydni looks at the universe. The universe offers no help.

"Uh… yeah," Elias says gently. "And you're Sloan?"

Sloan extends a hand with the gravitas of a man offering a treaty. "Correct. Sloan Hart. Sydni's… handler."

"SLOAN."

"Emotional handler," Sloan clarifies quietly, where Sydni can't hear him.

Elias laughs, not offended, not thrown. Just amused. "Good to meet you. I've heard a lot about you."

Sloan smacks Sydni's arm. "What did you say!?"

"Nothing bad!" She protests. (She absolutely said something bad.)

Elias lifts the plant slightly. "I was… trying to find something my sister won't kill within 48 hours. But the clerk asked me about hydration cycles, and now I'm questioning my entire lifestyle."

Sydni relaxes a *little*. "Are you holding it like it might explode?"

He looks at the pot. "Honestly? Yeah."

She grins. "Alright then."

Sloan steps between them like a referee. "Important question, Elias. What are your intentions with my soul mate?"

Sydni wants to dig a grave. Right on the shop floor. Next to the succulents. "SLOAN!" she hisses.

Elias blinks. "My… intentions?"

"Yes," Sloan says, folding his arms. "Intentions. Objectives. Tactical goals. Please provide a PowerPoint."

"SLOAN."

"No, Sydni, let the man answer."

Elias meets Sydni's eyes and something warm flickers there. He clears his throat. "Well… mostly I intend to not drop this plant. And maybe… enjoy some more tea or coffee with her next week."

Sydni feels her heart *trip.*

Sloan narrows his eyes. "Hmm. Acceptable answer."

"Thank you?" Elias says, confused but smiling.

"And," Sloan continues, "are you aware that she snorts when she laughs too hard?"

"I do NOT—"

Elias smiles wider. "I am."

"I hate this," Sydni mutters.

"Oh come on," Elias says, a laugh threading through his words. "It's cute."

She chokes on her own saliva. "I— what— no—"

Sloan gasps dramatically. "HE THINKS YOU'RE CUTE. IT'S CANON."

"Sloan," she hisses, face turning red, "leave. The planet."

Elias bites back a grin. "You two are something else."

Sloan leans closer, whispering loudly enough for half the store to hear. "Just know if you hurt her? I have access to a drill and a vendetta."

"I'd never—" Elias starts, but Sloan waves him off.

"Good. I'll allow your existence."

Sydni stands there with her mouth open. Her face red with embarrassment.

Elias stares at her over the top of the plant with an amused look. The kind that says he's not running, not weirded out, not even remotely bothered by the circus standing before him. In fact, he looks like he likes it.

When they leave the store, Elias gives her a little wave. "Text me when you get home?"

"Yeah," she nods.

Sloan waits until they're half a block away before turning on her like a soap opera villain. "HE. IS. IN. LOVE. WITH. YOU."

"He is NOT—"

"He called you CUTE."

"No he didn't."

"You heard the words. Your ears WORK."

She tries to hide her smile and fails miserably. But the moment she lets out a tiny laugh, Sloan's expression shifts "You okay?" he asks. It's so gentle it almost cracks her.

"Yeah," she says too quickly. "I'm fine. Just mortified."

Sloan doesn't push. But he walks a little closer, just in case.

CHAPTER NINETEEN

The moment they get back to Sydni's apartment, she kicks off her shoes and faceplants onto the couch with a dramatic groan that could win awards. Sloan follows her in, tossing his jacket over a chair and flopping down beside her like they've rehearsed this routine for years. Which, realistically, they have.

"Well," Sloan announces, "that was a masterclass in romantic tension."

Sydni's groan gets louder. "I hate everything. Throw me into the trash."

"Sweetheart, if I threw you into the trash, Elias would probably climb in after you, and then I'd have to deal with an entire sanitation department worth of paperwork."

She lifts her head just enough to glare at him. "He's not… like that."

"Oh, he absolutely is."

"He's just nice."

"He thinks you're cute."

She huffs. "He said the *snort* was cute. Not me."

Sloan gives her the look. The one that says *girl, seriously?*

"That man looked at you like you hung the moon," Sloan says, grabbing a pillow and swatting her with it. "And you're over here acting like you just tripped into a pothole and he politely helped you out."

Sydni can feel her face warming. "He was just being polite."

"NO." Sloan points at her like he's delivering a sermon. "Polite is holding the door. Polite is smiling awkwardly. Polite is 'have a good day.' What he did was *delighted surprise.* That is not politeness. That is 'I am happy to see you with my whole face.' There is a difference."

She hides behind the pillow. "Stop. I'm fragile."

He laughs, pushing the pillow down so he can actually see her. "Okay, real talk?"

She hesitates, but nods.

"You like him," Sloan says gently. Not teasing. Not mocking. Just truth. "And you're terrified."

Sydni closes her eyes. "I don't… I don't know what I'm doing. Or what this is. Or if I should even—"

"Hey." He nudges her shoulder. "You're not alone in this."

There's no judgment in his voice. Just care. Protectiveness. Steady male energy. The kind that doesn't want anything from her except to see her safe, despite a little sadness behind his eyes.

"Do you think he noticed…?" she asks, not finishing the sentence. She doesn't have to.

Sloan softens. "If he did, he didn't look freaked out."

She picks at the hem of her sleeve. "He didn't say anything."

"That might actually be a good thing."

"I almost wish he would've," she admits. "Just so I could know what he was thinking."

"It's Elias," Sloan says simply. "He was probably thinking something gentle. Something respectful. Something that wouldn't make you shut down."

She nods, swallowing a knot of emotion she didn't expect to feel today.

"You're allowed to like someone," he adds. "You're allowed to let someone like you back."

She stares at him, blinking. "You're being very emotionally intelligent right now. I hate it."

He grins. "Yeah, well, I contain multitudes."

She laughs, leaning her head onto his shoulder. Sloan bumps his head against hers, an unspoken *I've got you.*

After a moment, he clears his throat. "Also? Straight men don't usually memorize someone's coffee order unless they're into them. Just saying."

She groans and throws the pillow at his face. "Get out."

He catches it. "Love you too."

Later that evening, after Sloan heads home, Sydni curls up on her couch with a blanket and a mug of chamomile tea she's not fully paying attention to. Her mind keeps circling back to the shop. The almost touch, that smile, the way Elias's eyes had warmed when she stepped inside.

Her phone buzzes.

Elias:
So... ran into you today. Very unexpected.

She bites her lip, smiling despite herself.

Sydni:
Total coincidence. Sloan dragged me outside for "fresh air."

Elias:
Tell Sloan I appreciated his... enthusiasm.

She snorts. Damnit.

Sydni:
Oh God. He talked too much, didn't he? I'm so sorry.

Elias:
*No, he was great. Intense. Slightly terrifying. But great. A very...
devoted handler. And you two seem...close*

Sydni:
He's fired.

Elias:
Don't fire him. I like the way he looks out for you.

She swallows a small, unexpected ache in her chest.

Before she can respond, another message pops up:

Elias:
So... same time next week? Or earlier if you want.

Her heart thumps a little harder. God, is this how it is for
everyone?

She types back before she can overthink:

Sydni:
Earlier sounds nice.

Elias:
Good. I'll find a place that won't require plant-parenting skills.

She laughs so hard she snorts, loudly, alone in her apartment.

And then her phone buzzes one more time.

Elias:
Also… the snort is cute. In case you were wondering.

Sydni's face flames. Sloan would combust on the spot.

She pulls her blanket up to her chin, smiling into the fabric like an idiot.

She feels wanted. She feels seen. And she feels… hopeful.

CHAPTER TWENTY

The morning is colder than it has any right to be, the kind of cold that sneaks past her jacket and finds her bones. Frost clings to every branch, glittering faintly in the early sunlight. Sydni tucks her chin into her scarf and starts her 10-minute walk anyway. Resolve be damned, competition be damned. She's committed now.

Normally these walks steady her, make her feel like a person again. Today, her thoughts snag on something she doesn't want to look at.

Valentine's Day.
Two weeks away. A date holiday. A day for couples.

Her chest begins to hurt and not in a cute, rom-com way. More in a "this is going to require emotional endurance training" way.

She stops at the end of the block, the wind stinging her cheeks.

Someone like him doesn't end up with someone like me. Normal girls. Beautiful girls. Girls without scars. Girls who weren't broken open and stitched back together.

The thought hurts even though she tells herself it shouldn't.

Her phone buzzes in her pocket interrupting the spiral before it gains too much speed.

It's Elias.

Elias:
Still good for today? Earlier like we said?

A small smile cracks through the anxiety.

Sydni:
Yes. But define "earlier." I need time to prepare my social battery.

Elias:
Let's try 1 p.m. And trust me. You'll like the place.

Sydni:
I swear to God if it's ice skating—

Elias:
Please. I don't have the coordination to survive that.

She huffs a laugh and finishes her walk, still uneasy, but amused. Somewhere between spiraling and smiling. Somewhere between fear and hope.

~*~

The winter market is bursting with white lights, rustic little booths, and the smell of cinnamon drifting through the air. Couples wander hand in hand. Children race between aisles. Musicians play acoustic guitar near a fire pit. It's charming. Sweet. Cozy. It should feel comforting. Instead, it feels like everything around her is whispering: **romance**.

Elias stands waiting near a booth selling handmade mugs, bundled in a charcoal coat, hands tucked in his pockets. The lights overhead catch faint gold in his hair. He straightens a little when he sees her, his smile blooming slow and warm.

He is beautiful, damn it. The kind of beautiful that sneaks up on her. The kind that settles under her ribs and refuses to leave.

"Hey," he says.

And just like that, everything inside her chest loosens. They fall into step easily, like they've been meeting at winter markets their whole lives. She notices how he adjusts his pace to match hers without making it obvious. A tiny consideration that makes her feel light, more than the lights strung above them.

He buys them hot chocolate, complete with a ridiculous peak of whipped cream that nearly topples over.

She lifts a brow. "Are you trying to drown me?"

"It's festive," he protests, deeply serious.

"It's a weapon."

"It's a holiday beverage," he corrects.

She takes a sip, getting whipped cream on her nose. He tries not to smile and fails. One corner of his mouth lifts first, then the rest follows. It's stupidly charming.

"Don't," she warns.

"I didn't say anything."

"You didn't have to," she mutters, wiping her nose. "Your face said everything."

"My face is innocent."

"That's a lie and you know it."

Their banter fits between them like a familiar sweater, soft in all the right places. Easy. Effortless. A language they somehow both learned without ever being taught.

The air nips at her cheeks, but her limbs feel loose. Light. It's as though the cold can't quite reach her as long as he's beside her. For the first time today, she feels okay. She feels like she belongs here, standing with him, walking with him. Existing with him.

They weave through the booths, shoulders brushing now and then. The first time it happens, she thinks nothing of it. By the third time, she's pretty sure she's imagining the slight pause in his step. The tiny moment where he doesn't move away quite as fast as he should.

Each accidental touch sends a spark low in her belly, like her body registered something before her mind did.

He leans closer at one point to glance at a display of candles. The collar of his coat brushes her arm, warm wool against her skin, and her face reddens traitorously.

If he notices, he doesn't say anything. If he felt it too… he doesn't hide it very well. He looks at her like he's memorizing the way she looks under the market lights.

It's a little unnerving. She swallows hard and pretends she's very interested in a string of handmade ornaments shaped like vegetables.

Elias slows as they approach a booth displaying hand-carved wooden animals. Tiny bears. Little foxes. A lopsided penguin wearing a scarf.

He steps closer, eyes lighting with that excitement she's learned is rare from him. Something he doesn't give freely.

"My niece loves animals," he says. "Especially the weird ones. I think this penguin might actually make her cry."

Sydni laughs, and he glances at her again, and there's a flicker in his eyes she can't quite name. Fondness? Attraction? Something that makes her chest tighten and her pulse pick up?

Whatever it is, she feels it in the space between them. In the warmth radiating from his body, in the way he shifts just slightly closer like he's drawn in without realizing it.

Without thinking, she murmurs, "It's cute."

He doesn't look at the penguin. He looks at her. The cold air disappears, replaced by something different. It feels thicker. Her fingers tighten around the mug.

He clears his throat. "Yeah. It is."

She tries not to read into it. She tries of course and fails.

"I'm grabbing something for my niece," he says, eyes brightening as he leans in. "Don't move. You'll get lost in the mug section and I'll never find you again."

Sydni scoffs. "It happened ONCE. One time, Elias. ONE TIME—"

He shoots her a lopsided grin, the kind that kicks her heartbeat into a sprint, before slipping inside the booth.

She watches him for a half-second longer than necessary, her lips curving without permission. Then she takes a sip of her hot chocolate, letting the warmth seep into her hands, into her bones. The whipped cream has melted into a thick swirl, sweet and soothing. She closes her eyes briefly, breathing in cinnamon, pine, woodsmoke, cold air.

She lets herself be still and present. Almost content. She looks around at the lights, the rosy-cheeked families, the laughter drifting like smoke, the couples leaning into each other. And she can't help but wonder if that is what they look like together.

Her hair flutters in the winter breeze. She hugs the cup closer, smiling to herself. A small, private smile she rarely feels anymore. She's not sure if it's the cocoa, the lights, or Elias just twenty feet away picking out wooden animals with more concentration than anyone should have. She feels *hopeful*.

Then a male voice cuts through the air beside her.

"Hey there, sweetheart. You waiting for someone?"

The words are harmless on the surface. But the tone…The closeness…The smell.

Her chest constricts so sharply it feels like a fist closing around her ribs. Air stutters in her lungs. A startled, fractured breath she can't quite finish.

She turns her head slightly. The man is older, scruffy, his eyes glassy with alcohol. His breath carries the sour edge of cheap beer. When he steps closer, his jacket grazes her arm. A small, accidental touch that feels like an electric shock across her skin.

It's the way he *looks* at her. Like he's entitled. Like she's an opportunity. Like he's already measuring what he can get away with.

A ghost wearing someone else's face.

"No," she whispers. "I mean—yes. Yes, I'm meeting someone."

He leans in any way, invading her space, his voice dipping into something oily and intimate. "Didn't ask about them," he murmurs. "Asked about you."

The man steps closer, too close, and something inside Sydni folds in on itself so fast it steals the warmth right out of her hands.

The market's glow blurs at the edges. The music dulls. Her heartbeat spikes loud in her ears… that old, unwelcome drum of memory she never asked to hear again. This shouldn't be a big deal. A harmless line from a drunk man shouldn't undo her.

But her body reacts before her brain can catch up. Her fingers tighten around the paper cup. Whipped cream smears against the lid. Her breath comes out shaky and thin.

She forces herself to look around to anchor herself in the present. Children laughing. Lanterns swinging overhead. The smell of cinnamon and pine. Elias's laughter drifting faintly from the booth behind her. She tries to focus on that. On him. On safety.

But the man shifts closer again. "So who you waitin' on? A boyfriend?" he asks, tipping his chin toward her like they're sharing a private joke.

She stiffens. The word hits somewhere tender. "I— I'm meeting a friend," she manages. It comes out small. Too small. She hates how small.

The man leans in, his jacket brushing her arm again. It's barely a touch, but her skin reacts like it's been burned. Her pulse surges. She steps back automatically.

He follows without noticing or without caring. "You're awful pretty to be standin' out here alone," he slurs, smiling with too many teeth and not enough space.

Sydni swallows, throat tight.

Her vision narrows to a pinpoint the way it does when the past crowds in, uninvited and unwelcome.

Not again. Please not again.

Her hand trembles around the cup. Hot chocolate sloshes over her fingers, sticky and warm, grounding her just enough to take another breath. She reminds herself: This is a market. Public. Safe. She is not trapped. She is not powerless.

But her body doesn't know that. Her body remembers something else entirely. She inhales sharply through her nose, trying to steady her voice. "I—I'm fine. My friend will be right back."

He laughs like that's even funnier. "Well, hey, sweetheart, I'm just bein' friendly. No need to look so scared."

She flinches. Because she *is* scared. Or startled. Or triggered. Or something messy in between. She hates that he can see it.

Her free hand curls into a fist inside her coat pocket. Nails press crescents into her palm as a quiet reminder. You are HERE. Not THEN. You are okay. You are okay.

But her breath still comes shallow, and her eyes dart instinctively toward the booth where Elias disappeared. She can't see him yet. And the thought makes her chest tighten all over again.

His words slither down her spine. Her pulse spikes so fast it becomes a roar in her ears. Her hands go numb.

A different voice, harsher, crueler, flashes through her memory, pressed tight against her ear. The old terror rises so fast she tastes metal. Her vision narrows at the edges.

The man's hand lifts a little, like he might touch her arm. She jerks back on instinct again, a small flinch, but sharp.

"Hey."

Elias's voice slices through the moment. Steady and controlled. A tone that doesn't need volume to carry authority.

He steps between them without hesitation, not touching her, but forming a solid wall of warmth and safety. Sydni feels the shift immediately. The sudden barrier, the shield she didn't know she needed until it was there.

The man blinks at Elias, annoyed, sizing him up. "We were just—"

"No," Elias says, calm but immovable. "You weren't."

The man holds his hands up. "Relax, dude. She didn't—"

"No. Walk away." His voice was still low. Still even as he takes a step forward. The underlying steel would stop anyone paying attention.

The guy mutters under his breath, but he retreats, stumbling back into the crowd.

Elias doesn't turn around right away. He stands there for a second, making sure the man is actually gone before glancing over his shoulder and meeting her eyes. And even though he isn't touching her, Sydni feels the tremor easing in her hands.

Elias waits until he's fully gone before turning around. "Sydni." Concern softening every line of his face. "You okay?"

She tries to force a laugh, but it is brittle. It is obvious she is trying too hard. "Yeah. Totally. Just winter market creeps, right? Classic."

He doesn't buy it. Not even a little. But he doesn't push. "Do you want to go?" he asks gently.

She nods too fast. "Yeah. Yeah, that's probably good. It's getting cold. And I should... you know... work. Or something."

He offers his arm, not touching her until she takes it herself. She loops her hand around his sleeve. Her fingers tremble, and he pretends not to notice.

They leave the market. Walk back toward her apartment through streets filled with laughter and holiday lights. She cracks jokes. He responds. They talk about Sloan, the weather, the ridiculousness of New Year's resolution apps.

On the surface, it looks almost normal. But inside her chest, something trembles. A door she'd kept locked for years rattles on its hinges. And Elias, gentle, careful, attentive Elias, walks beside her like he senses the shift, even though he doesn't know the story behind it. Not yet.

When they reach her building, he pauses at the steps. "Text me when you're in, okay?"

She forces brightness into her voice. "Absolutely. And hey, thanks for, um… stepping in. That was… yeah. Thanks."

There is something utterly sincere in his eyes. "Anytime."

And she knows he means it. She watches him walk away with his hands in his pockets. She stands there until he turns the corner. Only then does she go inside. And only then does she let her knees feel weak.

Inside her apartment, the heat hits her like a wave. She closes the door behind her and leans against it, eyes shut, breath trembling before she can stop it.

She grabs her phone and types quickly.

Sydni:
Inside. All good. Thanks again for today.

A moment later, he replies.

Elias:
Glad you're safe. Let me know if you need anything, okay?

Sydni:
I'm fine. Promise.

She sends it before she can second-guess it. But the lie tastes metallic.

After a minute, she sets the phone facedown and walks further inside, the apartment dim and quiet except for the hum of the heater. She tries to tidy the coffee table. She tries to open her laptop. She even attempts to re-read a grant draft, but the words blur.

Her mind reruns the moment at the market. But more than that, it morphs. The drunk stranger's face flickers into another face. That voice becomes the other voice. The too-close body becomes the wrong body. The breath on her cheek becomes a memory she never asked for.

It's not a full flashback, just the edge of one. A shadow rising without fully swallowing her. But enough to rattle every bone.

She closes the laptop.

Her chest aches with something too familiar. Without fully thinking, she moves to the bathroom, flips on the light, and stares at herself in the mirror. Slowly, she lifts her shirt. She sees the softness. The fullness. But what she's really looking at? Are the scars.

The scars wind across her ribs and abdomen, faded but unmistakable. A pale line above her hip. Another on her lower abdomen. The small cluster near her ribs. The longer one on her side. The ones on her arms, half-hidden by ink.

She turns slightly. There it is, the long thin scar across the back of her shoulder. The one she covers with a tattooed cardinal. She hates looking at them. She hates remembering how they got there even more.

For a flicker of a moment, she wonders how Elias would react if he saw them all. Really saw them. Not just glimpses through clothing, but the truth. The thought makes her stomach twist.

She drops the shirt quickly, tugging it down, covering herself like she's freezing. She sits on the closed toilet lid, elbows on her knees, head in her hands. Trying to anchor herself back into her body instead of the memory.

She doesn't know how long she sits there before she hears knocking. Not frantic but purposeful. "Syd?" Sloan's voice.

She wipes her face even though she wasn't crying, straightens her shirt, and opens the door.

Sloan stands there with a plastic grocery bag and a suspicious expression. "I brought snacks. And Coke Zero. And emotional support mozzarella sticks."

She musters a smile. "You're absurd."

"Yes," he says, brushing past her and setting things on the counter. "Now tell me everything. How was the day date with Captain Cinnamon Roll?"

"It was good," she says quickly. Too quickly. "Really good. The market was cute. The hot chocolate was amazing. He's funny. It was just…nice."

Sloan narrows his eyes the way a cat stares at a suspicious noise. "Mm-hmm. And your voice did that thing."

"What thing?"

"The 'I am lying through my teeth and hoping you're too stupid to notice' thing," he says, crossing his arms.

"I'm not lying."

"You are one hundred percent lying."

She sighs and drops onto the couch. "It was fine. Really."

Sloan shifts immediately, sitting beside her. "Hey. Look at me."

She does, reluctantly.

"You're beautiful," he says simply. Not dramatic. "Inside, outside, all the weird places in between. If something happened today that made you forget that even for a second, I'm going to fight whatever or whoever caused it."

Her throat tightens and she looks away.

He studies her face for a long moment. "Did Elias do something?"

"No!" she blurts, horrified. "God, no. Elias was… perfect. He stepped in actually, when—" She stops.

"When what?" Sloan's voice sharpens just slightly, protective instincts waking like a guard dog.

"Just a guy," she says. "At the market. He… was too close. Said something gross. Elias handled it."

Sloan's eyes flash. "Handled it how?"

"Calmly," she says. "Just… stepped in."

Sloan exhales. Some tension leaves his shoulders. "Okay. And you? Are *you* actually okay?"

She tries to smile. "I'm fine."

He gives her a look that says he would tear the apartment apart searching for answers if she tried him. He wants to push, but he doesn't. He knows what happened to her. He knows that secrets that most don't know. He knows that marks under all of those tattoos.

So instead, he loops an arm around her shoulder and pulls her into a sideways hug. "He cares about you," he murmurs. "I could see it the first time. Anyone with eyes could."

Her heart stutters painfully. "Sloan…"

"You don't have to talk about anything you're not ready to," he says carefully. "But don't pull away from people who care. Not him. Not me."

She closes her eyes. The words hit too close. Too raw.

"Okay," she whispers. "I hear you."

But whether she believes it is a whole other story.

Later that night, after Sloan leaves, Sydni curls on the couch under a blanket, staring at the wall because she's too exhausted to stare at anything else.

Her phone buzzes.

She knows it's him before she even picks it up.

Elias:
Made it home. Just checking in... You sure you're okay?

Her chest cracks open again for a split second. She could answer. She could tell him she's shaken. She could admit she's scared. Instead, she locks the phone. Sets it screen-down. Doesn't respond.

A Resolve notification lights the display, glowing faintly through the blanket.

Elias added:
• **Community time**
• **Evening walk**
• **Journaling**

She doesn't open it. She rolls over, pulling the blanket tighter.

And for the first time in weeks, she lets the distance grow. Just a little. Just enough to feel safe. But enough for him to feel it.

CHAPTER TWENTY-ONE

The next morning is brighter than yesterday, but somehow colder. A brittle kind of cold that cracks against her skin as Sydni pushes herself outside for her walk. She wraps her coat tighter and steps onto the sidewalk, her breath drifting upward in white ribbons.

She turns on Resolve and taps **Start Activity: 10-Minute Walk**.

The notification chimes cheerfully, as if it's proud of her. She wishes she felt proud too.

The neighborhood is quiet. Frost coats the roofs. Little flakes of snow cling to mailboxes. Normally she takes this in, the details, the beauty, the tiny things she's been missing while locked inside her apartment for too long.

Today, everything looks slightly washed out, almost muted. Like someone dimmed the world by a few notches. She tries to shake it off. She tries to focus on the crunch of gravel under her boots, the way the sun glows golden between bare branches. But her chest feels heavy. Her mind drifts, uninvited, to the market. To that man.

She reroutes the thought, shoves it aside.

Her phone buzzes.

She expects another app notification. It's Elias.

Elias:
Saw your walk update. Nice job. I only did mine because Clementine stared me into submission.

A tiny smile pushes through the fog.

Sydni:
Your dog is oddly motivational.

Elias:
She's the backbone of my entire self-improvement journey.

Another buzz — a Resolve encouragement from him.

Resolve encouragement from Elias:
"Proud of you for getting out there today. Even when it's cold."

The words sink deeper than she expects. Her throat tightens.

She types back:

Sydni:
Thanks. Almost froze to death, but at least I moved my body.

Elias:
Hey, if you die of cold, I can't take you for tea again.

She laughs though it's weak, hollow-edged.

Sydni:
That's the true tragedy.

But even through the jokes, her chest aches. There's a strange distance in her own words, like she's texting from underwater.

~*~

Back inside, she decides to cook an actual meal for lunch instead of cereal or microwave ravioli. Something healthy, something meaningful, something that'll make her feel like she's still moving forward.

She attempts a simple chicken stir-fry. Halfway through, the garlic burns. The chicken sticks. The vegetables go from "vibrant" to "angrily charred." Smoke curls up from the pan, and she swears loudly enough that Mrs. Henderson downstairs probably clutches her pearls.

"Fantastic," Sydni mutters, waving a dish towel in the air. "I have invented sadness in skillet form."

She dumps the ruined mess into the trash and presses her hands to the counter, eyes closed. Why can't she do *anything* right today? She hates how quickly the thought arrives. She hates how familiar it sounds.

Her phone buzzes as she enters her Resolve task:

You completed: Cook a Meal
(Activity logged manually)

She stares at the screen. Petty victory. Still a victory.

She tries to work next, pulling up the grant she's writing for the DV shelter. This used to be just work. Now the words feel personal in a way she didn't ask for.

Not now. Not the memory. Not today.

Her laptop screen blurs. Then, her phone lights up again. This time, it's not jokes. Not light banter.

It's a much longer message.

Elias:
Hey… I've been thinking a lot about yesterday. I want you to know that I didn't step in at the market because I thought you needed rescuing. I stepped in because I care about you, because I like spending time with you, and I want you to feel safe when we're together. I hope I didn't overstep. I just… want you to know you aren't alone in things. And I hope we can meet again next week. If you're up for it.

She states at it. It's too sweet, too kind, and definitely too much. Not because it was from him. But because of her, for where her head is at.

She types the safest thing her brain can produce:

Sydni:
Thank you.

Two words. They were too small, she knew it. But it's all she has. She stares at the chat bubble, regret blooming instantly. But she can't bring herself to say more.

She locks her phone. Sets it face-down.

~*~

She glances at the Resolve widget on her home screen.
A little notification shows three new checkmarks from Elias:

• **Morning walk**
• **Journaling**
• **Social connection**

She doesn't tap it. She doesn't want to see the details. She doesn't want to feel the closeness creeping in again. Not when her chest still feels bruised from the day before.

She curls up on the couch under a blanket, staring at the wall. Trying to quiet her thoughts. Trying not to remember. Trying and failing, not to picture Valentine's Day glowing on the calendar like a ticking bomb.

CHAPTER TWENTY-TWO

The next few days pass in a strange, disorienting blur. Too fast in the moments she wishes she could slow down, too slow in the moments she wishes would pass. Time feels fickle and indecisive, unsure of how exactly it wants to torment her.

Every morning, Sydni forces herself outside for her walk. The winter air bites at her cheeks, sharp enough to make her eyes sting, but she does it anyway. Resolve chirping with cheerful enthusiasm each time she logs it, as if the little app alone could hold her upright.

She keeps her hood up, hands shoved deep in her pockets, shoulders tight. She tries to see the beauty she noticed in January. The frost clinging to fences like lace, the way sunlight catches on rooftops, softening dull edges. But this week, everything feels off. It feels like she's watching someone else's life through thick glass.

Still, she checks off the walk on Resolve. A tiny victory. A fragile one. She clings to it anyway.

On the third morning, her phone buzzes as she peels off her coat.

Elias:
Just saw your walk update. Look at you, beating the cold again.

Her lips twitch, not a smile, really, but the beginning of one. The praise lands gently, too gently, kind in a way she doesn't know how to hold.

She types:

Sydni:
Barely survived. I think my toes quit.

Elias:
Tell them to stick it out. We have a bookstore date to plan.

Date. The word moves through her like tiny electric current.
Light, warm, dangerous.

Sydni:
Maybe. I've got a lot going on this week.

Not a lie. Just… not honest. After she sends it, the heaviness
returns, seeping into her bones. The apartment feels too quiet, the
air too still, as if the walls lean in to listen.

She attempts lunch and produces a grilled cheese so burnt it looks
like a carbon sample.

"Spectacular," she mutters. "I've invented ash."

She logs **Cook a Meal** on Resolve anyway. Petty victories count
too.

She tries to work, pulling up the DV shelter grant. She scrolls
through statistics. Assault reports. Barriers to safety. Lines she's
read a thousand times before.

But today they feel heavier. Personal. Her chest tightens with
every paragraph. She rubs her sternum as if she can press the
discomfort back down.

Her phone buzzes again.

Elias:
*How's work going? Found a tea place we should try next week.
Totally indoors. Zero creepy-man potential.*

She shuts her eyes. His kindness is sharp, almost painful.

Her fingers hover over the keyboard.

Sydni:
Sounds nice. Busy with work right now.

After a pause, that seemed to last a long time, he messages back.

Elias:
You seem quieter than usual.

She stares at the message until the screen dims. She could tell him. She could try to explain what yesterday stirred up. She could say she hasn't felt steady since. She could say Valentine's Day is creeping closer like a threat she can't quite name.

Instead she just says:

Sydni:
Just tired.

He waits a few hours before trying again.

Elias:
If you need space, that's okay. I just want you to know I'm here.

The words unravel her in slow threads. She almost responds. She even types:

I'm scared. Yesterday reminded me of something I don't talk about. I don't know how to be close to someone without falling apart.

She stares at it until her eyes sting.

Deletes it.

Sends nothing.

~*~

Her walks shrink over the next few days, from ten minutes to eight, then five. Her Resolve updates turn sparse.

By midweek, she logs:

- **Walk (5 minutes)**
- **Work task**

Nothing more.

Two days later, she doesn't walk at all.

Her phone vibrates.

Resolve encouragement from Elias:
"Missed seeing your walk today. Hope everything's okay."

Sydni flips the phone face-down.

She nestles into the couch, wrapped in a blanket, the TV casting a glow across the room. Outside, her neighbor has hung a massive pink Valentine's wreath…glitter, bows, the works. It mocks her from across the hall. She groans into her blanket.

Every commercial is red-and-white couples smiling. Every email is SALE FOR YOUR SWEETHEART. Every aisle in every store is begging people to be in love.

And she feels like she's running out of time for something she doesn't even understand.

Her phone buzzes again.

Elias:
Still hoping we can see each other next week. But really, no pressure. Just wanted you to know I'm thinking of you.

It's simple. And she knows he's trying, but she doesn't know how to try back. So, she responds with the smallest message she can get away with.

Sydni:
Thank you.

It's all she has.

No Resolve checkmarks tonight. She hates that after so many great weeks, feeling warm, getting to know someone great, that she is spiraling.

She lies back, staring at the ceiling until her eyes blur. Caught between wanting to reach out and wanting to disappear.

~*~

A sudden knock rattles her door hard enough to make her jump. It wasn't a polite knock. Sloan's knock. The "I-will-break-this-door-down-if-you-don't-open-it" knock.

She closes her eyes. "Please go away."

The knocking grows louder. "SYD."

Three seconds of debate pass before she remembers he has a key and a dramatic streak. She shuffles to the door and opens it a crack.

Sloan stands there holding a six-pack of full-sugar soda, a grocery bag, and the face of a man ready to interrogate someone under a single swinging lightbulb.

"Hi," she deadpans.

He shoulders past her. "Okay. What did that man do to you?"

"What—what man?"

"Elias."

She nearly chokes. "Sloan, what? No! He didn't—nothing happened. He was… good. Really good."

Sloan narrows his eyes. "Then why do you look like the human embodiment of a raincloud? And before you lie, just know I can see the depressing bun."

"I'm just tired."

"You," he says, pointing dramatically, "are lying to my FACE."

She throws a pillow at him. "I'm having a bad week."

Sloan steps closer, expression shifting into something heavier beneath the theatrics. "Did he hurt you?"

"No!" she says again, voice cracking. "No, Sloan. He didn't hurt me. He helped. I just… I'm not okay. That's all."

"Then talk to me."

"I can't." The truth slips out too easily.

He studies her for a long, silent moment. It feels too intimate, too intense. "Syd," he says, "don't shut me out."

She tries to joke. "You just want the tea."

"No. I want you okay." He brushes a curl from her face without thinking, and she startles. He withdraws immediately, guilt flickering across his features.

"I'm on your side," he murmurs. "Always."

And she believes him. Too much. But it doesn't stop the rising panic.

"I'm fine, Sloan," she lies.

He doesn't call her out this time. He just sighs. "Fine. But I'm not leaving until you eat something and stop looking like you're narrating a tragic piano montage."

She almost laughs. So he talks while she drifts in and out, anchoring her with jokes and gentle nudges. It helps. Not enough, but enough for now.

When he leaves, he hugs her a beat too long. "Talk to me when you're ready," he says.

"Yeah," she whispers.

The apartment feels cavernous when he's gone.

Her phone buzzes on the coffee table.

Elias:
Hope you're resting tonight. If you need anything, even just someone to sit in silence, I'm here.

She locks the phone. Puts it face-down. She sees the Resolve icon glowing with new activity from him but doesn't tap it. For tonight, drifting feels easier than reaching for something that might break her open.

CHAPTER TWENTY-THREE

Elias notices the drift before he admits it to himself.

At first, it's small things. Longer gaps between her replies, shorter jokes, less spark in the words she sends. He tells himself she's busy. Tired. Cold. Winter is miserable for a lot of people. Nothing to worry about.

But when their weekly meet-up day arrives, and he hasn't heard from her since his last message three days ago, the truth settles in his stomach like a stone. He tries not to stare at his phone. And he fails. Repeatedly.

Clementine hops onto the couch, planting one determined paw on top of his hand like she's claiming it. When he doesn't react fast enough, she pushes harder. "Okay, okay," Elias mutters, scratching behind her ears. "I get it. Comfort me, you must."

Clementine blinks at him, deeply unimpressed with his tone.

"You're no help," he sighs, though he rubs her cheek.

He checks Resolve again. Sydni still hasn't logged anything in three days. Not a walk. Not a meal, or even a single check-in. A hollow ache opens beneath his ribs. That strange mixture of worry and helplessness he only seems to feel with her.

He knows she struggles with consistency. He knows she has hard weeks. He knows disappearing is something she sometimes… does. But this? This feels different.

He scrolls back through their last conversation. Short sentences, a clipped joke, her replying "Thank you" to a message he'd agonized over. He can still feel that hesitation behind her words. He exhales slowly, letting his head fall back against the couch cushion.

His mind drifts, unbidden, to the winter market. To the way she froze when that man stepped too close. To how her shoulders curled inward like she was bracing for impact. To the tremor he felt beneath his hand when he touched her arm, subtle, but unmistakable. To the faint, shiny scars he'd glimpsed earlier when her shirt shifted, pale lines disappearing beneath ink.

He hadn't asked. He wouldn't. Not unless she offered. But he's not an idiot. And he's not blind. Something had happened to her. Something that lived in her body the way muscle memory lived in his athletes except hers wasn't from training. It was from surviving. And the thought that she might be navigating that alone makes his chest ache in a way he doesn't have a name for yet.

He rubs a hand over his face. Maybe that's why she hasn't logged anything. Maybe she shut down. Maybe the week swallowed her whole. Maybe the Resolve app feels stupid when just breathing feels like too much effort.

He can almost see it, Sydni curled on her couch in an oversized sweatshirt, curls messy, eyes tired, slipping behind that invisible wall she builds when the world gets too heavy. He hates that he can picture her alone in it.

Clementine nudges his chin with her nose, unbothered and deeply concerned at the same time. "I know," he murmurs, scratching her head again. "I'm worried too."

He stares at his phone, thumb hovering over the screen, unsure if he should text her again. If he should check on her. If reaching out would help… or push her farther away.

But the image of her face at the market, the startled inhale, the way her hand shook around her cup, keeps playing in his mind.

He swallows, voice barely above a whisper. "She didn't just get overwhelmed," he says to Clementine. "She got scared."

Clementine offers the dog equivalent of a sigh.

He nods, more to himself than to her. "And I think she's still scared."

The truth settles heavy and real in his chest.

He wishes she'd said more. He wishes he knew what he did wrong. He wishes he didn't care this much.

He rubs a hand over his face and stands, pacing his living room. Clementine gruffs, offended by the sudden movement. "I know," he mutters. "I'm annoying myself, too."

He opens their message thread and types:

Elias:
Hey... I missed seeing you today. Just checking in. Hope everything's okay.

He waits. Three dots don't appear.

After twenty minutes, he forces himself to step away from the phone. He does dishes. He sweeps. He pretends to read an article. None of it sticks. When he checks his phone again, there's still no reply.

He tries one more time, the last attempt he'll allow himself before he becomes exactly the kind of pushy man women hate. He types carefully:

Elias:
I know next week lands on Valentine's Day, so if you want to skip or reschedule, I understand. No pressure at all.

He stares at the message, thumb hovering, thinking maybe he shouldn't send it. But he hits send anyway. The moment he does, a dull ache settles in his chest, like he already knows what the answer will be.

She doesn't reply. Not that day. Not the next. Not the one after.

~*~

Valentine's Day arrives wrapped in red and pink, loud and saccharine, aggressively cheerful in all the ways he's never cared about.

Normally, it wouldn't matter. Normally, it's just another day. But this year, every heart-shaped decoration feels like a reminder.

He checks his phone once that morning. Then again. Then again. And still nothing.

Resolve sends a notification:

"Your Accountability Partner didn't log any activities this week."

He swipes it away. By evening, he knows she isn't going to message him. Not today. Maybe not again.

He feeds Clementine, heats frozen soup, and sits on the couch, staring at the wall the way Sydni had done two nights ago without him knowing it.

He scrolls to his sister's contact and hits call. She answers on the second ring. "Hey, stranger," she chirps. "Happy Valentine's, loser."

He huffs a small laugh. "Thanks. Appreciate that."

"Why do you sound like someone stole your joy and punted it into a river?"

He hesitates. His sister waits, she's good at that. "There's someone I've been seeing," he says finally. "Not dating. Just… spending time with. My accountability partner on the Resolve app."

"Ooooh," she says, delighted. "And?"

"And I think I messed it up."

Logically, Elias knows the silence is probably because of what happened at the market, the way she froze, the tremor in her hand, the sharp edge of fear she hadn't been able to hide. He *knows* that. But logic has never stopped his brain from doing laps around the worst possibilities.

"And," he admits, "I keep thinking maybe I'm the problem."

"What?" his sister sputters. "How? You're like a cardigan personified. You don't mess things up."

He lets out a humorless laugh. "You'd be surprised."

Nora doesn't interrupt, doesn't tease and she just waits, and that makes it easier for the truth to slip out.

"I have this… stupid tendency," he says, rubbing a hand over the back of his neck. "When someone pulls back, even a little, I start assuming it's me. That I pushed too hard. Said too much. Scared them off. I stepped in when a guy made her uncomfortable," he says. "And afterward everything felt… different."

Nora's tone softens instantly. "Eli. That's not coming on too strong. That's basic human decency."

"Maybe," he says. "But I saw her face. It wasn't just discomfort. Something in her shut down. And what if—"

"What if it wasn't about you?" she says gently.

He closes his eyes, sinking back into the couch cushions. Clementine hops up beside him, pressing her warm weight into his leg as if to ground him. He absently curls his fingers into her fur.

"She's been quieter," he murmurs. "Distant. Barely checking the app. I don't want to push her. I know what it feels like when someone expects too much from you when you're already at capacity. But I miss her. And I hate not knowing if she's overwhelmed… or if I completely misread everything."

"Did she tell you she's not interested?" his sister asks.

"No."

"So you're assuming the worst," she says lightly, "because that's your hobby."

He huffs a laugh through his nose. "Maybe."

"Eli," she says, kind but firm, "maybe she's dealing with something big. Maybe something scared her. Maybe she's disappearing because she's hurting. Not because of you."

He knows she's right. But the ache in his chest doesn't ease. Because Sydni bent something inside him before he even realized it was bending. Now the silence feels like he's waiting for a door to close he never got the chance to step through.

He swallows. Hard. "I don't want to make things worse," he murmurs.

"Then don't push," she says. "But don't disappear completely either. Be steady. Let her know you're there. Quietly."

He rubs his thumb over the edge of his phone. "I think she needs space."

"Space isn't the same as abandonment."

He closes his eyes. He knows she's right. He also knows that reaching out again won't help. Not right now.

So when Valentine's Day ends, when the world goes dark again, he makes himself a promise. He won't chase her. He won't overwhelm her. He won't push past her boundaries.

But he'll wait. He'll hope. He'll be there when she's ready. Even if she never texts again.

That night, he opens Resolve one last time. His own checkmarks glow up at him. But hers, her side of the app, is empty. He closes it.

Clementine nudges his hand before curling her perfect fluff of a dog self next to him on the couch.

And now, Elias wonders if maybe…he wasn't what she expected. And maybe that's why she's gone.

CHAPTER TWENTY-FOUR

Sydni reads his message about rescheduling for Valentine's Day three times. Each time, it hits a little harder.

"I know next week lands on Valentine's Day, so if you want to skip or reschedule, I understand. No pressure at all."

She knows he means it kindly. Gently. Considerately. But her brain, the cruel one, the one shaped by years of bracing for pain, twists it into something else entirely.

He doesn't want to see you. He's relieved to have an excuse. You misread everything. He was just being polite.

She drops her phone onto the couch like it burned her.

For the next hour, she sits still. Too still. Her mind feeling like a room slowly filling with water. So she works because it's the only thing she knows how to do when she's drowning. She buries herself in grant language, statistics, budget tables. Words blur. Data twists. She types anyway.

Work is safe. Work is predictable. Work doesn't get disappointed in her.

She ignores the pain in her chest, the tightness in her throat. She keeps her eyes on the screen even when they burn. The rest of the day becomes mechanical: laptop, notes, coffee, silence repeat.

She doesn't check the Resolve app. She doesn't reply to texts. She doesn't reach out to Sloan. So when Sloan knocks around 8 p.m., she doesn't answer. She waits him out until he gives up, leaves a bag of takeout on her doormat, and texts:

Sloan:
Eat something, please.

She flips her phone over without responding.

By morning, she feels even worse.

Her alarm goes off for her walk. She stares at it. Lets it ring. Hits snooze. Then dismisses it entirely. It's the first time she's skipped it intentionally. She doesn't log anything on Resolve. Too much pressure. Too much shame. Too much not-enough-ness. She can't bear the idea of Elias seeing her empty checkmarks. Or thinking she's quitting.

Or thinking she's quitting him. Though maybe she is. Maybe that's safer.

She shuts her laptop only to open it again an hour later. The shelter grant calls her name. Trauma funding. Survivor stories. Safety statistics. It all sinks into her like ink.

By noon, her chest feels thick and heavy. Her phone buzzes once. Then twice. Then a third time.

She doesn't look. Not until later, when the buzzing stops, and curiosity or guilt or loneliness finally wins. Three messages.

One from Sloan:

Sloan:
I'm calling the police to perform a welfare check. Not joking. Ok maybe a little joking. But answer me, Syd.

One from her friend, Victoria:

Victoria:
Hey lady!! Birthday party planning is officially underway! 
Theme: Glitter, cocktails, questionable decisions.
You BETTER be there. Text me so I know what food to bring!!

She stares at that one for a long time.

Victoria's birthday is next week. And she knows she can't. She can't do crowds. She can't pretend to be normal. She can't smile and hug and be the fun version of herself that everyone expects.

She tucks the phone under a pillow so she doesn't have to see it anymore. Then she crawls back under her blanket, curled so tightly she resembles a comma in the sentence of her own life.

She tells herself she's fine. Just tired. Just overwhelmed.

But the truth keeps whispering, louder and louder, impossible to ignore:

You messed it up. You're too much. You're not enough. You scared him away. You should've kept your distance.

By evening, she hasn't eaten. She hasn't walked. She hasn't showered. She hasn't replied to anyone. The apartment is dim and slightly cold. She sits on the couch, wrapped in her blanket, staring at the wall. The air feels thick. Heavy. It presses against her lungs, her ribs, her scars.

She tries to journal, types a few words, then deletes them. Every thought feels too big. Too sharp. Too dangerous.

The night stretches on, long and unkind. Her Resolve app remains untouched. Her phone stays silent.

Sydni feels like she's slipping backward into a version of herself she hoped she'd left behind, the one who hides, who shuts down, who convinces herself she's safer alone.

Over the next several days, time becomes strange. Hours blur. Days blend. The sun rises and sets without permission. Sydni moves through it on autopilot, like she's detached from her own body, watching herself go through the motions of being alive without actually feeling any of it.

She works because she has to. Emails, drafts, data. Her fingers move, her brain half-engaged. She powers through because if she stops, the quiet gets too loud.

Her Resolve app remains unopened. Her phone stays mostly face-down.

Her apartment becomes dimmer each day, curtains drawn, lights rarely on. She eats when her stomach hurts too much not to. Drinks coffee because it's habit. A part of her knows that this is extreme. Not normal for the average person. Someone on the outside looking in may think this reaction is unbelievable. She knows. But she can't seem to get out of this funk.

Sleep is restless. Her walk alarm goes off every morning. Every morning, she stares at it. Every morning, she dismisses it.

Two days pass. Then three. Then five.

She responds to no one. Not Sloan. Not Victoria. Not a single person.

On the morning of Victoria's birthday party, she wakes with a knot in her chest so tight she can hardly breathe. The idea of people, of noise, of laughter, of being watched, makes her throat close.

Her phone buzzes repeatedly.

Victoria:
Party day!! You coming, right?? Please don't bail, I need your face there! 🖤 👻

Victoria:
Sydni?

Victoria:
You okay?

Sydni stares at the messages until her vision swims. She types nothing. She deletes nothing. She just lets them sit there like accusations.

She rolls over and pulls the blanket over her head.

By afternoon, her phone is silent again.

Sloan texts her twice that evening.

Sloan:
You better be getting ready for Victoria's thing.

And later…

Sloan:
Babe? You alive?

She ignores both.

Around six, there's a knock at her door. Not the usual knock. This one is sharper. Shorter. Concern wrapped in frustration. She doesn't move.

"SYD," Sloan calls through the door, voice low. "Don't make me use my key."

She squeezes her eyes shut. Then the sound of metal in a lock. The door opens.

"Sydni? I'm coming in."

There are footsteps. There is pause in the living room and a sound of rustling. Then a loud sigh. "Okay… where is my gremlin?"

She wants to laugh. She doesn't.

Her bedroom door creaks open. Sloan steps inside, eyes adjusting to the dark. He sees her curled in bed, knees tucked to her chest, wearing the same oversized sweatshirt she's had on for three days. His whole expression shifts. Anger melting into worry, sarcasm replaced with tenderness.

"Oh, Syd…" he sighs. He walks over and sits on the edge of the mattress. Not too close. Not touching her. Just… there. "You didn't answer any of my texts," he says gently.

"I know."

"You missed Vic's party."

"I know."

He swallows. "Talk to me."

She shakes her head.

"Sydni."

"I don't want to talk."

"You don't have to give me details," he says. "Just… something. Anything."

She lifts one shoulder, a tiny shrug. "I'm tired."

He studies her face in the dim light. "This isn't tired."

She doesn't answer.

"This is the spiral, isn't it?"

Still, no reply. She can't.

He exhales slowly, like his heart aches for her. "You should've said something."

Her voice cracks on the smallest whisper. "I didn't know what to say."

Sloan nods once, understanding in his eyes but helplessness too. He sits with her in silence for a long moment, the weight of the room settling between them. Then, "And you are sure he didn't do something?"

She looks over at him, her face pained. "No."

"Then something happened."

She doesn't reply.

His jaw flexes. "Syd, I can't help if I don't know."

"You can't fix this," she murmurs.

"I can't fix you," he corrects gently. "But I can sit in the dark with you so you don't have to be alone."

Her throat tightens. Her eyes sting. She pulls the blanket tighter.

Sloan finally lies beside her, not touching, just stretching out, shoulder to shoulder, staring at the ceiling. He says nothing else. He doesn't need to. His steady presence fills the silence she's been drowning in. At some point, he whispers, "I'm not leaving you like this."

She whispers back, "I know."

Hours pass and he stays. Only when she's half-asleep does he slide off the bed, tuck the blanket around her, and close her bedroom door behind him. Before he leaves the apartment, he sends one last text, even though she's in the next room.

Sloan:
When you're ready, I'm here. No pressure. No questions. Just me.

She reads it from her pillow, blinks hard, and turns her phone over.

She still doesn't open Resolve. She still doesn't text Elias. She still doesn't answer Victoria.

The days keep passing. And Sydni keeps sinking.

CHAPTER TWENTY-FIVE

The next few days slide by like mud, thick and slow and impossible to wade through. Sydni wakes up each morning feeling heavier than the last, as if gravity has singled her out for a personal vendetta.

She tries working on the DV shelter grant again. Tries reading the statistics, the survivor quotes, the description of the program timeline, but her eyes keep skimming past the same sentences without absorbing a word. Every paragraph feels like it grips her by the throat.

By noon on Monday, she slams her laptop shut and pushes it away, chest tight and trembling. She sits there for a long time, coughing out sob-like breaths that don't fully form.

"I can't," she whispers into her empty apartment. "I can't do this grant right now."

And she hates herself for that. She hates that her own trauma is getting in the way of work meant to help other people. So, she switches. She digs through her deadlines and selects the least emotionally triggering proposal she has. Something small, simple community education grant that's due next week. All logistics. All numbers. No trauma. No stories. No reminders. The kind of grant she can do on autopilot.

She starts typing with stiff, robotic fingers.

"Objective: provide three quarterly community training sessions…"
"Expected outcomes: increased awareness of…"

The words pour out empty and precise, like she's assembling IKEA furniture instead of writing. No creativity. No spark. Just… output. She keeps working until her neck aches.

At some point she gets up to refill her coffee mug and stops short.

The kitchen is a disaster. Dishes piled in the sink, stacked dangerously high. Plates with old crumbs. Bowls with dried cereal film. A pan from last week's failed grilled cheese attempt, still greasy, shoved half in the sink like it's decided to retire there permanently. A sour smell lingers near the trash can, something she's been ignoring.

She stares at it all, emotion swelling in her chest like a rising tide. She should do the dishes. She should clean. She should try. But the thought makes her legs feel weak. She fills her cup with water instead of coffee because the coffee maker is too dirty to deal with, and goes back to the couch.

The apartment feels smaller today. The air thicker. Everything slightly tilted. She wraps a blanket around herself and curls into the corner cushions like she's trying to disappear. The hours pass in a blur. She answers one email. Deletes three. Skims a spreadsheet until the numbers blur.

At some point, her stomach growls, but she doesn't move. At another point, her phone buzzes, but she flips it over. She doesn't even check who it is. She can't handle being needed. Not right now. Not with everything inside her feeling like splintering wood.

By Wednesday, the dishes have doubled. Laundry is in a heap near the bedroom door. Her hair is a messy, unwashed knot. Her Resolve app hasn't been opened in over a week.

Her walk alarm goes off. She throws her phone across the bed, face scrunching with frustration. She swallows hard.

No. No thinking about him. About anything that hurts.

She pulls her laptop back into her lap and opens the grant again. She forces herself into the rhythm.

"This program aims to…"
"The target demographic includes…"
"A projected 12% increase in…"

Mechanical. Efficient. Emotionless. It's the only thing she's good at this week. But she keeps drifting. Losing focus, rereading lines, staring blankly at the cursor like it might start typing for her. At one point she realizes she's read the same bullet point seven times. Her throat burns. She sits very still, staring at her screen until tears start to gather, slow and hot. She blinks them away angrily.

She will not cry. Not today. Not over something this stupid. Her phone buzzes again…short, sharp.

A part of her hopes it's Elias. A part of her fears it's Elias. A part of her hopes it's Sloan. A part of her fears that too.

She doesn't check it. She won't survive seeing his name pop up again with something kind, gentle, or worried. Not when she feels like she's failed at being the version of herself he liked. She presses her fingers into her temples.

She's sinking. She knows it. She's trying not to drown, but her limbs feel like wet sand. She goes back to typing. She has to. If she stops, the quiet thoughts will eat her alive.

Her chest hurts. Her stomach aches. Her home is cluttered. Her mind is worse. And still, she tells herself she's fine. Because collapsing now would require admitting how far she's fallen.

CHAPTER TWENTY-SIX

It is afternoon, and she doesn't even know what day it is. Sydni feels like her body is made of wet cement. Everything is heavy. Her limbs, her thoughts, her chest. Even blinking feels like work. She sits hunched over her laptop, staring at the same sentence for nearly ten minutes.

Her cursor blinks. And blinks. And blinks. She reads the line again. Adjusts a comma. Deletes it. Adds it back. Deletes the whole sentence in a burst of frustration and then immediately regrets it, her fingers trembling as she retypes the exact same words because her brain can't form new ones.

The apartment is silent. No music. No TV. No Resolve notifications. No texts she's willing to open. Just her shallow breathing and the occasional drip from her kitchen faucet. A sound she's been meaning to fix but hasn't touched.

Her coffee is cold. Her stomach is empty. Her hair is a knot she doesn't remember creating. She glances toward the sink where the dishes look less like a chore and more like a personal failure. The smell has worsened, faint but sour.

She should wash them. She doesn't move. Her chest tightens again, not sharp enough to be painful, but deep enough to be suffocating. A dull, constant pressure right behind her sternum.

She tries to inhale deeper, but her lungs only cooperate halfway.

She rubs her collarbone, trying to ease the tension, trying to move past the familiar panic that threatens to rise.

Keep working, she tells herself. *If you keep going, you won't think. Don't think. Don't feel. Just do.*

She refocuses on the grant.

"Training sessions will be implemented quarterly—" Her vision blurs. She blinks hard.

And that's when it happens, the thing so small and stupid, it shouldn't matter at all. She reaches for her glass of water on the coffee table, misjudges the distance, and knocks it over.

The glass falls, hits the edge of the table, and shatters against the hardwood floor.

Water spreads. Glass fragments scatter. The sound rings out like a gunshot in the stillness.

Sydni goes perfectly still. She stares at the mess. At the water soaking into the rug. At the glint of shards around her bare feet.

And then, something inside her breaks. An accidental noise escapes her throat. Not a sob, not exactly, more like a tiny, wounded sound she's been holding in for weeks. Her vision blurs again, not from strain this time but from tears welling too fast for her to swallow down.

She presses her hands over her face. And the tears come. It isn't loud or dramatic, but she can't stop them. She folds forward, elbows on her knees, hands covering her eyes as her body trembles under the weight of it all.

It isn't the broken glass. It isn't the spilled water. It's everything she hasn't let herself feel. The man at the market. The way Elias stepped between them. The way she felt seen for the first time in years and how that terrified her. The scars. The memories she never touches. Elias' gentle texts. Her own silence. Her own shame. The feeling that she's ruining everything good before it can reach her.

Her tears hit the blanket pooled around her legs. She tries to stop crying but her breath stutters, jagged and uneven. Her hands shake as she drags them down her face, trying to compose herself, failing miserably.

She whispers, cracked and hoarse, "I don't know how to do this."

The words hang in the room, heavy, and heartbreaking. Her chest tightens again, worse this time, her breaths short and rapid. She presses a hand to her sternum, trying desperately to ground herself.

"In… out," she whispers. Her voice quivers. She tries again. "In… out…"

She squeezes her eyes shut, shoulders shaking. Time bends. She doesn't know how long she sits there like that; folded into herself, crying, surrounded by broken glass and the sinking feeling that she is the broken thing in the room.

Eventually, when the tears slow to a damp ache behind her eyes, she forces herself upright. Her head throbs. Her throat is raw.

She wipes her cheeks with the sleeve of her sweatshirt and stares emptily at the Resolve icon on her phone. That stupid little app. That stupid promise of bettering herself. Of accountability. Of connection. Of him.

Her hand trembles as she picks up the phone. For a second, she just stares at the icon, thumb hovering.

Then with a breath that feels like surrender, she presses down on it. It wiggles. She presses the X.

A little box pops up:

**"Delete Resolve?
All data will be removed."**

Her eyes sting again.

She whispers, "I'm sorry."

She taps **Delete.**

The icon disappears. The screen goes blank.

Sydni's chest hollows. There is no relief. Only the terrible sound of giving up.

She sets her phone down beside her, curls into herself again, and hides her face in her hands as the last of her strength unravels.

And for the first time since the new year began, she feels completely, utterly lost.

CHAPTER TWENTY-SEVEN

Sydni doesn't remember falling asleep. One minute she was curled on the couch, tear-stained and hollow, and the next she's waking up to the sound of persistent knocking.

Three sharp knocks. There is a brief pause before three more come.

She squeezes her eyes shut. If she keeps still, maybe whoever it is and it can *only* be one person, will go away. But Sloan never goes away.

The knocking grows louder. "SYDNI BENTON, OPEN YOUR DOOR OR I'M CALLING THE NATIONAL GUARD."

She groans into her blanket.

Another knock. "Don't test me. I will assemble a *team.*"

She drags herself upright, her body heavy from crying. She doesn't bother fixing her hair or her face or the trembling in her hands. She shuffles to the door and cracks it an inch.

Sloan's eyes widen. "Jesus Christ."

"What?" she whispers, voice raw.

"You look like a raccoon who's been hit by a semi."

She tries to shut the door.

He wedges his foot into the frame, unimpressed. "Nope. Not today."

"Sloan—"

"Step aside. I'm coming in."

She doesn't fight him. She's too tired.

He pushes the door open and steps inside, and the second his eyes sweep over her apartment, his expression shifts from sarcastic to stricken.

Dishes piled in the sink. Laundry on the floor. Blankets half off the couch. Her coffee table cluttered with mugs. Her laptop open, screen frozen mid-sentence. Small pieces of broken glass glinting under the lamp.

"Okay," he says slowly. "Okay. Got it. We're doing this."

She sinks onto the couch, hugging her knees. "Please don't make this a thing."

"Syd," Sloan says, voice lower than usual, "this *is* a thing."

He walks to the kitchen without asking, grabs the broom and dustpan, and crouches to sweep the glass. He does it silently, carefully, like he's cleaning up something fragile.

When he stands, he sets the broom aside and looks at her. Really looks.

"You deleted Resolve," he says.

She freezes. "How—"

"I checked the app this morning." He lifts his phone. "Resolve friend data unavailable. Which means you deleted it."

She stares at the blanket bunched in her fists.

He sets his phone down and sits in the armchair across from her. Not crowding her, but close enough that she can't pretend he isn't here. "I need you to talk to me," he says. No sarcasm. No jokes. Just truth.

"I can't."

"Try."

She shakes her head. "I don't want to."

"Syd."

Her throat tightens. "It won't help."

"It will help *me,*" Sloan says. "Because right now, I'm scared."

Her eyes snap up. Sloan almost never says that word.

He leans forward, elbows on his knees. "You haven't answered anyone in days. You missed Vic's party without texting her. You ignored every one of my calls. You look like you haven't slept or eaten. And your apartment… this isn't you."

Shame burns her cheeks.

He continues, voice steady. "Talk to me. I don't need every detail. I just need… something."

She swallows, jaw trembling. "I'm tired."

"That's not enough."

"I'm overwhelmed."

"Still not enough."

She squeezes her eyes shut. Tears threaten. "I'm… I'm not okay."

Those three words crack something open. She keeps going, the words tumbling out like something finally breaking free. "I can't do the DV grant right now. Every sentence felt like it was choking me. I switched to something easier but even that feels impossible. The apartment's a mess. I can't get out of bed some days. I haven't walked. I keep thinking about—" She stops. Swallows. "—about everything."

Her voice shakes on the last word.

Sloan nods, slowly, like he's piecing a puzzle together. "Is this about him?" he asks gently.

Her chest crushes inward. She doesn't answer.

"I'm not asking if you're in love with him," Sloan says. "I'm asking if something happened."

"No," she whispers. "He didn't do anything wrong."

"But something happened to *you.*"

Sloan leans forward. "Sydni, I've known you a long time. And I know the difference between you being stressed and you drowning."

She wraps her arms around herself. "I'm fine."

"You are *not* fine."

Her voice cracks. "I don't know how to be okay."

Those words…He hears the truth in them. He feels it.

And his expression melts into something fiercer, more protective. "Syd," he says quietly, "you need help."

She flinches. "I don't want—"

"You need help," he repeats, firmer. "Not because you're weak. But because you've been carrying something enormous alone. And you're exhausted."

Her chin trembles. Tears gather again. She looks away, ashamed.

Sloan's voice softens. "I'm on your side. But I can't be your whole support system. I'm your best friend, not your therapist."

She wipes her face with her sleeve. "I don't want therapy."

"Why?"

She stares at her hands. "Because I'm tired of explaining myself."

"You don't have to explain everything," Sloan says. "Just start somewhere. Start small. Start by breathing. Start by talking to someone who can help you unload the stuff that's hurting you."

She shakes her head. "What if I can't do it? What if I fall apart?"

Sloan leans in. His voice is barely above a whisper. "Then you fall apart. And someone helps you put yourself back together. That's how it works."

Tears fall silently down her cheeks.

He reaches out, giving her a chance to pull away, but she doesn't. So he gently takes her hand.

"Listen to me," he says. "You're not broken. You're hurting. There's a difference."

Her shoulders shake. A sob slips out, small but sharp.

"And you're not alone," Sloan adds. "Not even a little."

She drops her forehead to her knees, finally letting herself cry. Not the contained tears from before. This is full-body crying. Shaking, breathless, messy.

Sloan moves from the chair to the couch, not touching her at first. He waits until she scoots toward him, barely an inch, and only then wraps an arm around her shoulders. She melts into him, crying harder.

"I'm here," he murmurs. "I'm not leaving. Not today, not tomorrow."

She cries until she can't anymore. When she's quiet again, Sloan wipes her cheek gently with the sleeve of his hoodie.

Then he says the thing she needs most:

"You deserve help, Syd. And I'll go with you if you want."

She nods once. It is a small but real nod. She is fragile and she knows she needs help.

Sloan squeezes her hand. "Good. We'll figure it out."

Sydni feels something shift. She knows she is not fixed and she is a long way from it. But maybe there is hope. She feels it. It's small. A single thread of hope wrapped around a trembling heart.

When Sydni's sobs finally fade into hiccups, Sloan gives her hand one last squeeze before standing up with a decisive clap of his hands. "Alright," he says. "Here's what's happening. I'm calling in reinforcements."

She frowns, exhausted. "…What?"

He gestures around the apartment. "This. This disaster. This—" he points to the kitchen "—crime scene."

"It's not that bad," she mutters.

"Syd," he says solemnly, "if the CDC showed up right now, they'd evacuate the building."

A tiny, unwilling laugh escapes her, a small puff of air, but it counts. Sloan catches it like a win, throws his hands up.

"See? She lives!"

"I hate you," she mumbles into her sleeve.

"No, you don't," he says, heading into the kitchen. "You tolerate me at a subpar level, and honestly? That's enough for me."

She watches him survey the damage like a general preparing for battle. He pulls his hoodie sleeves up past his elbows with exaggerated determination.

"Oh my god," he mutters, looking into the sink. "This is… wow. This is… a war crime."

"Stop," she says weakly, but the corner of her mouth twitches.

"Is this pan *alive*?" he asks, poking it with a wooden spoon.

"It's just grease."

"Sydni, it's glistening. In a threatening way."

She pulls her legs up onto the couch and wraps her arms around them, watching him without the usual shame that comes with being seen like this. Maybe because he's seen her worse. Maybe because he isn't judging. Maybe because right now, she can't care about pride.

He starts running hot water and squirting dish soap into the sink like he's baptizing it.

"Okay," he says, "we're doing this in stages. Dishes first, then trash, then… whatever that smell is."

"There is no smell," she mutters.

Sloan opens the trash can. "Sydni."

"…Fine. A small smell."

"A medium-to-large smell," he corrects. "Like a raccoon died and left a note that said, 'Clean your kitchen, babe.'"

She snorts, that actual snort that was once called cute, and Sloan grins triumphantly.

"See?" he says. "We're laughing AND we're cleaning. A two-for-one special."

He washes dishes with chaotic energy, humming off-key, making absurd commentary about each item he touches.

"Oh look, a mug that's been holding old coffee so long it has emotional trauma of its own."

"Is this a fork or a science experiment?"

"This plate has seen things. We need to get it counseling."

She rubs her face, feeling the tiniest flicker of warmth in her chest. "You're ridiculous."

"And yet," he says, rinsing a pan with flourish, "here you are. Benefiting from my ridiculousness."

She slides off the couch slowly, her limbs still heavy. "I can help…"

Sloan holds up a wet, soapy hand. "Nope. Sit your ass down."

"Sloan—"

"You cried so hard you lost a contact you're not even wearing. Sit."

She blinks. "…What does that even mean?"

"It means you cried VERY HARD," he says, sweeping another plate into the drying rack. "My point stands."

She retreats to the couch for a moment, but after a minute, she gets up anyway. She can't just watch him clean her mess, That feels too vulnerable, even now. So, she shuffles to the trash can, ties up the bag, and starts on another.

He notices. He doesn't comment. He just works beside her, shoulder to shoulder, like it's the most natural thing in the world.

When she reaches for a stack of dishes, he pauses. "Sure?"

She nods.

"Okay," he says, handing her a sponge. "Welcome to the team."

They work in comfortable silence. Water running. Clinking of dishes. A trash bag rustling. The apartment slowly becoming… lighter.

As the sink clears and the counters appear again, Sydni realizes she's breathing easier. Not fixed. Not okay. But less crushed.

Sloan wipes down the counter, looks at her, and says, "See? Helping isn't a bad thing."

That hits a tender place. "I… thank you," she whispers, her voice cracking again.

He shakes his head immediately. "Nope. I don't want a thank you."

"Sloan—"

He elbows her lightly. "Friends don't get thank-you for doing friend things. That's just the job."

Her throat tightens again, but not with panic this time. With something warmer.

Sloan cups her shoulder gently, no pressure, just grounding. "You're not a burden, Syd. Not to me. Not ever. So when I say I've got you? I mean it."

Tears prick her eyes again. She nods.

"Good," he says, patting her arm awkwardly. "Now let's take out this trash before the smell becomes sentient."

She laughs, actually laughs, and Sloan beams like he's won a championship.

Together, they take out the trash, scrub the last pan, wipe the counters, and light a candle that smells like clean laundry.

The apartment still isn't perfect, but it feels…livable. And Sydni, standing there in the warm kitchen light beside the person who knows her best, feels the smallest stir of hope.

Maybe accepting help doesn't mean she's weak. Maybe leaning on someone doesn't mean she'll fall apart. Maybe, just maybe, she's not as alone as she thought.

When they're done, Sloan tosses the dish towel dramatically over his shoulder like a 1950s housewife. "There. Domestic goddess levels restored."

She smiles, tired but sincere. "Thank you."

He rolls his eyes. "I said no thank-yous."

"Okay," she whispers. "Then… I'm glad you're here."

"Always."

CHAPTER TWENTY-EIGHT

Sydni wakes to sunlight brushing her cheek. A warm kind of light she hasn't noticed in weeks. Her eyes feel swollen, her head heavy, her throat scratchy. Sleeping after an emotional collapse feels like swimming up from the bottom of a deep, dark lake.

Her phone buzzes under her pillow.

Two messages.

Sloan:
Morning, babe. Proud of you for yesterday. Really.

And then:

Sloan:
And before you roll your eyes, here's the number to my therapist. She's amazing. Please call.

Attached is the contact:

Lena Wexler, PhD, LPC

A therapist, a real one, who will want her to talk about her feelings. It wasn't a checklist. Not a journal prompt. Not a friend trying their best. A professional. Someone she'll have to look in the eye. Someone she'll have to tell the truth to, even the pieces she doesn't want to see herself.

Fear blooms low in her gut. "What if I can't?" she whispers into the empty room.

But her thumb is already hovering over the number. Her hands shake as she taps **Call**. Her heart races against her ribs.

It rings once.

"Wexler Counseling, this is Marianne," a kind voice answers, warm and professional.

Sydni swallows hard. "Hi. Um… my best friend gave me your number. I'm… looking to make an appointment."

"Of course, sweetheart. What's your name?"

"Sydni. Sydni Benton."

"Well, Sydni," Marianne says kindly, "we're glad you reached out. Are afternoons okay? We had a cancellation for today at 2:30."

Today. Her pulse spikes.

That's too soon. She's not ready. She'll never be ready.

But her voice says, "…Yes. I can do today."

"Wonderful. We'll see you then. Come ten minutes early for paperwork."

"Okay. Thank you."

When she hangs up, she stares at the phone like it might burst into flames. But she doesn't cancel. Instead, she pushes herself out of bed and pads into the kitchen and stops short. The counters are clean. The dishes washed. The trash gone. A candle under a warmer, left by Sloan, gives off a vanilla scent.

Her apartment looks like someone cared about it. Someone cared about *her*.

A calmer, tentative feeling settles in her chest. She wouldn't call it relief. But maybe the first step out of the fog. She runs her fingers along the smooth countertop, remembering how hopeless it all felt yesterday.

Maybe she can rebuild from here. Maybe she doesn't have to do it alone.

~*~

At 1 p.m., she stands in front of her closet, overwhelmed by the idea of choosing an outfit. Everything feels wrong. Too tight. Too loose. Too bright. Too dull. Too revealing. Too plain.

Eventually she settles on jeans and a blue sweater. It's clean and modest, and most of all, safe.

She brushes her hair into a low, messy bun. Puts on mascara. Wipes it off. Puts on a tiny bit again. In the mirror, she looks like someone trying and trying counts.

Driving to the therapist's office is its own battle. Each red light feels like a moment where she could turn around. Each street she passes feels like she's leaving her comfort zone farther behind. But she keeps going.

~*~

The waiting room is surprisingly warm and inviting. Cool tone lamps instead of overhead lighting. Bookshelves lined with titles about relationships, trauma, healing. A faint scent of lavender.

Her hands shake as she fills out the intake form.

What brings you in today?

She writes slowly:

I'm overwhelmed. I feel like I'm disappearing. I don't know how to stop shutting down. I need help.

When Marianne calls her name, Sydni nearly jumps.

A woman in her forties steps out from a low lit hallway. Curly dark hair, warm brown eyes, teal blouse, and an expression that radiates calm.

"You must be Sydni," she says, her voice gentle enough to make Sydni's throat tighten. "I'm Dr. Wexler. Come on back."

The office itself feels like someone's cozy reading nook. A big window spills natural light across a patterned rug. Two plush chairs sit angled toward each other with a small table between them holding a box of tissues and a mug that reads *One Hour at a Time*.

Sydni sits stiffly, hands clasped so tightly her knuckles pale.

Dr. Wexler doesn't start with questions. She starts with presence.

"I'm really glad you're here today," she says. "Reaching out for help is a big step."

Sydni's throat burns. "It… didn't feel brave."

"That's usually how bravery feels," Dr. Wexler replies with a kind smile.

The first few minutes are awkward, stilted. Sydni tries to speak and only manages fragments — "bad week," "overwhelmed," "can't get out of bed," "something triggered me," "work has been hard."

Dr. Wexler listens like each word is worth hearing. No judgment. No pressure. Just patient, steady presence.

When the tears come, and they do, sudden and hot, Dr. Wexler hands her a tissue without interrupting the flow.

"You don't need to apologize," she says when Sydni tries. "This room is safe. You don't have to be strong in here."

Sydni cries harder. But it's different than the night before. Less like breaking. More like releasing.

They talk about grounding strategies. About breathing techniques. About trauma spirals and how the brain protects itself. About guilt. About the fear of being seen. About the terror of letting someone help her.

Dr. Wexler doesn't pry. She doesn't ask about the past she isn't ready to share. She simply creates a space where Sydni doesn't feel like a burden for existing.

By the end of the session, Sydni feels wrung out, like her emotions had been squeezed but not drained. She feels… lighter. Just a little.

As she stands to leave, Dr. Wexler pauses.

"Sydni?"

She turns.

"I want you to hear this," the therapist says gently but clearly. "You showed up today. Do you know how big that is? You did something incredibly hard for yourself and you should be proud."

"Thank you," she whispers.

"Same time next week?"

"Yes," Sydni says, surprising herself with the ease of it. "Absolutely."

~*~

Back home, Sydni drops her bag on the couch and walks straight to her laptop. She opens the smaller, easier grant. The one she's been too overwhelmed to finish and begins reading.

The words make more sense today.

She edits. Refines. Finishes the last section. Rechecks the budget. Attaches the documents.

When she clicks **Submit**, she feels light, with this feeling she hasn't felt in weeks:

Accomplishment. It wasn't perfection and that was okay. It was just… *I did something today.*

She leans back in her chair. The apartment is cleaner. The grant is submitted. Her first therapy appointment is behind her. And she survived it all.

She feels a small, real spark of hope. Something inside her has shifted. She is trying.

CHAPTER TWENTY-NINE

The morning after her therapy session, Sydni wakes before her alarm. It surprises her…she'd grown used to mornings where she clung to the bed like it was the last safe place on earth. But today, the sunlight creeping across her pillow looks gentler, less aggressive. The room feels slightly less oppressive.

She sits up slowly, pushing the blanket aside. Her body aches with the exhaustion of emotions she'd kept bottled for weeks, but something in her chest feels different. Not lighter, exactly, more like a loosening around the edges.

She decides to do one thing. Just one.

She gathers her sheets into a pile, stripping the bed entirely. The fabric is cool and wrinkled in her arms, smelling faintly of restlessness and too many nights spent numbing out. It isn't shame she feels, not today, but an awareness that she deserves better.

Fresh sheets go on next. Clean. Crisp. Smelling faintly of lavender and detergent. She smooths the corners, pulls the comforter up neatly, and stands back. Her bed looks almost inviting again.

A small accomplishment. But she feels it. She lets herself feel it.

Over the next few days, Sydni builds on that single step.

She showers. Every day. Not because she wants to, but because she promised herself small actions would count.

The first few showers feel mechanical, but on the third morning, she finds herself lingering as the steam fogs the mirror. She watches her reflection slowly appear, faint and shadowed, but present. There's something grounding in the ritual. Something honest.

She washes her laundry next, not all of it, because that would overwhelm her, but one basket at a time. She folds the clothes, placing each item in drawers instead of piling them on the chair she'd been using as a makeshift closet.

The sight of her room no longer cluttered with scattered jeans and sweaters feels… good.

~*~

Her second therapy session is harder than the first. She talks more about the knot in her chest that tightens every time she thinks she's getting too comfortable, too safe. About the way she flinches when strangers stand too close. About how quickly she shuts down when something feels unfamiliar or threatening. She also talks about how repetitive her actions are, both for the good and bad.

Dr. Wexler listens with gentle attentiveness, nodding at the right moments, offering grounding tools and affirmations. "You're rebuilding trust with yourself," the therapist says calmly. "That takes time. And patience."

"I'm not used to that," Sydni admits.

"That's why we practice."

When she leaves, she doesn't feel lighter. But she feels… real. And that is its own kind of progress.

~*~

At home, Sydni tries cooking again.

Attempt #1:
Chicken so burnt it crumbles under the fork. Smoke alarm screaming. Three curse words. She laughs through it instead of crying, which feels monumental.

Attempt #2:
Slightly under seasoned pasta with vegetables. Not great, not

terrible. She eats half while watching a YouTube video about "Basic Cooking Skills for People Who Fear Stoves."

Attempt #3:
A simple rice bowl with sautéed veggies and chicken. Balanced. Tasty. And miracle of miracles, actually intentional.

She takes a picture of her plate and sends it to Sloan.

Sydni:
Look what I made! Real food. Like an adult.

He responds instantly:

Sloan:
She COOKS! My girl is unstoppable. Proud of you, babe.

She rolls her eyes at the last part, her lips twitching despite herself.

~*~

Some nights, when her apartment feels too quiet, she walks next door to Sloan's. He always opens the door with a dramatic gasp, as if her arrival is the highlight of his day.

"Come in," he says one evening, gesturing grandly. "I made spaghetti. It is, objectively, awful. We will suffer together."

The spaghetti is terrible. The sauce is water and there is way too much garlic. There isn't enough salt. In reality, it was a crime against Italian cuisine.

She laughs so hard she snorts again.

"You actually ate this?" she wheezes.

"I created it," he says solemnly. "I am obligated to honor my own disasters."

They watch a cheesy action movie afterward, the kind with explosions every ten minutes and dialogue so bad it loops back around to entertaining. Sydni sits curled in the corner of his couch, comfortable in her hoodie and leggings. Sloan sprawls beside her, feet on the coffee table he refuses to dust.

Halfway through the movie he glances at her, really looks at her, and smiles. "You're doing better," he says.

She tucks her hair behind her ear. "I still feel like crap some days."

"Yeah," he nods. "But you're still here. Still trying. And I know how much you LOVE this, but I'm proud of you."

She looks away, her throat tightening. She doesn't cry, but she could. His words don't sting, they settle. She doesn't say thank you. It's not because she doesn't feel it. But because she knows he'd shoo it away with a joke.

Instead, she nudges his shoulder. "Your spaghetti is an abomination."

He gasps. "Oh absolutely. But you ate it, which means you love me."

She laughs again, lighter this time.

~*~

The next two weeks move in small, gentle waves.

She journals, not daily, but enough to leave trails of her thoughts scattered across the page. Some entries are short, others deeply reflective. She writes about therapy, about rebuilding routine, about how scary vulnerability still feels.

She picks up the DV grant again. Slowly. Cautiously. And it doesn't strangle her the way it did before. Instead, it challenges her in ways that feel manageable. She outlines sections, highlights important statistics, and even rewrites a paragraph she hated.

She doesn't feel crushed beneath the weight of her work.

She takes walks too, short ones, without pressure to hit a certain distance. Sometimes she goes outside just to stand on the sidewalk for a few minutes and breathe fresh air.

It counts. All of it counts.

Sloan notices every step forward, cheering her on with ridiculous enthusiasm.

"You folded your laundry? BABE! Superstar."
"You cooked rice? Michelin star."
"You showered twice in one day? Honestly iconic."

Sometimes she rolls her eyes. Sometimes she laughs. Sometimes she just lets the words land. But every single time, he means it.

One evening, Sloan pokes his head into her apartment without knocking and stops mid-stride when he sees her living room.

"Whoa," he says, blinking dramatically. "Did a responsible adult break in here?"

Sydni snorts. "Shut up."

"No, I'm serious. This is suspiciously tidy. Should I call someone? The Vatican? Ghostbusters?"

Sloan steps farther into the room, turning slowly like he's taking in a museum exhibit. "Look at this. Floors. Surfaces. The absence of doom piles." He presses a hand to his chest. "I'm emotional."

Sydni rolls her eyes but can't completely hide the small smile tugging at her mouth. "It's not that big of a deal."

"It is to me," Sloan says. "And to you."

She sinks onto the couch, hugging a pillow loosely. "It's just… small stuff."

"Small stuff is how humans function," he replies, plopping down beside her. "You think we level up in life with boss fights and power-ups? No. We do laundry and hope we don't shrink our shirts."

She laughs again, surprising herself. But after a moment, she picks at the edge of the pillowcase and says, "It feels like one of those cheesy rom-com books. You know the part where the heroine hits rock bottom, isolates herself, eats cereal straight from the box—"

"You mean Tuesday?"

"—and then," she continues pointedly, "she starts doing tiny things. Like… showering. Cleaning one corner of her apartment. Washing an actual dish without crying. And that's her big turning point. The 'she's starting to find herself again' montage."

Sloan leans back, crossing his arms. "So you're in your redemption arc?"

"Maybe," Sydni says, cheeks warming. "Or maybe I'm just living through a really crappy plot where one thing sets you off, your whole life spirals, and the universe expects you to magically fix it with bubble baths and self-reflection."

"Look, if this were a rom-com," Sloan says, "the audience would be rooting for you so hard right now. They'd be eating popcorn and yelling, *'Yes queen, fold those jeans!'*"

She laughs so hard she has to curl forward, her forehead nearly hitting her knees.

When she finally catches her breath, she sighs. "It just… feels good. I didn't think it would."

Sloan nudges her shoulder. "That's because progress isn't glamorous. It's boring, slow, stupidly uncinematic. But it's real. And you're doing it."

"Yeah," she murmurs. "I guess I am."

He bumps her knee with his. She looks away, blinking faster than she means to.

"And for the record," he adds, "your life isn't a crappy rom-com plot."

"No?"

"Nope. It's more like an indie film. Emotional, weird, filled with stunning character development…and questionable fashion choices."

Her smile lingers long after he stops laughing.

After Sloan returns to his place, she sits tackling the toughest section of the DV grant without spiraling, Sydni closes her laptop and sits in her clean kitchen.

The candle on the counter flickers, illuminating the space that no longer feels like a reflection of her worst days. She's not healed. She's not back to herself yet. She has to keep reminding herself this. But she's not drowning anymore. She's swimming. Slow, shaky strokes, but forward.

CHAPTER THIRTY

The days turn into weeks. Not one awkward lull. Weeks.

Elias stares at his phone again, thumb hovering over the empty Resolve chat thread that used to hold small bursts of encouragement. The app interface looks too clean without her goals popping up, without her tiny checkmarks, without her sarcastic commentary about his stretching routines.

It shouldn't matter this much. But it does.

She's not there. No new tasks or completed goals. No encouragements sent his way. He knows that he shouldn't be checking it repeatedly.

Her profile photo is gone too replaced with a generic silhouette, which only means one thing: She deleted the app.

Deleted *him*, really. He exhales slowly, leaning back on the couch while Clementine hops up beside him, dropping her head onto his thigh. Her golden retriever eyes lift to his face with worry, sensing the heaviness in him.

"Yeah," he murmurs, rubbing behind her ears. "I know. I'm being dramatic."

She huffs through her nose, nudging his hand until he continues scratching her head.

He should let it go. Move on. People drift all the time, especially when they barely know each other. But he can't shake the feeling that something happened. Something beyond simple disinterest.

Because the last time he saw Sydni… she seemed bright. Nervous. Funny. And for the first time in a long time, he had felt something in himself shift. Something hopeful.

Then she vanished.

Maybe he came on too strong. Maybe he wasn't what she wanted. Maybe she'd decided that their weekly meet-ups were nothing more than a silly New Year's experiment.

But the ache in his chest feels familiar. Too familiar.

He stares at the blank app screen again, the silence she left behind. No checkmarks, no goals, no little sarcastic notes echoing louder than any argument or breakup ever had. And then, like someone tilting a puzzle piece into the right light, something clicks.

This silence…
This disappearing act…
This sudden vanishing without explanation…

He's done it. God, he's *done* that exact thing. Retreat when something hurts. Pull back when things get complicated. Cut communication so he doesn't have to risk saying the wrong thing. Isolate to "get himself together," then realize he's only made the gap wider.

He closes his eyes. "She's doing what I do," he whispers, voice barely above air.

Clementine nudges his ribs gently, and he lets out a breath that feels half like understanding and half like heartbreak. He sees the situation clearly. Not through confusion or jealousy or hurt pride…but through recognition.

She didn't delete the app to erase him. She didn't pull away because she didn't care. She didn't retreat because she's cold or indifferent. She retreated because something scared her. Because something hurt. Because that's what people do when they've been through too much. Because she learned the same survival response he did.

And the knowledge hits him with a tenderness so sharp it almost hurts. He isn't angry anymore. Just… aching. And gentler with her in his mind than he was a second ago.

He tells himself that's okay. It's normal, it's just life.

Still, he thinks of her at odd moments. When he's buying groceries. When he passes a bookstore window. When he tries a new recipe and wonders what sarcastic comment she'd make.

Sometimes, when he stretches before bed, he wonders if she ever joked about it again, if she ever told Sloan about his "old man mobility routines" and laughed.

He misses the sound of her laugh. He didn't get to hear it nearly enough. He hadn't known her long but he still misses that sound.

~*~

Nora breezes into his apartment one Saturday morning like she owns the place — mostly because she does that everywhere. Her curly hair is piled on her head in a messy bun that somehow looks purposeful, and she carries a tote bag covered in enamel pins.

"Eli!" she calls out. "Are you alive?"

"I'm sitting right here," he says from the kitchen, stirring a pan of eggs. "You act like I'm one tragic breakup away from collapsing in my socks."

"First of all," she says, dropping her bag on the counter, "I've seen your sock collection. You absolutely *would* collapse in those green argyle ones."

Clementine bounds over to greet her, panting happily.

Nora grins. "See? Someone appreciates me."

Elias narrows his eyes. "What do you want?"

"I come to check on my big brother and that's the tone I get?" she asks dramatically.

"Yes."

She shrugs. "Fair enough. I came to fix your social life."

"No."

"Yes."

"No."

"Yes."

He sighs, giving up faster than he should. Nora has been bossing him around since she was five; resisting is pointless.

She folds her arms. "Elias Monroe, when was the last time you went out? With actual humans?"

"Work," he offers.

"That doesn't count."

"I walk Clementine."

"She's a dog."

"Well that's not nice."

She rolls her eyes. "Look, it's been months since you've been on a date, and honestly? You're starting to give quiet woodland hermit vibes."

"I like quiet."

"Yes," she says, "but you're also lonely."

He pauses at that longer than he intends. Nora's expression softens. "I'm not judging you," she adds gently. "I just… I want you to be happy. You deserve that."

He thinks of Sydni again. The warmth of her humor, the way she pushed her curls back when she was nervous, how she surprised him without trying. But she's gone.

"Okay," he says finally. "Fine. I'll consider going on a date. If the right person comes along"

Nora lights up. "YES! I knew you'd say yes eventually. I already have someone picked out."

"What?"

"She's sweet, funny, works at the front desk at the community center, and she's been asking about you. And she's soooooo pretty."

"You told her about me?"

"I may have shared some light details," Nora says, waving a hand. "Like the fact that you're a good guy, a great cook, and annoyingly introspective."

He groans.

She elbows him. "I'm setting you up. You're going."

He doesn't say no.

Even though something in him tugs backward. A thread tied to someone he hasn't seen in weeks.

~*~

Later that afternoon, Elias sits on his couch with Clementine curled up against him as he types out a message to the girl Nora set him up with.

Her name is Brielle. She seems nice. Maybe even normal.

Elias:
Hi Brielle, this is Elias. Nora said you wanted to maybe grab coffee sometime?

He stares at the message far too long before sending it.

His phone buzzes thirty minutes later.

Brielle:
Hi Elias! I'd love to! I've actually been hoping you'd reach out. How's Wednesday evening?

He swallows and types back.

Wednesday works. Would you like to meet at Perk & Gray?

Her reply comes quickly, enthusiastic, full of emojis. He should feel excited. Or at least… open. Instead, he feels a flicker of guilt, which is stupid. He doesn't owe Sydni anything. They barely knew each other. She left without a word.

Still…He finds himself whispering into Clementine's fur, "I just…thought she'd come back."

Clementine nudges him gently, tail thumping once in understanding.

~*~

Brielle calls a few hours later.

"Hey!" she says brightly. "Sorry, I'm more of a voice-not-text person. Is now a bad time?"

"No, it's fine," he says, sitting up straighter.

She launches into easy conversation. She's funny. Warm. Talks about her job, her hobbies, her love of hiking.

He responds politely, laughing when appropriate, even joking back once or twice. She seems like someone he could genuinely like. But somewhere in the back of his mind, in the place where his real thoughts live, he keeps seeing dark curls, bright blue eyes, and a crooked smile.

He keeps hearing the ghost of a laugh he hadn't heard enough of. He keeps wondering if she's okay.

When the call ends, Brielle sounds thrilled. Elias feels… conflicted. Hopeful and hollow at the same time. A strange combination.

He leans back against the couch, closing his eyes.

"New beginnings, right?" he whispers to himself.

Clementine licks his hand. And whether he wants to admit it or not…Some small part of him still misses the girl who disappeared.

CHAPTER THIRTY-ONE

By Wednesday evening, Elias feels something he hasn't felt in months. It wasn't dread or tension. It felt sharper. Maybe a little buzzier. Hope-adjacent if he lets himself call it that.

He stands in front of the bathroom mirror, adjusting the cuffs of his button-down like he's trying out versions of himself. His reflection looks steady enough, but inside, he can feel his heartbeat echoing in his ears. Clementine, sprawled dramatically across the hallway rug, seems to notice. "You could try being supportive," he tells her.

Her tail thumps once in a *Fine, but I'm watching you* kind of way.

"It's just one date," he mutters, even though he's not sure he believes that. "People go on dates when things don't work out with… other people."

His jaw tightens. Other people. He still can't say her name without something inside him pulling tight. Sydni hadn't disappeared abruptly. Not the kind of ghosting he might have shrugged off in another life. She had just… dulled. Gone from warm and quick-witted to distant and vaguely polite.

He has to remember that he she didn't block him, didn't send a dramatic goodbye, didn't even say *I need space.* She simply slipped backward into the kind of quiet that hurts more than words ever could and he knows that routine well, as an experienced veteran.

So now he's here. In the cologne that Nora suggested. Clean shirt. Heart at half-speed. Trying something new. Trying to move on. Trying not to think about how good it felt when she was close enough for him to hear her laugh without it sounding afraid.

Clementine sighs loudly.

"Yeah," he says. "I know." He scratches behind her ears. "I'll be back soon."

She watches him leave like she's not convinced.

~*~

The café glows warmly against the cold evening. Golden lights, fogged windows, clinking mugs. The world inside feels alive and hopeful.

He spots Brielle immediately. She sits near the window, blonde curls bouncing as she laughs at something on her phone. Her green eyes catch every bit of ambient light. Her sweater is a cream color, her cheeks faintly rosy from the cold.

She stands when she sees him, and her smile blooms like she's genuinely excited he's here. "Elias?"

He returns the smile, surprised by how easy it is. "Yeah. Hey."

Up close, she's all brightness and confidence, the kind of beauty that turns heads and the kind of warmth that makes people want to linger in her orbit. Nothing like Sydni. And the thought stings, so he sets it aside.

They sit. She tucks a piece of hair behind one ear. It's elegantly natural like she's done it thousands of times. "I'm always early," she says, grinning. "It's a flaw. I hate rushing."

"I should've guessed that," he says. "You chose the best table."

"I always do."

She winks. It's playful, practiced, but not in a bad way, like she simply enjoys the game of getting to know someone.

Elias exhales slowly. This feels… nice. Normal.

It turns out she's easy to talk to. She funny and quick witted. She is also comfortably self-assured. She works at the community center, mentors teens, volunteers with the sports league, hikes on weekends, and watches terrible reality TV with no shame whatsoever.

He laughs, actually laughs, when she describes a pottery project that exploded in the kiln. Her joy is infectious. Her confidence is soothing. Nothing like the way Sydni carries her walls in layers of sarcasm and softness. He doesn't realize he's thinking about Sydni until he forces himself to stop.

Brielle leans forward. "Nora talks about you all the time, by the way."

He groans. "That sounds… dangerous."

"No, it's sweet. She adores you."

"That's mutual."

"And she wasn't lying," Brielle says, stirring her drink. "You *are* handsome."

Heat crawls up his neck. He's not used to compliments like that, not delivered so boldly.

"Thank you," he says. It's disorienting, being seen so directly.

They share pastries, her choice, again impeccable. Talk about everything from holiday plans to awful dating app bios to the best breakfast food in the world (she insists it's waffles; he argues for pancakes; she threatens to walk out).

And throughout it, something inside him relaxes and let go. Unwinds in tiny increments.

For the first time since January, he feels the faint possibility that he might be allowed to enjoy someone else's company without guilt.

~*~

He notices it when it happens. A full minute where he isn't wondering if Sydni ate today. A moment where he isn't picturing her smile. A brief, flickering stretch of time where he isn't feeling the ache of her absence. He doesn't know if that makes him relieved or ashamed. Maybe both.

Brielle is lovely. Genuinely. Anyone would be lucky to sit across from her. So why does something in him still feel… untethered?

~*~

When the barista flips the sign to *Closing Soon,* Brielle stands and slips her coat over her shoulders.

"This was wonderful," she says. "Really."

He nods. "It was."

She hesitates, not shy, but thoughtful. "If you want to see each other again, I'd really like that." Her voice is hopeful.

Something inside him stirs, a cautious, warm flicker. "I'd like that too," he says gently.

Her delighted grin answers him. She steps outside, hair catching in the wind, and waves before heading toward her car.

Elias watches her go, his hands tucked into his jacket pockets. It felt good. He acknowledges it fully.

But beneath that good feeling…There's an ache curled up in his ribs. Not loud. Not sharp. Just… present. A reminder. A thread. One he isn't sure he knows how to sever or if he even wants to.

As he walks back to his car, he realizes that this could be the start of something. Something real. Something uncomplicated. Brielle is warm and steady and open. She wants him. She said so.

But when he turns the key in the ignition, the glow of the dashboard lights makes him think of something else instead, a woman with messy curls and quick wit and eyes she hides too often. Someone who deleted an app to disappear more gently. Someone he still wonders about at night. Someone who probably isn't thinking about him at all.

He exhales slowly. "I'm trying," he whispers to himself.

And he is. But some ghosts don't care how hard you try. They linger anyway.

CHAPTER THIRTY-TWO

Weeks pass. They aren't hurried. But they are shaped by small decisions, small victories, and the slow unfurling of a woman learning to breathe again.

Sydni wakes up one morning and realizes that she isn't bracing for the day. Her body isn't tensed in that familiar defensive curl. Her heart isn't pounding before her feet hit the floor.

She stretches, feeling the pull in her shoulders, the stiffness in her back, the warmth of her blanket. Her room is quiet, sunlight spilling across the comforter, turning the fabric into pale gold.

She whispers into the void, "Okay. Let's start here."

And she gets up.

~*~

Her routines come back slowly.

She showers. It feels good. The water washes over her, warm and steady, grounding her in her own skin, keeping up a routine that she is determine to keep.

The next morning, she showers again. Not because she must, but because the steam loosens something tight inside her. Because she feels a little more human afterward. Because it's a ritual she can rely on.

After a few days, showers become the first anchor of her mornings. Repetition is something she needs.

Then she starts making her bed gently, imperfectly. Tugging the blankets up. Smoothing out wrinkles. Fluffing pillows. A small gesture of order in a world that had felt chaotic.

After that, she continues to add a walk. One block. Then two. Sometimes three when the wind isn't too harsh.

She doesn't measure distance or time. She just walks. Her boots crunch against winter's leftover salt, the cold air bites lightly at her cheeks, and sometimes she looks up at the sky and thinks, *I'm still here.*

One morning, she realizes…she likes being outside again. Even if just for a moment.

~*~

Her apartment changes with her.

Slowly at first, a sink of dishes washed one night, a load of laundry folded the next. Then more. She vacuums the living room one weekend. Wipes down the counters another. Sloan helps her tackle the refrigerator, where they find a Tupperware container that smells like it has philosophical opinions.

"Burn it," Sloan says, holding it at arm's length.

"We can wash it," she argues.

"Sydni, that is *evil* in a jar."

She laughs so hard she has to sit down.

Piece by piece, the apartment starts to reflect someone who cares about where she lives. Someone who cares about herself.

She lights candles in the evenings. A bergamot, warm vanilla, fresh linen. Her space smells like calm. Like silent triumph.

Sometimes she stands in the doorway and just looks around, a tiny smile pulling at her mouth.

"This feels like mine again," she whispers.

~*~

Therapy becomes a steady rhythm in her weeks.

Dr. Wexler's office feels more familiar each time she visits. Familiar and predictable. The plant in the corner she hadn't noticed before. The woven rug that cushions her feet. The hum of the small diffuser in the corner.

In her third session, Sydni talks about control, how losing it terrifies her, how gaining it back feels impossible. Dr. Wexler nods, listening intently.

"You're rebuilding trust with yourself," she says. "And trust doesn't come back in a straight line. It moves like a wave."

Sydni sits with that. Feels it land. Feels it settle.

Some sessions leave her drained. Others leave her feeling lighter. One, surprisingly, leaves her laughing when Dr. Wexler shares a grounding tip involving humming a favorite song.

She tests it. It works.

"Baby steps," Dr. Wexler reminds her every week.

And Sydni finds that she's actually taking them. And agrees to up her visits to twice a week for awhile.

~*~

Work shifts too. At first, she avoids the DV grant like it's a wound she can't touch. But with therapy, with her apartment clean, with her routines in place, she revisits it cautiously.

She opens the file one afternoon, hands trembling, expecting the familiar panic to curl in her stomach. It doesn't. So she reads. And reads again. Then begins editing.

Some days she can only manage one paragraph. Other days she rewrites whole sections with clarity she couldn't access before. When she finally completes the first portion of the grant, the one she'd feared for weeks, she sits back in her chair with a slow exhale. The cursor blinks at the bottom of the page like it's congratulating her.

Submitting it feels monumental. Not because it's perfect but because she didn't quit on it. The first section of the grant is complete. Now she has to wait to see if she moves onto the next phase. But, she whispers, "I did it," and feels tears prick her eyes. Not sad tears. Not overwhelmed tears.

Proud tears. It's been a long time since she's felt proud of anything.

~*~

Sloan becomes her steady companion through the weeks.

He helps her grocery shop, because "left unsupervised, you will survive off cereal and vibes." He drags her to the farmer's market one Saturday morning when the weather finally shifts. He forces her to try a new tea that tastes like warm flowers and sadness.

They watch bad movies. Make worse food. Laugh constantly. Sit in comfortable silence when she needs it.

One night, they sit cross-legged on her living room floor surrounded by unfolded laundry, and Sloan says sincerely, "You're really doing better, aren't you?"

She doesn't look up from folding a towel. "Yeah, I think I am." And she's not lying. She feels steadier. More grounded. More herself. Maybe even a better version.

The most surprising part? She doesn't think about Elias.

Not in the way she used to. Not with longing or ache or spiraling what-ifs. Her mind is full of other things: healing, routines, therapy, work, friendship, her apartment, her life. The space that Elias once occupied has now shifted into a distant memory, not an open wound.

And for the first time in a long stretch of weeks, Sydni realizes she's not waiting for anyone to come back. She's building forward. Creating momentum. Choosing herself. And it feels…good.

Outside her window, early spring light stretches longer into the evenings. Inside her chest, something new grows with it.

Sydni Benton is coming back. Not as who she was, as who she's becoming. And she's proud of herself. Deeply proud.

CHAPTER THIRTY-THREE

As times passes, Elias feels something like steadiness returning to his life.

Work is work, spreadsheets, emails, cases, patients, the familiar rhythm of his days. Clementine keeps him grounded, nudging him awake when he oversleeps, dropping toys at his feet with relentless optimism, curling against him on the couch at night like she knows he needs the anchor.

But the biggest shift? He's actually going out. Leaving the apartment. Talking to people who aren't his coworkers or his dog.

It's a quiet unraveling of the fog he'd been swallowed by since the New Year. A slow disentangling from the stillness that had crept into his routine long before Sydni disappeared.

And a lot of that has to do with Brielle.

The second date was easy.

They meet for lunch at a cozy café near her work, and she talks animatedly about a pottery class she's taking, describing the disaster she made in terms so vivid he nearly chokes on his sandwich from laughing.

"You're judging me," she accuses playfully.

"I would never judge someone for trying to make a vase and accidentally creating a lopsided cup with a self-esteem crisis."

"It wasn't a cup," she insists. "It was… abstract."

"It was crying out for help."

She nudges him with her shoulder, grinning. "You're lucky I like you."

He's surprised by how good it feels to hear that.

She makes him laugh. She makes him feel… normal.

It's been awhile since he felt the ache in his chest, the one shaped like a girl with curly hair and blue eyes, doesn't feel so sharp.

~*~

The third date is even easier.

They walk around a local art event, sipping hot chocolate while hopping between vendor tents. Brielle stops at every booth, picking up handmade jewelry and examining paintings with the kind of bright enthusiasm he can't help but admire.

At one table, she holds up a small ceramic fox and says, "This reminds me of you."

"In what way?" he laughs because he's pretty sure he's not foxlike in any capacity.

"You're observant," she says simply. "And steady. And nicer than you pretend to be."

He swallows hard because that shouldn't hit him the way it does. But it does. He buys the fox.

When he walks her to her car, her cheeks flushed from the cold, she hugs him. Arms tight, warm, lingering just a little longer than necessary.

"I like this," she murmurs into his coat. "Us."

He hesitates for a fraction of a second, not because he doesn't like her, but because something inside him flickers.

Then he hugs her back. "Yeah," he says. "Me too."

~*~

Later that night, Nora storms into his apartment with a bag of takeout like she planned the invasion.

"Tell me everything," she demands.

Elias takes the food from her, trying not to smile. "You're worse than a reporter."

"Correct. Now talk."

He recounts the date: the art booths, the fox figurine, the hug. Nora bounces on the edge of the couch like a kid listening to a bedtime story.

"So, you LIKE her," she declares.

"I do," he admits slowly.

Nora gasps, then shoves half her pad Thai into her mouth. "Finally. Finally! I've been waiting for you to like someone for years."

"That's a bit dramatic, don't you think?" he asks.

"Maybe, but that doesn't make it any less true," she retorts.

He thinks about it, how long it's been since he let anyone in. He knows he tried with Sydni, but that didn't end well. And before that, the disastrous break up that caused him to retreat into a dark hole.

Nora leans over and nudges him with her foot. "You deserve happy things, Eli. And Brielle? She's good. She's warm. She's exactly the kind of person who won't break you."

He winces. "You make me sound fragile."

"Not fragile," she says. "Just… careful. And that's okay. You've been through enough."

He nods, not trusting himself to speak.

But later, after Nora leaves and the apartment grows quiet, he finds himself turning the little ceramic fox over in his hands. He smiles. He really does like Brielle.

She's easy. She's sweet. She's straightforward in a way that feels refreshing. She's everything he thought he wanted.

But then there's a moment. Small. Barely noticeable. A flicker in his chest he can't quite name. He tries to ignore it. Pushes it aside. Focuses on the good, and there is so much good.

He tells himself the flicker doesn't matter. That it's just nerves. That liking someone new takes time. That maybe the missing piece will fall into place on its own.

He sets the fox on his bookshelf, next to a candle and a framed photo of him and Nora as kids.

"Time," he murmurs to himself. "That's all it needs."

Clementine hops onto the bed, curling into a golden ball of warmth. Elias scratches behind her ears and whispers, "I think things might finally be changing."

He hopes it's true. He believes it could be. But somewhere deep inside buried beneath new beginnings and cautious optimism, something small shifts, tugging gently at the back of his mind.

Something missing. Something he can't quite name. He tells himself more time will fix it. He wants it to.

He hopes it will.

CHAPTER THIRTY-FOUR

Sydni wakes with a sense of clarity she hasn't felt in… she can't even remember how long. The kind that euphoric but steady.

She stretches beneath her clean sheets, listens to the muted hum of the radiator. Her room feels like her again, gently lived-in instead of suffocating.

It's a good morning. She feels grounded and capable. She even feels a little bit confident.

"Ten minutes," she says to herself as she pulls on leggings and an oversized sweatshirt. "Just ten. Easy."

Outside, the air is brisk but refreshing. Early spring light glows over the tops of the buildings, and small patches of melted snow sit in tired piles along the sidewalks. Sydni walks at a relaxed pace with her arms swinging gently at her sides.

One minute at a time. Then two. Then three. Each step feels like a small promise kept to herself. By six minutes in, she's smiling at nothing. Proud of herself, proud of her body for carrying her, proud of how far she's come without collapsing under the weight of it all.

She's rounding the corner near the small park when she hears the jingle of a collar. Before she can turn, something warm and furry barrels into her legs.

"Whoa—oh!"

A full-grown golden retriever plows into her with all the grace of a furry missile. Sydni grabs the dog's collar instinctively as excited paws press into her thighs.

"Hey!" she laughs, steadying herself. "Hi, sweet girl. Where did you come from?"

The dog is gorgeous. It has honey-colored fur, big brown eyes, tail wagging so hard her whole backside wiggles. And her leash is dangling freely behind her.

"Oh no," Sydni murmurs, crouching to pet her. "You escaped from someone, didn't you?"

The dog licks her cheek enthusiastically.

"Well hello to you too."

And then —

"Clementine!"

The name hits her like a shock. She looks up. And suddenly, Elias is jogging toward her. And he's not alone.

At his side walks a woman. Tall, blonde, elegant even in a puffer jacket and sneakers. She has big green eyes and the kind of classic beauty that turns heads without trying.

Sydni's heartbeat skips, but she wills herself not to flinch, not to shrink, not to disappear. She stands slowly, brushing fur from her leggings.

Elias slows to a stop just in front of her. "Sydni?" he asks, voice stunned.

Her heart swings upward. Not painfully, but with the strange recognition of a song she hasn't heard in a while. "Hey," she says, trying to sound casual and calm. "I think your dog attacked me."

He lets out a laugh. "Yeah, she does that. Sorry."

"She's perfect," Sydni says, still petting Clementine's head.

Brielle smiles politely. "She really likes you."

Sydni gives her a kind smile in return. "She seems like the type who likes everyone."

There's a brief, awkward silence. One of those moments where three people suddenly become too aware of each other.

Elias clears his throat. "Um — this is Brielle."

Brielle steps forward lightly and extends her hand. "Hi. It's really nice to meet you."

Sydni shakes it. "You too. I'm Sydni."

Elias hesitates, barely, but she sees it, as if he's not sure what label to give Brielle in this moment. "This is… a friend," he finishes.

Brielle doesn't react outwardly, but something flickers in her eyes. Understanding, maybe disappointment, maybe surprise. It's subtle.

Sydni doesn't dwell on it. Not today. She steps back, giving Clementine one last affectionate pat. "She's adorable. You should get her a GPS collar. Or a parachute. Something."

Elias laughs again, a different one this time, softer. "Probably both."

"Anyway," Sydni says, lifting her chin, "I should finish my walk. It was nice seeing you."

And it is. It really is. Even if the moment feels surreal.

"You too," he says.

"Take care," Brielle adds, warm and sincere.

Sydni nods, offers a polite smile, and continues on her route without turning back.

She doesn't look over her shoulder. Not once. Even though a part of her wants to.

Even though she can feel Elias still watching her walk away, even if he doesn't understand why.

~*~

She finishes her ten minutes with her spine straight and her lungs full. No spiraling. No sinking. No comparison.

She sees the blonde hair, the green eyes, the effortless beauty, and it doesn't break her. She knows she is not a model. She has more softness than that woman. Thicker thighs. More curves. And she accepts it.

Instead, she thinks:

She's beautiful. And so am I... just differently.

The realization made her feel proud. She didn't compare herself to someone else and immediately tear herself down. Yes, she should feel proud.

~*~

Back home, Sloan is stirring something in his kitchen that smells suspiciously like burnt rice when she knocks twice and lets herself in.

"Guess what?" she announces.

Sloan turns, eyebrow raised. "If it's about your walk, I will praise you dramatically."

"Better," she says, stepping in fully. "I ran into Elias."

Sloan freezes, spoon mid-air. "Where?"

"During my walk."

"Was he alive?"

"Yes."

"Did you kill him?"

"No."

"Do you want me to?"

"Sloan!"

He drops the spoon dramatically into the pot. "Babe, you can't just drop plot twists without details. Sit down. This is story time."

They sit at his small table while she recounts everything. Clementine bounding into her, the polite introductions, the presence of the beautiful blonde.

"And I didn't spiral," she finishes proudly.

Sloan's teasing melting into something warm and full of admiration. "Damn right you didn't," he says. "Look at you. Doing emotional stability like a champ."

She laughs, bright and real.

He reaches across the table and taps her hand. "Good for you, Syd."

~*~

Later, when she's back in her apartment, sitting at her desk with a cup of chamomile tea, she thinks about the Resolve app.

Not Elias. Not their competition or their brief almost-storyline. Just the app itself, the structure it offered. The accountability it gave her.

She's different now. She's stronger. She's doing this for herself, not for anyone else. So she opens the app store. Redownloads Resolve. Logs in.

Her profile is blank. A clean slate. But Elias is still there, listed as her partner.

She adds her morning walk:
10 minutes — Completed.

A chime sounds, and before she can close the app, a notification pops up.

Encouragement from: Elias M.
"Keep going."

She smiles, small and secret and warm, then locks her phone.

The past isn't pulling her backward.

But the future…maybe it's opening up again. Just a little.

CHAPTER THIRTY-FIVE

Sydni wakes with something that feels almost foreign…clarity. Not joy. Not excitement. But a peaceful steadiness that wraps around her like a blanket. She sits up slowly, rubbing sleep from her eyes, stretching her arms overhead until her muscles loosen.

The apartment is calm and clean. Light seeps in through the blinds. Today feels… possible. She is really in her redemption arc of the rom-com book.

She pads to her desk, opens her laptop, and logs into the Resolve app. The page is blank again, every goal she ever had wiped away the moment she deleted the app in a spiral. But she doesn't regret reinstalling it, not even a little.

She takes a sip of coffee and begins typing.

Walk 20 minutes a day.
Twenty feels bold, progressive but she wants something that challenges her gently.

Shower every day.
Not because she feels she has to, but because it anchors her.

Cook three meals a week.
Actual meals. Real ingredients. Something that reminds her she deserves nourishment.

Socialize twice a week.
Even if it's just being around another human. Even if it's uncomfortable.

Read one non-work book.
Something indulgent, purely hers.

Write or journal every day.
A way to release, not implode.

Laundry and house reset every Sunday.
A ritual she can rely on.

Complete the Food Bank grant by Friday.
Manageable. Concrete. Achievable.

She sits back, glancing over the list. These aren't punishments.
They aren't obligations. They're promises, small lanterns lighting
a path forward.

Then, without letting herself overthink it, she clicks "Edit
Profile" and uploads her new picture: hair loose and curly, cheeks
flushed from her walk last week, eyes bright. Confident in a way
she didn't know she could look.

She hits save. For a moment, she studies her own face on the
screen and feels something warm stir in her chest.

She likes this version of herself. Not perfect. Not healed. But
present. The mantra she has been repeating to herself.

A notification pings.

Message from Elias:
I'm glad to see you back.

She feels surprised to see his message.

Before she can process it, another notification pops up.

Elias has completed 'Morning Mobility and Stretching.'

She laughs a little and taps the encouragement button and a little
message.

Sydni:
Nice job. Look at you being productive.

She imagines him seeing that. Wonders if it will make him smile.
Then quickly shuts her laptop before she can spiral into what-ifs.

This is her fresh start. Her arc. The rest will sort itself out.

~*~

Sloan bursts into her apartment at six sharp wearing a button-down that looks like it was ironed precisely once in its lifetime.

"Get dressed," he announces. "Real clothes. Cute clothes. And if you pick those gray leggings again, I'm calling the police."

She rolls her eyes. "You're so dramatic."

"Dramatically correct," he counters, swiping a package of crackers off her counter. "Tonight is important."

"Why?" she asks, pulling mascara from her bathroom drawer.

"Because," he says, "you deserve a night out where you're not drowning."

She pauses with the wand halfway to her eyelashes. Then nods in agreement. Ten minutes later, she emerges in dark jeans, a soft emerald sweater, and her curls framing her face. She looks good. Surprisingly good.

Sloan whistles. "Ma'am. You're glowing."

"Shut up," she laughs, nudging him as they head out the door.

~*~

The restaurant he chooses is dimly lit, full of warm amber lights and hushed conversation. People are dressed nicely, couples sharing tapas, friends leaning in close, the smell of garlic and wine floating in the air.

Sydni slides into the booth opposite him, and for a moment, it almost feels… romantic. But she immediately shakes that off, but the lighting isn't helping.

They order drinks and appetizers. Sloan talks about work. She teases him about his tragic cooking attempts. He tells a story about accidentally locking himself out of his apartment wearing only pajama shorts and socks. She laughs so hard she snorts, and the table next to them stares.

Sloan grins. "Awe, I missed that sound."

229

She can't help but grin at that.

Throughout dinner, he watches her. Not in a heavy way, but in a noticing way. As if he's memorizing each piece of her progress, tucking it away like something sacred. And halfway through her second drink, briefly wonders if there's something she's missing.

After dinner, he pulls her toward an old arcade tucked between a bookstore and a nail salon.

"Really?" she asks.

"Listen," he says, nudging her, "therapy can do wonders, but Skee ball is cheaper."

He buys tokens, most of which she steals, and they duel in a wildly competitive game that ends with Sydni beating him by exactly ten points.

He clutches his chest. "Betrayed. In my own arcade."

"You dragged me here!"

"And you crushed me! I raised a monster!"

She laughs again, deep, and belly-warm and real. Just what she needed. Depression be damned.

By the time he walks her home, her cheeks glow from the cold and the joy.

When they stop outside her door, Sloan touches her arm gently. "I know you may not like hearing this again, but I'm proud of you," he says. "For trying. For showing up. For being here with me."

She whispers, "Me too."

If someone were watching from afar, they might think he's about to kiss her. He doesn't. But the moment lingers, close enough to be misread, warm enough to make the air buzz.

~*~

Across town, Elias stands on a cobblestone sidewalk outside a trendy Italian place while Brielle loops her arm through his.

She's stunning. She is funny and sweet. Her smile radiates genuine affection. Tonight is their fifth official date, and on paper, everything feels right.

Inside the restaurant, she keeps the conversation flowing. Talking about books, her love for early morning runs, how Clementine has adopted her as a part-time chew toy. Her green eyes shine beneath the candlelight, and she laughs at all the right moments.

Elias tries, truly tries, to let himself be fully present. He tells her about work. He tells her about Nora's meddling. He laughs when she says he needs a haircut.

It's nice and comfortable. It is what most people should be excited about.

And yet…

Something inside him stills. A part of him that used to spark during conversations, that used to wake up, brighten, lean in. He can't name why he feels it. But he does.

Mid-meal, Brielle lifts her wine glass and smiles at him. "You seem quieter tonight."

"I'm just tired," he lies.

She nods, but her smile dims. "If you ever want to slow down, we can. Dating doesn't have to be all at once."

He offers a gentle smile. "I know. I appreciate that."

She reaches across the table and squeezes his hand. Her fingers are warm. Kind. He squeezes back. It should be enough. She's everything a person could want. But somewhere, buried beneath politeness and effort and the easy comfort of a "normal" date…something feels off. Something is missing. Something he can't put into words.

He tells himself it's just nerves. Time will help. More dates. More connection. More chances. Maybe tonight is just a slow night. Maybe next time will be the click he's hoping for.

He repeats that thought until it feels true.

But when Brielle smiles at him again, bright and hopeful…he can't shake that feeling in his chest, that he knows is ridiculous.

CHAPTER THIRTY-SIX

By May, everything feels different.

The city has defrosted. Snowmelt has given way to green grass and muddy walking paths. Outdoor patios are opening again, and the air smells faintly of lilacs and distant barbecues. Warmth presses gently against Sydni's skin each time she steps outside, coaxing her into longer walks, more errands, more sunlight.

Her life, too, has thawed. The apartment looks nothing like the dim cave she once hid in. The windows are open most mornings. Plants she never thought she'd keep alive sit like tiny green trophies on the sill. Her laundry is folded, stacked neatly in drawers she used to ignore. Her bed is made every morning, not perfectly, but intentionally.

Therapy is steady. Work is steady. Her chest is steady.

There are still moments, flashes of memory that sting, sudden dips of self-doubt, but they pass. She has tools now. Breathing exercises. Distraction rituals. Sloan. Especially Sloan.

He's become a fixture in her days, more so than usual, slipping into her apartment after work or dragging her outside whenever the sun is too nice to waste. Some days they cook together; some days they wander the farmer's market and mock hipster mushrooms; other days they sit on her couch drinking sparkling water, that she still hates, and watching reruns of dramatic reality shows they pretend they're too mature to enjoy.

And sometimes, sometimes she catches him looking at her with a softness. She feels it too, that warm hum between them. Not romance, not really, but something tender all the same. Something deep. Something that could, in another timeline, be mistaken for the beginning of a love story.

Today, they are sitting in Sloan's living room sharing a carton of strawberries while he reads aloud from a terrible romance novel he found in the free library box outside the building. He uses ridiculous voices for each character, changing accents mid-sentence, making her laugh so hard that she nearly drops a berry on his couch.

"You're welcome," he says smugly, tossing the book on the coffee table. Therapy who? It's me. Hi. I am the coping mechanism."

She nudges him with her foot. "You are chaos in human form."

"And yet you thrive in my presence."

She rolls her eyes, but it's true. She does. Life feels… manageable again. Sometimes even good.

She's waiting to hear if her DV grant advanced to phase two. Checking her email anxiously every morning, sending up silent wishes to the universe, but she's proud of the work she turned in. And in the meantime, she's completed a Food Bank grant, one she finished with clear-headed confidence instead of panic.

A month ago, she never would've believed she could feel this way. Clear, organized, and more grounded. Then, one warm morning, while she's sitting at her kitchen table going over her to-do list for the week, her Resolve app dings.

Elias completed: 30-minute morning run
Send encouragement?

She hesitates. For months, their only communication has been this. Tiny digital affirmations sent through the app like echoes of the connection they once had. No texts. No calls. Just Resolve.

It's oddly comforting. She taps *Encourage.*

A few minutes later, another notification appears.

Message from Elias.:
Hey… uh, I know this is out of the blue, but would you want to meet up sometime this week? Just to catch up?

Sydni freezes. The request sits on her screen like a small, glowing ghost from a different life. She reads it again.

He wants to meet up.

She isn't sure how she feels. Nervous, flattered, cautious, curious? Part of her stirs with adrenaline, part of her stiffens with defensive instinct.

She stares at the message for a full minute before typing:

Sydni:
Sure. Friendly catch-up sounds good.

He responds within seconds.

Elias:
Great. Want to meet at Ridgeview Park? Afternoon works best for me.

She agrees before she can overthink it.

The day of the meetup is warm but breezy. The kind of afternoon where the light seems a little golden even before sunset. Sydni pulls on jeans and a simple white T-shirt, her curls wild around her shoulders. She considers long sleeves for a moment… then chooses not to hide.

It's too warm for that. Too honest a day.

Her ink coils beautifully across her arms, blending with the faint, jagged scars beneath. Not invisible but rewritten by color and meaning. Sloan once told her they made her look like she'd survived something and turned it into art. Today, she chooses to believe him.

She arrives at the park a few minutes early, finding a shaded bench just off the walking path. Butterflies flutter, but not the uncomfortable romantic kind.

When she sees him approaching in a dark gray T-shirt and sneakers, Clementine trotting beside him on a leash this time. He looks good. Healthier. Sharper around the edges in a way she hasn't seen since winter.

"Hey," he says, slowing to a stop in front of her.

"Hey," she echoes, standing to greet him.

There's a brief awkwardness. The polite kind, the kind where two people try to remember how they used to talk to each other.

"Clementine remembers you," he says after a beat. "She tried to drag me over here when she saw you." The dog yanks the leash in enthusiastic agreement, nearly pulling his shoulder out of socket. Sydni laughs, petting the golden retriever's head. "Hi, sweet girl."

They start walking slowly, casually, side by side. The familiarity grows, slowly warming between them like sunlight on chilled hands. She asks about work. He asks about hers. She tells him she's been finishing smaller grants and keeping busy.

He smiles, genuinely. "I'm glad you're doing better."

She nods. "I am."

They walk another minute before she asks lightly, "And… Brielle?"

He brightens, just a little. "She's great. We've been seeing each other for a couple months now."

"That's good," she says, and she means it.

He hesitates before asking, "What about you? Seeing anyone?"

She shrugs casually. "Just Sloan."

Elias tries, he *really* tries, to keep his expression neutral. He fails.

"Oh," he says, nodding once. "That's… cool."

She doesn't clarify or explain. She didn't see the point. So, their conversation drifts into comfortable banter. Teasing jokes, observations about weird joggers, laughing at Clementine's attempt to chase every squirrel in Illinois. It's friendly. Warm. Human.

When they part at the edge of the park, he smiles at her. "I'm glad we caught up," he says.

"Me too."

He hesitates, like he might say something more… but doesn't. "See you on the app?" he finally says.

"See you on the app." She turns and walks home, sunlight brushing her shoulders, a strange lightness blooming in her chest.

She's okay. They're okay. Maybe they can be friends after all.

~*~

Back at her apartment, Sloan is sprawled across her couch, half-asleep with a bag of pretzels on his chest.

She kicks his foot lightly. "I'm back."

He opens one eye. "From what I can only assume was a date with destiny?"

"Shut up."

He sits up, stretching. "Did you have fun?"

"Yeah," she says, smiling. "Actually… yeah."

He watches her for a long moment, something thoughtful in his expression, before his shoulders relax and he pats the seat next to him.

"Good," he says simply.

And Sydni realizes she means it: She feels good. She doesn't feel confused. That anxious feeling isn't lingering. She doesn't feel like she is on the verge of spiraling.

Just… good.

CHAPTER THIRTY-SEVEN

The waiting room smells faintly of warm linen and peppermint tea. Clean and welcoming. Too welcoming, in Sydni's opinion. Comfort makes her suspicious. Still, she sits in the same beige chair she chooses every week, legs tucked neatly to the side, hands twisting the hem of her sleeve like she's braiding her nerves into cotton.

This is her fourth month of therapy with Dr. Wexler. And somehow, even now, the air in this office still feels like it sees more of her than she's ready to reveal.

The door clicks open.

"Sydni?" Dr. Wexler calls gently.

Her therapist looks exactly as she always does. Brown curls pinned back loosely, a gentle cardigan that makes her look like a hug made of fabric and patience. Her presence alone could lower blood pressure.

"Come on in," she says.

Sydni follows her inside, settling onto the couch while Dr. Wexler takes her usual armchair, notebook balanced on her knee but never opened right away. She always gives space first.

"How has this week been for you?" Dr. Wexler asks, voice warm.

Sydni exhales slowly. Not the polite, automatic answer but the real one. "Good. Actually pretty good."

Dr. Wexler nods, encouraging her to continue. "What made it feel good?"

So, Sydni tells her. She talks about finishing the Food Bank grant, the way the writing felt steady instead of frantic. She talks about her routines becoming habits like the laundry on Sundays, the daily walks, the warm light through her clean apartment. She talks about Sloan: the laughter, the dinners, the grounding presence he's become in her life. She talks about how nice it is to have some repetition and routine back in her life. How it helps with the anxiety.

Dr. Wexler picks up on that warmth instantly. "It sounds like you've built a support system that works for you."

Sydni smiles slightly. "Yeah… I guess I have."

She waits until the very end to admit she ran into Elias.

There's no judgment in Dr. Wexler's face only curiosity. "How did seeing him feel?"

Sydni stares at a small plant on the side table. "Better than I expected. I didn't fall apart. I didn't panic. I was… okay."

"Were you surprised to feel okay?"

"Yeah," she admits. "I always assume I'll regress. Or shut down. Or do something embarrassing. But I didn't. I actually felt… proud."

"That's a significant shift." Dr. Wexler's voice warms. "Often when we do healing work, acceptance follows quietly behind it."

"I want that. Acceptance. But there's still… a lot in the way."

"Tell me about the 'lot.'"

Sydni twists her fingers together, picking at an invisible thread. Her throat tightens in warning. She hasn't shared all of this before. Not like this. "I've been thinking about… letting people in," she whispers.

Dr. Wexler's expression softens even more. "A big topic. What thoughts have come up around that?"

Sydni hesitates, but the truth feels like it's pushing its way out through the cracks she's been patching for years. "I don't think I ever learned how to let people stay," she says finally. "Because I kept losing them."

She swallows hard. "My parents died three years apart. Both suddenly. Both before I turned eighteen. My brother, Jonathan, passed unexpectedly shortly after. And there wasn't anyone else. No more extended family. Just me."

She looks down at her hands.

"After that, it felt like expecting anyone to stay was stupid. Like it was safer to hold people at arm's length. If I didn't need anyone... I couldn't lose them."

Dr. Wexler nods slowly, her voice gentle. "That kind of loss teaches us that connection is dangerous because its absence is unbearable."

Tears gather at the corners of Sydni's eyes. She blinks them away too quickly. "And then, on top of that..." she says softly, "there was what happened when I was nineteen."

The room seems to still, not from fear, but from reverence.

"You don't have to share details," Dr. Wexler says softly.

"I don't want to," Sydni whispers. "I just... want to say that it happened. And that it changed everything. It changed the way I trust men. The way I trust myself. The way I see myself."

She closes her eyes for a moment. "I couldn't look at myself without remembering him. So I covered the scars with tattoos. Tried to make them look like something else. And it helped but... not completely."

"Survival often comes with physical reminders," Dr. Wexler says. "But you took something marked by trauma and reshaped it into something you chose. That tells me more about your resilience than your pain."

Sydni shudders. "I want to believe that."

"I believe it," Dr. Wexler says firmly. "And I think a part of you is starting to believe it too."

Sydni presses her palms to her knees, grounding herself. Sometimes I wonder if I'm capable of letting someone love me. Or if I'm just too broken. Too scared."

"Trauma complicates closeness," Dr. Wexler answers, "but it doesn't erase your ability to love and be loved. And healing doesn't require you to be fearless. It just asks that you be honest, with yourself, and with whoever earns a place in your life."

"I'm scared of that," Sydni admits. "Of letting someone close and losing them. Or trusting the wrong person again. Of going through this same spiral over and over again."

"Being afraid isn't failure," Dr. Wexler says. "Fear is your body remembering the past. Healing is allowing the present to be different."

Those words land somewhere deep. Deep enough to sting, deep enough to soften. "I don't know if I'm ready for a relationship," Sydni murmurs. "But sometimes… I want to be. I'm thirty-one now. So I guess…"

"That wish is a powerful sign," Dr. Wexler says. "It means your heart is thawing. It doesn't mean it's rushing. Just opening enough to wonder."

Sydni wipes her cheek, catching another tear. "I want to feel normal. To not be ruled by what happened. To not feel like love is impossible."

Dr. Wexler's smile warms deeply. "You deserve connection, Sydni. You deserve gentleness. You deserve someone who cares for you without demanding your healing on their timeline. And you are allowed to move toward that slowly."

"Allowed," Sydni whispers. "That's a hard word."

"It's also the word that frees you."

They sit for a long moment. The kind of silence that feels like growth, not avoidance.

As the session winds to a close, Sydni stands, feeling unusually unsteady. Not because she's falling apart, but because something inside her has finally begun to shift.

Dr. Wexler places a hand over her notebook, meeting her eyes. "You did incredibly brave work today," she says. "Be proud of yourself for showing up."

Sydni feels that pride spread through her chest, slow and real. "Thank you."

Outside, the spring air tastes cleaner. She steps into the sunlight feeling a little more like a person who deserves good things and a little less like someone shaped entirely by shadows.

She starts to believes she might be allowed to be loved someday.

And maybe even love back. And maybe one day, she will quit stressing so much about it. Not likely, but maybe.

CHAPTER THIRTY-EIGHT

The restaurant glows with amber light, the kind meant to make everyone look a little more romantic, a little more mysterious. Brielle chose it. She always chooses the places with atmosphere and Elias tries, as he often does, to inhabit the mood she hopes will settle over them.

Tonight, the table between them is set with candlelight flickering across the polished wood. Brielle is talking animatedly about her sister's upcoming wedding, her curls bouncing around her shoulders when she laughs. She looks beautiful. She always does.

And he likes her. He really, genuinely does. He just wishes liking someone came with the same ease it used to, before… everything.

"…and I swear, if she makes me wear sage green, I'm eloping from the bridal party," Brielle says, rolling her eyes with a grin.

Elias smiles, a real one, but it feels like it stops somewhere short of reaching his chest. Still, he leans in, trying to be present. "It can't be that bad."

"It washes me out," she sighs dramatically. "Besides, you haven't even seen the shoes."

She launches into another story, and he listens, mostly. His attention drifts now and then to small details: the way her fingers curl around her glass, the way her voice lifts in that familiar melodic pattern when she's excited, the faint vanilla scent of her perfume.

It's all pleasant and nice. And yet…It's as though he's watching a movie instead of starring in it.

Brielle shifts in her chair, leaning slightly closer. Her knee brushes his under the table. She doesn't pull away. Neither does he. She's been sending these little signals for weeks now. The touch, the lingering looks, the subtle invites hoping he'll reciprocate.

He hasn't. Not really.

They've kissed twice. Both times brief. Pressed lips and nothing more. Both times initiated by her. He kissed back politely, the way you would return a smile from a kind stranger. Warm. Gentle. Not electric.

Brielle clears her throat, bringing him back to the moment. "So," she begins, her expression earnest now, "I wanted to ask you something."

Here it comes.

"Eli…" She pauses, chewing her lip. "We've been seeing each other for a few months now."

He nods. "Yeah."

"And I love spending time with you. I really do." She reaches across the table, her fingers brushing his wrist. "But I need to know… where you see this going."

His heart thuds once.

"I'm not asking for labels," she continues. "Just… clarity. I don't want to get ahead of myself if we're not on the same page."

The air grows thick around him. Pressure rising behind his ribs. He opens his mouth to respond—

—and his phone vibrates. A single buzz against the table.

He glances down instinctively, guilt already blooming because Brielle is mid-sentence. The notification lights up the screen.

Message from: Sydni Benton

The breath is knocked clean out of him. It's not an encouragement ping. Not a Resolve notification. A *text*. His thumb unlocks the phone without consulting him, and the message fills the screen:

Sydni:
Hey... was just thinking about you. You busy right now? Wanna go for a walk?

Time splits. The restaurant noise fades into static. The candlelight blurs. Even Brielle's face softens into shapes he can't quite put into focus.

He reads it again. And again. And again because his brain won't catch up. She texted him. She reached out, not through the app, not with a button press, but with actual words. His heart reacts before he can stop it.

He smiles. It's unfiltered. A smile he hasn't worn in months. And when he finally looks up, Brielle is staring at him motionlessly like she watched the shift happen in real time.

Her eyes drop to his phone. "Who's that?"

Elias straightens in his chair, clearing his throat. "It's—uh— just... a friend."

Brielle isn't stupid. She sees the lie by omission. She sees the glow in his expression he didn't mean to reveal. She sees the fault line splitting down the middle of something she thought was solidifying.

"Friend?" she repeats curiously.

He nods, but the hesitation gives him away.

Brielle takes a slow, steady breath, the kind people use right before bracing for impact. "Eli... is there something you want to tell me?"

He opens his mouth to answer, but everything is tangled. Too tangled to pull apart at the dinner table. Because what would he admit? That he hasn't stopped thinking about Sydni? That even their little Resolve encouragements have been the highlight of his days? That her message, eight casual words, shook something awake in him?

He doesn't know the full truth. But he knows enough. And so does Brielle. Her smile falters, slipping into something raw. "I felt something change just now."

"Brielle…" he starts, but the sentence withers.

She gives a tight, sad smile. "I think… maybe you should answer her."

The words cut through him. Not because she's cruel. But because she's right. He looks down at his phone again, Sydni's message still glowing. He shouldn't reply. It's a terrible idea. It's complicated and messy. But the thought of ignoring her feels wrong. It feels like leaving something unfinished, something important.

His chest tightens, not in panic… but in recognition.

Sydni.

He wonders if the connection he fought so hard to forget never actually fully died. And Brielle, seeing the truth in his eyes, looks away, pain flickering across her expression before she can mask it.

CHAPTER THIRTY-NINE

The apartment is calm in a way that feels earned. The overhead lights are off, leaving only the warm glow of the lamp beside the couch and the hum of her small tabletop fan. Sydni is curled under her blanket, half-watching a baking competition where contestants are wildly overestimating their ability to make croissants from scratch. It's the sort of lazy comfort she never used to allow herself.

She hadn't expected anything after sending the text. It wasn't a strategy. She wasn't trying to test him or begin a nervous fishing expedition. She just had a simple impulse that drifted through her like a warm breeze.

Sydni:
Hey... was just thinking about you. You busy right now? Wanna go for a walk?

She sent it, took a sip of tea, and went back to her show. So, when her phone chimes, sharp and sudden in the quiet room, she jumps slightly, glancing at it more out of reflex than hope.

When she sees his name, she is surprised.

Message from: Elias

She blinks once, then twice, and opens it.

Elias:
Sure. Ridgeview Park? I can be there in 20 minutes if that works for you.

A small, unguarded smile climbs onto her fac.. She hadn't expected him to say yes. She hadn't expected him to respond at all. And now... she feels something she hasn't felt in a while. A gentle, unfamiliar flutter that isn't anxiety, but curiosity.

She isn't chasing him. She isn't defining anything. She isn't expecting anything monumental.

She just wants to see him. And maybe it's okay to want that.

Sydni stands quickly, tossing off the blanket with a small laugh at herself for moving so fast. The clock on the stove reads 8:12 PM. The sky outside is still a dusky blue, not fully night, not fully day. That perfect in-between where the world feels softened at the edges.

She pulls on jeans and a light cotton T-shirt, runs a hand through her curls to fluff them into some kind of organized chaos, and glances at her reflection just long enough to make sure she looks like herself, the version she's learning to like.

She texts him back.

Sydni:
See you there.

~*~

Ridgeview Park at 8:30 PM is a different creature than the daytime version. The playground is empty now, the grassy fields dotted with silhouettes of people finishing their evening jogs or walking dogs. The air is warm enough that she doesn't need a jacket, and the last of the sunlight glows faintly at the horizon like a dying ember.

She spots him standing near the central path beneath a streetlamp that hums with a reassuring buzz. Clementine sits obediently beside him, tail sweeping the grass in hopeful arcs.

Elias looks… put together. He's wearing dark jeans and a charcoal button-down with the sleeves rolled halfway up his forearms. It's nicer than what someone throws on for a casual walk, which makes her both curious and amused.

He glances up at the sound of her approaching footsteps, and his expression shifts, brightens, just a little. Enough that she notices.

"Hey," he says, voice warm and steady.

"Hey," she returns, smiling as Clementine immediately trots toward her, tugging the leash from his hand.

The dog bounds up to her with unrestrained excitement, and Sydni crouches to scratch behind her ears. "Hi, beautiful. Miss me?"

Clementine responds with a happy whine and enthusiastically licks Sydni's cheek.

"She definitely remembers you," Elias says with a laugh.

Sydni stands, brushing dog hair from her jeans, her smile lingering. "I was beginning to think I interrupted something. You're dressed like you were at a Michelin-star restaurant."

He rubs the back of his neck with a sheepish smile that almost makes him look boyish. "I… uh… didn't really have time to change."

"For a walk?" she says teasingly.

"Yep," he replies, and something unspoken hangs in the air between them, something neither of them touches.

They fall into step on the winding gravel path, Clementine weaving between them until she decides Sydni must be protected at all costs and claims her side. The conversation starts slowly, like two people reacquainting themselves with a familiar rhythm. But with every step, the distance between them thaws.

"I'm still impressed you actually walk on purpose," he says after a while. "Like… for fun."

"Oh please. I saw your Resolve logs. You run five miles before breakfast."

"That was one time," he insists.

"You did it three days in a row."

He tries unsuccessfully to hide a smile. "Okay, but that's only because Clementine has main-character energy and demands a morning parade."

Clementine barks at a squirrel in agreement.

They keep walking, pace slow and easy. Fireflies start to appear in the dimming light, blinking around the edges of the path like tiny lanterns.

"How've you been?" he asks, glancing sideways at her.

"Good," she says honestly. "Actually good. Therapy's been helping a lot. And work feels more stable. I've been doing normal human things like… laundry and cooking and not hiding under blankets."

He laughs, but it's not mocking. "I'm glad. You seem… lighter."

"I feel lighter," she admits. "It's weird, but in a good way."

"And Sloan?" Elias asks, trying to sound casual.

"Sloan's great," she says with a small smile. "We've been hanging out a lot."

He nods once, too casually, but doesn't press. She doesn't elaborate either, and the only sound for a moment is the crunch of gravel beneath their shoes.

"What about you?" she asks. "How's work? How's life?"

He considers his answer carefully. "Busy. Good, mostly. Clementine's been a handful. But I've been getting out more. Doing more social things."

"Good," she says. "You deserve that."

He smiles at her, a small, sincere upturn of his lips that makes something settle beneath her ribs.

A calm settles between them as they walk, but it isn't awkward at all but speaks to a shared ease. They talk about mundane things:

terrible drivers, the best sandwich place in town, how he once ruined an entire batch of cookies by confusing baking soda with baking powder.

"No, no, I'm sorry," she says, laughing so hard she has to stop walking. "You made salt discs?"

"I made edible coasters," he corrects solemnly.

"Even the dog wouldn't eat them?"

"Clementine sniffed one and walked away offended."

They reach the loop near the park's lake, the lamplight shimmering across the water like melted gold. Neither seems to want to turn back yet. The conversation shifts into a familiar territory. It didn't feel heavy. It felt meaningful. The things you talk about with someone you feel safe with.

She mentions finishing another grant. He tells her a story about his sister trying to set him up with a yoga instructor who hated dogs. She makes it a point to not mention Brielle. She shares that she's been reading a book she actually enjoys. He confesses that he's been learning to cook something other than chicken or pasta.

They pause once more, watching a pair of bats swoop across the sky above the tree line.

"It's nice," he says, "talking like this."

"Yeah," she agrees. "It is."

By the time they return to the parking lot, the sky has deepened to a dark navy, and the park's lights have brightened against the approaching night.

"This was good," he says, turning to her with a sincerity that feels steady and warm. "Really good."

"Yeah," she echoes. "It was."

They stand there for a moment, not quite ready to leave, not quite able to stay.

He repeats that same phrase. "See you on the app?"

She smiles. "See you on the app."

And when she walks back to her car, she realizes her chest doesn't feel tight. Her head isn't spinning. She isn't stuck in old patterns or old pain.

She feels… hopeful. Ready. Capable of letting more than one person have a space in her world. *Maybe this is what healthy feels like.*

CHAPTER FORTY

The morning after their walk feels strange. Like the world woke up on a lower volume setting. Like someone turned the dial down a few notches and left behind something softer.

Sydni sits at her kitchen table with a mug of coffee cupped in both hands, watching the curtains sway gently in the morning breeze as though the apartment itself is breathing slower today.

She should feel normal. It was just a walk. Just two adults catching up. Just a few conversations and a few laughs on a perfectly ordinary afternoon. But nothing about the feeling in her chest feels *just* anything.

It settles under her ribs like a persistent hum. Gentle, not overwhelming, but undeniably there. Like the ghost of someone's hand brushing hers. Like possibility she doesn't trust yet.

Eventually, she opens her laptop and begins to type.

Journal Entry

I didn't expect to feel anything yesterday.

Twenty minutes after sending a text I regretted immediately, I somehow ended up standing in a park next to Elias, laughing about cursed cookies and squirrels that looked like they were ready to unionize.

I didn't think I'd feel safe. Or steady. Or comfortable. But I did.

And I hate that part of me noticed how nice he looked. And I hate that another part noticed how he looked at me. Not like I was something fragile, not like I was a problem to solve, but like he was actually happy I was there.

We talked about normal things. Work, books, dogs, life. And it didn't feel forced or complicated or heavy. It felt easy. It felt like being myself.

And that terrifies me because I don't know what I'm supposed to do with that.

Especially because he has someone. And she's beautiful. The kind of beautiful that makes people pause in public. Tall, blonde, elegant. Everything I'm not.

I'm not competing with that. I'm not anything next to that.

But something sparked yesterday. Something warm. Something real.

And I don't want to want anything from him. I can't want anything from him.

She stops typing as a tightness blooms behind her eyes. No tears fall, but honesty sits heavy and low in her chest. These are the moments that she has to remember that her mental health is important. She is allowed to feel. She is allowed to be on repeat. She is allowed to not know the answers. And she is allowed to be afraid.

She doesn't delete it. She doesn't think about editing it. She just closes the laptop gently and changes clothes for therapy.

~*~

Dr. Wexler's office is calm in the way good therapy offices always are. The same lighting and warm tones. The same faint eucalyptus. The loveseat is the same barely-blue as always, worn enough to feel inviting, plump enough to feel safe. Even the plant on the round table looks more confident than Sydni feels. But the consistency brings comfort.

Dr. Wexler wears a lavender blouse and wide-leg pants today, soft curls framing her warm, steady face.

"I'm glad to see you," she says as Sydni settles into the couch. "How was your week?"

"Good," Sydni says, fiddling with a loose thread on her sleeve. "Mostly. Productive."

"And emotionally?" Dr. Wexler asks gently.

Sydni lets out a small exhale. "Messy. But not… bad messy. Just… confusing."

"Confusing how?"

She swallows, then meets her therapist's gaze. "I saw Elias yesterday."

Dr. Wexler's expression softens, inviting more.

"It was… really nice," Sydni continues. "We walked. We talked. I didn't spiral. I didn't overthink. I just… existed. With him." Her voice dips, almost embarrassed. "It felt normal."

"That sounds like real progress," Dr. Wexler says.

"It does," Sydni admits. "But afterward… I didn't know what to do with what I felt."

"And what did you feel?"

Sydni hesitates only a moment. "Hope," she whispers. "Which is ridiculous. And dangerous."

Dr. Wexler nods slowly. "Wanting something can be frightening. Especially when your past has taught you to equate wanting with pain."

Heat blooms in Sydni's chest, but this time it's not embarrassment or shame. That is a nice change.

"You've survived more than most people," Dr. Wexler continues gently. "Losing both of your parents so young. No family support. The attack at nineteen. You learned to protect yourself by shutting doors before anyone could walk through them."

Sydni looks down at her hands. "I don't understand why this is happening now," she says softly. "Why him."

"Why do you think it's him?" Dr. Wexler asks.

"Because he's kind. And patient. And funny. And he listens. And he never makes me feel broken or difficult or like I'm too much. Being around him feels... easy. And I don't have easy with men."

"Maybe it isn't about him being perfect," the therapist says. "Maybe it's about you finally being in a place where your wounds aren't making every decision for you."

The words settle into her like a truth she didn't know she needed. "So what do I do now?"

"For now," Dr. Wexler says, "just let yourself feel what you feel. No judgment. No rushing. Curiosity alone is enough. And Sydni..." She leans forward slightly, her voice warm. "You are allowed to be loved. And you are allowed to go slowly. You don't owe anyone anything you aren't ready to give."

For a moment, all Sydni can do is nod. She was growing a little frustrated that her sessions were about a guy, she almost had to laugh.

~*~

That evening, after a long shower and fresh sweats, Sydni sits on her couch with a bowl of pasta and a comfort show playing low in the background. She tries very hard not to think about Elias.

She fails. A little before nine, she realizes that she has a missed text sent hours before. She glances down. Elias.

Elias:
Hey. Thanks again for yesterday. It meant a lot seeing you. Hope you're having a good night.

Very kind message. Not romantic but not entirely platonic either.

She stares at it for several seconds before typing carefully:

Sydni:
I enjoyed it too. Thanks.

When she hits send, her heart settles in a way that feels cautious and lovely at the same time.

~*~

Across town, Elias sits in the parking lot of the restaurant where he and Brielle just had dinner. The evening air hangs thick and warm around the car, and he feels a pressure building.

He runs a hand along the back of his neck, searching for the right words, the words Brielle deserves. She looks beautiful tonight, elegant in a lilac dress, her posture straight, chin lifted with that poised confidence he always admired. But her eyes… her eyes are tight with something she's trying not to acknowledge.

"Hey," he begins, "before we go, there's something I want to say."

She turns toward him, bracing.

"I'm sorry about last night," he says. "I was distracted, and you deserve better than half-present."

Her shoulders drop slightly in relief, but her expression doesn't ease entirely. "Thank you," she murmurs. Then, quieter: "But… I could tell your mind wasn't with me."

He doesn't respond. Because he can't lie. Not with the truth sitting so openly in the air between them.

His phone buzzes. He glances at it. A message from Sydni. And he smiles before he can stop himself. It is involuntary.

Brielle sees it. Her face falls just a fraction, the tiniest tremble in her breath. "Elias," she whispers, "is there someone else?"

He swallows, guilt and clarity tangling together in his chest. Tomorrow, he'll tell her everything. Tomorrow, he'll end it with honesty.

But tonight… he just grips the steering wheel tightly, the weight of the truth settling deep in his bones. He doesn't speak. Because the answer lives in the space between them. That was the plan now.

CHAPTER FORTY-ONE

For a long moment, neither of them speaks. The car idles in the glow of the streetlamp outside Brielle's apartment building. The engine hums, a low and steady vibration beneath them, but everything else feels suspended. Even the air seems afraid to move.

Brielle sits perfectly still, her hands folded in her lap the way she does when she's bracing herself. Her knuckles are pale, tendons drawn tight. Elias notices the way her shoulders slope inward just slightly, as if she's holding the weight of a truth she doesn't want but already knows.

She exhales…slow, measured, the kind of breath you take before walking into pain. "Elias," she says quietly, "I need you to answer me."

He closes his eyes, just for a second. Not to avoid the moment. To steady himself for it. When he opens them again, she's watching him with a mixture of resolve and fear that cuts straight through his chest. He had planned to do this tomorrow. Oh well, plans change.

"Brielle," he says, voice low, "you deserve honesty. Always."

Something flickers across her face, relief, maybe. Or the sorrow of having guessed right. She swallows. "Is it her?" she asks, barely above a whisper. "The girl we ran into. The one with the curls."

Her voice trembles on *curls*. Not jealousy, but the sting of realizing she was a footnote in something larger. He feels something twist inside him: guilt, affection, and regret. All tangled. "Yes," he says gently. "It's her."

Brielle nods slowly, like she'd prepared for this, rehearsed the hurt in her head. She turns toward the passenger-side window for a moment, blinking at the streetlights reflected in the glass. The prickling behind her eyes, the tightening of her jaw, the small battle to keep her dignity intact.

When she faces him again, her voice is steadier. "Tell me," she says. "Not the vague version. The real one."

Elias leans his head back against the seat, staring at the glow of the dashboard for a moment before he answers. He owes her clarity. Not the polite version. The truth.

"I wasn't looking for anything when we met," he begins. "I wasn't in a place to be looking. You know that."

"I do," she says.

He nods. "You've been… wonderful. Truly. You pulled me out of my shell after isolating myself. You got me laughing again. You made me remember what it feels like to enjoy someone's company without thinking too hard about it."

A sad smile touches her mouth. "But."

"But," he echoes. The word feels heavy. "There was someone I met before you. And nothing happened. I wasn't even sure anything ever would. I told myself I'd moved past it. That I should move past it."

She watches him intently, bracing.

"But when I saw her again…" He exhales. "It felt like something woke up. Something I thought I'd shut down for good."

Brielle's eyelashes flutter, a tiny crack in her composure. She looks down at her lap, smoothing the fabric of her dress with fingers that tremble once before she stills them. "So this isn't about her being yours," she murmurs, voice tight. "It's about what she… could be."

"Yes," he admits. "It's not fair to you for me to keep going when part of me is somewhere else. Even if she never feels anything for me. Even if nothing ever happens. I don't want to lie to you by omission."

Silence settles over them again. But this time it's not brittle. It's an ache, heavy but human. She nods, jaw working as she absorbs it. "I'm not angry," she says eventually, though her voice catches just slightly. "A little hurt. But not angry."

He feels that like a punch. Her grace is more than he deserves. "I'm sorry," he murmurs. "This isn't about you not being enough. You're… more than enough."

"I know."

It's not arrogance. It's truth. A woman choosing not to shrink just because she's hurting. Brielle turns toward him fully, her expression settling into something bittersweet and final. "Drive me home?" she asks.

"Of course."

~*~

The drive is quiet, but not cold. There are no shouted accusations, no slammed doors. It is an unraveling of something that wasn't meant to stay tied. And when he pulls up to her apartment, Brielle unbuckles her seatbelt but lingers for a moment. She turns toward him.

"I hope she knows," she says gently, "what kind of man she has orbiting her." Her throat tightens. "And I hope you don't hide from her. Let her see you, Elias. Really see you."

He feels something towards her in that moment. It's genuine and painful at the same time. "Take care of yourself, Brielle."

"You too," she whispers. She leans in, pressing a gentle kiss to his cheek. She didn't push for more. She just said goodbye…kind, final, and full of respect.

When she pulls back, she offers him a small smile. "Be honest with your heart. It'll save you trouble."

He watches her walk into the building before he pulls away.

262

The drive home feels different. It can't be described as light, exactly, but clear. Breakups aren't painless, even gentle ones. But this one leaves behind a space that feels honest, like something finally aligned instead of fractured.

When he opens the door, Clementine bounds toward him with her tail thumping against the wall like she's welcoming home a hero. He kneels down and buries his fingers in her fur, grounding himself in her uncomplicated joy.

"Hey, girl," he murmurs, forehead resting briefly against her warm head.

Later, he sits on the edge of his bed, elbows on his knees, letting the stillness of his room settle around him. He thinks of Brielle. Her grace, her steadiness, the way she handled something that could have been so much worse.

He thinks of the park last night, of Sydni tipping forward when she nearly tripped over the uneven sidewalk, her curls bouncing, her laughter bubbling out despite herself. He thinks of the way she said thank you, almost shy, like no one had looked at her with kindness in a very long time. He thinks of the way something inside him shifted the moment he saw her again, the way hope flickered in his chest before he could talk himself out of it.

He's not imagining a future. He's not planning anything. He's not assuming she'd ever see him that way. But he can't help but feel a twinge of quiet hope.

He lies back, Clementine hopping onto the bed beside him and resting her head on his chest. "Yeah, girl," he whispers into the dim room. "I know."

Her tail taps once against the blanket.

In the stillness, he lets his eyes close and allows himself, just for a moment, to imagine possibilities he'd been too afraid to picture before.

CHAPTER FORTY-TWO

The week after the walk arrives like a calm tide. Not forceful enough to drag her under, but steady enough that she can feel every shift in the water. Each morning, she wakes before her alarm and sits at the edge of her bed in a half-lit room, listening to the hum of pipes in the apartment building and the faint patter of footsteps above her.

Her world doesn't feel the same. It doesn't feel fixed, she knows better than to expect that, but something inside her has loosened. A knot that once felt permanent now feels like it might, with patience, unravel. She has to keep reminding herself that it's not going to feel like her life is right now.

But, there is still something stirring. It's unsettling and hopeful. And if she were honest with herself, it was also terrifying. She has no idea what to do with any of it.

~*~

On Wednesday morning, she puts on her walking shoes and steps outside into the damp spring air. The sidewalk is scattered with fallen petals and the faint smell of honeysuckle. She walks her usual loop, passing the bakery with the crooked sign and the row of brick townhomes where an elderly woman always sits on her porch feeding peanuts to the squirrels.

She logs her walk in Resolve. Not ten seconds later, her phone buzzes.

Elias sent an encouragement:
Great job today.

Something expands beneath her ribs. She tells herself it's just the app. Just a friendly nudge. Nothing meaningful. But the truth is that she feels seen.

~*~

Her therapy session that afternoon feels heavier than usual, as though she carried something inside her she didn't realize was weight until she sank into the familiar corner of Dr. Wexler's blue loveseat.

"Tell me what this week has felt like," Dr. Wexler says gently.

Sydni stares at a spot on the carpet for a long moment. "Different," she finally says. "Quieter. Not numb quiet… more like the space after a thunderstorm. Where everything is washed out and a little too bright."

"That kind of quiet can feel strange," Dr. Wexler says. "Sometimes even uncomfortable."

"Yes," Sydni murmurs. "Exactly. Like something inside me is… rearranging. And I don't know if I want it to."

~*~

Later that afternoon, Sydni sits at her desk with her laptop open and the cursor blinking at her like it's waiting for truth. She hesitates and then types.

I don't know what to call what I'm feeling. I don't know if it's longing or confusion or hope or fear or some terrible cocktail of all of them. And I was so proud of myself for not comparing myself to the blonde, but that seemed to fade today. It's okay to take steps back, right?

But I do know this, walking beside him made something inside me feel calm. And I know that I shouldn't even be thinking about him. Life is not about the men in your life. I already have a solid man in my life. Sloan has been by my side. Yet, here I am thinking about him.

I thought seeing him would hurt. I thought I'd crumble or shut down or pretend. Instead, I felt like a real person.

And that terrifies me more than anything. Because what if I can feel things again? What if I'm not beyond repair?

And what if… someday… someone sees me and doesn't run?

Why do I keep flip-flopping back and forth between, yay I'm okay, to wondering what else is going to go wrong and it is obviously because of me. This is exhausting. Dealing with my own head is exhausting, I can't imagine anyone else wanting to deal with it.

And what point does life feel normal? At what point does it feel like I'm allowed to not beat myself for feeling? At what point do I stop cycling through the same thoughts over and over again. Yea, I'm tired of myself.

She closes the laptop with a click, feeling the truth settle around her shoulders like a blanket she's not quite ready to wear.

~*~

Later, as she curls up on the couch with tea and a blanket pulled over her legs, her phone buzzes with a Resolve notification.

Elias completed: "Evening run — 3 miles."
You wish to send encouragement? YES / NO

Without thinking too long, she taps "YES."

Immediately, another notification:

Elias:
Thanks :)

Her heart flutters. Damnit. It's just a little, but it still happens.

~*~

Across town, Elias sits in the dim lighting of his living room, Clementine's head resting on his knee. He still smells a hint of the perfume Brielle wore, something floral, and yet his chest feels strangely hollow. Not regretful. Just… finished.

He thinks about the breakup. He thinks about how calm it was. He thinks about how right it was. And he thinks about the walk with Sydni. The spark, the comfort, the sense of coming home without expecting to.

He is definitely in his own thoughts more than he should be. He was always the guy who would talk himself out of something good and he has to wonder if she is going through the same spiral about all of this. Or if he was the crazy one, driving his dog crazy.

When his Resolve app buzzes with Sydni's encouragement, he smiles to himself. Should he feel guilt? He chooses not to and just accept the fuzzy feeling.

Clementine makes a small whiney noise. He scratches behind her ear. "Yeah," he murmurs. "I know. I know. I'm getting on my nerves too."

CHAPTER FORTY-THREE

May blends into June with a gentleness Sydni isn't used to. Not because her life has suddenly transformed into something magical, she's far too practical for that. Because it feels like it's actively falling apart.

Her mornings shift first. Coffee. A stretch long enough to feel her ribs expand. A walk around the neighborhood as early sunlight spills over the rooftops. Same routines. Routines are still important.

Sometimes she pauses, letting the scent of cut grass, warm bakery bread, and sun-dried concrete fill her lungs. Each inhale feels like it unspools a knot inside her chest she didn't realize she'd been living with.

When she finishes her walk, she logs it. Resolve dings. Another notification from Elias, encouraging, kind, thoughtful in the way he probably doesn't even realize is disarming. And every time, something flutters deep inside. She tells herself it's just caffeine. It isn't.

Work becomes possible again in a way that surprises her.

On Monday, she sits at her desk staring down a digital folder she's successfully ignored since December. The thing is a relic from a more chaotic version of herself: duplicate files, outdated drafts, attachments she told herself she might "get back to someday."

She clicks it open. One by one, she deletes old program outlines, messy spreadsheets, abandoned revisions. What begins as hesitation becomes momentum, and before she knows it, she's wiped the whole thing clean. Every unnecessary file, every silent reminder of burnout, gone.

A lightness blooms in her chest. Like space she didn't know she needed. And she keeps going. Her next task is a food bank grant she drafted last week. She rereads it expecting to find mistakes, disjointed paragraphs, foggy thinking, the kind of imperfections she's gotten used to seeing in her work during the harder months.

But it's… good. It's clear and organized. She knows it's strong.

She edits with confidence and prepares it for submission when her inbox pings. A new email from Melissa, another grant writer she partners with.

Subject line: *Do I need to call 9-1-1?*

Sydni snorts and opens it.

Did you mean to upload that file already? And did you actually update the budget line items?? And did you… respond to my last two questions from Friday?? I'm concerned. Blink twice if you're being held hostage.

Sydni rolls her eyes, grinning despite herself.

She types back:

Not hostage. Just trying to be a functional adult today. Please do not alert authorities.

She adds a winking emoji, rare for her, and hits send before she can overthink it.

A few seconds later, Melissa replies with a meme of someone fainting dramatically onto a sofa.

Sydni laughs and leans back in her chair. It feels good.

Her apartment continues to mirrors the internal shift. Stacking laundry instead of letting it drape decoratively over chairs, rinsing a mug instead of abandoning it to the sink, wiping the counters after dinner. She's never been a minimalist; she lives in her space, not around it. But now things feel intentional instead of overwhelming, like she's reclaiming pieces of herself one chore at a time.

Eventually, she buys a plant. Not a succulent or cactus. A leafy green plant that requires actual effort. She puts it on the windowsill and checks it obsessively: water, sunlight, soil, angle. Every morning, it's still alive feels like a tiny miracle.

"Look at us," she whispers to it one morning. "Surviving."

Maybe even growing. And she knows that as each day, week, month that passes that she sees progress, she is proud of herself. No matter how repetitive it is. The same feelings. The same thoughts. But, it's something.

~*~

Sloan shows up on a Thursday evening without warning, as usual, letting himself in with his spare key and calling out, "If you're naked, cough twice!"

Sydni groans from the living room. "I'm folding towels! Do you mind?!"

"Depends," he says, walking in with Thai takeout bags hanging from one hand. "Are you folding them the right way or the chaos gremlin way?"

"My way is perfectly acceptable."

"It's violent, Syd."

He steps into the living room and stops dead in his tracks, eyes trailing slowly across the tidy space, the clean surfaces, the order. "Holy shit," he says. "It looks like an adult lives here."

"I *am* an adult," she says, indignant.

"A questionable claim." He picks up the plant pot, holding it like a bomb. "Is this real?"

"Yes."

"And alive?"

"Yes!"

He narrows his eyes. "Are you bribing it? Whispering affirmations? Did Dr. Wexler assign you sentient greenery?"

She chucks a rolled sock at him. He ducks, grinning.

"Okay, okay," he says, hands raised. "I'm impressed."

And she can tell he means it. They spread takeout across the table: pad see ew, chicken satay, and dumplings. They eat comfortably, the way you can only eat with someone who knows your worst moments and still shows up.

Halfway through dinner, Sloan studies her more closely, his expression shifting. "You look good," he says. "Not hot, don't get weird. Just… good. Alive. In a good way."

She stares at him. "That was dangerously close to another genuine compliment."

"It *was* a compliment," he says, pointing his chopsticks at her. "You're just allergic to receiving them."

"I accept compliments."

"You do not."

"I totally do."

Sloan raises one eyebrow, and she deflates.

"Fine," she mutters. "I don't."

He bumps her shoulder gently. "Figure it out. Because you deserve them. You're doing good, Syd," he adds. "Really."

Her throat tightens. He has been her rock through these times. This is not the first time he's told her this. And it won't be the last time. But that is the thing with mental health struggles, right? You struggle to believe you are deserving of good things. Of good friends. Of people who care.

Then, because he can't resist, he smirks. "So… this new glow. Is it from walking, therapy, or a certain floppy-haired man and his golden retriever?"

"Sloan!"

"What? He's cute. Clementine's cute. You're cute. Suspicious."

She tries to glare but ends up laughing instead.

"Mmhmm." He studies her carefully. "And that makes you feel… what?"

She opens her mouth and stops. How she would have answered months ago, and how she would answer now would obviously be different. "I don't know," she says. "Or I do know, and it scares me."

His teasing fades instantly. He bumps her knee with his. "Then let it scare you," he says. "Just don't let it stop you."

A lump forms in her throat. He always sees right through her.

After he leaves, with dumplings, a lecture about proper hydration, and a suspiciously long glance at her plant, Sydni curls up at her desk.

The apartment is a good kind of peace. She opens her journal. Her fingers fly.

I think I'm finally coming back to myself. Not all at once. But piece by piece.

Things don't feel impossible anymore. Maybe because I'm actually doing the things I avoided for months. Cleaning. Walking. Breathing. I feel a sense of déjà vu that I've done all of this before. The same conversations with Sloan. I'm not sure what to think about that.

Or maybe because I'm letting myself enjoy things again.

Elias flickers into her thoughts. His voice, the way he listened that day, the way he didn't rush her or flinch.

I know I have baggage. Enough to fill a cargo ship. And I'm not ready for anything romantic. But seeing him again didn't hurt the way I expected. It felt... hopeful. Like maybe there's a version of my life where letting someone in doesn't end in disaster.

Maybe one day I'll even be brave enough to try. I have to wonder if other people are writing in their journal somewhere repeating themselves over and over again. I can't be the only one, right? Maybe this is why people are in therapy. To break the cycle of I'm good, I'm good, I'm not good, I'm not good. Oh look, I am okay, I'm healing. Maybe I'm enjoying things, or maybe I'm not allowed.

This is why we write, so we don't bore people with a constant and consistent thoughts. God forbid someone read this one day.

She rereads the entry, feeling the truth settle into her chest. She closes the laptop gently.

And her phone buzzes. It's not a Resolve notification but a text..

Elias:
Hey. I hope this isn't weird... but I was thinking about you. Just wanted to check in. You doing okay?

It's simple, nothing out of the ordinary, right? That's what friends do. But it shifts something inside her.

She doesn't reply right away, not out of hesitation, but because she wants to feel this moment fully. She is trying not to go down a spiral of wondering what that means that he was thinking about her. This has to be easier for other people.

CHAPTER FORTY-FOUR

The text from Elias sits on Sydni's phone like a tiny electric spark, humming under her skin.

Sydni:
Not weird. Actually really nice. I'm good tonight. Had dinner with Sloan.

After a moment, he responds.

Elias:
He didn't grill you about vegetables again, did he?

She laughs, curling her legs under her on the couch.

Sydni:
Nope. This time he judged my plant. The one that's miraculously still alive.

Three dots appear. Pause. Appear again.

Elias:
Plants are liars. They look easy, but they're basically tiny drama queens. I murdered basil last month by looking at it too aggressively.

She laughs. God, it feels good to laugh like this. Over nothing important.

Sydni:
How was your day?

A longer pause. Long enough she wonders if she said the wrong thing.

Elias:
Quiet. Nice. Clementine figured out how to open the treat drawer. So that's fun.

Sydni:
A criminal mastermind.

Elias:
She misses you, by the way.

Before she can answer, her email dings. She almost ignores it. Emails can wait, but the subject line makes her sit straight up.

"CONGRATULATIONS — ADVANCING TO PHASE TWO"

"No way," she whispers, hand flying to her mouth. It's the DV grant. The big one. The one she nearly drowned under. The one she thought she ruined.

She squeals. Absolutely squeals and texts him without thinking.

Sydni:
ELIAS! OH MY GOD!! MY DV GRANT MOVED TO PHASE 2 I'M FREAKING OUT

She expects him to text back. She does *not* expect her phone to start ringing. She stares at the screen like it's grown legs.

"Elias is calling me," she whispers into the empty room, then scrambles to answer before she drops dead from shock.

"Hello?" she manages.

His voice is warm, and bright in that way that makes her chest tight. "Hey. I'm sorry—I just… texting didn't feel like enough for this."

Her throat tightens instantly. "I can't believe it," she whispers. "I thought, I didn't think I'd finish it. I didn't think I could do it. Not after everything."

"You didn't just finish it," he says, voice low and proud. "You pushed through hell and made something incredible. This is *huge*, Sydni. You earned every bit of it."

Her eyes burn. She presses her palm against them. "Thank you," she whispers. "Really. Thank you."

She hears him smile. Actually hears it. "I knew you'd get it."

"You didn't know that."

"I strongly believed it," he corrects. "Like ninety percent confidence."

She laughs louder than she means to.

He continues, "You sound happy. Like… truly happy."

"I am," she admits. "It feels like I'm finally doing things again. Like I'm myself again."

"You are," he says. "And honestly? You're even better than before."

AAAAND she is receiving a call, Sloan, that she chooses to ignore. Two phone calls at one time?

She goes back to the moment. Not awkward, not heavy. Just two people sitting in it together.

"So," he asks gently, "how are you celebrating?"

"I, oh God, I'm not," she says. "I don't celebrate. I panic. Don't you remember?"

He chuckles. "Try celebrating instead. You deserve a win."

"Maybe I'll… I don't know… drink a soda?"

"A wild woman."

"I contain multitudes."

He laughs and she wants to bottle the sound. Before she can say anything else, she hears something muffled on his end.

A door opening and then footsteps. Fast, uncoordinated ones.

"ELIAS!" a voice shrieks.

Sydni jumps. "What was that?"

He groans. "My sister just broke in."

The voice gets closer. "ELIAS YOU CANNOT JUST LEAVE A WOMAN LIKE THAT—"

"Nora," he mutters into the phone, "I'm on a call."

Sydni can hear her now, loud, and dramatic. "You broke up with Brielle and didn't tell me?!"

"Oh my God," Sydni whispers, eyes widening.

Elias sighs hard. "Sydni? I'm so sorry. She's… she's Nora."

"It's okay," she says, biting back a smile. "You should probably go rescue your house from her."

"Yeah," he says. "I'll call you later?"

 "I'd like that."

"Goodnight, Sydni."

"Goodnight, Elias."

She remains sitting on her couch, holding the phone against her chest, amazed at the fact that he called her, but she got the grant she struggled so hard to write. Pride was an understatement.

~*~

Meanwhile, in Elias's living room, Nora paces like a tiny storm.

"You left Brielle?!" she demands, hair wild, eyes huge. "BRIELLE! Who makes fresh bread and folds fitted sheets and is NICE TO DOGS?!"

Elias drops onto the couch, exhausted. "Nora—"

"She's perfect! Perfect! Why would you—"

"Because it wasn't right," he says simply.

Nora stops mid-rant and blinks at him. "You look happier."

He exhales. "I am."

She narrows her eyes like she's trying to see inside his soul. "Is this about curly hair girl…Sydni, the Resolve girl?"

He scrubs his hands over his face, groaning. "I don't know."

"You DO know," Nora declares. "Your face knows. Your voice knows. Your dog knows."

At the mention of her name, Clementine barks once.

Nora points triumphantly. "SEE?!"

Elias laughs despite himself. And when he thinks about the sound of Sydni's excitement, her laugh breaking through. He realizes he's smiling again.

CHAPTER FORTY-FIVE

Sydni sits frozen long after the call ends, phone still in her hand, thumb resting lightly against the screen as if touching the last place his voice lived there.

The apartment around her glows with warm lamplight, and she feels that same warmth humming inside her chest. Something less like anxiety and more like… possibility. She exhales slowly and leans back into the couch, staring at the ceiling.

Elias called her. Because he *wanted* to celebrate with her. And did she hear that right? He isn't with the blonde bombshell anymore?

She presses her palm over her heart and shakes her head at herself. "Get a grip," she mutters. But she's smiling.

The phone buzzes.

Elias:
I'm really glad you told me. And sorry about the interruption.

She grins so hard she has to set the phone down for a second. It's ridiculous, how easily he can pull a reaction out of her. But it's also… nice.

She picks the phone back up and replies, more honestly than intended:

Sydni:
Thanks again for calling. I didn't realize how much I needed someone to be excited with me until you were.

She hits send before her brain can stage a protest. And she is careful to not address what she overheard.

Elias:
It wasn't a courtesy call. I wanted to hear you say it. You sounded really happy.

Her cheeks redden. She bites her lip, typing slowly.

Sydni:
I was. Am. I guess it means more than I thought it would.

Elias:
It should. You did the work. It's okay to let yourself feel the good stuff.

She leans back, staring at that line far too long. The good stuff. God, when was the last time she let herself have any? She's still staring when her phone suddenly rings again…Sloan.

She groans, then answers. "Heyyyyy."

"I swear to God," Sloan says dramatically, "if you ever ignore your phone this long again, I will repossess it."

She laughs. "I didn't ignore you. I was… on the phone."

"Oh?" A smirk she can *hear* through the speaker. "With who?"

She hesitates. Just a second. But Sloan doesn't miss anything. "Oh my God," he gasps. "You were on the phone with him."

"Sloan."

"YOU WERE ON THE PHONE WITH ELIAS, WEREN'T YOU? CONFESS YOUR SINS."

"Sloan, why did you even call me? You live across the hall!"

"Hang up immediately. I'm coming over."

"What? No you're—"

But he hangs up.

"Oh my God." She slumps back. "He's actually coming over."

Before she can even process that, her phone buzzes again.

Elias:
You disappeared. Did Sloan call? He seems like the type to call.

She snorts.

Sydni:
Yes. He has summoned himself to my apartment.

Elias:
Should I fear for your safety? Or mine?

Sydni:
Probably yours. If he ever finds out how much you make me smile, he may challenge you to a duel.

There's a long pause before his next text.

Elias:
You smile because of me?

Sydni:
Occasionally. Don't let it go to your head.

Elias:
No promises.

She presses a hand to her chest, laughing, and flinches from a loud knock at her door. She stands, opens the door, and Sloan barrels past her like he owns the place.

"Okay," he says, dropping onto her couch. "Explain everything. Now. From the beginning. Use small words so I can follow."

"I talked to Elias. He called when I got the DV grant update."

Sloan freezes mid-settle, eyes going wide. "He *called*?"

"Yes."

"With his voice?"

"People often call with their voices, Sloan."

He grabs a throw pillow and screams into it.

When he lifts his head, he points dramatically. "Sit down. Tell me everything. Start from his greeting and end with how your heart combusted."

"Sloan—"

"Sit."

She sits. And he listens to everything: how Elias sounded, how proud he was, how gentle, how happy he seemed to hear from her again. Sloan's expression shifts from playful dramatics to something more serious… admiring, almost.

"So he really does care," Sloan murmurs.

"Yeah." The admission hovers between them, fragile and real.

Then Sloan nudges her knee with his. "I'm proud of you too, you know."

She looks down, voice small. "For what?"

"For letting people in again. Even if it's just inches."

"So much pride coming from you both. I don't know what to do with that."

Before she can respond, her phone buzzes again. Another message from

Elias.

Is he there? Blink twice if you need extraction.

She covers her mouth.

"What?" Sloan demands.

"Nothing."

Sloan narrows his eyes. "He's texting you again, isn't he?"

She doesn't answer, which is answer enough.

Sloan gasps. "OH MY GOD, YOU HAVE A TEXT SITUATIONSHIP."

"Please leave my apartment."

"Never," he says, draping himself dramatically across her couch. "I live here now."

She laughs, fully and loudly. It feels good. Really good.

Her phone buzzes once more.

Elias:

Goodnight, Sydni.

She types back:

Sydni:

Goodnight, Elias. And thank you. For everything tonight.

She hits send, leaves Sloan on the couch after covering him up, and heads to her bedroom and lays down and closes her eyes. She worries for him, for his heart. But she falls asleep not afraid of what tomorrow will bring.

CHAPTER FORTY-SIX

Elias doesn't hear Nora's car pull in the next morning, but Clementine does. She lifts her head from his lap with a soft *whuff*, ears perked, tail thumping once, warning enough.

A second later, there's a knock that doesn't wait for permission. Elias sighs. "She really needs to learn boundaries."

Nora steps inside wearing sunglasses even though it's cloudy, carrying a reusable grocery bag full of items he didn't ask for. She takes one look at him slumped on the couch and snorts.

"You look like you slept twelve hours and are still confused by it."

He rolls his eyes. "Good morning to you too."

She tosses the bag onto the kitchen counter and kicks off her shoes. "So. How does it feel?"

"How does what feel?"

"Being a newly single man again." She wiggles her eyebrows. "Do we need to get you a leather jacket? Maybe a motorcycle?"

"For the love of God, Nora."

She laughs and sinks into the armchair across from him, folding her legs under her. Clementine immediately abandons Elias to sit loyally at Nora's feet. Traitor.

Nora pushes up her sunglasses. Her expression shifts subtly, still playful. "Seriously, though… how are you?"

"Better than I should be, I think."

She nods. "That tracks."

"What's that supposed to mean?"

"That you didn't end things because Brielle wasn't enough. She *is* enough. She's great. You ended it because you were somewhere else entirely."

He runs his hand across his face. "It's not that simple."

"Actually," she says gently, "I think it is."

He doesn't answer. For a moment, neither of them speaks.

Then Nora asks, lightly but knowingly, "So… have you talked to her?"

He doesn't pretend not to understand. "Sydni? Yes."

"And?" Nora prompts.

"And it was good," he says, surprising himself with how easily the truth comes out. "Really good. She got big news on a project she's been working on. I didn't want her to celebrate alone."

Nora smiles like a woman who already guessed every detail. "I like who you are when you care about someone. But be careful Eli, you know how you can…pull back," she says.

He looks down, embarrassed by the earnestness of it. "Don't start," he mutters.

"No, really." She leans forward and decides to drop it. "Ok, but when you do care about someone, you get less… calcified."

"What does that even—"

"You smile," she interrupts. "You joke. You breathe differently. It's like someone cracks a window open in your ribs."

He wonders if Sydni is dealing with Sloan constantly badgering her with these types of conversations. It is getting painful.

Nora watches him for another beat, then lowers her voice conspiratorially. "So… is she seeing anyone?"

He blinks. "Why would I know that?"

"Because men do weird competitive research when they like someone," Nora says. "Like checking their Instagram stories at ungodly hours."

"I do not—"

Nora raises a single eyebrow.

"...often," he finishes.

She grins. "So? Do you know?"

"No," he says honestly. "But I don't know. I don't... think so."

"Well." Nora stretches her legs. "For what it's worth, you're allowed to be honest about wanting someone. You don't have to stay in limbo to protect everyone else from discomfort."

He absorbs that. Then he asks, "And you? Are *you* seeing anyone?"

She stiffens in a way that catches him off guard.

"Oh. Um." She clears her throat. "Maybe."

"Maybe?"

"Possibly."

"That's not an answer Nora. You don't get to come in here and demand answers about my life and then not return the sentiment."

She picks up Clementine, who is far too big to be a lap dog, and hides behind her fur. "It's new. And private."

"Do I know him?"

"No."

"Is he nice?"

"Yes."

"Is he sane?"

"Mostly."

Elias narrows his eyes. "You're being very cagey."

"And you're being very invasive," she fires back. "So we can both mind our business."

He huffs a laugh. "Fine."

Nora stands and brushes off her jeans. "Listen. Whatever you're feeling about Sydni… it's not going to magically disappear because you ignore it. And it's not going to break her to let her decide what she wants."

He feels that one.

She grabs her purse. "Okay, I have a yoga class to pretend to enjoy. Are you going to ask her to meet up again or just stare at her name in Resolve until New Year's?"

Elias glares. "I don't stare at—"

"Bye!" she sings, slipping out the door.

The apartment settles back into quiet. Clementine climbs onto the couch beside him, resting her head on his thigh with a little sigh. He strokes her ears, staring at his phone.

His thumb hovers over Sydni's name. A long moment passes. Then another.

Finally, he types:

Elias
Hey. I was thinking… if you're up for it, maybe we could get back to our weekly meetups? No pressure. Just… would be nice to see you again.

He reads it twice. Three times. His heart thuds harder than it should. He hits send. Clementine nudges his hand as though congratulating him.

CHAPTER FORTY-SEVEN

Sydni is already half-asleep when her phone vibrates on the nightstand, its buzz barely audible over the hum of her bedroom fan. Sloan is snoring on the couch. Loud enough to reassure her that he's definitely not dead. The apartment smells faintly of pizza, cupcake icing, and the vanilla candle she accidentally left burning too long.

She reaches for her phone, blinking at the screen.

Elias:
Hey. I was thinking… if you're up for it, maybe we could get back to our weekly meetups? No pressure. Just… would be nice to see you again.

She types back:

Sydni:
That sounds nice. Let's plan it tomorrow. I'll text you in the morning. Goodnight.

She hesitates a second, then adds:

Sydni:
Really glad you reached out.

She hits send before she can talk herself out of it. Then she turns off her lamp, settles into her pillows, and drifts into a sleep that feels better than anything she's had in months.

~*~

The next morning, Sydni wakes to sunlight warming her room and the faint sounds of Sloan rummaging in her kitchen like he pays rent. She groans, grabs a hoodie, and pads out into the living room.

Sloan is leaning against her counter, still half in pajamas, typing furiously on his phone with a dumb grin plastered on his face.

His grin, the suspiciously pleased one, is rare. Dangerous. Possibly illegal.

She narrows her eyes. "Who are you texting and why are you smiling like a raccoon who found cake?"

He immediately locks his phone. Too fast. Criminally fast. Then he tries to cover by stretching dramatically.

"Morning, sunshine!"

"That didn't answer my question."

"Nope," he agrees cheerfully. "And it never will."

She squints. "Is it a girl?"

Sloan freezes like a startled deer. "Why would you—no. Absolutely not."

"Uh-huh."

"It's work stuff. Work is funny sometimes."

"Sloan, you work in accounting. Nothing about accounting is funny."

He tosses a piece of toast at her. "Get out of my home."

"This is *my* home," she says, catching it.

"Not when I'm here."

His grin says *don't dig*, so she lets it go. (But she files it away. Because something is definitely up.) He grabs his jacket and heads for the door.

"Okay, I have to go pretend to be a functional adult. You look happy, by the way."

"I do not."

"You do," he insists. "Suspiciously so. Almost like someone texted you last night."

She throws the toast at him. He dodges.

"BYE," he shouts, letting himself out.

She rolls her eyes, but she's smiling as she shuts the door.

~*~

After coffee, Sydni pulls on her sneakers and steps outside for her morning walk. Spring has shifted into early summer. Warm breeze, bright sun, a sky painted bluer than it has been in months.

Her therapist's words echo in her mind:

It's okay to want things, Sydni.
It's okay to want connection.
It doesn't make you weak.

She passes the old coffee shop with the crooked sign, the tiny community garden sprouting tomatoes, the bookstore that's become her escape. Every part of this walk feels less like a challenge and more like a ritual.

Her phone vibrates. Resolve notification.

Encouragement from Sloan: (who does no tasks of his own, just monitors hers as her "friend" on the app)
Keep it up, champ! (Also, you owe me coffee.)

She laughs and keeps walking.

Another notification follows. This one from Elias.

Elias:
Morning. Hope your walk is good. Thought maybe we could meet up Friday? If that works for you. Coffee or a walk. Your pick.

A slow smile curls across her face.

She types back:

Sydni:
My walk is good. Sun is perfect today. And Friday sounds great. Coffee would be nice :)

His reply is instant.

Elias:
Coffee it is. Pick the place. And the time. I'm flexible.

She walks for three more blocks before it hits her all at once. A blend of excitement and nerves and something tender she hasn't let herself feel in a long time. Something like hope.

She stops by the big oak tree near the park, heart fluttering in a way she's still getting used to. This time… she doesn't push it away. She just lets herself feel it.

CHAPTER FORTY-EIGHT

The first thing Sydni notices when she wakes up Friday morning is the warm light spilling across her bedroom floor. Early summer sun, bright and confident, pressing through the thin curtains like it's reminding her to breathe.

She yawns, stretches, and immediately feels the flutter in her chest. Today. She's seeing Elias today.

And she was not stressed about the *we're-definitely-going-to-kiss* thought that she had had in the past. It was just friendly coffee. Just… everything she's been both wanting and avoiding for months.

She pushes the covers back and stands, shaky but steady, and starts getting ready.

~*~

By midday, the sky is blue and sharp, the kind that makes the world look more hopeful than it usually allows itself to be. She spends too long picking out an outfit. Not dressy, not too casual, not too "I'm trying," but definitely "please notice that I exist."

She settles on lightly distressed jeans, gray fitted t-shirt, her favorite sneakers, hair half-up so the curls look intentionally chaotic, tattoos fully visible for the first time around him

She studies her reflection in the mirror. Her ink climbs across her arms, down her ribs, peeks from the curve of her hip, wraps delicately along her collarbone. The scars beneath them. Some softened by time, some still ridged, whisper their history quietly.

She inhales. Today, she won't hide. She grabs her purse, locks the door, and starts toward the coffee shop.

~*~

The little café sits on the corner of Maple and Fifth, with wide windows and hanging plants and that too-expensive-but-worth-it smell of roasted beans. Through the glass, she sees him immediately.

Elias is sitting at a small table by the window, fidgeting with the paper sleeve on his coffee cup. Clementine isn't with him, but he keeps glancing toward the door like he's waiting for an earthquake instead of a person.

And when he sees, he stands. He isn't dramatic about. He also isn't performative "I'm such a gentleman" way. He just does it, like his body made the decision before he could.

"Hi," she says, stepping up to the table.

"Hi," he echoes, smiling in a way that's small, but real. They linger there awkwardly for a beat too long before he gestures to the chair. "Um…sit?"

She laughs. "Yeah. Sitting is a strong choice."

He clears his throat like he's embarrassed, and she sits across from him, sliding her bag onto her lap.

"Did you order yet?" she asks.

"I got a cold brew," he says. "I wasn't sure what you'd want so I didn't want to assume."

"Well," she says, "I'm going to get something with way too much sugar."

He stands. "What do you want? My treat."

"Oh, you don't have to—"

He shakes his head with a confidence that surprises her. "I want to."

That flutter hits again. She gives him her order, an iced almond latte with vanilla and cinnamon, and he nods, memorizing it with an attentiveness that shouldn't make her stomach flip, but does.

While he's at the counter, she exhales shakily, palms damp. The nerves aren't panic, just anticipation tangled with the fear of wanting something again.

When he returns, he sets her drink down carefully, like it's meaningful. And maybe it is. She takes a sip. "This is perfect."

"Good," he says.

Silence stretches between them, not uncomfortable, just fragile, like they're both afraid of stepping on something important.

Finally, he breaks it. "So… June snuck up fast."

She smiles. "Somehow, I blinked and missed spring."

His gaze flicks briefly to her arms, the tattoos, some darker than others, some layered over old scars. He doesn't stare. He doesn't ask. His eyes just warm, gentle, and curious without prying.

She surprises herself by saying, "You can ask if you want."

He looks up. "About your tattoos?"

She nods.

He hesitates, respectful. "Only if you're okay with it."

"I am."

"Okay. Um… they're really beautiful. I've always wondered if they…if they mean something. Or if you just like the art."

His voice is soft. She traces one faintly with her finger. "They all mean something. Even though some were just impulse decisions. Some were… cover-ups."

He nods again, slow and steady. The kind of nod that says he's listening without needing all the details. "I like them," he says. "They suit you."

Her cheeks warm. "Thank you."

"And the curls are having a great day," he adds lightly.

She laughs. "Stop, please, I can only emotionally handle so many compliments in a week."

He grins. A real one, bright and boyish. "I'll try to pace myself."

And just like that, the tension melts. They talk. Really talk. About work. About coffee preferences. About Sloan being… Sloan. About Nora's yoga obsession. About Clementine's new hatred of mail carriers. About the first time they met on New Year's Eve, the shoulder bump, the almost-kiss, the weirdly electric moment they both pretended didn't exist.

They laugh at all the same times. They pause in the same places. They fall into a rhythm that feels like two people who didn't mean to orbit each other but are now held together by gravity they don't dare question.

At one point, he asks, "Do you feel okay? Being here?"

It takes her a second to understand what he's really asking. "Yeah," she says honestly. "I actually… really do."

And he smiles, making her feel immediately relieved. When they finish their drinks but neither of them moves.

Elias clears his throat. "I, um. I know we usually walk, but… want to go for one now? If you feel up for it?"

She thinks of the sunny sidewalk, the changing seasons, the way being near him feels like steady warmth instead of fear. "Yeah," she says. "I'd like that."

They walk side by side out of the café, the summer air wrapping around them like an invitation into something gentle and new. The air outside is warm with the hint of humidity that signals June settling in for real this time. Sunlight filters through the trees lining the sidewalk, dappling the concrete in gold. As they start walking, the sounds of the café fade behind them replaced by quiet streets, distant lawnmowers, and the occasional dog barking as if offering commentary on their pace.

For a few steps, neither of them speaks. It's not an awkward silence, more like the kind that belongs to people figuring out how close to walk beside each other.

Finally, Elias clears his throat. "By the way… you said iced almond vanilla cinnamon latte? That's not your usual drink, was today a bold lifestyle choice?"

She laughs. "It's not my usual but I like my coffee to taste like dessert and poor boundaries."

He grins. "I respect that. Mine tastes like self-loathing and dark roast."

"Yeah well… you look like the type of guy who orders black coffee because you think adding sugar is weakness."

"It is weakness."

"It is joy, Elias."

He smiles, that small smile that presses dimples into his cheeks when he isn't trying to hide them.

As they walk, a breeze sweeps through, lifting strands of her curls and brushing them across her cheek. She tucks them behind her ear automatically and he watches her and lingers for half a heartbeat too long.

"Do you have a favorite?"

"Favorite what?"

"Tattoo."

"Do you have a favorite organ? Because picking a favorite tattoo is like picking a favorite lung."

He barks out a laugh, a real one, loud enough that she startles and bumps his shoulder. "I'm sorry," he says, still laughing. "Did you just compare your body art to pulmonary anatomy?"

"Look, I panicked. It's been a long day."

"It's eleven a.m."

"And I've been awake since nine," she says, dead serious.

He shakes his head, smiling down at the sidewalk. "God, I missed talking to you."

She freezes for a fraction of a second. Missed. She recovers with a small, shy smile. "Same."

They walk several more blocks like that. Side by side, shoulders occasionally brushing, each touch shooting a tiny spark through her chest. It's nothing dramatic. Nothing that would make anyone else look twice. But to her? It's everything.

When they reach the small farmers market that pops up every Friday, he glances toward it. "Want to walk through?"

"Only if we avoid the man giving out free samples of raw honey. Last time I did that I almost got roped into sponsoring a beehive."

He grins. "I feel like you'd make a great beekeeper."

"Oh my God. Stop."

"I'm serious. You have beekeeper energy."

"Explain."

"Hm." He studies her with a thoughtful squint. "You're gentle. And patient. And bees would trust you with their lives."

Her mouth falls open. "Elias, that is, without exaggeration, the strangest compliment anyone has ever given me."

"And yet," he says lightly, "you're blushing."

"I'm not."

"You are."

~*~

They stop at a small booth selling fresh flowers: sunflowers, wildflowers, and pale pink peonies. Sydni brushes a fingertip along the petals, lifting one to smell it.

"They're beautiful," she murmurs.

"They are," he says and she realizes too late that he's not looking at the flowers.

She steps back, flustered but smiling. "Should we keep walking? Before you compare me to insects or organs again?"

He chuckles. "Lead the way."

After a while, the crowd thins and the sidewalk widens. The sun hangs warm above them, and the scent of freshly cut grass sweeps through the air.

"Can I ask you something?" Elias says.

"Sure."

"What made you get your first tattoo?"

She considers this. "Impulse."

He hums. "And the second?"

"Fear."

He slows slightly, turning his head. "Fear?"

"It's… complicated."

He nods once not pushing, not prying. "You don't have to explain."

She looks up at him. He means that. And somehow, that makes her want to explain more.

"I think a lot of them were a way to take back something," she admits. "To choose what goes on my body instead of letting… life decide for me."

He stops walking and she turns to face him. "That makes sense," he says. "A lot of sense."

She looks away, swallowing.

"And they look incredible," he adds.

She laughs. "Thank you."

"I mean it."

When she looks back up, his eyes are already on hers, steady and so much kinder than she knows what to do with.

Her pulse skips in her throat. She steps away first. "We should, um, keep walking."

"Yeah," he says, clearing his throat. "Okay."

They fall into step again. This time, a little closer. By the time they loop back toward her street, they're deep in conversation about movies and childhood snacks and the absolute superiority of cinnamon over nutmeg.

He tells her about the time Clementine chewed up his work shoe. She tells him about the time she accidentally joined a yoga class because she thought it was a sound bath. He laughs until his eyes crinkle and she laughs until her cheeks hurt.

And with every minute that passes, the distance that once existed between them shrinks. Not physically, but in a way she can feel. They're not the people they were in January. They're not the strangers they were in March. They're not the ghosts they were in April. They're something… new.

When they finally reach the corner where they'll part, she almost wishes the walk were longer. He turns to her, shoving his hands into his pockets in a way that makes him look boyish and nervous and painfully endearing.

"I really liked today," he says.

"Me too."

He hesitates. The kind of hesitation that feels like he's holding back twenty different things he wants to say. They linger…too long, too close. And for one impossible second, she swears he's leaning closer.

But then he steps back instead, clearing his throat. "I'll text you?"

"Please do."

"I will. Back to work for me. Patients need tending."

And the look he gives her is almost enough to undo her. Almost enough to crack her open, almost enough to make her reach for his hand. She turns and starts walking first, cheeks warm, heart full. She makes it half a block before glancing back over her shoulder.

He's still there. Watching her. Not leaving until she turns the next corner. And she does turn, smiling like someone who just found something she wasn't sure she deserved anymore.

CHAPTER FIFTY-TWO

August arrived warm and thick. The kind of month that clings to your skin and slows your steps. Sydni felt it as soon as she opened her blinds one morning: that late-summer heaviness that wasn't quite melancholy, but wasn't quite hope either. Something in between. Something she couldn't name.

She made her usual cup of coffee, stood barefoot in her kitchen, and watched the steam rise. A small routine. A steadying one. And yet… it didn't feel as grounding as it did a week ago.

She checked her phone out of habit. Nothing from Elias.

Not that she expected anything. Not that she *should.* But she still checked. She'd sent a small message two days earlier. Nothing dramatic, nothing vulnerable.

Sydni:
Hope work's been good this week. Stay hydrated, it's gross outside.

The little "delivered" status sat there. Unanswered. Somehow that tiny silence needled deeper than she thought it would.

She dropped her phone face-down on the counter, took a sip of coffee she suddenly didn't want anymore, and told herself out loud, "It's fine." Because she *was* fine. Mostly.

~*~

She dressed in shorts and an oversized T-shirt, grabbed her headphones, and forced herself outside for her walk. Ten minutes, like she told Dr. Wexler she would keep doing. But today she didn't hit ten. She hit nine. Then eight. And she stopped.

She didn't spiral. She refused to spiral. But she was tired. Bone-tired in a way that didn't quite match how well her life had been going. She made it back to her apartment with the awareness that progress wasn't linear, and that still frustrated her.

Sydni hears the knock before she sees him. Three soft taps. Not his usual obnoxious "I'm barging in" rhythm. This one is careful.

She opens the door just enough to see Sloan on the other side. Hands in his pockets, hood up, shoulders slumped like he's bracing for winter or judgment. Maybe both.

"Hey," he says.

Sydni crosses her arms. "Hey."

He swallows, glancing at the floor. "Can I come in?"

She hesitates. Then steps aside. Sloan enters slowly, like he's afraid he'll break something by existing too loudly. He stops in the middle of her living room, turns toward her, and then, very unlike him, he doesn't rush into words.

"Syd…" His voice cracks on her name. He clears his throat. "I'm sorry.

She says nothing.

He nods, accepting that. "I know you're mad. You should be. I was… I was a jerk." The word sounds too small for what he's trying to admit.

He starts pacing, fingers dragging through his hair. "I didn't mean to snap at you. Or make you feel like you did anything wrong. That was me being… me."

"Sloan. Don't do that. Don't make it a joke."

And for a moment, she sees it. The guilt eating him alive.

"I'm not joking," he whispers. "I just… I don't like saying things that make me sound weak."

Sydni's shoulders drop. "You're not weak."

He lets out a shaky breath. "I felt like I was losing you."

Her heart lurches as he keeps pacing, words spilling faster now, desperate.

"Not in a romantic way. Just… you're my person, Syd. My safe place. And when you started opening up to someone else, I panicked. I hate that I did. I hate how it came out. But I wasn't angry at you. I was scared."

He stops again, this time looking at her like he's afraid she'll disappear. "Robin left," he says quietly. "And I didn't see it coming. Not really. And the whole time after, I kept thinking… if I had been better, she wouldn't have gone."

He looks at her and exhales loudly. "I know you're not her," he continues, voice fraying. "I know that. But my brain still… grabs onto that fear." He presses a hand to his chest. "And when I saw you getting close to Elias, and actually doing things for yourself, and smiling in ways I haven't seen in months… I felt that same panic. Like I was waiting for the day you'd wake up and realize I'm just… excess baggage."

"Sloan," she whispers.

He shakes his head fiercely. "No. Let me say this. Please. I should have talked to you instead of blowing up. I should have asked what you needed instead of assuming I was losing my place in your life. You didn't deserve that. Not after everything we've been through. You deserve someone who cheers for you, not someone who falls apart the second you grow."

He finally meets her eyes. "And I'm sorry. For all of it."

The room feels heavier and lighter all at once. Sydni steps closer. "You're not losing me. But," she adds gently, "you can't… tear me down because you're scared I'll leave. That's not fair to either of us."

"I know." He nods quickly. "I swear, I know. And I'm working on it. I really am. I just—" His voice cracks. "I don't want to be the reason you stop trusting people again."

She reaches up, touches his arm. "You won't be. Not if you keep talking to me like this."

He looks down at her hand, then at her. "Can you forgive me?" he asks.

Sydni lets the pause sit. Harshness has never been their language, honesty was. "Yeah," she says finally. "I can."

His shoulders sag in relief.

She nudges him lightly. "But if you blow up at me again, I'm hiding all your hoodies and replacing them with glitter sweaters."

His horror is immediate. "Sydni. Please. I'm fragile."

She laughs, rolling her eyes. "Come here, idiot."

He pulls her into a hug, not the goofy side-hugs he gives when he's deflecting. A real hug. Arms tight. Head buried against her shoulder like he's grounding himself.

"I'm really glad you're not going anywhere," he murmurs.

She closes her eyes, hugging him back.

"Me too," she whispers.

CHAPTER FORTY-NINE

A week passed before Sydni really noticed how steady her days had become. Therapy is down to once a week, morning walks six days a week, a grocery run she didn't panic her way through, and even a clean kitchen. Sloan had gone home on Saturday with a heroic flourish, declaring himself "Saint Sloan of Domestic Resurrection," and she'd laughed so hard she cried.

She wasn't back to her old self; maybe she never would be. But she was something new. Something steadier. Stronger.

Still, on Tuesday afternoon, sitting cross-legged on her couch with grant notes sprawled around her, she caught herself checking the Resolve app without thinking. She had completed her walk. Marked off journaling. Did laundry. All good things.

But what jumped out was **his** little green check-mark from earlier that morning.

Elias completed: 15-minute stretch & mobility.

She was fine. Totally fine.

That illusion shattered when her front door flew open so loudly she jolted upright.

"HELLO, MY BELOVED DISASTER RACOON," Sloan announced, striding in like he was a sitcom character entering on a laugh track. He tossed his keys somewhere in the vicinity of her bowl by the door, but missed by a good foot. "We have to talk."

Sydni blinked. "First of all, boundaries. Second of all, what?"

"Get dressed."

"I am dressed."

"Dressier."

"For what?"

He sat beside her, leaning in dramatically. "We're going to Trivia Night."

"No, we're—"

"Yes, we are. Because," he held up a finger, "I have made an executive best-friend decision."

"Oh God."

"I need to vet Elias."

Her jaw dropped. "You're kidding."

"I would never joke about vetting a man who might destroy your heart, or worse, has bad taste in movies."

"Sloan—"

He cut her off with a raised hand. "It's not about jealousy."

"It sounds like jealousy."

"It's protective affection with flair."

Sydni groaned and buried her face in a pillow.

"And," he added, "I told him to bring his sister so he has backup. Or emotional support. Or someone to glare at me when I ask the real questions. Oh and I got his number from your phone. Oops!"

"You WHAT?!"

"Don't worry, his sister agreed."

"I didn't even agree!"

He placed a hand over his heart. "But I *felt* your future agreement in my soul."

"Sloan…"

"It's Tuesday Trivia. At The Crooked Lantern." He shuddered. "God help us all."

She stared at him. "Why? Why are you like this?"

"Because you let random men get too close in grocery stores and someone has to supervise."

"That happened *one time*."

"ONE TIME TOO MANY."

She threw a pillow at him. She is always throwing things at him. He dodged like a cat.

Still… a part of her felt something warm flicker at the idea of seeing Elias again. A part of her felt terrified too.

"Okay," she said finally. "Fine. Trivia. But you're buying dinner."

He gasped. "Rude. How dare you."

~*~

They arrived early…well, Sydni arrived early. Sloan had dragged her out the door twenty minutes before the acceptable meeting window so he could "scope the place." The Crooked Lantern wasn't much to scope: low ceilings, buzzing neon signs, mismatched tables, and a jukebox stuck permanently between 80s rock and early 2000s pop.

By 6:55 p.m., she was fidgeting with her sleeve, trying to look casual.

By 6:57, Sloan was rearranging the chairs "strategically."

By 6:58, she considered faking a tummy issue.

By 7:00, she heard his voice.

"Hey."

She turned. Elias stood in the doorway with Nora beside him, the bar's dim lighting catching on his hair in a way that made him look somehow different than she remembered. His expression warmed when he saw her, though something guarded flickered underneath. This was a terrible idea. Why did she agree to this?

"Hi," she said, hoping her smile didn't look as shaky as it felt.

Before she could move toward them, Sloan swooped in and placed a hand on her lower back like a protective boyfriend in a 90s drama. "Elias. Glad you could make it."

He didn't say it warmly. Or neutrally. It was… territorial.

Elias blinked, surprise tightening his shoulders. "Yeah. Thanks for inviting us."

Nora crossed her arms. "Is this a casual vetting or an interrogation? I'd like to prepare my resting facial expression accordingly."

Sloan brightened. "I like you."

Nora did not return the sentiment.

They sat. Sloan directly beside Sydni, leaning into her space. Elias across from her, right beside his sister. The moment was already bad.

~*~

Trivia began with a man in suspenders who yelled the rules like a drill sergeant and encouraged groups to pick punny team names.

"Team name?" he barked, slapping a sheet onto their table.

Sydni opened her mouth, but Sloan slapped the table first.

"Team Emotional Damage."

Nora snorted. Elias looked pained. Sydni wished the floor would open and swallow her whole.

The host nodded approvingly. "Love the self-awareness."

The first round started smoothly enough. Then Sloan and Elias began silently competing for Sydni's attention. When she answered a question correctly about sitcom theme songs, Sloan leaned over and whispered dramatically, "She's brilliant. A genius. A scholar."

When Elias got a geography question right, Sydni smiled at him, and Sloan loudly cleared his throat, putting his hand on the back of Sydni's chair. Nora's eye twitched.

Halfway through round two, a waitress approached for drink refills. A tall brunette with a glossy smile and a voice that could charm a roomful of drunk college students. She rested a hand on Elias's shoulder. "What can I get you, sweetie?"

Sydni's stomach plummeted.

Elias startled. "Uh—just a beer."

The waitress winked. "Coming right up, handsome."

She walked away, and Sydni stared very hard at her trivia sheet.

Sloan noticed. He leaned closer, voice low and smug. "You okay?"

"I'm fine."

"Because I could tell her to back off."

"Sloan—"

"I could hiss."

"SLOAN."

But Elias's gaze drifted between them, Sloan's arm slung insistently across the back of Sydni's chair, Sydni trying to act normal, Sloan leaning in like a possessive boyfriend. And something in Elias's expression dimmed. Something tight. Something jealous.

Nora noticed too. She folded her arms tighter.

When the music round started, Sloan and Elias both leaned toward Sydni to explain their answers. Their heads nearly collided. They glared at each other like middle school rivals.

At one point, Sloan muttered, "We get it, Elias. You know bands. Congratulations."

Elias shot back, "We all have strengths. Some people have… volume."

Sydni kicked Sloan under the table to stop him from replying. It did not work. Because during a question about Oscar winners, Nora corrected Sloan. He scowled, and she gave him a flat, unimpressed stare. Sydni could *feel* the mutual tension even if she couldn't interpret it correctly.

Then, for the lightning round, teams had to assign a captain.

"Elias will do it," Sloan said instantly.

"Actually," Elias countered, "Sydni should."

"I wasn't asking you," Sloan replied sweetly.

"Then ask her," Elias said.

Both looked at her. She wanted to disappear.

"Um… Elias can be the captain" she said weakly.

Sloan beamed. Elias tried to hide his disappointment. Nora scribbled something on her napkin so aggressively it tore.

The waitress comes back over, her hand resting on Elias' shoulder, "Hey handsome, another beer?"

Elias' shakes his head no and thanks her politely, and she smiles warmly at him and slides a piece of paper over to him and bends over and whispers something in his ear that makes his face turn red.

Sydni and Sloan both stare and then casually try to look away like they weren't shocked.

When the final scores were announced, they placed third. Third wasn't bad. The walk out to the parking lot, however? Worse than any loss.

"Thanks for inviting us," Elias said, but his voice was polite more than warm.

"Of course!" Sloan answered loudly, stepping closer to Sydni again. "We'll do it again sometime."

Nora muttered, "God, I hope not."

"Goodnight," he said.

"Goodnight."

He and Nora walked off together. Sydni and Sloan watched them disappear.

After a moment, Sloan broke the silence. "Well," he said brightly, "that was a dumpster fire wrapped in a tragedy."

"Sloan…"

"You still like him," he sing-songed.

"I do not."

"You're lying."

She shoved him, but he grinned.

"You're jealous," he added triumphantly.

"I am NOT."

"Uh-huh."

"Sloan, shut up."

"Never."

~*~

Back home, she opened her laptop, curled on her couch, and wrote.

I don't know what tonight was. I don't know what Sloan is doing. I don't know how Elias feels. I don't know why that waitress bothered me or why I wanted to drag Sloan out by his ear half the night.

I only know that seeing Elias again did something. Something small. Something warm. Like a spark that didn't burn but reminded me heat exists.

She marked off her "non-work writing" goal on the Resolve app, closed her computer.

She didn't know what came next.

~*~

The moment he and Nora were far enough from the bar, Elias sighed. Nora, walking briskly beside him, was uncharacteristically silent.

"That was…" Elias started, searching for the right word. A disaster? A fever dream? Some bizarre emotional obstacle course?

"Something," Nora finished flatly.

They walked another half block before he finally asked, "Do you think Sydni and Sloan are dating?"

Nora stopped dead in her tracks. "What?" Her voice pitched upward. "Dating?"

"He's just… really protective," Elias said, rubbing the back of his neck. "And close. And he kept touching her back and leaning into her, and she didn't pull away. And I don't know… maybe I read everything wrong back in January."

Nora stared at him with an expression that hovered between irritation and disbelief. "You think Sloan is her boyfriend?" she asked.

"I mean…" Elias exhaled. "It looked like it."

"No. No." Nora resumed walking, her steps sharp. "No."

"Then what was that?" Elias pressed. "Because that wasn't normal friend behavior."

"You don't know what normal friend behavior looks like," she snapped before she could stop herself.

He blinked. "Okay… ow."

Nora's jaw clenched. "Sorry." But she didn't sound sorry. She sounded… offended. Somehow.

Elias tried again. "Nora, just tell me. If they're together, I need to—"

"They're not," she interrupted. "Trust me."

"How do you know?"

Her mouth opened, then promptly closed. Instead, she threw her hands up. "I just do, okay? Sloan is—he's a mess. And dramatic. And clingy. And loud. And—ugh, you saw him tonight!"

"That doesn't answer the question."

"It answers enough!" she snapped.

Elias stared at her, baffled. He'd known his sister his entire life. He could count on one hand the number of times she'd been truly rattled. Something about tonight had crawled under her skin, and he couldn't figure out why. "I just…" he said. "I don't want to screw things up. Again."

Nora's expression shifted just a fraction. "Maybe ask her," she suggested. "Like a normal person."

"Yeah," he murmured. "Maybe."

They reached the parking lot, the air cool with a slight breeze. Elias looked back toward the street where Sydni had disappeared minutes earlier. He hadn't imagined that spark. Not in January. Not last week. Not tonight. But after watching Sloan hover around her, and seeing how easily Sydni allowed it, he wasn't sure what any of it meant.

As they reached his car, Nora buckled herself in, muttering, "Dating… honestly. Men are so dense."

"What did you say?"

"Nothing," she snapped.

But he saw the faint pink on her cheeks before she turned away. "Okay," he murmured. "Let's go home."

He started the engine, his thoughts looping in hesitant circles. If Sydni and Sloan weren't dating…why had tonight felt like they were? And if they were…why did it hurt so damn much?

CHAPTER FIFTY

July crept in with warm mornings, humid evenings, and the kind of sunlight that made the sidewalks glow a gentle gold. Sydni woke each day with a little more steadiness than the one before. Therapy sessions with Dr. Wexler continued to unravel the tight knots inside her. Her grants were organized, scheduled, and shockingly, even turned in early.

She wasn't drowning. She was floating. Sometimes even gliding. And in the middle of that slow, unexpected peace were her Friday lunches with Elias.

They never planned them until the day before. Never talked about what it meant. Never acknowledged that the pattern had become something almost sacred. It simply existed like muscle memory, like something her life had been waiting to make room for.

Friday One — July 5th

Elias chose the spot, an outdoor seating area behind a downtown deli that served sandwiches bigger than her face. He was already seated when she arrived, lifting his iced tea in a small wave. The smile he wore was warm and a little shy, the kind that settled somewhere behind her ribs before she could stop it. He had gotten a haircut since their last lunch. The shorter sides made his eyes look even brighter, and she tried very hard not to stare. She failed immediately.

"You survived the Fourth?" he asked as she slid into the chair across from him.

"Barely. Sloan bought sparklers and set off the fire alarm in my hallway. I thought we were going to meet our ancestors."

Elias laughed, leaning back with the kind of ease that made his whole body look relaxed. "That sounds about right."

She noticed Clementine curled under the table near his feet. He had brought her today, claiming she had separation anxiety, though Sydni suspected the golden retriever simply preferred her company. Clementine's tail thumped the moment she leaned down to scratch behind her ears.

They talked about nothing important at first, letting the conversation drift without pressure or direction. Reality TV betrayals. Work emails. Why iced tea always tasted better out of plastic deli cups. Which flavor of chips counted as elite. Sydni felt herself relaxing in ways she didn't expect. Her laughter came easily with him, so easily it almost startled her.

"You always drink the lemon part first. I noticed that last time."

"Maybe I'm predictable," she teased.

He shook his head. "No. Just observably consistent."

She hid her smile behind her cup.

As they finished eating, Clementine nudged her hand, demanding one last ear scratch. Elias watched the interaction with an interest that she didn't entirely understand.

"Sloan would steal her," Sydni said without thinking. "He thinks every dog is destined to be his."

Elias's expression shifted. Barely noticeable. A tiny wrinkle between his brows, a flicker of something uncertain before he covered it with a polite smile. "Oh. Sloan likes dogs?" he asked, voice light, but not casual.

She nodded, oblivious. "He likes anything that doesn't bite him back."

"Right," Elias said, and looked down at Clementine, though he seemed to be thinking about something else entirely. It was a brief moment. Quick. Gone almost as fast as it appeared.

They stood to leave, and he walked her halfway to her complex. Their arms brushed once, and neither moved away. Clementine trotted between them, tail wagging like she approved of whatever was happening.

Before they parted, Elias glanced at her for a moment longer than necessary, as though memorizing something he didn't want to misplace.

"Same time next Friday?" he asked.

She nodded. "Yeah. I'd like that."

And the way he smiled at her made her wish next Friday wasn't so far away.

~*~

Friday Two — July 12th

Sydni chose the spot this time, a tiny taco truck tucked behind a hardware store that looked vaguely illegal but smelled like heaven. Elias arrived right on time, hands in his pockets, hair pushed back like he had run his fingers through it on the walk over. A strand had fallen loose over his forehead, and Sydni had to remind herself not to stare at it for too long.

"This place has… personality," he said, eyeing the truck.

"That's Yelp Elite language for 'please don't poison me,'" she replied.

He laughed, and she felt it all the way down her spine.

They sat on the curb with foil-wrapped tacos balanced on their knees. The sun was bright enough to make her squint, and Elias kept glancing at her like he wanted to shield her eyes with his hand but was too polite to risk it.

He told her about a coworker who microwaved salmon. She almost died laughing.

"That's a felony," she wheezed.

"He claims it was organic," Elias said. "As if that makes my suffering poetic."

318

When she nudged him for being dramatic, he nudged her back, but his touch lingered a heartbeat longer than last week. Not enough to be blatant. Just enough to make heat crawl up her neck.

"Do you always find the weirdest food places?" he asked.

"Yes. It's a gift. Yelp is a sacred calling."

"Then I am honored to be chosen for your journey," he said with an exaggerated bow of his head.

A gust of wind suddenly blew curls across her face. She tried to push them away but only succeeded in making them stick to her lip gloss.

"Hold on," Elias murmured. He reached toward her slowly, giving her time to pull back if she wanted to. She didn't. His fingers brushed her cheek as he tucked one curl behind her ear, the touch featherlight and unbearably gentle.

Her breath stalled. So did his. He pulled his hand back quickly. "Sorry. That was— sorry."

"It's okay," she said, touching the place where his fingers had been. "Really." His ears went pink, and she felt a strange, fizzy warmth in her chest because of it.

They ate the rest of their meal with a comfort that felt dangerous in its simplicity. She found herself wanting to stay longer. Wanting to sit closer. Wanting to learn the shape of his smile in every shade of sunlight.

When they stood, she casually mentioned, "I should probably help Sloan move some furniture later."

Elias stiffened almost imperceptibly. "Sloan again," he said lightly, but something in his tone tightened.

"He's helpless," she added without thinking. "Someone has to keep him alive."

"Oh," Elias said. "Right. Of course."

The seed deepened. But he still walked her back to her building, hands brushing once, almost twice. When their shoulders bumped, neither of them apologized.

"Same time next week?" he asked.

"Yes," she said immediately.

His smile told her he had been hoping for that.

~*~

Friday Three — July 19th

Rain pushed them indoors to a cafe that smelled like cinnamon and warm sugar. The owner greeted Sydni by name the moment they walked in, and Elias raised an eyebrow.

"Well, well," he teased. "Celebrity status."

"I come here for the muffins," she said.

"You come here enough for them to know your coffee order."

She tossed a sugar packet at him. It hit his shoulder and bounced into his lap. He looked down at it like it had personally offended him.

They ordered one muffin to split, because neither wanted to commit to a full dessert but both wanted a taste. When Elias tore it in half, he gave her the larger portion without comment.

"You are a secret gentleman," she said.

"If I were a gentleman, I wouldn't have eaten the top of yours first," he replied.

"You are a menace."

"Thank you. I work hard."

His cheeks flushed, the pink that had become her new favorite color.

320

They talked about work, about summer storms, about Clementine's ongoing feud with the neighbor's cat. At one point she made a comment about Sloan texting her nine times this morning.

"He worries too much," she said.

"Sounds like the two of you are close," Elias said. His voice was casual, but his eyes gave him away.

"Yea. He's just dramatic." She sipped her coffee. "Extremely dramatic."

Elias laughed, but his shoulders loosened in a way that told her he had been holding something tense without realizing it.

They lingered far longer than a lunch break allowed, conversations looping into comfortable silences. Twice she caught him watching her. Twice she pretended not to notice. When she finally stood, brushing crumbs from her jeans, Elias lingered like he wasn't ready for the moment to end.

He opened his mouth, closed it, tried again, and then defaulted to, "Same time next week?"

She nodded, "Yes."

He exhaled, almost relieved.

As they stepped out into the drizzle, he held the door for her, not out of politeness, but like he simply liked looking at her while she walked past him.

She didn't dare think about what that meant.

Friday Four — July 26th

Their last July Friday had become a ritual without either of them acknowledging it. They met at a park bench downtown, sunlight filtering through the leaves above them.

Elias brought sandwiches again. Sydni brought cookies she had baked that morning, which she nervously warned him might be "technically edible." He took a bite, blinked dramatically, and declared, "These are the greatest cookies ever made by human hands. I would challenge the gods for another one."

She snorted. "You are ridiculous."

"But you are smiling, so I consider this a win."

She swatted his arm with the back of her hand, and he pretended to be wounded.

Partway through lunch, two joggers passed. One waved at Elias. "Hey man!" he called. Then he looked at Sydni and added, "Your boyfriend's a great guy!"

Sydni inhaled sharply, coughing on her cookie. Elias went bright red. "We're not—" he started.

"Definitely not," Sydni blurted.

"Oh," the jogger said, unfazed. "Could've fooled me."

"Client," he says. And they avoided eye contact for a solid twenty seconds. Then she giggled. Then he laughed. Then everything felt easy again.

Still, the jogger's words lingered between them like static. Neither addressed it. Both remembered it.

After lunch, they wandered toward her office at a lazy pace. At one point she tripped slightly over a broken bit of pavement, and Elias instinctively reached for her elbow. His hand rested there, and when he let go, his fingers brushed her arm in a way that felt intentional and not accidental at all.

He walked her all the way to her building even though it added several blocks to his route. She noticed. He pretended she didn't.

When they stopped, he held her gaze for a long, warm moment. She could feel something humming between them, fragile and wonderful.

"I really like Fridays," he said quietly.

"Me too."

He looked as if he wanted to say something more, something he wasn't ready to risk. Instead, he said, "Same time next week?"

She nodded. "Please."

He smiled. It was genuine, and almost tender. The kind of smile that made her feel like he had already fallen without realizing he was falling.

And neither of them dared break whatever magic they were building.

~*~

July slipped away in sunlight and sandwiches and laughter. Neither asked the question they both felt hovering in the space between them. Neither risked the answer.

But every Friday, their steps fell a little more in sync. Every Friday, the air between them warmed just a little more. Every Friday, something bloomed carefully, but real.

Summer was half over. And neither of them realized how close they were to the moment everything would change.

CHAPTER FIFTY-ONE

Tuesday nights used to be Sydni's sanctuary. Laundry humming in the background. Pasta is eaten directly from the pot. Silence that felt comfortable, not accusing. But lately Tuesdays have turned into emotional catch-basins. Therapy reflections are still raw. Monday's momentum fading. Friday lunches with Elias feeling like an eternity away.

She was loading the dishwasher when her front door unlocked. Sloan slipped inside, his eyes too bright. The look he wore when fear crawled up his spine.

"Syd," he said, voice thin, "we need to talk."

She wiped her hands on a dish towel, approaching him slowly. She knew this version of him. The pacing. The tight jaw. The way he stood like someone had yanked a chair out from under him.

Her heart softened. "What happened?"

He didn't answer. Just paced once, twice. Then stopped abruptly. "You're pulling away from me."

There it was. Not anger. Fear. The fear she'd known since they first met. The fear stitched to every abandonment he'd lived through: His dad leaving. Robin moving out. Every friend who got married and forgot him. Every relationship that fizzled without warning.

Sydni exhaled gently and stepped closer, voice low. "Sloan… honey… no. I'm right here."

"No," he said quickly, backing away like her reassurance physically hurt. "You're somewhere else."

"Sloan—"

"I can feel it." His voice shook. "I know when people are about to leave."

Her chest tightened. This wasn't about Elias. This was old. Deep. A wound re-opening. Sloan, always fun, always funny, always the best friend, has wounds that she may not have seen were re-opening.

She reached for his arm. He flinched, then let her hold him. "Sloan," she whispered, "I'm not going anywhere."

He stared at her, searching her face like trying to predict a storm. "Don't say that unless you mean it."

"I do mean it."

"No." His voice was a razor. "People always say that. And then they go anyway."

"Sloan…"

"I can't lose you," he blurted. "Not you. Not the one person who's never given up on me."

She swallowed hard, squeezing his hand. "You're not losing me."

But he wasn't hearing her. Not the rational part, anyway. "You're choosing him," he said.

"What?"

"Elias." The name cracked out of him. "You're choosing him."

She felt herself twist with surprise, guilt, fear all tangled. "Sloan, I'm not choosing anyone right now. I don't even know what I feel."

"But you DO feel something," he insisted. "And I'm not stupid."

She tried to stay steady. "Sloan, we can talk about this—"

"That's all it ever is now!" he snapped. "Talking about him. Comparing things to him. Wondering what he meant by this or that. Pretending you don't care."

Her face flushed hot. "That is not fair, and I don't even know where this is coming from, you are my best friend!"

"It's the truth," he said, voice rising. "And it's driving me insane because he shows up and suddenly *I'm on the outside of us.*"

"Sloan… this is not you losing me."

He laughed, a bitter, broken sound. "But every time someone new comes into your life, I get pushed to the edges. Every damn time."

Her heart splintered. She cupped his cheek. Sydni knows that is not true. Sydni knows that Sloan has his moments of spiraling too. Sydni knows that he is in a place where he is projecting past pain into their situation. "Sweet boy… that isn't happening."

"It is," he whispered fiercely. "And I'm scared. So scared."

She pulled him into a hug before he could stop her. His arms tightened around her immediately, almost desperately. She murmured, "I'm not going anywhere, Sloan. I swear."

But he shook his head against her shoulder. "You say that," he choked, "but I know what happens next. You start caring about someone romantically and I become second place."

She froze. "Sloan…"

He stepped back, eyes wild. "You like him."

"Sloan—"

"You do," he said, voice cracking. "And you're terrified of that."

Her pulse thundered. "Stop."

"You think I don't see it? The way you look at him?"

"Stop it."

"The way you light up when you talk about him?"

"Sloan—"

"You want him!"

"STOP!" she cried.

"And you're pulling away from me because you don't know how to want us both."

"STOP IT!" Tears surged abruptly behind her eyes. "You don't know what you're talking about."

"I know EVERYTHING," he shouted, voice shaking. "I know you. I know your patterns. I know how you get when you feel something real."

"Sloan…please—"

"And I know you're running from him because you're scared he'll see what you went through!"

She froze. The air punched out of her lungs. "Don't," she whispered.

But Sloan couldn't stop. Not anymore. "He'll see the scars," he said, voice trembling. "He'll ask what happened. And you don't want to tell him."

Her chest caved in. "Stop."

"He'll find out how you flinch when someone moves too fast, or how you panic when you're touched unexpectedly, or how you still wake up shaking some nights—"

"STOP IT!" she screamed, voice breaking entirely.

"—and you think that makes you unlovable!"

Her knees buckled. She grabbed the edge of the counter to stay upright. "You don't understand," she choked. "You have NO idea what it feels like to carry this around."

"Syd—"

"You have NO idea," she cried, tears finally breaking loose, "what it feels like to know someone hurt you so badly you flinch at your own shadow! To have scars you can't hide! To feel like damaged goods wearing a pretty tattoo!"

"Syd—stop—"

"And you think it's easy?!" she sobbed. "To just… let someone in? To let someone SEE that?!"

Sloan's face crumpled. "It's not easy," he whispered. "I know it's not."

"No, you don't," she whispered harshly. "You don't understand what he makes me feel. And how terrifying that is."

Sloan swallowed, voice wrecked. "I know you love him."

She shattered. "GET OUT," she whispered, shaking.

"Syd—"

"GET OUT BEFORE I SAY SOMETHING I CAN'T TAKE BACK."

"Sydni—"

"GO!"

He took a step. Stopped. Turned to her with tears in his eyes. She knows this spiral with him, but this one stung deep. "I'm scared," he whispered, coming back to his senses. "That's all this is. I'm scared of losing you."

"You're not losing me," she whispered. "You're hurting me."

His jaw trembled. And then he said the wrong thing. The worst thing. "I don't want to lose you because you'll choose him."

"Sloan…"

He grabbed the doorknob to leave. He pulled it open—

And Elias stood there. Bakery box in one hand. A folded note in the other. And a look on his face like someone had just knocked the wind out of him.

His eyes darted from her tear-streaked cheeks to Sloan's red eyes to how close they were standing.

"…So it's true?" he whispered.

Sloan froze.

Elias stood frozen in Sydni's doorway like some ghost conjured at the worst possible time. His eyes darted from her tear-bright face to Sloan's rigid posture, then down to the bakery box in his hand, as if suddenly remembering he was holding it.

He swallowed. Hard. "I… uh…" His voice cracked. "I was just dropping this off."

Sydni blinked rapidly, wiping her face with her sleeve. "Elias—"

But Sloan stepped forward like a shield. "You don't have to say anything."

"Don't," Sydni whispered, panicked. "Sloan, don't."

But Elias didn't move. Didn't speak. Just stared. And the hurt there. God, she felt it like a physical blow.

Sloan dragged a hand across his face. "This is my fault," he muttered to Elias. "You didn't hear—"

"I heard enough," Elias said. His voice wasn't angry. It wasn't cold. It was worse. Soft, wounded, confused. He lifted the bakery box weakly. "I… um… Nora made cookies. She said you liked the ones Sydni brought to lunch last month. I was just going to drop them off and—" He trailed off, because nothing he said made sense in this moment.

Sydni took a shaky step toward him. "Elias, please, it's not—"

"Syd," he said, and the nickname alone nearly split her open.

Sloan visibly winced.

"Are you two…?" He didn't finish the question. Maybe he couldn't.

Sydni felt the room spin. "No. We're not. That's not—"

But Sloan, still trying to fix the unfixable, jumped in. "Look, man, I messed up, okay? I shouldn't have—"

"Yeah," Elias whispered. "I know."

Sloan's face crumpled.

Elias looked at Sydni again with a quiet devastation, and she hated herself for it. "You don't have to explain anything," he said. "You don't owe me that."

"But I want to—"

"It's okay." His voice broke, barely audible.

No, she thought. *No, it's not.*

He shifted the bakery box in his hand, suddenly unsure what to do with it. "Just wanted to drop these off. That's all."

Her throat tightened. "Elias—"

But he stepped back. Slowly. Carefully. Like he was afraid any sudden movement would shatter her. Or himself.

Sloan moved forward, desperate. "Hey, man, really…this is a misunderstanding."

"It's fine," he said again, though everything in his expression screamed it wasn't.

He turned to leave.

Sydni's heart lurched. "Please don't go."

He paused, shoulders tense. For a heartbeat, she thought he might turn around. But he didn't.

"I'll see you around," he whispered.

Then he walked away.

And the click of her apartment door closing behind him felt like the loudest sound Sydni had ever heard.

~*~

She stood there long after he disappeared down the hall, her chest tight, her body locked in place.

Sloan turned back toward her, guilt spilling from every haunted line of his face. "Sydni…"

She shook her head. "Don't."

"I didn't mean for that to happen."

"Don't," she repeated, voice cracking.

"Syd…" Sloan's voice was small now. "I'm so, so sorry."

Her chest tightened painfully. Because he was sorry. Because he was right. Because she hated hearing the truth when she wasn't ready for it. Because Elias had seen something she had spent months trying to bury. Because she saw the way he looked at her when he said, *You don't owe me that*. Because he believed she and Sloan were together. Because she didn't know how to fix this.

She covered her face with both hands, tears slipping hot down her cheeks. "I can't—I can't do this right now."

Sloan stepped closer, reaching out tentatively. "Let me—"

"Please go," she whispered.

He froze. "Sydni, please don't shut me out."

"I just…" She swallowed the ache in her throat. "I need space."

He hesitated. "Okay."

But not before saying quietly, brokenly, "I'm still on your side."

Then he slipped out of her apartment, closing the door gently behind him. Just leaving her alone in the hollow silence that followed. And for the first time in months, Sydni felt herself collapsing into old patterns. Fear, shame, and grief curling around her ribs like vines.

She slid down the wall, hugging her knees to her chest. God, this was the worst part of any rom-com, she thought to herself.

Her thoughts spiraled:

He thinks I'm with Sloan.
He thinks I'm a liar.
He thinks I don't care.
He thinks… he thinks…

But the worst one, the one she couldn't outrun, the one that echoed loudest in the empty apartment.

I think I wanted him to know. I think I wanted someone to see how I feel. I think I'm the one who's been running.

~*~

Elias didn't remember walking down the hallway.

Not really. He remembered the carpet pattern in a strange, hyper-focused way, as if his brain was desperate to latch onto anything other than the sound of Sloan's voice saying:

"That's all this is. I'm scared of losing you."

Those words echoed so loudly he wasn't sure if they'd been shouted or whispered or simply carved into his bones. He remembered Sydni's panic. He remembered Sloan's protective stance. He remembered the look they shared. Brief, charged, meaningful to someone standing outside that door.

Meaningful to him.

He didn't remember the elevator ride. Or the parking lot. Or the drive home. Only when he was sitting in his car, engine still running in his driveway, did he realize he'd made it there at all. Clementine barked from the other side of the door, her happy thumps vibrating the wood.

Elias didn't get out. He gripped the steering wheel, knuckles pale. Jaw tight. Chest aching in a way he wasn't prepared for. Because what he'd overheard felt like a puzzle snapping into place. A painful one. Just panic. Just fear of being exposed. And Sloan. God, Sloan standing there like a boyfriend defending his territory.

Elias leaned his forehead against the steering wheel. Of course. Of course, Sydni and Sloan were together.

Why hadn't he seen it sooner? The touch that lingered a beat too long. The private jokes. The familiarity. The way Sloan always stepped in front of her when he got protective. The way he looked at her sometimes, not as a friend, but as someone who carried a piece of his heart.

Elias felt something twist inside him. He wasn't angry at them. He wasn't even angry at her. He was angry at himself. *Nora was right. He should've asked.* He should've clarified months ago. But instead he'd built hopes in small, cautious layers: Friday lunches, inside jokes, encouragements, a walk at sunset He'd let himself believe that maybe…*Maybe she saw something in him, too.*

He finally shut off the car and opened the door. Clementine bounded out into the yard, tail wagging, unaware that anything in her person's world had shifted. Elias leaned against the side of the car, staring at the sky as the first stars peeked out.

He let the truth settle. She's not mine to want. She never was.

Inside, Clementine dropped her leash at his feet, nudging his knee with her nose. He knelt and buried a hand in her fur, using her steady warmth to keep himself grounded.

"You'd tell me if I was being stupid, huh?" he whispered into her neck.

She licked his chin. He huffed out a laugh that didn't feel like one. "Yeah. That's what I thought." He rubbed her ears, staring at nothing.

He wasn't going to text Sydni. Not tonight. Maybe not again. She deserved whatever love she'd found with Sloan. And Sloan, despite his territorial attitude, was clearly someone who would fight for her, protect her, stand by her.

Elias couldn't resent that. He admired it. He envied it. He wished, selfishly, that he had been that for her. But he wasn't. So he did the only thing he knew how to do when something hurt: He folded it up gently, like a letter he wasn't meant to read, and tucked it away somewhere deep.

Clementine pressed her forehead to his shin. He inhaled shakily. "Yeah," he whispered. "I know. We'll be okay."

But even as he said it, he couldn't shake the feeling that tonight, that moment in the doorway, had changed something he couldn't get back.

CHAPTER FIFTY-THREE

By mid-afternoon, her work laptop stared at her with the unforgiving glow of a half-finished grant. She reread the same paragraph four times. The words danced, thinned, blurred. It wasn't burnout; she knew burnout. This was more like her brain was walking through wet cement. She was happy that things were settling with Sloan.

She typed a sentence. Deleted it. Typed it again. Deleted it again. This wasn't like her, not the *new* her.

When her phone buzzed, her pulse jumped… and immediate disappointment followed. Not Elias. Just spam about car insurance.

"Fantastic," she muttered.

~*~

Sloan popped in later without knocking. His sunglasses were still on, and he was holding a bag of takeout. "You look like a Victorian ghost who hasn't eaten since June," he announced.

"Wow," she replied dryly, "you really know how to make a girl feel alive."

He dropped the bag on her counter, studying her face. "How's the grant going?"

"Fine."

"How's therapy?"

"Fine."

"How's your brain?"

"…also fine."

He crossed his arms. "You've said 'fine' three times, which statistically means nothing is fine."

She smirked despite herself. "You're annoying."

"And you're deflecting," he shot back gently. "Anything you want to—"

"Nope," she cut in. Too quick. Too sharp.

He paused. Something flickered behind his expression, concern, maybe. Or recognition. But Sloan didn't push. He never pushed until he *really* needed to. "Okay," he said finally. "But at least eat the food. I'm pretty sure you've survived on caffeine and unspoken feelings all day."

She threw a napkin at him, but she did smile. A small one. But still, a smile.

Sloan watched her for another moment, a quiet evaluation passing over his features, then let it go.

~*~

That night, Sydni sat on her couch with her laptop open, trying, and failing, to journal. The blinking cursor felt accusatory. She typed two words, deleted them, closed the document entirely.

She was doing well. She *was*. But she felt slightly… crooked inside. Like she was walking while holding something off-center. She checked her phone again. Still nothing. Her chest didn't ache, exactly, but it tightened. Something small and private and easily hidden.

Before bed, she forced herself to complete one task: laundry. She folded it. Put it away. Didn't leave it in a pile. Didn't let it grow. A tiny victory. Except victories didn't feel triumphant tonight. They felt like reminders of something she couldn't name.

As she turned off the lights, she whispered into the dimness of her bedroom,

"I shouldn't care this much." And because she said it out loud…she knew it wasn't true.

~*~

September arrived without asking permission. Quiet mornings, earlier sunsets, warm days that pretended summer wasn't fading. For Sydni, it felt like moving through a slow, humming fog. Not dark. Not crushing. Just… muted.

She kept going. She always kept going. Her routines slipped in tiny ways at first. Not enough to alarm anyone. Not enough to undo the progress she'd fought for. Just… small shifts.

Her ten-minute walk became eight. Eight became seven. On a few mornings, she didn't go at all. She stared at the wall instead, telling herself she'd walk after lunch. She didn't.

She still showered daily, still made her bed, still showed up to therapy every week, still hit her work deadlines. But the *lightness* she'd felt in July? It had thinned around the edges. The things that used to feel like forward motion now felt like maintenance. Like holding ground instead of hiking upward.

She tried to reach out again. Once. A short message. Nothing loaded or emotional.

Sydni:
Hope Clementine's still being a menace. How's your week?

Delivered. Read. No response. This time, the silence didn't needle. It landed heavy.

She placed her phone face down, then flipped it back over. Facedown again. Then back. A stupid little dance. She told herself she didn't expect anything. She told herself it didn't matter. But something inside her whispered, *It mattered.*

She shut that voice off.

Work helped. At least that's what she told herself. Her new project, a mid-sized grant for afterschool programming, should've been an easy lift. The kind she used to knock out in a couple days.

Instead, she drifted. She wrote a paragraph. Rewrote it. Rewrote it again. She caught herself staring out her window, mind blank, hands still. She tried to focus. She made lists. Color-coded them. Reorganized them. And when she caught herself hovering her cursor over Elias's name, she snapped the laptop closed like it was radioactive.

"Nope," she whispered. Firm. Final.

She didn't need distraction. She didn't need hope. She didn't need the tug in her chest that had started the moment she'd looked at him during trivia night.

Nope. Absolutely not.

~*~

Sloan noticed. Of course he noticed.

He noticed she laughed at his jokes but didn't laugh *through* them. He noticed she made coffee but let it grow cold. He noticed her walks got shorter. He noticed she didn't ramble about her latest grant statistics the way she usually did.

He gave her space at first. Then, one afternoon, he didn't. He let himself in with his key, again, and leaned in her doorway with a grocery bag hooked on his wrist. "You alive?"

She raised an eyebrow from the couch. "Define alive."

He didn't smile. Not yet. He scanned her. Messy bun. Blanket cocoon. Laptop untouched. Eyes tired.

"You want to tell me what's going on?"

"Nothing's going on."

"Okay, rephrasing: you want to tell me what's *actually* going on?"

She groaned and covered her face with a pillow. "No, Sloan. I don't want to talk about anything. I just want… quiet."

He stared at her for a long beat, jaw flexing like he was trying to hold back a thousand questions. Then, gently, "Did you tell Elias the truth? Did you tell him that we aren't together?"

She sat frozen. And Sloan saw it. "Syd?"

"Nothing happened," she said quickly. Too quickly. "Seriously. We're just… you know. Busy. It's fine."

He opened his mouth. Closed it. Sat beside her on the couch, placing the grocery bag down. "Okay," he murmured. "If you say so."

But he didn't believe her. She knew he didn't.

He stayed anyway. Not pressing. Not prying. Just… existing beside her.

~*~

Nights were the hardest. That's when the silence got louder. She didn't spiral back into her old patterns. No disappearing from the world, no collapsing into her bed for days, no dishes piling into mountains. She'd worked too hard to let herself fall that far again.

But she felt the wobble. The unevenness. The fragility of the emotional scaffolding she was still building. And late one night, after staring too long at her ceiling, she opened her laptop, clicked on her journal file, and typed a single sentence before deleting it:

I think I miss him.

Her throat tightened. She shut the laptop.

~*~

Therapy helped. But she was tired of crying in that room. Dr. Wexler noticed immediately. Sydni kept conversation surface-level, overly polite. Guarded. Not resistant. Just… weary.

"Sydni, it's okay if this season feels heavier than the ones before it. Progress isn't a straight line."

"I know."

"Are you letting yourself feel what you need to feel… or are you trying to outrun something?"

"…maybe both."

"You don't lose the ground you've gained just because you feel unsettled," she said. "Your progress is still real."

Sydni nodded, though she didn't entirely believe it. Not yet.

The month faded away. She went on five-minute walks and called it victory. Because, for her, it was. She finished her grant and submitted it. She kept her apartment tidy. She had dinner with Sloan once a week. She breathed. She survived. She kept moving.

But every so often—

Her fingers hovered over her phone. Waiting for encouragement pings that didn't come. Wondering if she'd misunderstood everything. Wondering if maybe she shouldn't have reached out. Wondering if vulnerability always carried this weird afterburn.

And she hated that she wondered at all.

As September closed, she typed one journal line before bed. Honest, unfiltered, and even bold:

I miss him. And I hate that I do. But pretending I don't hurts worse.

She closed the laptop gently, like shutting a truth back inside.

Another month done. Another season shifting.

CHAPTER FIFTY-FOUR

October drifted in with leaf-smelling breezes and front-porch pumpkins, the kind of month that made the world feel calmer than it actually was. Sydni moved through it somewhere between steady and uncertain. Functional, present, improving… but still carrying the echo of August and September in her chest.

She wasn't sinking anymore. But she wasn't soaring, either. She was *floating.* And for the first time in weeks, that felt like enough.

Sloan, naturally, disagreed. He sprawled across her couch one evening, legs crossed, eating an entire bag of kettle corn he swore he didn't buy for himself. Sydni sat across from him, typing on her laptop, pretending she couldn't feel him staring.

Finally, he spoke. "You know what would fix everything?" he said.

"No," she replied without looking up. "And I'm not asking."

"Honesty. Radical honesty. Soul-baring honesty. Preferably directed at one tall, early-thirties man who owns a golden retriever. You know, telling him that you aren't dating your best friend. Your platonic soulmate?"

She stopped typing. Slowly closed her laptop. "Sloan," she said carefully, "I'm not dragging Elias back into the trenches. Not after the summer he had. Not after the silence. Not after— everything."

"I'm not saying you need to confess undying love," he said. "Or medium-dying love. Or light allergic reactions of love. Just talk to him like a functioning human before you develop permanent neck tension."

"No."

"You sure?"

"Yes."

Sloan sighed dramatically and flopped backward like a wilted fern. "You're killing me. Slowly. Painfully. Like death by paperwork papercuts."

She threw a pillow at him. He pretended to die. Their friendship, after everything, felt whole again. Not perfect. But stronger in the way things get when they're broken and put back together intentionally.

~*~

Then the invitation arrived. Victoria's Annual Halloween Bash.

A massive group chat message filled with emojis, glitter confetti GIFs, and the very firm statement:

COSTUMES REQUIRED.
NO BORING EXCUSES.
I KNOW WHO YOU ARE.

Sydni snorted. "She's terrifying."

"She's magnificent," Sloan corrected, reading over her shoulder. "And also terrifying. We're going."

Sydni blinked. "We are?"

He tilted his head toward her. "Do you want to go?"

She hesitated. A month ago, she would've said no. Two months ago, she would've disappeared into her blanket cocoon. But now? She wasn't really drowning. She wasn't frozen. She wasn't fragile glass anymore. "I… think I do," she said.

Sloan grinned. "Then we're going. And we're getting stupid costumes."

~*~

Costume shopping turned into chaos within three minutes.

They entered the seasonal store, and Sloan immediately sprinted toward the inflatable section. "Oh my god," he gasped. "SYDNI. You could go as a T-Rex."

"I am not wearing an inflatable dinosaur."

"Okay, but imagine the photos."

"No."

He grabbed another package. "Fine. Then go as this very angry slice of pizza."

"I am also not going as pizza."

"Why not? Pizza is universally loved."

"I don't want to be universally eaten."

He held up a sexy vampire costume. "This?"

"Absolutely not."

A giant pickle suit. "This?"

"No."

A disco ball. "This?"

"…maybe."

Sloan froze. "Wait. Are you serious?"

"No," she laughed, finally laughing the way she used to. Freely, without thinking about whether she deserved to.

They wandered the aisles for almost an hour, trying on ridiculous hats and masks, posing in front of the funhouse mirrors, quoting horror movies badly. Sloan put on a full-body cow suit and mooed loudly enough that a child cried in the next aisle.

Sydni couldn't stop laughing. Real laughter. Whole-bodied laughter.

She ended up choosing a vintage-style witch costume: flowy black dress, celestial-patterned shawl, and a pointed hat that looked less tacky and more whimsical.

Sloan chose a vampire costume that made him look like he'd stepped out of an 80s music video. His cape sparkled. His hair swooped dramatically.

"You look like a villain from a soap opera," Sydni said.

"You say that like it's an insult."

That's when his phone buzzed. A very specific buzz. A text he read quickly. Too quickly. Sydni noticed immediately.

"Who's that?"

"No one."

She raised a brow. "Really."

"Yes, really," he said, stuffing the phone into his pocket. "Focus on the fact that I'm going to be the most stunning vampire at this party."

"Sloan…"

"We are not doing this," he said firmly, but not unkindly. "Not tonight."

She let it go. He let the subject drop. But the flicker of something: nervousness, excitement, something else entirely lingered on his face.

CHAPTER FIFTY-FIVE

By the time Halloween night arrived, Sydni felt… steady. She tamed her hair into waves under the witch hat, applied dark lipstick she normally avoided, and adjusted the shawl draping over her shoulders. Her ink showed beautifully, colors weaving down her arms like constellations.

She looked in the mirror and whispered, "You're allowed to have fun." And for once, she believed it.

Sloan emerged from her bathroom wearing his ridiculous vampire getup, fangs, and all. He struck a dramatic pose. "Do I look mysterious?"

"You look like you drink expired wine and seduce people by accident."

"Perfect."

He studied her for a moment. Really studied her. "You look amazing, Syd."

She rolled her eyes. "Stop."

"I'm serious."

She smiled. "Thank you."

They headed to Victoria's party side by side, costumes swishing, the crisp October air cool against their cheeks. Neither of them, not even a little, had any idea what was waiting for them inside that party.

Sydni adjusted her witch hat, smoothed her celestial shawl. She did look… good. Good in a way she hadn't felt in a long time. Her ink glowed under the light, colors rippling over her shoulders and down her arms. Her lips were dark plum. Her eyes rimmed lightly with gold. She looked like someone who belonged at a party and not someone who'd spent months unraveling and stitching herself back together.

"You okay?" he asked, quiet beneath the theatrics.

"Yeah," she said. And for the most part, it was true.

He smiled. "Then let's go let Victoria shriek at us."

Victoria's Halloween party was already an ecosystem of chaos by the time they arrived. Fog machines pumping like dragon breaths, purple and orange lights crisscrossing the ceiling, someone's toddler in a Frankenstein costume running rogue between the snack tables.

Music thumped under Sydni's feet, bass humming through the floorboards. Laughter rose in waves. A punch bowl bubbled ominously like a Wiccan prophecy gone wrong.

They stepped inside and Victoria descended like a glittery Cleopatra tornado. "There you ARE!" she shrieked, hugging Sydni so hard her hat tilted. "My cosmic witch queen! Sloan, my undead problematic king! Kiss my ring!" She offered her hand. Sloan bowed and kissed it with far too much commitment.

"Drama king," Sydni muttered.

He winked and Sydni felt… light. Like the version of herself she'd almost forgotten existed. They drifted toward the drink table, Sloan yammering about mist density while Sydni scanned for a safe corner—

—and then her world tilted.

Someone walked past her. Close enough that his shoulder brushed hers. Close enough that she caught the familiar scent of cedar and cold air. She turned. And Elias was standing there.

He wore a ranger-style costume. Dark green flannel, leather straps across his chest, boots that looked far too normal to be part of a costume. His hair was pushed back, his jaw clean-shaven, eyes warm but startled.

The moment he sees her, he freezes. Like he wasn't prepared. Like she wasn't supposed to be here, but suddenly he can't imagine the room without her in it. "Sydni," he says.

Her heart thumps painfully. "Hi."

The fog machine hisses like God requested a dramatic effect. He took her in slowly, not in a way that made her shrink, but in a way that made her feel seen, fully seen, which was somehow worse and better at the same time.

She opened her mouth to say something…anything.

Sloan materializes beside her a second later, posture shifting like a guard dog spotting a squirrel.

"Oh," Sloan says flatly. "You."

Elias lifts an eyebrow. "Hello to you too."

"Sloan," Sydni whispers sharply.

"What? Someone has to defend your honor."

"From what? A forest ranger?"

"EXACTLY."

Before she can argue, a devil costume sidles up behind Elias—the eyeliner, the smirk, the attitude unmistakable. Nora. She sips her drink. "Wow. Did I walk into a live episode of emotional chaos? Or is this just a costume theme?"

Sloan sputters. "YOU."

Nora sips again. "Tragic."

Sydni stares between them. "Okay. I missed something."

Sydni stepped between them, palms out like a middle-school teacher. "Everyone. Please. Don't make this a scene." But her voice faltered when she turned back toward Elias, because now he was watching her. Really watching her.

"Can we talk?" he asked.

"Yes. Please."

Sloan made a strangled noise. "I'll just be… over there. Simmering."

Nora stalked after him. "Someone has to supervise your simmering."

"Don't follow me!"

"Don't walk away from me!"

They bickered into the fog.

And Sydni followed Elias into a quiet hallway, heart pounding. The noise of the party dulled behind them, music replaced by flickering lights from fake candles lining the wall. Fog curled around their ankles like curious ghosts.

Elias leaned against the wall, arms crossing loosely over his chest. He was calm but seemed a little guarded.

Sydni wrapped her shawl tighter. "You look good," she said before she could stop the words.

He blinked, surprised, pleased. "You look… stunning."

Heat crept into her cheeks. "I'm sorry about that night."

He opened his mouth, but she lifted a hand. "Let me get this out, because I've replayed it a hundred times," she said. "That fight with Sloan… it probably looked like something it wasn't. It was intense and messy and loud, but it wasn't—" she swallowed, "it wasn't relationship drama."

"Okay."

"And I should've explained sooner," she said. "I know it looked like we were… something. But we're not. We never have been."

A sound of relief escaped him. Almost a release. But he didn't smile. He looked down. Then back at her. "Thank you for telling me," he said. "I… wasn't sure how to ask."

"You didn't have to ask," she whispered. "You deserved clarity."

He nodded. And then, he pushed off the wall, rubbing the back of his neck, exhaling slow and shaky. "I owe you an apology too," he said.

"For what?"

"For not answering you."

Her fingers curled into her shawl, grounding herself.

He kept going. "You reached out. More than once. And I saw every message." A long pause. "I even opened the chat a few times just… staring at the words. Trying to figure out how to respond."

Her heart twisted. Not from hurt, but recognition. "I typed replies," he said. "Deleted them. Rewrote them. Deleted those too. Not because I didn't want to talk to you. I did. I really did."

He lifted his eyes, apology written in every line of his face. "The truth is… I'm bad at not retreating."

Sydni blinked. Elias continued, almost embarrassed:

"When something hits me emotionally, I go quiet. I don't push through it, I pull back. I shut down until I think I've sorted myself out." He tapped his chest once. "It's not about the other person. It's me trying not to make things worse."

He shook his head. "But this time? Retreating did make it worse. And you didn't deserve that. You were trying, and I… wasn't." A beat. "I'm sorry, Sydni."

The vulnerability in his voice cracked something open in her. Relief, understanding, and the realization that maybe they weren't so different after all. Immediately, something inside her unclenched. Something that had been knotted for weeks.

"Thank you," she said. "That means more than you think. It seems we are a lot more alike than we realized. Rinse and repeat, right? Spiral and pull way. And then do it again. I get it."

He nodded, shoulders easing. A silent moment stretched between them. Then, lightly…tentatively: "Are we… okay?" he asked.

She didn't answer immediately. Because the real answer was layered. She wasn't okay. Not yet. But also… yes. She wanted to be. She offered him a small, real smile. "We're… getting there," she said. "If you want that."

His eyes warmed, slow and sure. "I do," he said.

"Then we're okay," she whispered.

They were not instantly back to who they were, and that's okay. Her mind drifted to those movies. The ones where the two people overcome their issues, and it almost feels too easy. This wasn't as easy as it seemed. This whole year has been insane. But she smiles at him anyway.

Sydni and Elias had just settled into a quiet, relieved silence when of course that's when Sloan appeared, bursting through the fog like a Victorian ghost with unresolved issues. "Sydni!" he cried. "I have made peace with your forest man!"

"Sloan—"

Nora dragged behind him, muttering, "I tried to stop him. He has no brakes."

Sloan planted himself dramatically beside them. "I have something to say."

"Oh God," Nora groaned.

Sydni pinched the bridge of her nose.

Elias smiled, amused.

"For being a territorial troll," Sloan said, gesturing vaguely at his own body as if it were the problem. "And for acting like a badly written Hallmark boyfriend. And for—" he motioned at Sydni "—whatever the hell that was at the door that you overheard."

"Sloan," Sydni groaned, "stop talking."

"No," he insisted, hand still on his chest. "Let me finish, this is my character growth arc."

Nora snorted. "You don't have an arc. You have a repeated loop."

Sloan whirled on her. "I will NOT be disrespected in my own monologue."

"You're in a community center dressed like a glittery vampire," Nora said. "Let's not overstate the setting."

He gasped like she'd stabbed him. "My CAPE is AUTHENTICALLY SOURCED."

Sydni's head dropped into her hands. Elias smiled, looking amused. The tension had completely evaporated.

Sloan cleared his throat, regaining his tiny scrap of dignity. "Anyway," he said, turning back to Elias, "I thought, incorrectly, that you hurt Sydni. And because I love her—"

"Sloan—"

"—as a SISTER, Sydni, relax—"

She exhaled.

"—I overreacted. In a way that was both… theatrical and unnecessary."

"That's one way to put it," Nora muttered.

Sloan ignored her again.

"So," he said, standing straighter, "I'm apologizing. Because you didn't deserve that. And because Syd deserves people in her life who don't act like territorial houseplants."

Elias huffed a warm laugh. "I appreciate that. Really."

"Good," Sloan said, relieved. "Because it was exhausting being mad at you. You're annoyingly nice."

Elias shook his head. "Thanks. I think."

"And just for the record," Sloan added, voice lowering to a normal tone, "she and I are not a thing. Never have been. Never will be."

Elias nodded. "I know. We cleared it up."

"No thanks to *you*," Nora chimed in, elbowing Sloan. "You created the confusion."

"EXCUSE ME?!" Sloan snapped. "If SOMEONE hadn't shown up that night to deliver cookies like a Disney prince—"

"Oh my God," Nora said. "You're impossible."

"You're impossible."

"You started it."

"You *exist,* so technically YOU started it—"

Sydni stepped between them like a kindergarten teacher pulling apart two children arguing over markers. "Okay!" she announced brightly. "How about everyone takes ONE step back, breathes, and maybe gets a snack?"

Sloan and Nora glared at each other over her shoulders. Elias looked at Sydni with warm amusement.

"You really wrangle the two of them well," he murmured.

"I deserve a medal," she replied.

For the next hour, the four of them orbited in a strange, hilarious balance. Sloan tried to act chill around Nora. Nora tried (and failed) to disguise being irritated-but-interested. Elias hovered near Sydni in a comfortable, easy way. Sydni felt lighter with every passing minute

At one point, Sloan loudly declared, "NO ONE HERE IS DATING ANYONE," which caused three separate people at the party to stop and stare.

At another, Nora whispered to Elias, "He is insufferable," and Sloan immediately yelled across the table, "I HEARD THAT."

And somewhere in the middle of the chaos, Sydni realized, *she wasn't anxious. She wasn't scared. She wasn't pretending to be okay.* She *was* okay.

Talking with Elias felt natural again. It was easy and they needed easy. And when the night ended, Elias walked her and Sloan to the door. There was no tension. No awkwardness. Just the warm promise of something healing, something starting fresh.

At the doorway, he paused. "Sydni?" he said.

"Yeah?"

He hesitated and she could feel the moment balancing between friend and something more. "Maybe we can… try again," he said. "Not everything we were before. Not all at once. Just… talking again. Checking in. Letting things be easy."

The gentleness in his voice made her chest ache. "I'd like that," she said. "Friends?"

He smiles, small and warm. "Friends. Goodnight, Sydni."

"Goodnight, Elias."

They stepped apart. But her heart did not.

As she and Sloan walked toward the car, Sloan whispered, "You still like him."

She smacked his arm. "Shut up."

He grinned smugly. But Sydni didn't deny it. Because she didn't feel afraid of wanting something.

And the look Elias had given her as he walked into the misty October night? It felt like a door not wide open, but cracked. Not a promise, but a possibility. Hopeful. Exactly what she was ready for.

CHAPTER FIFTY-SIX

The apartment felt strangely silent when Sydni got home. Not heavy, not hollow, just… still. The kind of stillness that comes after a storm finally breaks apart into sunlight. She kicked off her boots, hung up her shawl, and stood in the middle of her living room with her witch hat dangling from one hand.

Her cheeks were still a little pink. From the laughter. From the embarrassment. From the relief. From Elias.

She set the hat on her table. Then she crossed the room, opened her laptop, and pulled up her journal file. For a moment she just sat there, fingers poised above the keys, heart full but unsure where to begin.

Finally, she wrote.

Tonight was… unexpected. Good. Strange. Warm. A little embarrassing. A little healing.

I didn't think I'd be able to face Elias after what he overheard at my apartment. I was convinced he'd think less of me, or think I was a mess, or think Sloan and I were hiding some ridiculous secret romance.

But instead… he listened. He understood. He apologized. I apologized. And it felt easy. Not like stepping onto old ground, but stepping onto something new.

Sloan was ridiculous. He always is but even he managed to (eventually) say something decent. Nora is… something else entirely. I don't know what's going on with her and Sloan, but the tension feels like a sitcom waiting to happen.

But the part that keeps replaying is the way Elias looked at me when I told him Sloan and I never dated. It wasn't relief exactly, not just that. It was something careful. Something like: "Oh. Okay. That changes things."

And then he said he wanted to start fresh. And I didn't realize how badly I needed to hear that.

I'm not sure what this means. I'm not expecting anything. I'm not hoping for anything. But tonight, for the first time in a long time, I didn't feel broken or behind or too much.

I just felt... me.

She read the words twice before saving the file, a smile tugging at her mouth. Her fingers trembled, not in panic, but in something gentler. Something like relief.

This time, journaling didn't feel like dragging feelings out of her. It felt like letting them breathe.

She reached for her phone.

Resolve App → "Non-Work Writing" → Completed

She tapped the checkbox. A little chime sounded, definitely satisfying. Two seconds later, her phone buzzed again. A notification banner slid across her screen:

Encouragement from Elias
"Good job writing tonight."

She curled up on the corner of her couch, pulling a blanket around her shoulders, letting herself savor the tiniest warmth blooming in her chest.

And before she could talk herself out of it, she sent him an encouragement in return.

Encouragement sent to Elias
"Thanks for being kind today. Hope you got home safe."

She didn't expect him to respond. She didn't need him to. But when her phone buzzed again a few seconds later, she smiled.

CHAPTER FIFTY-SEVEN

November arrived the way Sydni liked things to arrive. Gently, without demanding anything of her. The air turned crisp, the sky had that late-autumn gold tint, and for the first time in a long while, she woke feeling almost… balanced.

She stretched beneath her comforter, blinked at the pale morning light, and then felt her phone buzz on the nightstand.

She wasn't expecting anything. Which was why her heart skipped when she saw his name.

Elias:
Morning. Hope this week is kind to you. Clementine says hi and apologizes for shedding aggressively on everything I own.

The smile that spread across her face was involuntary. She typed back:

Sydni:
Tell her she's doing important work.

The reply came immediately.

Elias:
I keep telling her that. She believes she's a gifted visionary.

Sydni:
How's work?

Elias:
Trying to have a productive Monday, but Mondays are unionized and refuse to participate.

She hugged her pillow, warmth settling low in her chest. It wasn't the frantic, emotional messiness of June. This was steady. Comfortable. A rhythm she didn't know she'd missed until this moment.

~*~

Over the next two weeks, something surprisingly effortless happened. They didn't text constantly, but they texted enough. They didn't overshare, but they shared enough. Encouragements on the Resolve app came and went with tiny sparks of connection that felt safe.

And the Friday meet-ups returned naturally, as if the universe had placed them back in her life and said, *Try again, but slower this time.*

There were no declarations. No questions about labels. No pressure. Just two people finding each other again at a comfortable pace.

~*~

Their first Friday outing of November, they wandered the aisles of Warm Oak Books, each holding a paper cup of far-too-hot coffee. The place smelled like dust, vanilla, and nostalgia.

"This section is dangerous," Sydni said, tapping the spine of a fantasy novel with dragons on it. "I'll end up buying something with a twelve-book commitment."

Elias held up a thick hardcover. "Is this the one you once declared 'a crime against literature'?"

She stopped mid-sip. "It is. Burn it."

He put it back immediately. "I would never betray your moral compass."

"Good," she said. "I take book recommendations seriously."

They drifted slowly, comfortably, shoulder occasionally brushing shoulder. At one point she reached for a book on a low shelf and her shirt shifted, revealing the faint ink wrapping her side. Elias didn't stare, he'd seen her tattooed skin before. There was no shock, no hesitation, no pity in his expression.

He simply asked, "What's that one mean?"

She looked down at the piece. Bold lines, soft shading, a symbol she rarely explained. "It's… a reminder," she said.

He nodded thoughtfully. "A beautiful one."

The ease in his tone loosened something deep inside her ribcage.

~*~

Their second Friday meet up, the farmer's market was buzzing with late-fall energy. People bundled in scarves, kids dragging parents toward kettle corn, dogs sniffing everything.

Sydni accepted a sample of apple cider, took a sip, and sighed dramatically. "This tastes like autumn wrote a love letter to itself."

"That is… absurdly poetic," Elias said. "I'm concerned."

"Oh hush—"

A pumpkin rolled off a vendor's table, barreling straight toward a fragile stand of handmade earrings. "NO—NO—NO—" Sydni lunged, catching the pumpkin just before it destroyed an entire artisan's livelihood.

The vendor gasped. "You are a hero!"

Elias clapped with theatrical flair. "A savior of produce."

"I'm ignoring both of you," she said, breathless and laughing.

The vendor rewarded her with a free mini-pumpkin. Sydni named it Phyllis.

Elias gave her a very serious nod. "She looks like a Phyllis."

~*~

The next Friday, the café table wobbled like it had a personal vendetta. Every time Elias shifted, the salt shaker nearly leapt into her lap.

"This table is clearly possessed," he said.

"I told you not to anger the furniture."

"I breathed."

"Exactly."

They ate sandwiches, talked about nonsense and meaningful things at the same time, and somewhere between his sarcastic commentary and her eye-rolling, Sydni caught herself watching him with the kind of fondness that used to terrify her.

He leaned back, watching her, unable to hide his smile.

~*~

By mid-November, grocery stores were already sold out of half their pie crusts, and Sydni found herself wandering through the aisles with Sloan at an ungodly hour. Midnight grocery shopping was their sacred tradition.

Sloan tossed a box of stuffing mix into their cart. "This is the brand you hate, yes?"

"I despise it."

"Perfect. It's tradition."

The cranberry sauce made a loud *thunk* as she tossed it in.

Sloan gasped dramatically. "You wound me. That was aggressive."

"You'll survive."

"We'll see."

They giggled like overtired children. It felt… normal. And she felt fully present.

~*~

Thanksgiving Eve

They cooked until 2 a.m., making the kitchen look like the site of a culinary explosion. Sloan narrated the chaos like a Food Network dropout. "This turkey is judging me," he muttered.

"It's dead, Sloan."

"Even more reason to fear its power."

By the time Sydni crawled into bed, exhausted and smelling like butter and grief counseling brochures, her phone vibrated with an encouragement from the Resolve app.

Elias:
Happy almost-Thanksgiving. I hope tomorrow brings you peace and lots of carbs. You deserve both.

Sydni pressed her phone to her chest and whispered into the dark, "Yea, maybe I do."

Thanksgiving morning crept into Sydni's apartment slowly, like the sunlight knew better than to burst in uninvited. She woke to the smell of cinnamon and the faint clatter of something metallic in the kitchen.

For a moment, she panicked. Then she heard Sloan mutter, "Why does every spatula in this apartment betray me?"

She smiled into her pillow. Dragging herself out of bed, she pad into the living room wearing mismatched socks and an oversized sweatshirt. Sloan stood at the stove in plaid pajama pants and a shirt that read: *Gobble Gobble, Witches.*

He looked oddly dignified, considering he was cooking potatoes with the confidence of a man who'd watched one YouTube video at 2 a.m.

"Well, good morning, Sleeping Beauty," he said without turning. "I trust your dreams were full of mental stability and healthy coping mechanisms?"

"They were full of you burning my kitchen down," she replied, rubbing her eyes.

He pointed a wooden spoon at her. "I have not burned down a single kitchen. In my entire life. Yet." The "yet" hung ominously in the air.

But Sydni, instead of worrying, laughed. It felt like a stretch of joy in her chest.

"Coffee?" he asked, already reaching for her favorite mug.

She nodded, sitting at the counter. "Please make it strong. Like emotionally unavailable strong."

"Say less," he said, and began the sacred ritual of over-caffeinating her.

They spent the next hour working in quiet partnership, the only sounds the low hum of the fridge, the simmer of butter, and Sloan's occasional dramatic gasp whenever he thought a dish was "too ugly to live." At one point he paused, watching her with something gentle in his eyes.

"You doing okay today?" he asked.

She felt the question beneath the question. The check-in. The care.

"I think so," she said. "Better than last year."

He nodded. "You're allowed to feel good about that."

"I'm… trying."

"Good. Try harder."

"How are you, Sloan? You good?"

Sloan looks at her, knowing that she truly cares. "I'm okay. Besides, I have my favorite Thanksgiving partner who will cry at the parade. Why wouldn't I be?"

She threw a napkin at him, always throwing something. He grinned.

They curled up on the couch with plates of too-hot breakfast and watched the Macy's parade. Sydni pretended not to tear up at the big Broadway numbers. Sloan pretended not to notice but handed her tissues anyway. When a giant Snoopy balloon drifted across the screen, Sloan whispered, "I would die for him."

Sydni snorted into her coffee. "You need therapy."

"I do. And unlike SOME people, I actually go."

She kicked him lightly. He laughed. The apartment felt full.

~*~

Before starting lunch, they sat on the floor under the window, a tradition they'd invented the first year she and Sloan spent Thanksgiving together. Two cups of tea. One moment. And space to say the thing that hurt most.

"You don't have to share," Sloan said. "But if you want to…"

Sydni swallowed. The steam from her cup curled in front of her. "I miss them," she whispered. "My parents. And Jonathan. It hits me every year. But… this year feels different. Not easier. But different."

Sloan didn't interrupt. He didn't fill the silence. He was just *there*. "That's growth," he finally said. "Pain staying the same doesn't mean *you* haven't changed."

Her eyes filled. "Why are you so good at this?"

He shrugged. "I learned from the best."

Her throat tightened. "Thank you," she said. "And you know I'm always here for you, no matter what, right?"

"Always."

~*~

Lunch preparation devolved into chaos.

Sloan dropped a spoon into the mashed potatoes and screamed like it was a crime scene. Sydni nearly burned the rolls because she got distracted judging a stranger's casserole recipe online.

They danced to 90s pop while cleaning up, badly, loudly, off-rhythm. It was messy. It was imperfect. It was real. And somewhere between setting the table and carrying the turkey to the counter, the heaviness in her chest loosened. They sat down, plates full, and clinked glasses of sparkling cider.

"To survival," Sloan said.

"To progress," she said.

"To not setting anything on fire."

"That was on you," she said, pointing at him.

He gasped dramatically. "Slander!"

They ate. They laughed. They talked about everything and nothing. Holidays were always the hardest without her family. But for a few precious hours, Sydni felt… okay.

~*~

When the sun dipped low and the apartment glowed an amber color, Sydni curled into the couch and opened her laptop. Sloan dozed in the recliner, one hand over his face like a father recovering from holiday chaos.

She wrote slow, honest, tender.

I'm realizing today that family doesn't always look the way I thought it would. Sometimes it's the people who stay, even when I fall apart. Sometimes it's the friend who refuses to let me disappear into the fog. Today hurt. But today was also good. Both things can be true.

Grief is an ugly thing. And this year has been a roller coaster, so much back and forth. But it was a good Thanksgiving.

She logged it into Resolve. A moment later, her phone buzzed.

Elias:
Happy Thanksgiving

And she smiled…small, tired, real.

CHAPTER FIFTY-EIGHT

The Saturday after Thanksgiving crept in slow and gray, the kind of morning that made the whole world feel like it was wrapped in a blanket. Sydni woke to the sound of rain tapping her window and the faint ache of having laughed too hard the night before.

She made her way into the kitchen to find Sloan already awake, sitting at her counter with a bowl of cereal and an expression that suggested he'd been doing "deep thinking" which usually meant he had approximately one brain cell left functioning. "Morning," she said, grabbing a mug.

He squinted. "Why are you up? It's Saturday. We hibernate on Saturdays."

"It's noon."

He checked his phone and gasped. "Tragic."

She slid into the seat across from him as he pushed the cereal box toward her in offering. She declined with a smile.

"You good?" he asked, surprisingly gentle.

"I think so," she said. "Yesterday was… good. Really good."

Sloan nodded. "You needed a win."

"I did. So did you" She hesitated, then added, "And it kind of felt like… we deserved it?"

He set his spoon down. "Look at you having breakthroughs before breakfast."

She rolled her eyes, but warmth bloomed low in her chest.

They spent the late morning cleaning up the small mess left from the holiday: rinsing mugs, folding blankets, arguing about whether cinnamon rolls counted as a balanced lunch, "they're round, that's geometry," Sloan insisted.

In the late afternoon, after Sloan headed out for his shift, Sydni sat on the couch with her laptop, her Resolve goal sheet glowing on the screen. She'd been keeping up with her routine: walking, journaling, and cleaning in little bursts. Something about that consistency made her feel tethered in a good way.

Her phone buzzed.

Elias:
Hope your Thanksgiving was good.

Sydni:
It really was. Quiet. But good. Hope yours was too.

Three dots appeared, vanished, and reappeared.

Elias:
It was. And, um… I made your cookie recipe. It didn't turn out as good as yours. I think you're hiding steps from me.

She laughed out loud, the sound bouncing around in the empty apartment.

Sydni:
I would never sabotage you. …On purpose.

Elias:
That's comforting.

Elias:
Want to do coffee again this coming week? If you're free?

Sydni:
Yeah. I'd like that.

Her reflection in the black window glass looked hopeful. Calmer than she expected. She didn't overthink it. Didn't spiral. Just let herself smile.

She spent the rest of the evening curled up with a book. A romance Sloan had bullied her into reading and found herself lingering on lines about second chances, timing, and people finding their way back to each other unintentionally.

When she finally crawled into bed, she felt settled. And as she drifted to sleep, she let herself imagine, just for a moment, what December might bring.

~*~

And before she knew it, December arrived the way it always did in Illinois. With a wind sharp enough to slap someone across the face and apologize for nothing. Sydni braced herself against it anyway, her scarf wrapped twice around her neck as she made her way down the sidewalk.

Her steps were steady. And her Resolve app buzzing cheerfully as if it weren't twenty-five degrees outside.

10-minute walk completed!

She rolled her eyes but smiled anyway. Progress was progress.

Back in her apartment, she dropped her coat onto the hook and shook the cold from her fingers. Sloan was perched dramatically on her couch, one leg flung over the back like he owned the place

"You look like a woman who faced certain death and won," he said, sipping his coffee.

"It's Illinois in December. Everyone outside is a survivor."

He nodded gravely. "Heroes, all of us."

She laughed, setting down her phone, only for it to buzz again.

Elias:
Coffee tomorrow? Same spot? Unless you're sick of me. Totally valid.

She bit back a grin.

Sydni:
Not sick of you. Coffee sounds good. 11 work?

Elias:
11 works. Looking forward to it.

She let her phone drop onto the table, and Sloan raised a brow.

"'Looking forward to it,' huh?" he said, wiggling his eyebrows. "Sounds like somebody likes you."

"Sloan."

"All I'm saying," he continued, "is that the man responded in under ten seconds. Men only reply that fast when they're either A) avoiding work, or B) interested. Given his whole emotionally-stable-forest-ranger vibe, I'm going with B."

"Sloan."

"And considering he looks at you like you hung the moon—"

"SLOAN."

He put both hands up. "Fine. Fine. Pushing nothing. Saying nothing. Observing everything."

She glared at him until he took a dramatic sip of coffee and shut up. But inside her chest, a warm spark flickered anyway.

~*~

The café was cozy in a way that felt almost purposefully arranged, dim lights reflecting off gold accents, smooth jazz drifting like warm air, the windows fogged from people escaping the cold. And there was Elias, already waiting by the window, hands wrapped around a mug, looking up at her like she was the person he had hoped would walk through the door.

When he saw her unwinding her scarf, brushing snow from her curls, he stood.

"Hi," she said.

"Hey," he replied, eyes bright. "You are going to freeze to death walking around like an underprepared woodland creature."

She snorted. "I will have you know I am adequately layered."

"You are wearing Converse in December."

She looked down at her shoes. "I like my Converse."

"I know," he said, and he smiled in a way that made her world tilt for just a moment. "They're cute. Impractical. But cute."

Her cheeks warmed as she sat down, and he followed suit, something in the air settling. Not tension exactly. More like anticipation.

"So," she said, stirring her latte. "What's new? Work still chaotic?"

"Oh yeah," he said, leaning back in that relaxed way that always made his shoulders look broader. "Everyone wants to squeeze in appointments before the holidays. Who knew physical therapy was the hot December activity."

"Humanity at its finest."

"Truly." His eyes drifted toward her mug, then up to her. "But aside from work, December has been... good."

Her lips lifted. "Really?"

He nodded slowly. "Getting out more. Seeing people. Doing things. I guess I forgot how easy it is to fall into a routine and call it a life."

She raised a brow. "Look at you. Poetic philosopher."

"I am wise," he said, voice completely serious. "Once every seventy-two hours."

She laughed, and his eyes moved to her mouth like he wasn't supposed to, then away quickly.

"So how's therapy going?" he asked gently, fingertips brushing the rim of his mug.

She didn't flinch. Not anymore. "Good," she said honestly. "Hard sometimes. But good. I'm learning myself again."

"That's brave," Elias said, and something in his voice made her pulse misbehave.

"What about you?" she asked. "How are you? Really?"

He hesitated, and she watched him decide how honest to be. "I'm… good too," he said slowly. "Trying to move on from things. Trying to move toward others."

"Oh?"

He smiled. Small, knowing, almost shy, and she felt the heat beneath it. Felt it bloom.

~*~

When they stepped outside, snow fell in spirals, clinging to the ends of her curls. Elias noticed. Of course he noticed.

"Come on," he said, offering his arm. "I'll walk you home before your Converse revolt."

She rolled her eyes but took his arm anyway. His coat was warm beneath her fingers. His body heat curled around her like an invitation she didn't know how to answer yet.

They walked slowly, talking about nothing important. Sloan's inability to cook, Nora's holiday chaos, the neighbor who collected garden gnomes like they were priceless artifacts. He kept glancing at her as she talked, like he was memorizing her expressions, saving each one for later.

At one point her hand slipped from his arm, and he caught it without thinking. Just a quick touch, a light brush of skin against skin, but it sent a clean spark through her. He let go as if realizing what he'd done, but his cheeks flushed, and she couldn't help smiling.

Outside her building, the snow muffled the world around them until it felt like they were standing in their own small pocket of quiet. "So, coffee again next week?"

She nodded. "Yeah. I'd like that."

His smile warmed. "Me too." He hesitated like he wished he had the nerve to say something else, something more explicit, something he wasn't quite brave enough to risk yet. He reached up and brushed a little snow from her curls. Then he stepped back, giving her one last look. A lingering thing that settled behind her ribs long after he walked away.

Sydni stood there for a moment, hand pressed to her scarf, trying to understand why her heart felt like it was opening again… and why this time, she wasn't afraid of it.

CHAPTER FIFTY-NINE

The city in early December was a contradiction. Glowing store windows and bitter, bone-deep cold, festive cheer, and dark gray skies. The world looked ready for a holiday postcard, but the wind had the personality of an insult.

Sydni pushed into the café for their next Friday get together, with a puff of icy air trailing behind her, stomping snow from her shoes. Her hair immediately puffed in the humidity, curls blooming like she'd been electrocuted by the holiday spirit.

She muttered, "Perfect," and tried to smooth it down.

Elias was already at their usual spot. The two-person table near the window that overlooked the street. The garland above the window shimmered, catching the glow of the hanging lights. He looked up at the exact moment she was doing battle with her curls and grinned.

"There she is," he said warmly. "My Friday friend."

She froze halfway through pushing her hair back.

"…your what?" she asked, sliding slowly into her seat.

"Friday friend," he said again, still smiling, oblivious, earnest, and unbothered. "It feels like a little ritual now, you know? I need this in my week. It's good having someone to decompress with."

He meant it sweetly. Genuinely. He was trying. But the words still hit somewhere tender. Friday friend. Friend. Something in Sydni's chest deflated so softly she wasn't sure she even felt it. Just a small shift, a click of understanding.

"Oh," she said lightly. "Yeah. Totally. Friends are good."

He didn't notice the shift. He never did when she was trying to hide something.

"Exactly," Elias said, obliviously cheerful. "It's honestly one of the things I look forward to most during the week."

She nodded, but her throat felt tight. Why did that sting? It shouldn't sting. He was allowed to want friendship. She was supposed to want nothing more. Right?

A barista dropped off their drinks, and Sydni wrapped her hands around her latte like it might anchor her.

"How's work?" he asked, leaning back in his chair.

She inhaled. Okay, if she was just a friend, she could do this. Friends could chat. Friends could be normal. "It's good," she said, genuinely. "Actually good. I finally submitted that DV grant."

"Oh, the big one?"

"Yeah." She smiled. "Final round. I'm… surprisingly proud of it. Three rounds for one grant and excessive."

"You should be," Elias said simply. "You're really good at what you do."

Her cheeks warmed an embarrassing amount, as she hid behind her cup. "And you?" she asked. "How's work on your end?"

"Chaos." He sighed, rubbing his forehead. "One guy cried because I couldn't see him on Christmas Day. I get it, I'm great my job and all, but we are closed on Christmas."

"Oh dear God."

"Oh, it gets better," Elias said, eyes widening. "Another guy told me that I had the hands of an angel. That I was a physical therapy angel and asked me out on a date. I politely turned him down and he kicked the copier."

"Kicked it?"

"Twice."

"Why?"

"Maybe because he felt like kicking me might mean that he loses these magic hands."

Sydni laughed so hard she nearly spilled her drink. The sound escaped her chest freely, light, and bright. God, he really was handsome when he looked at her like that. Too bad she had to stop thinking about that.

"So Nora is apparently making eight kinds of fudge this year," Elias said as he sipped his drink.

Sydni's eyebrows shot up. "Eight?"

"Eight."

"Why?"

"She said, and I quote, 'because I can.' And because she is watching bake off shows."

"That woman needs a hobby."

"She has one. It's fudge."

"That's a cry for help."

Elias grinned. "I'll tell her you said that."

"No, you will absolutely not."

"Yes, I will."

"Oh my God."

He chuckled and leaned in, lowering his voice. "She thinks I need to take some home to give to you."

"Why?"

"Because she says you look like someone who appreciates sugar."

Sydni blinked. "I… don't know how to interpret that."

"It's a compliment, I think."

"You think?"

"She's confusing. But she likes you."

Her heart fluttered uneasily. "Does she… think something is happening between us?" Sydni asked before she could stop herself.

Elias shrugged. "No. I told her we're friends."

She nodded almost too quickly. "Good. I mean…yeah. Right. That's right."

His brow furrowed just slightly, but he didn't question it.

When they finish up their coffee and it's time for Elias to get back to work, they step outside into the sharp winter air, Elias automatically falls into step beside her. "You going straight home?" he asked.

"Probably. Sloan is doing some… bizarre wrapping ritual tonight. He's been watching tutorials."

"Oh God."

"Exactly."

They walked in silence for a moment, snowflakes drifting onto their coats. "Oh, I should tell you," Elias said, adjusting his scarf. "I'm going to be out of town Christmas week."

She felt a small twitch inside. A small, unexpected pang.

"Oh," she said. "That'll be nice. Where to?"

"My aunt's place in Colorado. Cabin. Big family thing. Loud. Messy. Everyone trying to talk over each other." He chuckled. "It's chaos, but it's the good kind."

"That'll be great for you."

"Yeah. I'll be back after New Year's, though," he added quickly, glancing at her. "We'll pick up our Fridays again then."

There it was again. *Fridays. Friends.* A routine. Nothing more.

She nodded. "Sounds good."

He gave her a small smile. And it should have hurt more. But weirdly…It didn't. Not the sharp ache she expected. Acceptance she didn't know she needed.

They reached her building, and he paused. "Thanks for today," he said. "I always feel better after we talk."

"Me too," she admitted.

And because they were friends, she stepped forward and hugged him. He froze for half a breath, then returned it. Her heart didn't race out of control. Her palms didn't sweat. She felt… calm.

"See you next week?" he asked as they pulled apart.

She smiled. "Yeah." She believed she could survive wanting someone she couldn't have, and oddly enough, it was sort of a relief.

When she walked into her apartment, Sydni found Sloan standing in the middle of her living room surrounded by wrapping paper like he'd lost a war to an elementary-school art class.

He had a dead-serious expression on his face, holding a mangled piece of tape between two fingers like it had personally wronged him. "Okay," he announced as she walked in. "I'm convinced scissors are a government conspiracy."

She dropped her keys. "I've been gone an hour, Sloan."

"An hour too long," he said dramatically. "I am fighting for my life."

Sydni surveyed the carnage. Three rolls of wrapping paper, all somehow ripped at weird angles; tape stuck to the coffee table;

two nice gift boxes that now looked like they'd been attacked by raccoons. "What… exactly happened here?"

"I tried to wrap your present," he said, gesturing to a lumpy, misshapen thing covered in Santa paper. "And then physics betrayed me."

"You didn't, I don't know… look up a tutorial?"

"I did!" he said, offended. "But the lady in the video had demonic levels of skill. Her tape stayed where she PUT it."

"With… tape?" she asked.

"Do NOT start with me."

She tried so hard not to laugh. It didn't work. "Okay," she said, wiping tears of laughter. "Step one. Stop using seven pieces of tape on one corner."

"I LIKE OVERKILL."

"And step two. Wrap on a flat surface, not your thigh."

"I reject your authority."

"Sit," she said, pointing to the floor.

He groaned like she'd asked him to climb Everest, but he obeyed.

Sydni knelt beside him, pulling a fresh sheet of wrapping paper. "Okay," she said, "put the box in the center."

He did.

"Fold up the long sides like this."

He copied her.

"Then tuck in the corners—"

The box slipped and shot sideways like a hockey puck. They both stared at it.

"What was that?"

Sloan shrugged, "Maybe your floor is haunted."

"Maybe *you* are."

He sighed, defeated. "Just… do it for me."

"No," she said. "I'm teaching you like a functioning adult."

"You're asking too much."

"You're thirty-three."

"AND?"

She laughed again. These moments, ridiculous and tender, were the reason Sloan was her person. Her platonic soulmate. Her family.

Eventually, after many sighs and several minutes of muttering ("How do children do this? Are they wizards?"), Sloan managed an okay-looking present. It wasn't great. But it was passable. And he looked so proud that Sydni didn't dare point out the crooked seam.

"Let's move to cookies," Sloan declared, tossing the tape aside like he'd won the battle.

"Have you ever baked cookies?" she asked.

"Absolutely not," he said immediately. "But how hard could it be?" Famous last words.

Twenty minutes later, the kitchen looked like a baking apocalypse. Flour spilled on the counter. On the floor. On Sloan. Somehow on the ceiling. "How did you even—?"

"I don't know!" he shouted defensively. "The flour had MOMENTUM!"

They finally got the dough on the sheet and into the oven. Sydni set the timer. Sloan stared into the oven like it was a wild animal that might bite.

"You know," he said, "this is kinda nice."

"Baking?"

"No," he said, bumping her shoulder. "Just… this. You and me. Doing dumb stuff. Feeling normal."

"Yeah," she whispered. "It is nice."

The fire alarm went off.

Sydni yells, "What did you do?!"

"NOTHING! I EXISTED!"

They flung open the oven to find the cookie edges smoking.

"Abort!" Sloan shouted, waving a towel dramatically.

"We're never baking again."

"We don't speak of this."

They opened windows. They laughed until it hurt. They rescued the edible middle parts. It was perfect. And later, after the smoke cleared and the cookies were salvaged, they collapsed on the couch to watch a Christmas movie.

"I picked this one," Sloan said.

"Oh no."

"It has time travel."

"Oh *no.*"

An hour later, Sydni found herself crying into a throw pillow because the time traveler reunited with his lost love during a snowstorm.

Sloan noticed immediately. "You okay?" he asked.

She wiped her cheeks. "Stupid movie."

"It *was* stupid," he agreed, nudging her side gently. "But you're allowed to feel."

"I know," she whispered.

"You're doing really good, Syd."

She swallowed hard. "Thanks, you are too," she whispered back.

And she let herself rest her head on his shoulder. Friendship was safe. Friendship was love too. Just a different kind.

CHAPTER SIXTY

By mid-December, the city had transformed the outdoor market into a glowing maze of color and noise. Strings of golden lights drooped from booth to booth, flickering against the night sky. The air smelled like cinnamon, pine, roasted chestnuts, and the faint but undeniable hint of burnt sugar.

Sydni inhaled it all with a surprised kind of contentment. She hadn't expected this year to feel… light. Not joyful, exactly, but not crushing either. Somewhere in the middle. Somewhere steady.

Beside her, Sloan shoved his gloved hands into his pockets and squinted at the first booth. "Okay," he declared, "we are NOT buying anything ugly. I'm putting my foot down."

"You have terrible taste," Sydni reminded him.

"I have VISION."

"You bought a candle called Frosted Masculinity."

"It smells like confidence."

"It smells like Axe body spray and wintergreen gum."

"Rude."

She laughed, looping her arm through his. "Come on. Let's look around."

They stepped forward into the bustle. Families holding paper cups of cider, couples walking arm-in-arm, teenagers shrieking over glittery ornaments, and a group of carolers who were aggressively enthusiastic but pitch-impaired. It was beautiful. Overwhelming. Alive. Sydni felt like she was part of it.

The first booth they stopped at was run by a man in a Santa hat and a flannel shirt, who greeted them with a booming, "WELCOME TO SCENTED DESTINY!"

Sydni blinked. "Scented… destiny?"

The man nodded fiercely. "Your future lies in wax."

"Oh my God," Sloan whispered reverently. "We've found my people."

The vendor shoved jars toward them enthusiastically.

"This one's called Midnight Kiss!"

Sydni sniffed. "It smells like cotton candy and regret."

"This one's Alpine Lumberjack!"

Sloan inhaled deeply. "Mmm. Smells like a man named Sawyer who chops wood shirtless."

Sydni slapped his arm. "Please behave."

"No."

The vendor thrust another candle forward. "THIS ONE," he said dramatically, "is our bestseller… Cozy Cabin Confessions."

Sydni hesitated. "That sounds… oddly specific."

Sloan's eyes lit up. "We're buying it."

"We don't even know what it smells like."

"We're buying it."

She gave in.

The candle smelled like cedar, vanilla, and the warmth of someone leaning too close in a small room. It was unfairly good. Of course they bought it.

They moved deeper into the market, stopping at a booth decorated with gingerbread men that looked a little too smug. "Let's decorate one," Sydni said.

Sloan gasped. "LET'S DECORATE TWENTY."

They bought two kits. The table was small, crowded, and chaotic. Teenagers next to them were slapping gumdrops on their cookies like they were in a food fight.

Sydni carefully piped buttons onto her gingerbread. Sloan slathered frosting across his like it was spackle. "What is that?" Sydni asked, horror creeping in.

"Art," he said seriously.

"It looks like your cookie has seen things."

"It HAS. He's a survivor."

Her laughter burst out, loud and warm, catching her off guard. And Sloan's expression softened.

"You're laughing a lot more this month," he said.

She paused. "Am I?"

"Yeah. It's good to hear."

"Thanks."

He averted his eyes, busying himself with sticking a crooked smile onto his cookie. "Just saying."

The next booth sparkled with handmade ornaments. Glass, ceramic, wood-carved, all delicate, all beautiful.

"Ooooh," Sydni said, reaching for a little glass snowflake.

Sloan reached for the same moment. Their hands bumped. The snowflake wobbled. The vendor gasped. Both of them froze.

"We are NOT breaking anything," Sydni whispered.

"I would never," Sloan said quickly, slowly retracting his hand like he was defusing a bomb.

They each chose an ornament. Sydni picked a simple, hand-painted star. Sloan picked one shaped like a raccoon wearing a scarf.

"His name is Mister Jingles," Sloan insisted.

"Why?"

"Because he told me so."

"You're unwell."

They stopped for hot chocolate from a booth where the vendor sprinkled cinnamon hearts on top "because it adds whimsy." They sat on a bench, sipping in silence. The cold curled around them, but it didn't feel harsh. Not with Sloan beside her. Not with people laughing and lights flickering and music muffled through the winter air.

Sydni let her shoulders relax. "This is nice," she murmured.

Sloan nudged her knee with his. "Yeah. It is."

"Thanks for coming with me."

"Thanks for inviting me."

They shared a mutual smile. Familiar, genuine, full of years of chosen family. And in that moment, Sydni realized that she didn't *need* romance to feel loved. She didn't need Elias to be happy. She didn't need to push for more. Being his friend was enough. Being herself was enough. She'd built a life here. Messy, chaotic, imperfect, but hers. And she wasn't lonely in it.

Not with Sloan beside her. Not with growth happening in small, steady steps. Not with hope whispering inside her chest.

They had just finished their hot chocolate when Sloan suddenly cleared his throat loudly, dramatically, the way he always did when he was trying to mask nerves with theatrics.

"So," he said, tone artificially casual, "hypothetically speaking… if you were buying a Christmas gift for a woman. A completely random woman with no distinguishing features or identifying details…what would you get?"

Sydni blinked. "That was… weirdly specific."

"Was it?" he asked, staring at a nearby wreath like it held all the answers. "I meant it in a general, non-specific, extremely broad sense."

"Okay… what's she like?"

"No idea."

"You don't know the hypothetical woman?"

"Nope."

"But you want to buy her a gift?"

"It's hypothetical!" he insisted.

She stared at him. He stared at the air.

"Sloan… are *you* okay?"

"Never been better," he lied. Poorly.

She tried again. "What are her interests?"

"Uh…" Sloan shifted his weight. "She, um… she might… like baking."

"'Might'? Or does?"

"She does," he blurted, then winced like he'd confessed something scandalous.

"Okay," Sydni said slowly, stepping into the role of supportive best friend. "Baking is a great starting point. Maybe something for the kitchen?"

"No!" he said quickly. Too quickly. "I mean… not something practical. Something… nice."

"Nice?"

"Yes. Not weird. Not too personal. But also… meaningful. But not too meaningful." He dragged a hand down his face. "This is hard."

Sydni bit back a smile. Was he… blushing?

"Okay," she said, sliding seamlessly into helper mode. "So something thoughtful but not romantic."

"Yes," he whispered, relieved.

"Something sweet but not intimate."

"Exactly."

"Something that says 'I see you' but not 'let's elope.'"

"Wow," Sloan said, impressed. "You're good at this."

"It's my job," she said with a shrug.

He exhaled dramatically, tension leaving his shoulders.

"Okay," he said. "Lead the way."

She looped her arm through his. "Let's find this hypothetical woman the perfect gift."

For a moment, Sloan hesitated for just a second then followed her, trying not to look suspicious, trying not to look hopeful, and trying very, very hard not to smile too much.

When Sydni got home that night, sending Sloan to his home with an adorable heart shaped baking dish, the apartment felt warm in a way she hadn't expected. Maybe it was the twinkling lights she'd strung around the windows. Maybe it was the lingering heat of laughter from the market with Sloan. Or maybe it was simply the feeling of *moving forward* again even if she wasn't sure where forward led.

She changed into her coziest sweatshirt, made tea, and opened her laptop. The blank document stared back. She hadn't journaled in days.

Tonight was good. Really good. I forget sometimes that life can be simple like that. Hot chocolate and cold air and someone who cares enough to drag me into crowds even when I pretend I hate it.

Sloan is ridiculous. And loud. And absolutely the best person to go Christmas shopping with, even with his mysterious "no identifying details" hypothetical woman.

But the truth is... I felt calm today. Steady. And I don't always feel that way.

And when I got home, I realized I hadn't spiraled in a while. I haven't lost myself. I've been here...present...for weeks now.

She paused. The cursor blinked.

I am just going to keep showing up for myself and trust that whatever is meant to happen will find its way.

She reread it. It was honest. Painfully so. But it felt like exhaling.

She saved the entry, tagged it as **"Non-Work Writing,"** and updated it in Resolve.

A second later, her phone buzzed.

Elias:
Hey, hope you don't mind me messaging tonight. I was thinking... before I head out for the holidays, would you want to meet up one more time? Maybe same place as usual? Let me know if you're free.

She typed back:

Sydni:
Yeah, I'd like that. Just tell me when.

The reply came faster than she expected.

Elias:
Lunch on Friday? Same cafe? I can shift my schedule if I need to.

She smiled despite herself.

Sydni:
Friday works. And no shifting. I can make it to you just fine.

Elias:
Good. Looking forward to it.

CHAPTER SIXTY-ONE

Sydni stood in front of her bathroom mirror, holding two sweaters up to her chest. One forest green, one light gray, and groaned. "This is stupid," she muttered to her reflection. "It's lunch. With a *friend*. A friend who is leaving town. A pre–holiday goodbye. Normal. Platonic. Not at all something to stand here agonizing over like I'm prepping for a rom-com montage."

She tossed the green sweater onto the bed. Gray it was.

Her curls cooperated for exactly four seconds before rebelling, so she pinned half of them back and hoped for the best. Cute, but not *trying too hard*. She put on jeans with zero distressing her "emotionally balanced adult" jeans and grabbed her coat.

"Totally casual," she told herself as she locked the apartment door. "Just lunch."

The December cold slapped her cheeks awake as she walked toward the café, boots crunching over patches of leftover snow. The café's windows glowed warm from the inside, fogged around the edges. A couple kids pressed their hands to the glass, pointing at pastries they begged parents for.

It was cozy. Familiar. A good place to land. She pushed open the door, letting the jingle of the bell spill into the morning. Their usual table near the window was open, so she claimed it and set her gloves aside.

She wasn't nervous. She wasn't excited. She was… fine. Shockingly, totally fine.

A few minutes later, the door chimed again. Elias stepped in, brushing snow from his hair, cheeks pink from the wind. His coat was unzipped, scarf crooked, and he looked a little harried, but the moment he spotted her, his shoulders relaxed. "Hey," he said, slipping into the seat across from her. "You beat me."

"Miracles happen," she said. "Sometimes I even show up early just to give the universe a thrill."

He laughed, rubbing his hands together for warmth. It was a friendly laugh. She didn't melt. She didn't float. She was fine.

"How's packing going?" she asked.

"Chaotic. Nora's bringing enough winter gear to survive the Arctic. We're going to Colorado, not Everest."

"So, when are you leaving? Tomorrow?" she asked.

"Yep. We'll be gone a little over a week." He paused to warm his hands around the water glass. "And… you know… today's also my birthday."

She blinked at him slowly. "I'm sorry… WHAT?"

He lifted one shoulder. "Yeah. Didn't want to make it weird."

"You're sitting here across from me, on your ACTUAL birthday, and you didn't tell me?" she gasped.

He laughed, startled. "I didn't think it mattered."

"It absolutely matters!" she hissed. "You can't just spring a birthday on someone like a surprise tax audit!"

"It's not a big deal."

"It's your BIRTHDAY, Elias! That is LITERALLY the definition of a big deal."

He covered his face with one hand, embarrassed and amused. "Okay, okay. I'm sorry."

She narrowed her eyes. "We're circling back to this."

He smiled at her. "I'm sure we are."

Before she could continue scolding him, he asked, "So… when's *your* birthday?"

She looked down at her hands. "August."

He froze. "August… this past August?"

She nodded, "Yep, every August."

His expression dropped into full horror. "Oh God. Sydni, I'm so sorry, I didn't—"

"Well, we weren't exactly on great terms," she reminded him gently. "And I wasn't exactly… celebrating. So don't feel bad."

But he still looked gutted.

"So," she added brightly, "I think we're even."

He shook his head, unconvinced, then signaled the server. They placed their usual lunch orders, grilled cheese for her, turkey-avocado for him, and as the server picked up the menus, Elias pushed back his chair.

"Be right back," he said. "Bathroom."

The moment he disappeared down the hallway, Sydni shot out of her seat like she'd been launched. She bolted to the counter, leaned in, and whispered, "Hey. I need a cupcake. Like. Immediately. A birthday cupcake."

The barista's eyes flicked toward the pastry display. "Chocolate or vanilla?"

"Whatever screams 'you forgot to tell me it was your birthday and now I'm panicking.'"

"Chocolate it is."

"And," Sydni whispered, scanning the counter for anything candle-adjacent, "I need a candle."

"Sorry. We're out."

"Something candle-shaped?"

The barista pointed to a jar full of individually wrapped toothpicks.

Sydni grabbed one like it was a sacred relic. "Perfect. Thank you. I owe you my life."

She hurried back to the table, slipping into her seat just as Elias returned. Their sandwiches arrived moments later… along with a small plate. A chocolate cupcake. Centered perfectly. Waiting.

Elias blinked. "What's—"

Sydni slammed the toothpick into it like she was christening a ship.

"Happy birthday," she declared.

His mouth fell open. "That… that is a toothpick," he said.

"It is a minimalist candle representing the *idea* of flame."

He started laughing. Helpless, joyful, warm laughter that pulled the attention of the entire café. "Oh my God, Sydni."

"Nope," she said, clearing her throat. "No comments. Only birthday spirit."

And she started singing. He covered his face. She sang louder. Someone at the next table chimed in. A toddler clapped. The barista even chipped in.

When she finished, Elias shook his head, still laughing. "That was… very public."

"Birthdays should be public!" she proclaimed.

He looked at the cupcake. Then at her. "Thank you."

"Eat your fake-fire dessert," she nudged.

Instead, he picked up the plate and slid it halfway back toward her. "Half for me," he said. "Half for your August birthday. Since I missed it."

"That's… actually really sweet."

"That's how friendship works," he said simply.

They split the cupcake, sugar sticking to their fingers, and settled into easy conversation. How Nora keeps threatening to knit him a full-body sweater. How one of his patients insists on calling him "Dr. Monk" even though he has corrected him 57 times. How Sydni finished two grants this week and only cried once. How Sloan tried to wrap a gift and used an entire roll of tape.

Every topic drifted into laughter or teasing. And when their time ran out, they bundled up and stepped outside. Snow flurries drifted through the air, collecting in Sydni's curls.

Elias gave her a small smile. "Thanks for lunch," he said. "And for… the birthday surprise. I won't forget it."

"Anytime."

"I'll see you next year?" he asked.

The question was warm. Hopeful and not romantic, at least, not intentionally. But meaningful all the same.

Sydni smiled. "See you next year, Elias."

He walked away, glancing back once with a faint, lingering grin. Sydni stayed there for a moment, letting herself feel the peace of it.

They were friends. That was exactly what she needed.

CHAPTER SIXTY-TWO

Morning arrived with a pale winter light stretching across Sydni's bedroom as if encouraging her to get up gently, not abruptly. She yawned, stretched, and slid her feet into fuzzy socks that had long since lost their elasticity. "Okay," she mumbled to the empty room. "Let's do the whole functional adult thing."

She bundled herself into her coat and stepped outside. The air was cold enough to sting her cheeks. Her steps crunched over thin frost as she started her usual morning walk.

Ten minutes she'd chosen for herself, ten minutes that had become a ritual of choosing her own well-being. Christmas decorations were everywhere: wreaths, lights, a plastic reindeer who'd clearly given up and was now lounging sideways in someone's yard.

When she reached the corner before looping back, she opened her phone and logged the walk into Resolve. A tiny animation of confetti burst across the screen.

You did it! Great job showing up today!

And even though she knew the app didn't *care*, she still smiled.

She had just walked back into her apartment building when Sloan appeared behind her like a six-foot hurricane in flannel. "HEY." He dramatically dropped two grocery bags into her arms. "Emergency supplies."

She staggered. "Sloan! I'm literally still defrosting from outside!"

"We have exactly—" he checked his phone, "—thirty-six hours until Christmas. We need a plan."

"For what?"

"For *Christmas Eve*, Syd. Obviously."

He barreled into her apartment like he owned the place, tossing his coat at absolutely nothing. It fluttered to the floor.

She sighed. "You're not allowed to have caffeine today."

"No promises," he said, already rummaging in her kitchen. "Tomorrow: ugly pajamas. Hot chocolate. Tacky movies. The works."

She leaned against the counter. "You're planning chaos."

"Yes. Festive chaos. You're welcome."

They bickered through half the morning while he reorganized her spice cabinet for the fifteenth time in five years, claiming it "just makes more sense alphabetized." She rolled her eyes but let him ramble. His brand of loud concern was comforting.

After he left, with threats of returning with their "tradition," Sydni sank onto the couch with a warm blanket and a sigh.

That's when her phone buzzed.

Elias:
Just landed. Nora is already complaining about the dry mountain air. Clementine is making new friends at baggage claim. You survived your morning walk?

Sydni laughed as she typed back.

Sydni:
Barely. Frostbite almost claimed me. But yes, still alive.

Elias:
Glad to hear it. Would've been tragic if I flew across the country only to return and find you turned into an icicle.

Sydni:
A very stylish icicle.

Elias:
Hope you have a good Christmas Eve tomorrow. Do something fun.

Sydni:
I've got Sloan coming over. So "fun" is guaranteed.

Elias:
Send my condolences.

She laughed and tucked her phone away, warmth lingering long after the conversation ended.

~*~

That evening, Sloan arrived carrying a cardboard box labeled *CHRISTMAS DISASTER KIT*.

"Oh my, it lives."

"Our tree," he announced. "And our ornaments."

"I can't believe it survived another year?"

"It's a classic," he said with pride. "A vintage three-foot artificial wonder with—" he dug around, pulling something out, "—a branch that falls off if you breathe too hard."

He wasn't exaggerating. She was amazed this tree had any life left in it. The tree leaned like it had lived a hard life. It was tradition, and they loved it.

They set it up in the corner, adjusting it three times before giving up and declaring the lean "charming." Sloan opened the ornament box, revealing a chaotic collection: a glittery donut, a cracked snowman, a strange ornament shaped like a hot dog, a paper star Sloan made during a particularly dramatic breakup in 2020.

Sydni laughed through the entire decorating process. Sloan narrated each ornament's tragic backstory. She countered with dry commentary that made him wheeze.

By the time they finished, the little crooked tree glowed in the corner like a drunk Christmas miracle. Sloan flopped onto the couch. "We did good."

"We did something."

"Same thing," he said, stretching out.

She turned to look at him, softer now. "You okay?"

He blinked at her, caught off guard. "What? Yeah. Course."

"Sloan…"

He sighed and rubbed the back of his neck. "Yeah. I'm fine. Just… holidays are weird, you know? A lot happening. A lot not happening. But I'm good. Promise."

She nudged him with her foot. "You know you don't have to be funny all the time, right?"

He smiled, but it was tired around the edges. "Don't tell anyone. Would ruin my brand."

She rolled her eyes, but warmth slipped through her chest. "Well… I'm here. For whatever you need."

He stood, grabbed his coat, and tapped her forehead gently. "Right back at you, Benton."

When he left, the apartment felt but not empty. Sydni grabbed her laptop, curled up under her blanket, and opened a new journal entry.

Tonight was good. Sloan is chaotic and dramatic and exhausting in the absolute best way, and I think the weird little tree makes my apartment feel… alive. I forget sometimes how much connection helps. Even if it's just decorating a leaning tree with a man who alphabetizes spices like a psychopath.

Elias texted. Just a check-in. Friendly. It shouldn't have meant anything, but it made me smile like an idiot.

I'm trying to stay grounded. Trying to stay realistic. He said friend. And it's okay. It really is.

But the way it felt when he said "hope you have fun tomorrow"… I don't know. Something in me lifted a little.

Anyway, I'm ending the night grateful. And warm. And maybe a tiny bit hopeful about whatever the new year will bring.

She saved it and logged **Non-Work Writing** in Resolve.

Confetti burst onto the screen again. And she let herself smile.

CHAPTER SIXTY-THREE

Sydni woke to Sloan pounding on her door like a debt collector.

"OPEN UP, HOLIDAY GREMLIN! I COME BEARING CHEESE."

She groaned, stumbling out of bed. "You're early."

"It's 9:04," he said when she opened the door. "You're welcome for the extra four minutes."

He barreled inside carrying two bags from the corner market and a third bag filled exclusively with different types of chips.

"Why do we need five bags of chips?" she asked.

Sloan dropped everything onto her counter. "Because life is unpredictable, Syd. What if we get trapped in a blizzard? What if the power goes out? What if Santa wants a snack?"

She stared. He stared back. They both burst out laughing.

Within twenty minutes, her kitchen looked like a toddler with ADHD had planned a dinner party. Sloan declared himself in charge of "festive snacks," which translated to him dumping marshmallows into hot chocolate like he was fueling a rocket.

"You can't even see the liquid," Sydni said, horrified.

"It's cocoa *adjacent*," he replied, stirring the marshmallow mountain.

After their mugs were more sugar than beverage, they changed into their ugly pajamas. Sydni chose a pair covered in miniature sloths wearing Santa hats. Sloan's were red plaid with a shirt that read **SLEIGH ALL DAY** in glittery letters.

"You look like a drunk elf on probation," she said.

"You look like a zoo exhibit escaped," he shot back. "Adorable, but concerning."

They flopped onto the couch, queuing up the worst Christmas movies they could find. The kind with terrible special effects and an overworked single mom who inevitably found love with a man who owned three reindeer.

Around noon, Sydni's phone buzzed. It was a picture. Clementine, golden retriever perfection, sitting regally beside a beautifully decorated Christmas tree, wearing a candy cane bandana.

Sydni squealed. "LOOK."

Sloan leaned over. "I would die for her. Immediately. Without hesitation."

Elias:
Clementine wishes you both a Merry Christmas Eve. She's been on the naughty list since 8 AM. She ate a decorative pinecone.

Sloan clutched his heart. "I'm framing this."

Sydni, without thinking, typed back:

Sydni:
Tell her she's perfect and can do no wrong.

A moment later:

Elias:
Already done. She agrees.

Sloan grabbed her phone. "We HAVE to send a picture back."

"What picture? I look like an exhausted troll."

"Exactly. It's authentic." He shoved her onto the couch. "Sit. Smile. Don't ruin this."

He angled the phone, tugged the sloth-ear hood on her pajamas up over her head, and made her hold a bag of Doritos in one hand and a candy cane in the other.

Sydni grinned despite herself.

Sloan posed beside her, holding a mug of marshmallow sludge like it was fine wine. He snapped the photo. The result? Pure, chaotic Christmas joy.

Her hair a curly halo, him looking like an unhinged children's entertainer, their little crooked Christmas tree glowing haphazardly behind them.

They sent it. Seconds later, her phone buzzed.

Elias:
That… is incredible. Easily the best picture I've seen all holiday season.

Sydni's heart did something completely unnecessary. A little flip, a little flutter which she ignored immediately.

Hours passed in a swirl of movies, snacks, and Sloan's constant commentary:

"Why is he proposing? They met YESTERDAY."
"That is not how gingerbread works."
"Why is there snow inside the house? Is this a horror movie?"

They laughed until their stomachs hurt. They ate too much junk food. Their tiny tree blinked crookedly in the corner.

At some point, the room grew quieter. The lights dimmed. An instrumental version of "O Holy Night" played from the TV.

Sydni felt her eyelids droop. Sloan stretched his legs onto the ottoman. Both of them drifted, heavy and warm, under the weight of full bellies and cheesy movies.

She didn't know when she fell asleep. Just that when she woke, her head rested on Sloan's shoulder, the blanket half-tucked around them both. He was snoring softly.

She smiled. For a moment, a brief, golden moment, life felt perfect.

~*~

Back in Colorado, Elias sat cross-legged on the couch in the cabin, fire crackling in the stone fireplace. Clementine snored beside him. Nora sat at the dining table behind him, wrapping gifts with the concentration of a bomb technician.

He tapped the screen and the photo from earlier filled the display again. Sydni and Sloan in ridiculous pajamas, grinning in front of their misshapen Christmas tree. He didn't know why he opened the picture again. But he did. Maybe because her smile looked real. Like something that reached her eyes. Like something he hadn't seen in a long time.

Nora looked up. "What are you looking at?"

He turned the screen toward her without thinking. She stared at the picture. Her face shifted. Just a flicker. Something warm, something wistful, something he couldn't read.

"She looks happy," Nora said thoughtfully.

"Yeah," he replied, voice low. "She does."

He went quiet after that. Staring at the picture a little too long. Because suddenly, in the dim glow of a Colorado cabin, he realized something.

He missed her. More than he expected. More than he knew what to do with. And Nora, watching him from across the room, saw it too. She didn't say a word.

CHAPTER SIXTY-FOUR

Christmas morning came without fanfare. There were no alarms, no obligations, no frantic rushing. Just the winter light creeping across Sydni's apartment walls.

She blinked awake to the sound of her door opening. She didn't even know Sloan had left, yet here he was again.

"IT'S CHRISTMAS AND I BROUGHT CARBS," Sloan announced, letting himself in like he always did. He held up a grocery bag triumphantly. "Also, you're welcome for the early morning joy I bring into your life."

"It's 10 a.m.," she muttered, stumbling out of her bedroom. "You're late."

"I'm fashionably on time," he said, kicking the door closed behind him. "Now. Presents."

He dropped an absurd pile of gift bags onto her couch. She stared at them. "Sloan… we said ONE present."

"I lied," he said cheerfully. "Open something before I combust."

She rolled her eyes and dug into the first bag. Inside was… a pair of fuzzy sloth slippers. "Sloan…"

"They match your pajamas," he grinned. "I'm building a brand for you."

She hugged them to her chest, laughing.

"And now," he said, rubbing his hands together like an evil scientist, "your turn to shower me in gifts."

She handed him a neatly wrapped box, one she'd worried over for a week. He tore the paper like a raccoon with no self-control and then froze. Inside was a framed photo of the two of them from their first Christmas together. Standing in her kitchen, laughing so hard they were doubled over, flour smudged on both their faces from a failed attempt at Christmas cookies.

"You kept this?" he said, voice catching in his throat.

"You're my people," she shrugged. "You deserve to know that."

He blinked hard, looked away, and sniffed. "Ugh. Gross. Feelings." Then he set the picture carefully, reverently, on her coffee table.

They spent the next few hours in full chaos mode: Sloan burning the first frozen pizza, Sydni burning the second, both of them loudly blaming the oven, Sloan spilling hot chocolate on her rug ("it adds character"), Sydni accidentally spraying whipped cream directly into his eye ("aiming is hard!")

The tiny, crooked Christmas tree flickered happily in the corner as they watched movies, exchanged more small gifts, and argued over which holiday song was objectively superior.

By mid-afternoon, they were full, tired, and cozy. Sloan stretched across the couch, feet in her lap. "Good Christmas?"

"One of the best," she said truthfully.

He smiled at her, not the chaotic grin he threw around all day, but the real one, the only one she ever saw. Chosen family.

"It's going to be a big New Year's Eve," he said, wiggling his eyebrows. "Victoria's parties always bring danger."

"Danger?"

"Emotional danger," he clarified. "Which is worse. Now…help me put away the pizza boxes, my legs are asleep."

They cleaned up the kitchen while making fun of each other the entire time. Exactly what she needed.

~*~

New Year's Week

The days after Christmas slipped by faster than Sydni expected.

Snow melted into slush. Lights stayed up on balconies. People shuffled home with returns and gift cards. Life slid toward the holiday lull where everything felt suspended, waiting for midnight on the 31st.

New Year's Eve was coming. Victoria's big, ridiculous, over-the-top party was coming. Elias will still be out of town, so that takes THAT pressure off. She felt calm about it.

Meanwhile, Sloan grew increasingly… suspicious.

He kept texting someone when he thought she wasn't looking, smiling at his phone in that secret little way he never did. When she asked who it was, he would blink dramatically and say things like:

"No one."
"You don't know them."
"Mind your own business, Nosey McNoserson."

Which did *not* help.

One afternoon, they were sitting on her couch when she nudged him with her foot. "You're being weird."

"I'm never weird," he lied.

"You're texting someone."

"I text lots of people."

"You only text me, your sister, and your landlord, and only when something is broken."

"Which is often," he said solemnly.

"Sloan."

He looked at her, eyes wide with faux innocence. "You're imagining things."

Which was exactly what someone would say if they *weren't* imagining things. "Fine," she said, crossing her arms. "Be mysterious."

"I always do," he said, smuggling his phone deeper into his hoodie pocket.

Despite the banter, Sydni knew she was doing well. Like she'd climbed out of something dark and found level ground again. And now, with the party approaching, her life felt like it was shifting toward something. Something new. Something she couldn't name yet.

On the night of the 30th, she wrote in her journal:

Tomorrow is Victoria's party. Part of me is nervous. Part of me is excited. Part of me feels like something is changing like something is coming for me in the best possible way. I don't know what it is, but I feel ready for it. For the first time in a long time… I feel ready.

She saved it. Closed her laptop. Turned off the lamp.

New Year's Eve waited on the other side of sleep. And something in her heart whispered: *This year will be different.*

CHAPTER SIXTY-FIVE

Sydni woke with a knot in her stomach she couldn't quite identify. It wasn't dread, but it wasn't really excitement. It was something in between. That jittery, unpredictable feeling that comes right before the most emotional holiday on earth.

New Year's Eve.

"Okay," she muttered as she sat up. "It's just a party. A normal, slightly flashy, extremely loud party. With people. Lots of them. Probably glitter. Possibly danger."

She exhaled into her hands. The room felt cold in that particular December way that made getting out of bed feel personally offensive. But she stood anyway, because Sloan would storm through the door any minute like a caffeinated tornado.

She drug herself into the kitchen, turned on the kettle, and glanced toward her little crooked Christmas tree still twinkling in the corner. She couldn't feel happier if she wanted to.

Then she remembered something. She should text Elias. Just… politely. As friends. Her thumbs hovered over the screen.

Sydni:
Happy New Year's Eve! 🎉 Hope you have a good night wherever you're celebrating.

She read it three times. It felt normal. Friendly. Safe. She hit send.

No response. She told herself it didn't matter. He was busy. Traveling. Spending time with Nora. Trying to avoid literal altitude sickness. It didn't matter. But part of her chest tightened just a little. She pushed the feeling down and focused on tea.

At 10:07 a.m., Sloan burst into the apartment like he'd been shot from a confetti cannon.

"Benton! It's New Year's Eve! Get up, get dressed, get emotionally stable!"

She stared at him over her mug. "I'm drinking my tea."

"No time," he said, marching straight toward her closet like he paid rent here. "We have outfits to coordinate, hair to tame, eyeliner to apply, existential crises to manage—"

"Sloan."

He whirled around, finger in the air, already in mid-speech.

"No. Don't 'Sloan' me. This is Victoria's party. And I refuse to let you go looking like 'I worked from home all year and no one can stop me.'"

"That's… accurate though."

"Exactly. Which is why I'm here. To fix you."

He returned to the closet, muttering dramatically. "Black dress? Too intense. Green blouse? Too seasonal. This sweater? Why does it exist?" He tossed half her wardrobe onto the bed.

She sighed. "You know, normal friends just send 'want a ride?' texts."

"You don't have a normal friend," he said over his shoulder. "You have me. A blessing and a curse."

She shook her head, hiding a small smile. Eventually, after hunting through her closet like an archaeologist searching for treasure, Sloan held up an outfit with triumph.

"There. Perfect." A deep plum wrap top and dark jeans that fit her just right. It was stylish without trying too hard, soft without looking childish, subtle but undeniably flattering.

She blinked. "Where did that even come from? I don't remember buying it."

"You didn't. I bought it for you last spring."

"What?"

"You were depressed," he said with a shrug. "And the color made me think of you. But the timing never felt right to give it to you."

Her chest tightened in the way it always did when she remembered how deeply she was loved even when she didn't feel like she deserved it.

"Sloan…"

"Don't get mushy," he said immediately. "Try it on before I change my mind and make you wear sequins."

When she stepped into the bathroom to change, she paused at the mirror. The plum color really did suit her. It made her eyes brighter, made her skin glow. She turned sideways. Her curls framed her face wildly, stubbornly. Her tattoos peeked down the length of her arms. Some scars, lightened by time, curved beneath the ink.

She was… herself. She returned to the living room. Sloan gasped dramatically, hand to his chest.

"YES. You look like a competent adult and a slightly mysterious goddess."

She snorted. "Great. Exactly the vibe."

He flitted around her like an overexcited stylist, adjusting her collar, smoothing her hair, applying a bit of lip color before she could protest. "Where did you get makeup?" she asked.

"Your bathroom," he said. "Don't ask questions."

By noon they were cleaning up the apartment, prepping snacks "just in case," and playing loud music while trying to perfect the right hair and makeup combination.

Around 1 p.m., his phone buzzed. Sloan snatched it up quickly, too quickly, and spun around to hide the screen.

Sydni raised an eyebrow. "Oh? Mystery texter again?"

"Nope," he said. Way too fast.

He opened a cabinet and stuck his head inside like the person texting him lived in the Tupperware shelf. "It's nothing," he said, voice slightly echoey. "Mind your business."

"You're suspicious."

"You're suspicious."

"That doesn't even make sense."

"It made sense in my head," he snapped, grabbing a stack of plastic cups.

She stared. He refused to meet her eyes. Fine. Two could play this game. "Okay," she said lightly. "I'll stop asking." A lie. But he accepted it gratefully.

They spent the afternoon snacking, laughing, and rewatching half of a terrible holiday rom-com they'd already seen twice. Sloan made sarcastic commentary every five seconds. "She's falling for him because he saved her from a rogue ornament. That's the plot."

"That tree is a fire hazard and a metaphor."

"Why are they wearing sweaters indoors? No one sweats in movies. It's unrealistic."

By six p.m., they were finally ready.

She looked in the mirror one more time, not to pick herself apart, but to remind herself that she had survived. Thrived, even. She had grown. She had even changed, becoming stronger. She was allowed to enjoy a party.

"Ready?" Sloan asked, jingling his keys.

She nodded. "Let's go ring in the new year," she said.

~*~

Victoria's building was already glowing when they arrived, warm lights strung across the entrance, voices carrying down the corridor, music thumping faintly from her apartment on the fourth floor. Sydni smoothed the hem of her blouse, suddenly nervous.

"You doing okay?" Sloan asked, bumping her shoulder gently.

"Yeah," she said. "Just… crowds."

"I'll be glued to your side," he promised. "Like your emotional support golden retriever."

"That's Elias' dog," she corrected.

"Fine. Your emotional support ferret."

"That's worse."

He wiggled his eyebrows.

They reached Victoria's door just as it flew open, confetti bursting outward. "Sydni! Sloan!" Victoria shouted, glitter already in her hair. "Get in here! Drinks! Food! People who talk too loudly!"

They stepped inside into warmth and chatter and too many fairy lights and a playlist that could only be described as "chaos with a beat." Sydni relaxed slightly. It wasn't too overwhelming. Not yet. She grabbed a sparkling water, that still tastes like static. Sloan grabbed something neon and concerning.

They mingled. Laughed. Posed for photos Victoria demanded. Sloan danced terribly to a remix of "Auld Lang Syne" while Sydni pretended not to know him. Everything was good.

Then, midway through a conversation with a woman from Victoria's book club, the front door swung open. Cold air rushed in.

Victoria turned, squealed, and shouted —

"ELIAS!!"

Sydni froze.

She didn't turn immediately. She couldn't. But she felt it, like a shift in the room's gravity. And then she heard it. His footsteps. Low greetings. Nora's voice beside him. Her heart pounded.

Finally. Finally she looked toward the door. He was standing just inside, removing his coat, cheeks still pink from the cold. Nora beside him, shaking snow from her hair.

But Elias wasn't looking at Victoria. Or the crowd. Or the drinks table. He was scanning the room. Eyes searching, intent, warm. Until they landed on her.

He'd been looking for her on purpose. Like she was the one he came to see. The room hummed around her. Laughter, music, clinking glasses, but none of it seemed to touch the moment suspended between them.

Because all at once, Sydni realized, her year wasn't ending the way she expected.

CHAPTER SIXTY-SIX

For a heartbeat, the party stopped existing. Sydni stood frozen in the glow of twinkle lights, breath caught in her chest, every sound in the room muffled under the weight of one realization:

Elias was here. Not in Colorado. Not arriving "next year." Here.

Her heart thudded painfully, but not in fear. In shock. In something warm and bright she didn't dare name yet. She took one involuntary step back, bumping into Sloan, who steadied her gently. He met her eyes, and instead of smirking or teasing, he gave her a knowing nod. Then, quietly, almost imperceptibly...

"Go."

There was no jealousy in his tone. He was just a friend pushing her toward something she deserved. She stepped away from Sloan and walked forward.

Elias had started moving too, weaving through clusters of people and clinking glasses and the muffled throb of music. His eyes didn't leave her once. Not for a second. When they finally stopped in front of each other, close enough she could feel the cold still clinging to his coat, neither of them spoke at first.

Then she exhaled a shaky laugh. "What are you doing here? You...you weren't supposed to be back until next year."

His eyes were almost heartbreakingly sincere. "I know," he said. "I wasn't."

He reached into his coat pocket, pulled out his phone, tapped the screen, and turned it toward her. It was *the photo.* The one she and Sloan took in ugly pajamas on Christmas Eve.

Sydni looked confused. "You... came back because of that?"

"No," he said with a smile forming. "I came back because of what I felt when I saw it."

He lowered the phone but didn't step back. "I was sitting at that cabin, and everyone was laughing and wrapping gifts, and I just… kept staring at that picture. At you. And I realized something."

He swallowed, cheeks flushed, not from the cold this time. "I missed you." He continued, voice steadier now. "I missed you when we stopped talking in the summer. I missed you when you deleted the app. I missed you in a way I couldn't name back then."

Her stomach dropped, then soared, both at once.

"And when we started talking again… when I saw you again… when we had lunch… it all came back. And this time I knew what it meant."

"Elias…"

He took her hands, carefully, gently, like she was something fragile he didn't want to startle. "I know you've wanted to tell me something," he murmured, eyes flicking briefly to the tattoos that climbed her arms, the faint edges of scars beneath the ink. "But you don't have to explain any of it right now."

She opened her mouth, ready, terrified, to tell him everything, about the attack, the scars, the fear, the trauma—

But he squeezed her hands and shook his head. "You can tell me all of that when you're ready," he said. "Because none of it changes how I see you."

Her vision blurred. He stepped closer, lowering his forehead toward hers but stopping just shy of touching. "And somewhere along the way," he whispered, "because of a stupid accountability app, I found my best friend."

Sydni lifted her eyes to his.

"And I'm pretty sure," he continued, voice almost shaking, "that I'm falling in love with my best friend. And I just couldn't mess this up again on another New Year's Eve."

Her lips parted. Her heart cracked open. She had spent months terrified to want anything. Terrified to risk anything. Terrified to feel anything. But standing here, hope blooming in her chest like a new season, she felt something she hadn't felt in years:

Safe.

Her eyes glistened as she whispered, barely audible, "Elias…" She hesitates, but looking into his eyes, the truth falls out, "I think I'm falling for you too."

A collective roar swelled in the room behind them.

"TEN! … NINE! … EIGHT!"

Sydni startled and blinked, realizing…

The countdown had started.

She glanced instinctively over her shoulder and saw Sloan and Nora standing close together in the corner, his arm around her waist, her hand fisted in his shirt, both smiling in a way that felt like a secret lit from the inside.

They were…Oh. They were something. Maybe had been for a while. Before she could process it, her attention snapped back to Elias.

He gently brushed a curl away from her cheek.

"SEVEN! … SIX!"

His thumb traced the soft line of her jaw.

"FIVE! … FOUR!"

His forehead touched hers.

"THREE!"

She exhaled.

"TWO!"

He whispered, "Happy New Year, Sydni."

"ONE!"

At midnight, he kissed her.

It was warm and deep and slow, a kiss that felt like healing, like home, like a new beginning all wrapped in one breathless moment.

Her hands slid into his hair. His arms wrapped around her waist. The noise of the party dissolved to static.

She didn't notice Victoria shrieking happily somewhere behind them. She didn't notice the confetti. She didn't notice anything except him. And he didn't notice, just over Sydni's shoulder, Sloan leaning into Nora for a quiet, stolen New Year's kiss of their own.

Two kisses. Two beginnings. Two hearts finding their way exactly where they were meant to be.

Sydni and Elias broke apart slowly, foreheads touching, breath mingling, both smiling like they'd stumbled into something they hadn't planned but desperately wanted.

"Hi," he whispered.

She laughed softly. "Hi."

And the new year began.

Sydni was halfway through taming her hair when Sloan burst into her apartment without knocking. He didn't even start with hello.

"Okay, I have arrived," he announced, swinging the door shut with dramatic flair. "Prepare yourself emotionally, because my Valentine's Day outfit is… frankly iconic."

She turned, wide tooth comb still in hand, and promptly choked on air. "Sloan, what *are* you wearing?"

He posed like he was on a runway. Red trousers. Pink suspenders. A button-up shirt covered in tiny cartoon hearts with googly eyes. And, dear God, light-up Cupid wings strapped to his back. "Fashion," he said. "Look it up."

She laughed so hard she had to sit on the bed. "Those wings are going to get you arrested for disturbing the peace."

"They're tasteful," he protested, flapping them once. The LEDs blinked in epileptic fury. "And festive."

"They look like Cupid died tragically on your spine."

He gasped. "Wow. On this, the holiday of love? You wound me."

She tossed a pillow at him. He caught it one-handed, smug.

Their banter rolled easily, comfortable, familiar, safe. The same rhythm they'd built for years. Except now… everything was a little lighter. A little healthier. Both of them finally standing on solid ground.

Sydni turned back to the mirror, adding the last touch of eyeliner. Sloan leaned in the bathroom doorway, arms crossed, pretending to judge her technique like a beauty influencer.

"And…" she whispered, placing a final flick of mascara. "Done."

He grinned. "Hot."

She rolled her eyes, but her cheeks warmed despite herself.

"Selfie time," he declared, pulling her to her feet.

"No filters," she warned.

"No promises," he said, already lifting her phone.

She reached for it—then paused. Her lock screen lit up. Not a generic background. Not a landscape photo.

Her and Elias. Taken last week at the park, his forehead pressed gently to her temple, her smile genuine in a way she hadn't seen on her own face in years.

Sloan's grin spread into a loving look. "Well. Look who's disgustingly adorable now."

She swatted him with the back of her hand, but couldn't hide the smile tugging at her lips.

"Let's go before you blind someone with those wings."

~*~

The pub was warm and loud, packed with early-evening Valentine's Day celebrators, twinkle lights, and the faint smell of fried food. Nora spotted them first, waving wildly from a booth. Elias stood beside her, and the moment he saw Sydni, his face lit up in that way he tried, and failed, to hide.

When they reached the table, Elias leaned in and kissed her cheek, lingering just long enough to make her heart stutter.

"You look incredible," he murmured.

"And you're—" She stepped back to take him in. "—wearing the tie."

He tugged at the ridiculous physical therapy–themed Valentine tie she'd bought him: little cartoon spines holding hands inside heart shapes.

"Well, my girlfriend got it for me," he said, pretending to whisper. "Very exclusive designer."

She nudged him with her shoulder—trying and failing to hide the blush blooming across her cheeks.

"And you're wearing the necklace," he whispered.

She touched the delicate chain around her throat—the tiny silver heart engraved with a crescent moon inside it. A morning gift from him. Simple. Thoughtful. Perfect.

Their eyes held for a beat too long.

Then Sloan cleared his throat obnoxiously. "Okay, enough flirting. Some of us are single by choice—"

Nora snorted so loudly her water nearly went up her nose. "By *whose* choice, Sloan, what are you trying to say?"

"Oh please," he shot back. "As if you're the poster child for—"

"Children," Sydni and Elias said at the exact same time. They both blinked, then burst into laughter.

Nora rolled her eyes but she was smiling—and when Sloan sat beside her, their shoulders brushed deliberately. She smiled at Sloan, telling him she liked his wings. He tells her, he likes her face, and they share a quick kiss.

The overhead speaker crackled.

"Trivia will begin in five minutes! Teams, choose your name!"

Sloan shot to his feet like a man possessed.

"Okay. Last time our team name was terrible. This time, I'm taking charge."

Elias muttered, "Oh God."

Nora asked, "Is this going to be humiliating?"

"Yes," Sydni said. "Absolutely."

Sloan dramatically slapped a sticky note onto the table and announced:

"OUR TEAM NAME IS: **The Cerebral Assassins.**"

There was a full beat of silence. Then everyone groaned at once.

"Sloan—"
"No."
"Please get help."
"I refuse to be on that team."

He crossed his arms defiantly. "It's a power move."

"It sounds like a cult," Elias said.

"A *nerdy* cult," Nora added.

Sydni leaned in, voice flat. "Absolutely not. Pick again."

Sloan sighed—deeply—as if the weight of artistic genius was a heavy burden.

"Fine," he said. "How about…" He scribbled something new.

"Love Actually Sucks (Except For Us)."

Nora snatched the note out of his hand. "That's it. That's the one."

Elias groaned louder. "Please no—"

But Sydni was laughing so hard she could barely breathe. "Well," she said, wiping her eyes. "At least it's honest."

Elias leaned closer to her, voice low, warm. "Just try not to distract me with how cute you look tonight."

She choked on nothing. Sloan threw a pretzel at Elias's face.

"Boundary violation!" he declared. "Technical foul!"

Nora kicked him under the table. "Stop flirting with their relationship and flirt with your girlfriend," she hissed.

He leans over and whispers something in her ear that makes her blush and giggle.

The trivia host stepped up to the mic.

"Teams ready?" They nodded.

"Then welcome, lovers and losers, to Valentine's Trivia Night!"

Sydni grins at Elias.

He grins back. He mouths, "I love you."

She mouths back, "I love you, too."

For the first time in a long, winding year, everything felt exactly right.